replica

replica

JENNA BLACK

**TOR®
TEEN**

A TOM DOHERTY ASSOCIATES BOOK
NEW YORK

This is a work of fiction. All of the characters, organizations, and events portrayed in this novel are either products of the author's imagination or are used fictitiously.

REPLICA

A Tor Teen Book
Published by Tom Doherty Associates, LLC
175 Fifth Avenue
New York, NY 10010

www.tor-forge.com

Tor® is a registered trademark of Tom Doherty Associates, LLC.

ISBN 978-0-7653-3371-1 (trade paperback)
ISBN 978-1-4668-0489-0 (e-book)

Tor Teen books may be purchased for educational, business, or promotional use. For information on bulk purchases, please contact Macmillan Corporate and Premium Sales Department at 1-800-221-7945 extension 5442 or write special markets@macmillan.com.

First Edition: July 2013

Printed in the United States of America

0 9 8 7 6 5 4 3 2 1

For Dan, the world's greatest husband

replica

CHAPTER ONE

The limo pulled up to the curb at the entrance of Chairman Hayes's Long Island mansion, and Nadia dug deep in search of an untapped reserve of energy. Her throat scratched with the early warning signs of a cold, and if she had any choice she'd be cuddled up in bed with a good book and a cup of hot tea, not spending the next four or five hours at a wedding reception. However, this was *the* event of the season, and she'd heard her mother's lecture on the duties of an Executive enough times to know it by heart. Attending state events was on the top of that list, so staying home was not an option.

A liveried attendant hurried to open the limo's door. Gerald and Esmeralda Lake, Nadia's parents, exited first, posing and smiling for the photographers while Nadia stayed momentarily hidden behind the limo's tinted windows. She wrinkled her nose at the stately mansion, hating the place. Chairman Hayes had built it shortly after Paxco had bought out what was then the state of New York. It had been the first in a long line of dominoes that had eventually led to the transformation of the United States of America into today's Corporate States. The mansion was a monument to the Chairman's ego, not an actual home meant to be lived in.

Too bad she would have to live in it someday.

Nadia plastered a smile on her face and exited the limo.

Cameras flashed from all around her, and the photographers called out orders for her to turn this way and that. The good news was that only the most respected—and well-behaved—reporters had been invited to cover this event, so everyone was being very polite, and if her smile drooped or she blinked at an inconvenient moment, those photos wouldn't show up on the net.

The mansion was positively aglow, golden light flooding every visible window. White bunting draped the marble-columned porch, and a bloodred carpet drew a path between the driveway and the front door. From outside, Nadia could hear the lively music that said the reception was in full swing. The atmosphere might have been festive, if it weren't for all the armed guards who tried futilely to fade into the background. Even at its most joyful and relaxed, the mansion had teeth, and only an idiot would forget that.

Nadia kept the polished smile plastered on her face as she and her parents made their way through the gauntlet of photographers, and she didn't let it slip while going through the endless receiving line. Her cheeks ached by the time she and her parents stepped into the ballroom, a vision of antique elegance with its crystal chandeliers, soaring ceilings, and large parquet dance floor on which no one was yet dancing. Arrangements of white flowers abounded, with the occasional splash of pink or yellow for contrast. The mingled scents of gardenias and roses made her nose itch. Liveried waiters made the rounds, offering cocktails and hors d'oeuvres, and the Executives of Paxco and Synchrony mingled to celebrate the alliance between their two states that would be cemented by this wedding.

As soon as they entered the ballroom, Nadia and her parents went their separate ways. She was expected to mingle, but she was on the lookout for an inconspicuous corner she could park herself in. Her cold was gaining ground, and the last thing she wanted to do was engage in a round of social sparring. She snagged a glass of champagne punch from one of the servers and edged her way toward the wall, eying one of the enormous flower arrangements. It might be tall enough to completely hide her from view if she stood in just the right spot. Then she wouldn't have to—

"Nadia!" cried a delighted voice from behind her, and Nadia fought a sigh.

Forcing another smile, she turned to face Jewel Howard, who looked painfully perfect with her blond ringlets and her frothy pink gown. As always, Jewel was flanked by her younger sister, Cherry, and their mutual friend, Blair. The Terrible Trio never failed to show up at any event where they might find fodder for their favorite pastimes of malicious gossip and intimidation. Unfortunately, their families were the cream of the Executive crop, so protocol required Nadia to act as if they were all best friends.

"Your gown is simply stunning," Jewel said while giving Nadia the requisite air kisses. "I could never wear that color without looking like a ghost."

Jewel's skin was the same unblemished alabaster as Nadia's, and while Nadia was confident her royal-blue gown wasn't too dark for her skin tone, she hated the frisson of doubt Jewel's comment triggered. The society columnists would eviscerate her if they felt she'd chosen the wrong gown for the occasion. There was an edge in Cherry's and Blair's smiles as they enjoyed their leader's backhanded compliment. Ordinarily, Nadia would have shot back an appropriate rejoinder, but tonight she just wondered if she could give them all her cold if she breathed on them enough. The image of Jewel with a runny red nose was almost cheering.

Nadia took a sip of her punch, which was watery and way too sweet. The bubbles in the champagne irritated her throat on the way down, and she stifled a cough. "Wasn't the ceremony beautiful?" she said in her best imitation of a gush, knowing the Terrible Trio couldn't resist the opportunity to dissect every moment of the wedding. Nadia might not enjoy the gossip and small talk that were the most prized skills of girls of her station, but that didn't mean she wasn't good at it. She put in just enough commentary to keep the conversation going, and though she internally winced at some of the Trio's most vicious critiques, at least their malice wasn't aimed at her. For once.

Nadia let her attention stray from the conversation, her eyes scanning the ballroom, and that's when she saw him.

Nathaniel Edison Hayes, Chairman Heir of Paxco, was flat-out gorgeous. His dark, unruly hair had been slicked back for this formal occasion, and he wore the standard black tux, but there was always an aura of contained energy around him that made him stand out in a crowd. His deep blue eyes sparked with mischief.

Nate was talking to some stuffed shirt Nadia didn't know, but he seemed to have a sixth sense where she was concerned, his eyes straying unerringly to hers practically the moment she caught sight of him. He grinned at her, and there it was, that glint in his eyes. He said something to the stuffed shirt—something offensive, or at least not particularly polite, based on the man's outraged expression—then turned away from him as if he didn't exist, making his way through the crowd toward her. As future Chairman of Paxco, Nate could get away with behavior that would have lesser Executives ostracized.

Nadia smiled back at the boy she was destined to marry, enjoying the view more than she liked to admit. He would be any girl's dream husband: rich and powerful and handsome. And Nadia was more than happy with their betrothal. Well, not betrothal, exactly. Their parents had agreed to the match when Nate was six and Nadia was four, but they couldn't be legally betrothed until they'd both reached eighteen, and Nadia still had two more years to go. Two more years of watching every well-bred girl in Paxco throw herself at him—or be pushed at him by ambitious parents. Two more years of not just good behavior but *perfect* behavior on her part to ensure no action of hers would discredit her family before the arrangement became legally binding.

Nadia knew the moment the Terrible Trio caught sight of Nate, because their inane banter suddenly stopped. Out of the corner of her eye, she saw all three of them stand up just a little straighter, hold their chins just a little higher. Jewel even took an extra deep breath so the tops of her breasts peeked out of her décolletage. Nadia resisted the urge to roll her eyes. If only Jewel knew how little her assets interested Nate.

"Be still my heart!" Nate declared when he was within earshot, sweeping all four of them with a lascivious look. "Such beauty will surely blind me." His voice dripped with so much exaggeration Nadia almost laughed out loud.

"You are too kind, sir," Jewel simpered, leaning forward so Nate could look down her dress if he wanted.

Always happy to play the role of the charming rake, Nate glanced downward and smiled, and though Nadia knew he was only playacting, she couldn't help bristling. If Nadia or her family were to commit some gaffe and the Chairman were to choose another bride for Nate, Jewel would be one of the top candidates.

"Shouldn't you be off talking to important dignitaries instead of flirting?" Nadia asked Nate.

Nate frowned, but at least he stopped looking down Jewel's dress. "I believe that's my father's job. I'm the ne'er-do-well son, remember?"

How could she forget? While she painstakingly navigated the protocol and etiquette of Executive society, careful never to set a foot wrong lest disaster strike, Nate barreled through life as though he were invincible.

But in many ways, he was.

"Shall we dance?" he asked, holding out his elbow to Nadia.

Uh-oh, she thought. There was a reason no one else was dancing, and Nate knew that as well as she did. "I don't think the bride and groom have danced yet," she said cautiously, hoping that didn't sound like a rebuke. She knew from experience how Nate reacted to even subtle rebukes. "But I'll be sure to save you a dance later."

His exaggerated pout told Nadia immediately that she'd made a tactical error. There was nothing like telling Nate he shouldn't do something to make him stubbornly determined to do it. "This is supposed to be a party," he said. "There's supposed to be dancing."

His elbow was still raised, as if he couldn't conceive of the possibility that she might turn him down. Nadia was painfully aware of the Terrible Trio watching her, enjoying her dilemma.

Nate didn't give a damn about protocol, but the rest of Executive society did. Protocol demanded that the bride and groom be allowed the first dance. Protocol also demanded that Nadia dance with her future husband when he asked her to. No matter which option she chose, people would talk, and her parents would later critique her decision. Nadia's mother would invariably decide that Nadia had made the wrong choice, and her father would agree because that was the path of least resistance.

Nate dropped the grin, his eyes filling with earnestness. "Dance with me," he said more softly. "Please."

Internally, Nadia sighed. She was never any good at saying no to Nate, and he knew that. She really should put her foot down. The more she gave in, the more he would take. Plus, she had the uneasy suspicion there was something more to this invitation to dance than met the eye. Some deeper trouble Nate planned to get into, dragging her along for the ride.

Nate plucked the champagne cocktail from her hand and downed it in three swallows, handing the empty glass to a passing waiter. Nadia shook her head.

"You shouldn't have done that," she told him. "I'm coming down with a cold."

Nate shrugged it off. "Will you dance with me, or won't you?"

Despite all her natural caution, she found herself taking his elbow and allowing him to lead her to the dance floor. If people were going to talk no matter what she did, then she'd rather dance with Nate than endure the Trio.

Nadia was painfully aware of the eyes following their progress. She imagined every whisper of conversation was about her, about the breach of etiquette she was about to commit. An exaggeration, of course. Most of the partygoers were no doubt oblivious, locked in their choreographed pleasantries or Machiavellian scheming. Until Nate swept her into the dance, that is. The background mutter of conversation faded for a moment, then came back at renewed volume.

"I'm never going to hear the end of this," she murmured, already second-guessing her decision. But then, if she'd refused to dance, he might have asked Jewel instead. Nadia knew he despised Jewel almost as much as she did, but that wouldn't have made it any more fun to watch him dancing with her.

Nate smiled down at her. "People would be disappointed if I didn't do something shocking and inappropriate at least once this evening. I have a reputation to uphold."

"Your father would be over the moon with joy," she countered. Nathaniel Sr., Chairman of Paxco, was humorless and unyielding, Nate's exact opposite. She was glad that she would one day be Nate's wife, but the prospect of having Nathaniel Sr. as a father-in-law was considerably less appealing.

"My father is off somewhere meeting with his cronies. You don't think he'd waste his precious time enjoying himself at a party, do you?"

That was probably true. The heads of over a dozen of the Corporate States had gathered to celebrate this wedding, and they weren't here because of their affection for the happy couple. The whole grand affair was merely a pretty façade masking a bunch of political and business meetings. The alliance with Synchrony had major implications for Paxco's technology division, making it possible to incorporate Synchrony's more advanced microprocessors into Paxco's currently second-rate hardware. If Nate were acting like a proper heir, he'd be sitting in on those meetings, learning the ropes, instead of making a stir on the dance floor.

"So, were you really so impatient to dance, or did you have some other reason for making a spectacle of yourself?" Nadia asked. Out of the corner of her eye, she saw a few other couples edging toward the dance floor indecisively.

"You looked like you could use a rescue," Nate said, and Nadia felt a flash of gratitude. "Besides," he continued, "I don't need an ulterior motive to dance with the most beautiful girl in the room."

Nadia snorted, an undignified sound she was glad no one but Nate could hear. "Yeah, because you're such a ladies' man."

Nate laughed, and she smiled at him ruefully. He played at being a ladies' man whenever he was in public, flirting shamelessly. Most of the unmarried Executive girls would swoon if he so much as looked at them, and Nadia was very much aware that not all of the jealousy aimed her way was because of her future husband's status. What girl *wouldn't* dream of having someone so handsome and charming in her bed? But any girl who shared his bed would spend a lot more time sleeping than she expected.

Nadia tried to ignore the sudden tightness in her chest. In just a few short years, *she* would be that any girl, lying untouched by Nate's side. Or lying alone in bed while Nate cavorted with someone more to his taste.

"Cheer up," Nate said into her ear, no doubt appearing to onlookers as if he were whispering sweet nothings. "Not only did I rescue you from death by gossip, I made sure we stole all the attention. You know how the Trio hate that."

Nadia couldn't help laughing. She glanced at the Trio and saw them huddled together like witches over a cauldron. They were all smiling, but the expression rang slightly false. Other couples were venturing out onto the dance floor, but the Trio would be too worried about their reputations to join in the fun. In one fell swoop, Nate had deprived them of their prey, their fun, and the attention of the state-approved photographers in discreet attendance. And he'd made her laugh when she felt miserable. All in all, it was probably worth the parental disapproval she was sure to face.

Nate and Nadia were no longer the only couple on the dance floor. The bride and groom had ventured out first, and then the other couples found their courage. The music came to an end, and Nate spun Nadia to a finish. The next song started up almost immediately, but it seemed Nate had lost interest in dancing once the shock value was used up.

"Let's give our audience even more to talk about," Nate said as he led her off the dance floor.

Nadia didn't know what he meant until she realized he was leading her toward a doorway at the back of the ballroom. A pair of security guards flanked the doorway, and as if their presence wasn't enough to clue everyone in that the rooms behind were off-limits, the lights in the hallway were off. Once again, Nadia had to suppress a groan. *Everyone* would notice the two of them sneaking off into the residential part of the mansion, and *everyone* would draw conclusions about what they were doing back there. Conclusions that would help Nate's camouflage, to be sure, but that wouldn't do her reputation a whole lot of good.

"I'd like another glass of punch," Nadia said, though she'd barely taken two sips of her first and hadn't enjoyed them.

Nate gave her his most wicked grin. "What's the matter? Afraid to be alone with me?"

The problem with Nate was that once you gave him the inch, he went for the mile every time. Sometimes Nadia just wanted to shake him. She stopped moving toward the shadowed hallway, forcing Nate to stop with her.

"One scandal a night is all you get." She said it with a smile, keeping her voice down so that no one watching them would know they were arguing. If that was what they were doing.

"You don't want to mingle any more than I do," Nate countered, "so let's not."

"What I want doesn't really matter," she said, hoping he didn't hear the hint of bitterness in her voice.

"You said you were coming down with a cold. I'm sure polite society will forgive you for not spreading it around."

Nadia wavered. The fact that she was sick wouldn't protect her from scandal. But her nose *was* feeling stuffier, and the thought of spending the rest of the evening forcing smiles exhausted her.

Nate reached up and tucked one finger under his collar, pulling at the bow tie like it was choking him. "I've been on my best behavior for hours," he said, sounding truly put upon. "I spent all morning schmoozing with my father and his cronies, and I even managed not to make more than one or two rude and inappropriate jokes. I dressed up, I showed up to the ceremony on time, and I've had only one drink. If I don't let off some steam, I'll probably end up doing something truly shocking in front of all these people. Far more shocking than leaving the room with my bride-to-be."

She suppressed a shudder. When it came to making trouble, Nate could be remarkably creative. And because he was Chairman Heir, his bad behavior would reflect poorly not just on him and his family but on Paxco itself. Nadia might hate politics, but she cared enough about her state not to want Nate causing an international incident.

"This is blackmail," she muttered, giving him a narrow-eyed glare that failed to make an impression.

His eyes twinkled. "Is it working?"

Her shoulders slumped in defeat. "Of course it's working,"

she grumped. Not for the first time, she wondered what her life would be like if she weren't destined to be Nate's bride, if the Chairman had chosen some other family to honor. And, as she had every time she'd questioned her fate before, she dismissed the thought. Nadia's role in life as her father's second daughter, and therefore not his heir, was to marry well and bring even greater wealth, prestige, and power to her family. Nate was far and away better than most of the men she was likely to be paired with.

Nate put his hand on her shoulder blade and guided her toward the hallway. She kept her chin up, not glancing right or left, trying to pretend she wasn't doing anything improper and that she didn't notice people watching her every move. Wandering off alone with Nate in such a public setting was an epic risk. Executive society operated on a set of social conventions that hearkened back to the nineteenth century, and though girls were able to inherit and hold power the same as boys, they were held to very different standards of behavior. If her engagement to Nate should fall through, she would be forever tainted in the eyes of Executive society. Damaged goods, sloppy seconds. All because of false assumptions about what she and Nate were doing when they were out of the public eye.

The guards pretended not to notice as Nate and Nadia slipped into the darkened hallway. Within a few steps, it was so dark Nadia couldn't see a thing, but Nate guided her with complete confidence, turning two corners before reaching a hallway in which a few dim lights glowed.

Nadia's eyes were drawn immediately to the figure who stood artfully posed in the halo of one of those lights, and her heart sank even lower as she realized exactly why Nate had dragged her away from the party.

Kurt Bishop was possibly the most inappropriate boy-friend Nate could have chosen—which was no doubt part of his appeal. Born and raised in the Basement, Bishop had been rescued from his life of depravity and squalor when Nate had accompanied his father on one of his routine re-cruitment campaigns there. Twice a year, a handful of young Basement-dwellers were given a chance for a better life, be-ing brought into the ranks of the Employees, generally as menial laborers. Nate had taken an instant liking to Bishop and had hired him as his valet.

Even dressed in his formal livery, Bishop looked like a barbarian. His hair was a scraggly mane he refused to cut. A multitude of silver rings pierced one of his ears from top to bottom. Another pierced his eyebrow. And then there was the little silver ball in his tongue. Nadia couldn't imagine let-ting someone jab a needle through her tongue. Every time she saw that piercing, she had to fight a cringe.

Bishop wasn't wearing his livery tonight, Nadia noted, as an embarrassed blush rose to her cheeks. Tonight, he looked like the Basement-dweller he was, wearing skin-tight black leather pants and a mesh shirt that displayed his tattoos to all the world. He looked like a predator on the hunt, and Nate was his more-than-eager prey.

Nadia shook her head. "No," she said firmly as Nate and Bishop met each other's eyes, their gazes hot enough to scorch her.

Bishop raised his pierced eyebrow at her and smiled. "Nate didn't tell you he was coming to meet me?"

"Of course not," she snapped. "If he'd told me, I wouldn't be here."

"Nadia—" Nate started in a coaxing tone, but there were limits to how far she would allow herself to be pushed.

"I said no, and I mean it." Earlier, she'd thought she wanted to shake him; now, she wanted to slap him.

"We'll make it quick," he promised. "All you have to do is stand guard for a few minutes, let us know if someone is coming."

Bishop snickered at the double entendre, but Nadia was far from amused. She shook her head at Nate, amazed at his gall, though maybe she shouldn't have been.

"You mean you're so desperate to get laid you can't even wait until after the reception?" she asked in a furious undertone.

"Where would the fun be in that?" Nate asked with a hard glint in his eye, and Nadia realized that there was more to this liaison than just a little mischievous fun. As much as he might enjoy provoking people, Nate never quite dared stage a full-scale rebellion against his father and the rules of Executive society. But sneaking off to screw his Basement-dweller boyfriend during a state event must have seemed a pretty satisfying substitute.

Nate had told her the truth about his sexual preferences when she was fourteen, when she was old enough that he could trust her to appreciate the importance of keeping it secret. Homosexuality was all right for the Employees and the Basement-dwellers, but it was an inexcusable flaw in an Executive. If anyone learned of Nate's practices, he'd be subjected to an extensive regimen of "reprogramming." Nadia had no idea what that "reprogramming" entailed, except that it was draconian and it would destroy the Nate she knew.

Ever since he'd told her the truth, Nadia had fought to resign herself to a future of looking the other way. But she would *not* put herself through that until she had to.

"You didn't really come to rescue me from the Trio after

all, did you?" she asked, tears burning her eyes, though she refused to let them fall. "It was just a lead up to this."

Nate's eyes widened in what looked like dismay. "Of course I did! I wasn't planning to meet Kurt until later."

Nadia bit her tongue to stop herself from telling Nate for the millionth time not to refer to Bishop by first name. He insisted on doing it when in private, but it upped the chances that he would let it slip in public someday.

"So it's a coincidence that he's waiting here for you now."

"I've been here for almost an hour," Bishop interrupted. "I had no idea when he'd be able to get away."

Maybe it was true. Maybe Nate had had mostly good intentions when he'd asked her to dance. But that didn't change the fact that what he wanted to do now wasn't just *reckless,* it was *dangerous.* She should never have let him talk her into leaving the party.

"You don't give a damn about anyone but yourself, do you?" she asked, and, despite her best intentions, angry tears spilled from her cheeks. Her cold was ramping up its attack, her sinuses clogged and achy, and crying wasn't helping things.

"Nadia—"

"You don't care that if someone caught us, I'd be ruined and Bishop . . ." She shook her head. "I don't even know what would happen to him, except that he probably wouldn't live through it." As a former Basement-dweller, Bishop would have no family of any consequence to stand up for him, to make a stink if he were to disappear off the face of the earth. And Nate would be too busy being "reprogrammed" to help him.

"That's why I'm asking you to keep watch," Nate said, and the flush of color in his cheeks said he was getting angry, too. He was not used to being denied, especially not by her. "We won't get caught as long as we have you for a lookout. You'll stand at the corner of the hallway and make some kind of noise if you see someone coming."

"Oh no, I will not!" She'd never been good at standing up to Nate, but she was going to do it this time. She *had* to. There was too much at stake. She glared at Bishop, who was leaning against the wall with his arms crossed over his chest, smirking like he was enjoying the show. "Why are you encouraging him?" she asked. "You could get killed over this."

Bishop shrugged. "I guess I just have more faith in our Nate than you do," he said simply.

"I think you're confusing faith and stupidity."

"If you want to go back to the party, be my guest," Nate said. "Have fun chatting with the Trio." He turned his back on her and pushed open a door that led to a small powder room. "We'll carry on without you. If anyone asks why you're coming back alone, you can just tell them we argued. It's the truth, after all. And you won't have been gone long enough for them to think we've done anything truly scandalous."

His eyes flashed and he fixed her with his most challenging gaze. It was another attempt at blackmail, an attempt to make her worry about what greater trouble he would get into without her help. It had worked in the ballroom, but it wasn't going to work here. Somehow, someday, she had to teach Nate that she wasn't a doormat. Apparently, now was the time.

"Fine," she said, though her nerves fluttered at the thought of what might happen. "Do whatever you want. It's what you always do anyway. But you're not going to drag me down with you."

She whirled and hurried toward the darkened hallway that would lead her back to the ballroom. Nate called to her once, but she couldn't make out the words over the roaring of her pulse in her ears.

nadia awakened from a deep sleep when she felt the bed dip under someone's weight. Her bedside lamp turned on, and she blinked in the brightness as she fought off the remnants of sleep to see her mother sitting beside her on the bed, looking pale and grave.

"What is it?" Nadia asked breathlessly, pushing herself up as her pulse suddenly raced. *Someone caught Nate and Bishop,* she thought in panic. *He's been sent to reprogramming because I refused to stand watch for him.*

"It's Nathaniel, dear," her mother said, and Nadia's chest tightened painfully. But the next words were not at all what she expected to hear.

"He's been murdered."

nate awakened, gagging and choking, as a long plastic tube was removed from his throat. He tried to open his eyes, then quickly shut them again when something wet and sticky dripped into them. He wanted to wipe whatever it was away, but something was wrapped around each of his wrists, holding them down.

What the hell . . . ?

He struggled to free himself, but his limbs felt sluggish and weak, and he wasn't getting anywhere.

"Take it easy, sir," a male voice said, and then someone wiped Nate's face with a steaming hot towel and he was able to open his eyes.

He was in a sterile white room, sitting in a coffin-shaped vat of slimy green goo. Tubes and wires connected the vat to a terminal in the wall. He blinked in confusion. The last thing he remembered was coming to the Fortress for his monthly backup. How had he gotten . . . ?

The thought trailed off in his mind as he realized what waking up in this tub of goo meant.

"Oh, shit," he whispered. His head spun, and he feared he was going to be sick. "I'm a Replica."

He looked at the white-coated lab tech who had wiped the slime from his face, a forty-something Employee with brown eyes and discreetly graying hair. The lab tech gave him a single nod of confirmation, then continued unhooking Nate from the machinery that had created him.

If Paxco had gone to the enormous expense of creating a Replica, that meant the original Nate Hayes was dead.

"What's the date?" Nate asked, holding back panic as his brain tried to process what was happening.

"March fourteenth, sir," the lab tech said. "Now hold still so I can get you out of there."

Nate closed his eyes and took a deep breath, his heart hammering. He'd gone in for his backup scan on March 1st. As a Replica, he had all of Nate's memories up to the date of that backup, but anything that had happened between then and now was gone, erased by Nate's . . . death.

"I'm dead," Nate murmured under his breath, trying the words on for size.

"You're very talkative—and very reluctant to hold still— for a dead man," the tech said drily, and Nate forced his eyes open once again.

Legally and practically, he *was* Nathaniel Edison Hayes, even if he was only a lab-created Replica, born in this vat of primordial ooze, constructed as a perfect facsimile of his original by the proprietary technology that made Paxco the richest and most powerful of the Corporate States. He tried a few tentative stretches, concentrating hard on the sensation of his muscles bunching and releasing. His joints were stiff and a little achy, like he'd been lying unnaturally still for hours on end, but the sensations were familiar. Normal. He still *felt* like himself, as far as he could tell.

The tech finally finished unhooking Nate from the mechanical womb. Nate felt weak and shaky as the tech helped him climb out of the ooze, which sucked at him as if reluctant to let him go. He wiped at the goo that clung to him, shuddering at the feel of it against his skin. Some of it glopped off onto the floor, but he was still coated with slime. Panic tried again to take over, but he shoved it down to be dealt with later.

"There's a shower in there," the tech said, steadying him by holding his elbow.

Nate shook him off. He could stand by his own damn self.

"What happened to me?" he asked, unable to wrap his brain around the idea that he had died. He'd have said this was a practical joke, if anyone he knew had that kind of sense of humor. How could he be a lab-created Replica of a dead guy and feel so *normal*?

"Your father will brief you after you've showered and dressed," the tech said, glancing at his watch. "He's scheduled to arrive at five o'clock, so you have half an hour to get ready. Do you need any help?"

Nate frowned at him. "I've been taking showers by myself for quite some time now," he said, trying for a tone of dry humor. His memory insisted he'd taken a shower a couple of hours ago, right after he'd eaten breakfast and before he'd come to the Fortress for his backup. But these memories were from two weeks ago, and they weren't really *his*, they were the real Nate's. The real Nate who was *dead*.

Nate shook his head. He'd drive himself nuts if he let himself think about it too much.

"As you wish," the tech said with a shrug. "I'll be right out here, so give a shout if you need anything."

"I need to know what happened to me," Nate said.

"Your father will explain when he arrives, sir."

Nate sighed. Patience had never been one of his virtues, but the tech had no doubt been ordered to keep his mouth shut. "Will you at least tell me whether it was an accident?"

Surely it was an accident. Nate did enjoy taking risks, and if one of those risks came back to bite him, it wouldn't be a complete surprise.

The tech hesitated, then lowered his voice. "It wasn't an accident."

Half an hour later, Nate felt a lot more like himself, the slime scrubbed from his skin and hair, his mind clearer, the panic mostly subdued. He'd examined himself closely in the bathroom mirror, and everything was just like he remembered it, down to the tiny tattoo on his ass he'd gotten for Kurt. (And because he enjoyed thinking about the fit his father would throw if he ever found out about it.) No doubt the tech had seen it, since Nate had come out of the ooze stark naked, but Nate doubted he would go blabbing about it.

Nate dressed in the stylish dark business suit that had been left for him, though he skipped the tie and shoved it in his pocket. He was more relieved than he could say to find the antique oval locket he always wore under his shirt stashed in a bag with his phone, wallet, and other personal effects. As far as anyone knew, the locket was a gift from Nadia. There was even a photo of her inside, and she'd always played along with the fiction. But in truth, it was from Kurt—Nate didn't want to know where the money had come from, because a solid gold antique locket was definitely outside Kurt's price range.

The tech—whose name, Nate discovered when he had enough wits about him to ask, was Gregson—led Nate to a small conference room deep in the heart of the Fortress. Getting into the Fortress required enough security checks to discourage all but the most determined, but only a handful of people had clearance to set foot this deep inside, where the

Replicas were made. The technology behind the Replicas was the most closely guarded secret in the universe. No one had duplicated Paxco's success, and without access to the extraordinary mind behind the technology, no one ever would.

Nate was not surprised that his father hadn't yet arrived. Nathaniel Sr. would never miss an opportunity to make a subordinate wait, and he always made sure Nate knew he was a subordinate.

Gregson left Nate alone in the conference room with a cup of foul-tasting tea that was supposed to help him regain his strength faster. After one sip, Nate decided he'd regain his strength at his own pace.

The tea had stopped steaming by the time the conference room door opened and Nate's father stepped in, followed closely by Nate's second-least-favorite person in the world, Dirk Mosely, Paxco's chief of security. A product of the Chairman's Basement reclamation project, Mosely was fiercely loyal, dangerously intelligent, and a sadistic bastard who enjoyed his work far too much. He was frighteningly good at his job—which was to uphold the law, except when the law got in his way.

Nate stood still as his father looked him up and down with a frown of concentration, examining him for flaws. Nathaniel Sr. was a pro at finding flaws. He frowned at the open collar of Nate's shirt, but he could hardly have been surprised that Nate had forgone the tie.

"It never ceases to amaze me," Nate's father said finally as he gestured for Nate to take a seat. "Such a perfect likeness." If he felt any grief over the real Nate's death, he was doing a great job of hiding it. But Nate had never really mattered to his father as a *person*, merely as an heir. And thanks to Replica technology, that heir still existed even though the person was dead. Not that Nate was bitter about their relationship or anything.

As far as Nate knew, he was only the third human Replica ever to be created. The technology was only about ten years old, and the astronomical fee Paxco charged for storing back-ups and creating Replicas assured that only the wealthiest of the wealthy were able to afford the privilege. Not to mention the considerable number of governments, moralists, and religious groups that considered Replicas an abomination, the ultimate example of playing God.

"What happened to me?" Nate asked, remaining on his feet just because his father had gestured for him to sit.

His father gave him a disapproving look as he sat at the head of the table, adjusting his chair so it was just right. Another little power play, letting Nate know he wasn't getting answers until he sat down as ordered.

Grinding his teeth to keep from saying anything that would annoy his father and cause further delays, Nate pulled back a chair and sat, clasping his hands in front of him on the table like an obedient schoolchild.

"What happened to me?" he asked again, meeting his father's cold gray eyes. He suppressed a shudder as he realized nothing had happened to *him*: it had happened to the real Nate Hayes. But damn, he *felt* like the real Nate Hayes.

"You were murdered," the Chairman said, no trace of emotion in his voice.

"Murdered," Nate murmured, hoping he sounded surprised despite Gregson's tip-off. He shook his head. "Murdered." The word tasted sour in his mouth. How could someone possibly have *murdered* him? Nate knew he had a gift for rubbing people the wrong way—it was a gift he cultivated with great care—but he couldn't imagine ever annoying someone so much that they would kill him for it. And it wasn't like killing him accomplished anything, when he was sure to be brought back as a Replica. It seemed a hell of a lot to risk for very little reward.

Mosely, standing behind the Chairman's shoulder, took over explaining. "You were last seen last night, leaving the reception with Nadia Lake. She returned to the reception alone. Presumably, you argued."

Nate had to think a moment to figure out what reception Mosely was talking about. Then he remembered today's date and realized the big state wedding must have been the day before.

The implications of Mosely's words sank in, and Nate's eyes widened. "You don't think . . ." Nadia wouldn't hurt a fly, no matter how badly they'd argued. He shook his head. "There's no way I was murdered by a sixteen-year-old girl," he said, almost laughing at the absurdity of it.

Mosely shrugged. "She isn't a suspect, though of course she is being questioned. You were found stabbed to death in a hall closet at the mansion just after midnight. There were no witnesses to the murder itself, but three people confirm seeing a man who matches the description of Kurt Bishop fleeing the hallway in an agitated state with blood on his hands. They didn't stop him at the time because he was holding his nose, and they thought he had a nosebleed. Only after the body was found did they realize they let a killer escape. His current whereabouts are unknown."

A chill ran down Nate's spine, and his pulse kicked up. "There is no way in hell Kurt killed me," he said as calmly as possible, but warning bells were clanging away in his head. He knew beyond a shadow of a doubt that Kurt would never hurt him. But Kurt made the perfect scapegoat, born and raised in the Basement and refusing to shed the trappings once Nate made him an Employee. How easy it would be for everyone to believe that Nate had been taken in by a predator, to believe that Kurt had bitten the hand that fed him like the disreputable Basement-dweller he was.

It wasn't until he noticed the look that passed between his father and Mosely that Nate realized he'd just made the mistake Nadia had always warned him he'd make: he'd used Kurt's first name in public. An Executive did *not* address or refer to a servant by first name. Then again, Nate had never met a social convention he didn't want to break, so perhaps they would think he was just being his usual self.

"You don't know that," Mosely said. "You're missing almost two weeks of memory. Maybe something happened during those weeks, something that put you and your valet at odds. I know you fancied him something of a friend." There was no missing the sneer in Mosely's voice, and for a moment Nate feared Mosely knew exactly what was going on between him and Kurt. But no. If Mosely knew, then Nate's father knew, and if Nate's father knew, Nate would be in reprogramming right now.

"Bishop did not kill me," Nate repeated.

"Then where is he?" Mosely asked. "Why did he go missing on the very night you were murdered?"

"Because he knew he'd be the prime suspect," Nate countered, fighting to keep his temper in check. "And he knew there was no way he'd get a fair trial."

"And he was seen fleeing the scene with blood on his hands because . . . ?"

"Because those 'witnesses' were lying. Or because he touched the body, trying to help me."

"You have an explanation for everything, don't you," Mosely

said. "So tell me: if Mr. Bishop isn't the murderer, then who is?"

"How the hell should I know? Figuring it out is your job, last I heard."

"Give me a suspect. Someone who had access to the residence and who had a reason to kill you even knowing there'd be a Replica."

Nate wished he could snap back a quick answer, but he had to admit he was stumped. If he really stretched, he could think of people who might want to get rid of him, but none of them would even consider trying it when they knew he'd be almost instantly replaced by a Replica. Cold logic suggested Kurt killing him in a moment of passion was the most reasonable explanation. But cold logic was wrong.

"Enough, Nathaniel," his father said. "If you wish to believe in Bishop's innocence, feel free. But the evidence says otherwise. He murdered you. Stabbed you to death and then left you in a pool of your own blood. For that, he will die."

There was no give in the Chairman's voice—not that there ever was—and Nate knew his father's mind was closed and sealed up tight. His father had disapproved of Kurt from the beginning, considering him unworthy of being a valet for *any* Executive, much less the Chairman Heir. If he saw a way to dispose of Kurt, he'd jump at it, whether Kurt was the killer or not.

Guilt niggled at Nate's conscience. Kurt's life in the Basement had been predictably ugly, but he was a natural-born survivor. He'd carved out a place for himself, and he'd been secure in it, no matter how unappealing it might seem to an Employee or an Executive. Nate had told himself he was doing Kurt a favor, rescuing him from that life. He'd been confident he could protect him, as long as they were careful. Had he been fooling himself all along?

"I'm telling you, you've got it wrong," Nate said, wishing the third time could be the charm. "Bishop didn't do it, and if you decide in advance that he did, you'll never get the real killer."

Nathaniel Sr. pushed back his chair, shaking his head. "I'm glad to see my son's Replica is as naive and foolish as my son himself was."

The paternal affection was overwhelming. Nate glared at his father's retreating back. "I'm not as naive as you think," he said. If his father truly knew him, he'd know just how far from the truth he was. Thanks to Kurt and repeated clandestine visits to the Basement—or Debasement, as its residents called it—Nate knew more about the ugly side of life than his father ever would. And someday, when the Chairmanship of Paxco passed to him, Nate was going to do something about it.

The Chairman didn't even bother to acknowledge Nate's words as he jerked open the conference room door and stepped out. Mosely stopped to give Nate a quick, sly smile over his shoulder before leaving. Nate refused to let the bastard see how much that smile chilled him.

He *had* to find Kurt before Mosely's security team did.

NO one had openly accused Nadia of having murdered Nate or of being an accomplice to his murder. From the moment the security team had come to her apartment and asked her to come to the station for questioning, they'd been unfailingly polite. She certainly couldn't blame them for wanting to talk to her when she was apparently the last person to see Nate alive. But being questioned three times by three different officers made her feel very much like a suspect all the same.

She couldn't be sure exactly how long she'd been at the station, except that it was a long time. There was no clock on the interview room wall, she wasn't wearing a watch, and they'd confiscated her phone. They'd brought her lunch, and the door wasn't locked, but she was under no illusion that she would be allowed to walk out.

Where were her parents? When the security officers had come to the house, her father had been at work, despite it being Sunday, but her mother had hugged her—an unusually affectionate gesture—and sworn they'd have her home in no time. But the moment they'd set foot in the station, Nadia and her mother had been separated, and she'd been alone ever since. Her understanding of proper legal procedure was slim, but Nadia thought that as a minor, she would have been allowed to have at least one parent with her at all times. The enforced isolation seemed like a very bad sign, and her imagination filled with images of dank prison cells and iron chains. Which was ridiculous, of course, but also no doubt what the security team wanted her thinking about.

Her cold had worsened overnight, her throat painfully raw and her sinuses so stuffy her head felt like it would explode. She wanted desperately to crawl into bed and sleep for a week. Her requests for cold medicine were ignored, though one of the nicer officers had brought her a box of tissues and a trash can.

The lights in the room dimmed sometime in what Nadia guessed was the late afternoon, and her heart fluttered. Creating a Replica took so much power it could cause a citywide blackout if not managed properly. She hoped the dimming lights meant Nate's Replica was being created.

Tears stung her eyes as the stark, awful reality slapped her in the face yet again. Nate was dead. Sure, there would be a Replica, and it would be just like him. But it wouldn't be *Nate*. Not the Nate she'd known all her life. Not the Nate who was her best friend, who was the only person in the world who didn't care about her social standing or her political value. Worse, the last conversation she'd had with him had been a bitter argument. She'd been so angry with him last night. . . . And now he was gone.

How could anyone believe she had anything to do with Nate's death? Couldn't they see she was heartbroken?

She couldn't possibly fall asleep, not sitting in this cold, stark interview room, and not with her constant need to grab for the tissue box, but she did drowse a bit, her mind wandering. Unfortunately, it didn't wander anywhere she wanted to go. This extended stay at the security station and the veiled suspicion that she might have had something to do with Nate's death would cast a pall on her and on her family, no matter how unfair. Her parents were going to be furious with her for wandering off with Nate last night and giving the authorities reason to detain her. Perhaps that was why they weren't working harder to get her freed, or at least get her an attorney. When she'd asked for one herself, she'd been told an attorney wasn't necessary because she wasn't under arrest.

Nadia jumped when the door to the interview room squealed open. She wondered if the squeaky hinges were part of an insidious torture technique designed to drive detainees mad. If so, it was working.

Her heart gave a nasty thud when she saw who had entered the room: Dirk Mosely.

Nadia had had little contact with Paxco's chief of security, but she'd heard the rumors, and they weren't pretty. A middle-aged man of average height, with a bald spot and just a hint of a paunch, Mosely didn't look particularly dangerous. If anything, he looked like a mild-mannered accountant, the kind of person who went through life barely being noticed by those around him. But if Nadia were to believe even half of the whispered stories, he was a monster, one barely controlled by the tight leash the Chairman kept on him.

Nadia's nose started to run; she grabbed for the tissue box, using that moment of distraction to pull herself together. She was the daughter of Gerald Lake, one of Paxco's most powerful Executives. Mosely wouldn't *dare* do anything to harm her. Not unless she were guilty of a crime, which she wasn't.

"I hear you've been under the weather," Mosely said as he pulled out a chair and sat at the table across from her.

Nadia blew her nose and tossed the tissue into the trash can, which was already halfway full. She figured that was answer enough to his inane observation. She pulled another tissue out, knowing she'd need it sooner or later.

"I'm sorry for the . . . inconvenience," Mosely said, sounding not the least bit sorry. "However, you were the last person to see Nathaniel alive, and you could hold the key to us capturing his killer."

She shook her head, deathly tired of all this. "I've been over this at least three times," she said. "Yes, I went off alone with Nate, and yes, we argued."

"About what?"

Nadia was certain Mosely had already read the transcripts of her last three interviews and knew the answer she'd given. She was also certain he'd insist she answer again. "He wanted to take more liberties than I would allow." Which was sort of true, if you thought about it, though not in the way Mosely and his officers would take it.

"Surely you knew he planned to take liberties when you left the party with him."

"Yes, I knew." As had everyone else who'd noticed the two of them leaving the room. "I just didn't know exactly *what* liberties."

"So what liberties did our Chairman Heir have in mind?"

Nadia felt a chill of alarm. No one else had asked her that, having made natural assumptions of what Nate was after. She had the immediate suspicion that Mosely already knew more than he should, that he might be testing her honesty. He was said to be uncanny in his ability to tell when people were lying, which meant she had to stick as close to the truth as possible.

"I don't see that that's any of your business," she said. "It's personal."

"The Chairman Heir was murdered," Mosely said, staring at her intently as if he thought she would burst out with a confession at any moment. "Everything about last night is my business."

"I'm not answering any more questions without a lawyer present."

Mosely smiled, but there was a hard—and strangely self-satisfied—glint in his eye. "Very well," he said, pushing back his chair and standing up. "It should take about a week for legal counsel to be arranged and all the paperwork properly filed. I will have you transferred to the Riker's Island Detention Center while the arrangements are being made."

Nadia hugged herself, shivering. "You can't do that," she said, though not with any certainty. "My father is—"

"A citizen of Paxco, subject to the same laws as every other citizen of Paxco. As are you."

In theory, perhaps, but everyone knew how unequally the

laws were applied. Still, if they thought she'd had something to do with Nate's murder, then her family connections couldn't protect her. Nadia's pulse was racing, and dread was a cold lump in her stomach. She didn't want to imagine what it would be like to spend a full day—much less a full week—at Riker's Island. And never mind the kind of taint being sent there would cast on her and her family. You didn't have to be guilty of anything to be socially ruined.

"Fine," she said, her stuffy head aching. She blew her nose for the millionth time. "I'll answer your questions."

Mosely smiled at her. "I knew you could be reasonable. Now, tell me *exactly* what happened between you and Nathaniel last night."

Nadia took a deep breath, organizing her thoughts before she spoke, planning her words to avoid any outright lies. "Nate wanted to have sex," she said, her cheeks heating with a blush as she stared at her hands. A true statement, even if it wasn't *her* he'd wanted to have sex with. "I turned him down. I knew when he asked me to leave the party that he meant to, um, take liberties. I just didn't know he was going to try to take things that far."

"What happened after that?"

"Nate threatened to do something scandalous if I didn't give in. I wouldn't let him manipulate me, so I left."

"Something scandalous? Be more specific."

"He threatened to do it with or without me." Her cheeks burned even more as she let Mosely draw the natural conclusion that Nate had threatened to go find another woman.

Mosely raised an eyebrow. "And you called his bluff?"

Nadia nodded. If she hadn't called Nate's bluff, if she hadn't left him and Bishop to their own devices, would they both be alive and safe right now? Was whatever had happened to them her fault?

"You are a remarkable young woman," Mosely said with an oily smile. "You would rather your presumed husband-to-be sleep with another than give up your own virtue? Such admirable strength of character."

Nadia wanted to throw her snot-covered tissue right in Mosely's smug face, but she was in quite enough trouble already. "I didn't think he would actually do it."

She realized with a start that that was true. As reckless as Nate was, Nadia hadn't believed he'd take the risk of hooking up with Bishop during the party if he didn't have her around to make sure they weren't caught. He took a risk every time he and Bishop were together, but nothing like doing it under the noses of the entire Executive class of Paxco and all the visiting dignitaries.

"During your disagreement with Nathaniel, did you by any chance see his valet, Kurt Bishop?" Mosely asked.

Nadia's palms began to sweat, and once again she wondered if Mosely had somehow known all along exactly what had happened last night. "He was there," she answered cautiously. "Nate wanted someone to serve as a lookout."

"And was he still with Nathaniel when you made your grand exit?"

She ground her teeth. Mosely's lips twitched with amusement, and Nadia hated that she'd given him the satisfaction.

"Yes. Yes, he was. And you already knew that, didn't you?"

Mosely smiled benignly, and once again Nadia was tempted to do something imprudent.

"If you knew he was there, then you know that someone saw Nate alive after I left. Why are you questioning *me* instead of Bishop?" Not that she'd wish Mosely on Bishop, of course.

Mosely's smile hardened. "Because Kurt Bishop is missing. Evidence suggests he stabbed Nathaniel to death and then fled the scene. I am trying to ascertain whether you might have been Mr. Bishop's accomplice."

Nadia's mouth dropped open in shock. She was hardly Bishop's biggest fan. As far as she was concerned, he was a bad influence on Nate, and there was a hard, bitter edge to him that made him difficult to like. But he would *never* hurt Nate.

"You're way off target, Mr. Mosely," she said. "I had nothing to do with Nate's death, and I'm sure Bishop didn't either."

Mosely rolled his eyes. "Yes, yes, I've already heard about Mr. Bishop's saintly innocence. The fact remains he is the prime suspect, and his refusal to turn himself in and account for his actions is most suspicious."

Nadia didn't find it suspicious at all. Mosely had already threatened to detain her, the daughter of a president and the presumed fiancée to the Chairman Heir. If he dared issue such a threat to someone of her station, God only knew what he would do to a nobody like Kurt Bishop. She refrained, however, from sharing that opinion with Mosely.

"Why would you suspect *me* of conspiring with Nate's valet?" she asked instead. "What could I possibly stand to gain from Nate's death? For that matter, what would *Bishop* have to gain?" Especially when they both knew Nate's death would be temporary, thanks to the Replica technology.

"One assumes it was a crime of passion of some sort. Perhaps Nathaniel threatened to dismiss him and Mr. Bishop reacted violently to the news."

Nadia shook her head. "That's ridiculous."

"Nathaniel's Replica shares your conviction in Mr. Bishop's innocence," Mosely said. "I believe he will make his own attempt to locate Mr. Bishop, with the intention of helping him escape justice."

If Nate's Replica was just like the real Nate, then yes, he probably would. There was no way he'd believe Bishop was guilty, and he would do everything in his power to protect his boyfriend. Including reckless, dangerous things that could get him killed again.

"You are Nathaniel's confidant," Mosely continued, and Nadia shivered in premonition. "If you would agree to share with me whatever you might learn about his efforts to locate Mr. Bishop—or about any contact he might have with Mr. Bishop—then I would be inclined to release you into the custody of your parents."

The blood drained from Nadia's face as she absorbed the implications of Mosely's words. "You want me to spy on him. To betray him."

"He is a young and foolish boy, blinded by idealism. Bishop is a murderer, and he must be brought to justice, despite the stars in Nathaniel's eyes. You wouldn't be betraying him—you'd be doing him a favor. And he would never have to know."

She shook her head. Even if she believed Bishop were the killer, she couldn't betray Nate like that. The Nate she'd grown up with might be dead, but if she helped Mosely locate Bishop, she'd be betraying his memory. Not to mention his Replica, whom she'd one day find herself married to.

"I won't do it," she said, shaking her head. "I *can't* do it. Nate would never forgive me."

Mosely folded his hands on the table and leaned forward, pinning her with his stare. "Let me make the situation perfectly clear. You *will* do this. You will learn Nathaniel's every plan, and you will share them with me. For Nathaniel's own good. If you refuse, you will spend at least a week at the detention center, where you will be questioned more rigorously about your involvement with the murder."

"You can't do that," Nadia said in a horrified whisper. "I haven't done anything wrong."

"Oh, I assure you, I can. The assassination of the Chairman Heir is an act of treason, and where cases of treason are involved, my department has the latitude to detain and question anyone we deem necessary. In truth, I am doing you a favor by allowing you to prove your loyalty to your state by helping us capture the killer."

Nadia's eyes filled with tears of hopelessness. "Please don't make me do this," she begged as those tears spilled over, though she knew better than to expect mercy from a man like Dirk Mosely. She couldn't bear the thought of betraying Nate, but she was going to end up betraying him one way or another. She had no illusions that she could withstand a week of "rigorous questioning" without spilling everything she knew about last night's events, including Nate's true sexual preferences. Whatever she did, she would damn Bishop, and Nate would hate her for it.

Mosely stood up, still staring at her with baleful eyes. "If I walk out that door without your agreement, you will be transferred to the detention center within the hour."

Mosely turned on his heel, striding purposefully toward the door.

Maybe he's bluffing, Nadia thought desperately. But she knew he wasn't. And if he sent her to the detention center, it would ruin not just her own life, but Nate's and her entire family's as well. A taint of that magnitude could never be overcome.

Mosely grabbed the knob and pulled the door open.

"Wait!" she cried, just before he stepped out of the room. "I'll do it." She felt like a pathetic coward for giving in, but she just couldn't face the consequences of refusing.

Mosely turned back to her with a vicious smile. "You've made the right decision," he said, then took his seat across from her again.

Nadia wished she could believe him.

CHAPTER THREE

After the unpleasant meeting with his father and Mosely, Nate hoped to go home and get his thoughts lined up, but of course things were never so easy when you were the Chairman Heir of a powerful corporate state. So instead of having time to rest and recuperate, he found himself running a gauntlet of press conferences, interviews, and debriefings.

The press asked the most intrusive and obnoxious questions, of course, focusing on the lurid details and constantly asking him how he felt about everything. He'd been Chairman Heir all his life, so Nate was used to the media circus. That didn't mean he liked it, and as the day wore on, his responses grew rather more abrupt than was politically wise. When he got asked for what felt like the thousandth time how he felt about having been murdered and brought back to life as a Replica, he snapped.

"How the fuck do you *think* I feel?" he snarled, then batted the microphone out of his way, fighting the temptation to shove it down the reporter's throat.

Nate's press secretary gave him a dark look as his security detail tried to confiscate all the cameras that had caught his little indiscretion for posterity. Nate put the odds at fifty-fifty that the film would wind up on the net anyway.

Screw it. He might be a Replica, but he wasn't a machine, and there was only so much shit he was prepared to swallow.

He left the press conference only to find a cluster of demonstrators waiting for him at the Fortress's front entrance. The entrance was sealed off with a double set of gates, and the security forces were keeping the protesters well away from the gates and the street, but that didn't stop Nate from seeing the signs being waved as his limo pulled out.

REPLICAS AREN'T PEOPLE.

ABOMINATION!

THE DEAD SHOULD STAY DEAD!

YOU WILL BURN IN HELL!

He suspected some of the stuff they were screaming and chanting was even worse, though he couldn't make out the words. The protest was peaceful enough, and there was no sign that the crowd wanted to fight past the barricade and rush the limo, but their anger was a palpable force. Nate tried to look straight ahead and ignore it all, but it was still a shock to the senses.

Nate was used to being well liked. Even his scandalous behavior was usually treated as roguish charm by the press and the public. The vehemence of the crowd's anger was more than a little unsettling, though perhaps he should have expected it. Even he had to admit that Replicas were a bit disturbing. The idea that anything he remembered in his entire life actually happened to someone else was going to drive him insane.

It was well past dark by the time he finally escaped and was able to drop the forced smile he'd been wearing all day. He still struggled with the idea that someone had actually stabbed him to death the night before. He could be an asshole sometimes, he knew that, but generally that wasn't a crime punishable by death.

His bodyguards performed a thorough examination of his

penthouse suite before allowing Nate to enter, but once he was inside, they retreated to the vestibule and he was finally able to close the door on the outside world. He had moved into the penthouse on his eighteenth birthday, a little more than six months ago. His father thought his eagerness to move out from under the same roof had been an act of rebellion, and it had. But more importantly, it had granted Nate the only modicum of privacy he was ever likely to have.

His knees feeling suddenly weak, his chest tight, Nate helped himself to a tumbler of expensive whiskey, closing his eyes and savoring the smooth burn as the alcohol slid down his throat. Technically, he was under the legal drinking age, but no one was going to refuse to sell to the Chairman Heir. His hands were shaking, his heart pounding. The pain and the panic he'd been fighting all day tried to swamp him as he finally had a chance to face them without an audience.

Nate gulped the rest of his whiskey, not caring that it was supposed to be sipped. He'd never developed a connoisseur's palate, despite the expensive tastes he was expected to cultivate, and he didn't make much of a distinction between the finest aged single malt and rotgut. They both contained alcohol, and that was all that mattered. He smiled tightly, thinking how his father sneered at his lowbrow tastes. The Chairman considered him to be about as cultured as a Basement-dweller, and Nate took pride in it.

The whiskey helped soothe away the panic attack, and Nate paced in front of the floor-to-ceiling windows that fronted his living room, looking out at the twinkling lights of the city. He had a breathtaking view of what everyone still called the Empire State Building, despite the fact that it had been officially renamed the Paxco Headquarters Building.

Usually, he appreciated the view, but tonight he was struck by how vast and dangerous the city was.

Kurt was out there somewhere, alone, hunted. Nate put his hand on the glass and closed his eyes, wishing he could sense Kurt's presence, wishing some magic would flow into his body and show him where to find him. Surely, Kurt would contact him eventually, would reach out for the help only someone of Nate's station could offer. All Nate had to do was wait and be ready when the time came.

He'd feel a lot more ready if he had some concrete plan for how he was going to help Kurt when he found him. Obviously, he would have to find some way to smuggle him out of Paxco. Even if Nate could find the real killer, Kurt would never be safe in Paxco again. He was supposed to be presumed innocent, but that wasn't how things worked in the real world, and the stain would never wash off.

"Hurry up and contact me," Nate whispered, as if willing Kurt to do it would actually make it happen.

Kurt had friends in the Basement, Nate reminded himself. Well, maybe calling them "friends" was a bit on the generous side, but he had connections. People who'd be willing to hide him and protect him from Mosely's security forces, as long as he had money.

As soon as the thought hit him, hope surged in Nate's chest. To survive in the Basement when he was being hunted, Kurt needed money. And Nate knew exactly where he could have gotten his hands on what he needed if he'd been daring enough to try for it.

Setting his empty glass down, he closed the drapes to protect from any unwanted watchers, then crossed to the bar with its impressive array of bottles and decanters. The floor of the bar was rich green marble, but the bar itself was of carved mahogany. Mahogany doors hid a minifridge from view, and beside the fridge was a decorative carved panel that looked like solid wood.

Nate felt along the sides of the panel until he found the little metal protuberance, then pushed. Something clicked, and the panel came loose in his hands. He laid the panel on the floor behind the bar, then peered into the thin vertical compartment the panel had hidden.

Ordinarily, the compartment held stacks of neatly banded hundred dollar bills. Real dollars, not company scrip. Scrip was the currency of choice for all legal transactions, and your ordinary Employee never laid eyes on a real dollar bill. But if you were going to spend any time in Debasement, you wanted the real thing. Oh, the black marketeers and sundry criminals in Debasement were perfectly happy to relieve you of your scrip, in epic quantities. But if you had real dollars, you could buy just about anything your heart desired. Without any official record of the transaction.

Nate, in his official capacity as Chairman Heir, had access to dollars that would make any Basement-dweller's eyes gleam with greed, and he'd been squirreling them away ever since he'd gotten old enough to understand their significance. He and Kurt had always tapped into that supply whenever they'd made their illicit trips to Debasement together, so Kurt knew exactly where the stash was hidden.

His eyes told him that the hidden compartment was empty, but, like an idiot, Nate had to reach in there and feel around anyway. But no, there was not a single dollar bill left in the compartment. Which was good news. It meant that Kurt had enough money to buy his way out of Paxco. Human smuggling was big business in the Basement, and Kurt would know just who to contact.

The less heartening news was that Kurt hadn't left anything for Nate. No note, no good-bye, no explanation. Kurt was a beginner at reading and writing—skills that weren't highly prized in the Basement—but Nate had been steadily teaching him. Kurt could have managed a note, even if it would have been clumsily written and riddled with spelling errors.

For half a second, Nate wondered if he was being the most naive human being on the face of the planet. To anyone but Nate, the theft of all those dollars with no explanation would be evidence of the most damning kind.

Was there a chance Kurt was guilty?

Nate dismissed the thought. He didn't care what anyone else thought. He knew Kurt, and Kurt hadn't done this. He'd taken the money, but Nate could hardly blame him for that. Every second he'd spent at the apartment would have increased the danger that he would get caught. So Nate couldn't hold it against him that he hadn't taken the time to write out a letter of explanation.

But the thought that Kurt was now forever out of his reach, doomed to live the rest of his life in hiding, sat heavily on Nate's shoulders. As did the realization that without Kurt's account of what had happened on the night of his murder, Nate might never know who had really killed him.

BY the time Mosely finally allowed Nadia to go home, the heat in her cheeks and the weakness in her knees told her she was running a fever, and she felt like she was at death's door. When she was escorted down to the security station's lobby, her mother was waiting for her, sitting rigidly on the edge of a straight-backed chair, her chin held high and her eyes flashing with fury as she worked to maintain her fabled aura of superiority. No doubt she'd been sitting in the station's lobby all day, but you'd never be able to tell by looking at her. Her makeup was still perfect, her hair neatly coiffed, her clothes unwrinkled. Nadia didn't even want to think about how *she* looked right now.

Apparently, she looked as wretched as she felt, because as soon as her mother caught sight of her, the anger in her expression eased and a hint of concern entered her eyes. Nadia wanted to fling herself into her mother's arms and sob, but of course the daughter of a president would never *dream* of doing something so undignified in public. No, Nadia's eyes were merely watering because she was sick and exhausted.

"Please take me home," she begged before her mother could say anything. "I need to lie down." She sniffled loudly, playing up her illness in hopes of staving off a maternal lecture. She was rewarded by even more softening of her mother's expression.

"My poor baby," Esmeralda Lake murmured, reaching up to touch the back of her hand to Nadia's forehead. "You're burning up." She glared at the two officers who had escorted Nadia, her face conveying the impression that she would hold them personally responsible for Nadia's illness. Nadia noticed that neither of the men would make eye contact with her mother, both shifting awkwardly where they stood, and she suppressed a smile. Esmeralda might derive her status from her husband's rank rather than her own, but she knew how to wield that status to devastating effect. Even big, bold, alpha-male security officers squirmed on the receiving end of her displeasure. Now, if only Nadia could somehow keep all that displeasure from being aimed at her.

Her mother put an arm around Nadia's shoulders, and it took everything Nadia had not to lean into her and let the tears loose. She was holding on to her self-control by the most fragile of threads. Nate had been murdered. Nadia had been questioned like a suspect, threatened with a stay at Riker's Island. Bishop was running for his life. And she had allowed herself to be bullied into spying on her best friend and future husband. It was all too much to handle, and yet somehow she had to hold it all inside.

"Where's Dad?" she asked, the cold having turned her voice into a hoarse croak that would embarrass a frog.

"He's in a meeting," her mother answered. Nadia fought a wave of hurt that her father would allow himself to be called away at a time like this. "With the Chairman," her mother hastened to add when Nadia gaped at her. "He couldn't very well refuse to see Chairman Hayes, now could he?"

No, of course he couldn't. And Nadia couldn't help suspecting that Chairman Hayes had deliberately separated Nadia from her support system. It was clear to anyone who had eyes that her father was the softer, more sympathetic of her parents. Her father would take one look at her now and immediately cosset her like a sick child. She doubted her mother would let her off so easily.

Naturally, the press were camped out in front of the station. When the security team had arrived in the morning, Nadia had been wearing no makeup and had on drawstring pants and a light, boxy sweater. They hadn't allowed her to change before bringing her in, and no doubt she looked the worse for wear. The idea of having her picture taken when she looked like that made her want to crawl away and hide.

Her mother apparently didn't like the idea much, either. At her command, the security officers walked them to the waiting limo, using their jackets to shield Nadia from view. She had no doubt that tomorrow's gossip columns would be filled with those photos, even if all they showed was the cluster of security officers.

Nadia let out a breath of relief when she climbed into the limo. Then she saw the look on her mother's face and braced herself for the lecture she'd known was coming.

"Really, Nadia," her mother said with a shake of her head, "what *were* you thinking, running off on your own with Nathaniel last night?"

Nadia groaned and closed her eyes, leaning her flaming cheek against the cool glass of the dark-tinted window. The coolness felt momentarily good, until it shot a chill through her entire body and she shivered violently. She wasn't even trying to manipulate her mother this time, but it worked anyway.

Esmeralda sighed. "Never mind. We'll talk about it later, when you're feeling better."

Nadia huddled in on herself and wished for oblivion. She didn't want to think about anything, least of all about what the future would bring. How she wished she could turn back the clock and change the decisions she'd made last night. If she'd refused to let Nate bully her in the first place, maybe things would have turned out differently.

By the time the limo pulled up in front of the Lake Towers—named after Nadia's grandfather, who had been the first president in their family line—Nadia was barely conscious. Someone—she was so out of it she wasn't sure who—carried her into the building and up to her family's apartment. She had the vague impression of someone else helping her out of her clothes and into her nightgown, and then the next thing she knew, it was morning.

Nadia's eyes were crusty, and her head felt stuffed with cotton. When she reached up to rub the grit from her eyes, she noticed the IV stuck into the back of her hand. She blinked in confusion, having no memory of having seen a doctor.

"Someone lied about getting her flu shot this year."

Nadia wondered what drugs were dripping into her blood from the IV, because she felt like she was reacting in slow motion. She heard the voice, then had to take a moment to figure out which way to turn her head to face the speaker. With an involuntary groan, she turned to the right and saw her older sister, Geraldine, sitting in the corner armchair Nadia liked to use for reading.

"Gerri?" she asked, noticing that while her voice was still hoarse and croaky, it didn't hurt to talk. The improvement was certainly welcome. "What are you doing here?"

As eldest daughter, Gerri was their father's heir, a role she took very, very seriously. Gerri might take a day off from work if her husband or children were on their deathbeds, but she surely wouldn't do it because Nadia had a nasty cold.

Gerri smiled ruefully. "Mother drafted me. She has a dinner party to plan and didn't feel she had time to properly, um, debrief you."

Nadia closed her eyes and prayed she'd slip back into a deep sleep. She'd dodged the proverbial bullet last night when her mother cut the expected lecture short. She should have known that wasn't the end of it. And she knew exactly why Esmeralda had chosen Gerri as her weapon. From what Nadia could tell, all mothers learned how to wield guilt like a deadly weapon, and Esmeralda liked to make certain Nadia was always aware of how her actions affected not just herself, but her entire family—including Gerri's two kids, Rory and Corinne.

Gerri rose to her feet and came to sit on the edge of Nadia's bed. She wore a ruby red power suit that said she planned to go to work after she was finished "visiting." With the red suit, alabaster skin, and nearly jet black hair, she looked like an evolved version of Snow White: beautiful and deadly, instead of beautiful and fragile. She was twelve years older than Nadia, so they hadn't exactly grown up together, but Nadia had always admired her sister's strength and certainty.

Gerri's marriage was an arranged one, of course, and her husband was—in Nadia's opinion—a nasty little toad of a man. But Gerri never complained or seemed unhappy. She did her duty as an heir, as a wife, as a mother, with never the slightest hint that she might want something more. Gerri was the ideal Nadia strove to emulate, but she always seemed to fall a little short.

All of which meant Gerri would have little sympathy for Nadia's dilemma. Nadia's duty was clear: protect her family at all costs. If the only way to protect her family was to give in to Mosely's demands and stab Nate in the back, then so be it. She would just have to figure out how to do it without him ever finding out.

"How are the kids?" Nadia asked her sister. It was a long shot, but maybe if she could get Gerri talking about her kids, she could squirm her way out of the "debrief" Gerri was supposed to give her.

Gerri's ironically raised eyebrow said she saw right through the ploy. "They're little demons sent from hell to torment me," she said with a fond smile. "Corinne has an ear infection, and Rory is in one of those everything-goes-in-the-mouth phases.

And if you think you're going to divert me that easily, I'll have to ask the doctor to check your meds."

So much for delaying the inevitable. Nadia stared at the nearly empty IV bag. She had no idea what the doctor had given her. The label had been blacked out, which meant whatever it was had come from the black market. Thanks to import taxes, some medications manufactured by rival states were preposterously expensive and best bought under the table. Illegal, of course, but it was a rare Executive who used no contraband. Nadia wondered if she could pretend the drugs were making her too loopy to handle a serious conversation.

"I'll give you the rundown of what happened, but please skip the lecture," Nadia said. "I know I shouldn't have gone off alone with Nate at the party, but you know how he is. I tried to stand up to him, but he's a force of nature."

Gerri gave her a hard look. "You're going to be his wife. You'd better learn to stand up to him or he's going to walk all over you for the rest of your life."

Easy for Gerri to say. She'd inherited their mother's backbone and their father's power. She had no trouble issuing orders, and no trouble having those orders obeyed.

"You try standing up to Nate someday," Nadia grumbled. She wasn't sure who would win a battle of wills between Nate and Gerri, but if she had to bet, she'd place her money on Nate against just about anyone.

"I don't have to. You do."

Nadia flopped over onto her side, facing away from Gerri. "Fine. Tell me how inadequate I am. There's nothing I'm more anxious to hear right now."

Gerri sighed. "Don't be like that. I'm not saying you're inadequate." She laid a hand on Nadia's shoulder and squeezed. "I love you, you know. I'm just trying to help. I know Nathaniel would be a handful for anyone, but I also know that you're the one who's going to be stuck with him, and you're the one who's going to have to learn to live with him without being miserable."

Nadia sniffled, though the black-market mystery drug seemed to be knocking out her symptoms with remarkable speed. Illness would not be her cocoon for very long. "Most girls would laugh at the idea that I'm 'stuck' with Nate."

"Most girls don't have enough of an imagination to see what a pain in the ass he is."

Nadia turned over to face her sister, surprised by the words. But then, maybe she shouldn't be. Gerri was the heir to their father's presidency. Nate was far from the most dutiful heir in the world, but he had no choice but to fulfill *some* of his obligations, which no doubt meant he and Gerri had attended many a business meeting together. Clearly, Nate hadn't made the best impression.

"I know you like him, Nadia," Gerri continued, "but to be perfectly honest with you, I can't see why. He's nothing but a spoiled brat with an enormous chip on his shoulder and a deeply rooted conviction that he's God's gift not just to women, but to the universe itself."

Nadia blinked. Gerri was not a kiss-ass, but it wasn't like her to be so openly critical of someone who outranked her—and who held the future of their entire family in his hands. As long as nothing went wrong in the next two years and Nadia ended up formally engaged to Nate, their father would eventually be promoted and given a seat on Paxco's board of directors—a seat that Gerri would inherit, when the time came. The power and prestige that came with becoming a board member were considerable, but there was another perk to the position, perhaps the most important perk of all: board members and their immediate families were eligible for periodic backup scans, and if there was a preventable death in the family, there was a high likelihood a Replica would be animated. Gerri had almost lost Corinne to a particularly virulent strain of flu that had swept the continent last year, and she was more aware than most of how fragile a human life could be.

Gerri smiled tightly. "I'm sorry to be speaking ill of your future husband. I just can't help thinking that if he'd behaved like a responsible adult, you wouldn't have been dragged into this mess."

On that, Nadia and Gerri could agree.

"There's no use wishing Nate didn't act like Nate," Nadia said. "I'm not stupid enough to think he's magically going to change."

"You're right, he's not. Which means *you* have to."

Nadia wanted to slap herself. She'd walked right into that one.

"I did what I thought was right at the time. Nate suggested he was going to make some kind of trouble if I didn't leave the party with him. If I'd known what was going to happen, of course I'd have called his bluff. But I didn't know. How could I?"

Gerri pursed her lips. "I know hindsight is twenty-twenty. But still, even if Nathaniel behaved like a complete boor, that would have reflected poorly on *him,* not on you."

"And if he'd created some kind of international incident, it would have been my fault."

"Don't be ridiculous!" Gerri snapped, her narrowed eyes and the intensity of her disapproval making her resemblance to their mother more obvious. "No one's going to hold a sixteen-year-old kid responsible for the Chairman Heir's actions."

Heat rushed into Nadia's cheeks, and she wasn't sure if it was because of her sister's dismissive reference to her as a "kid" or because she realized the ridiculousness of her own argument. She might have felt guilty if Nate had done something scandalous in retaliation for her refusal, but that hardly would have made his actions her fault.

"You went off alone with him because you *wanted* to," Gerri concluded. "I was sixteen once myself, you know. I understand the lure of hormones, and I even understand Nathaniel's appeal to a girl your age. But you're not some little nobody Employee who can afford to indulge her every whim. You have to think about consequences, not just to yourself, but to all of us."

Nadia wanted to sink into the softness of her bed and disappear. How could Gerri simultaneously be so right and so wrong? Obviously, Nadia's hormones had nothing to do with why she'd let Nate draw her away from the party, but she was pretty sure there *had* been some part of her that had wanted to go with him, despite the risks. If she were being perfectly honest with herself, she'd have to admit that she sometimes enjoyed—or at least envied—Nate's recklessness. The idea of taking part in it could be . . . supremely tempting.

Unable to think of a good reply, Nadia settled for silence, picking at the loose edge of the tape that held her IV in place. She was ready to have the thing out and get out of bed, if only to escape Gerri's penetrating gaze.

"I guess you already know you made a mistake," Gerri continued in a conciliatory tone, "even if you won't admit it. But what's past is past. Tell me what happened at the security station. Mother never could get a decent explanation for why they held you for more than fifteen hours. I refuse to believe even a black-hearted bastard like Mosely would think you're an assassin."

Nadia felt sure Mosely had at least briefly entertained the notion, as ridiculous as it might be. Slowly, reluctantly, she told her older sister about her interview with Paxco's chief of security. It was like picking at a scab, and though the fever was gone, she started shivering anyway.

"What are you going to do?" Gerri finally asked, chewing on her lip.

Nadia fought to contain another shiver. "I don't have a whole lot of choices," she said morosely. It probably would have been better for her if she hadn't received medical treatment last night. As long as she was sick and feverish, she couldn't be expected to spend much time with Nate, and the less time she spent with him, the less Mosely would expect her to learn.

"No," Gerri agreed. "But you're going to have to be very careful. Nathaniel would not take well to you conspiring with Mosely, even under the circumstances."

That was something Nadia didn't need to be told. If something Nadia did or said helped Mosely locate Bishop, Nate would never forgive her. It wouldn't matter that her future and the future of her entire family rested on her shoulders. He would never stomach betrayal, not unless his Replica was a substantially different person from the one she'd known. Their marriage had been arranged by their parents, and Nate and Nadia didn't have much say in it, but she was sure Nate would find a way to convince his father to pick someone else if he got angry enough.

"Don't be afraid," Gerri urged, taking Nadia's hand and giving it a squeeze. "We'll get through this. Do you know *anything* about Kurt Bishop that Mosely isn't likely to know? Anything that might help?"

"He's Nate's valet," Nadia said. "Why would I know anything about him? Other than that he was born in the Basement and isn't ashamed of it."

Gerri thought about it a moment, then fixed Nadia with a frank look. "If you knew anything more, would you tell me?"

Nadia swallowed hard, not sure how to answer. She loved her sister, but Gerri would never stick her neck out for someone like Bishop. Not because she was a bad person, but because she would tolerate no risk to the family.

"I was questioned for fifteen hours yesterday," she finally said. "I'm not an idiot. I know how much trouble I'm in, even though I had nothing to do with the murder. I told Mosely everything I know."

"I thought there might be things you'd be willing to tell me that you wouldn't tell him," Gerri prompted. "I have my own resources, you know. Maybe I can help find Bishop without you having to tell Mosely anything. If Bishop could be captured without you having revealed anything to Mosely . . ."

Nadia took a deep breath and squelched her knee-jerk, angry response. Gerri was just being practical, trying to protect their family from Mosely without destroying the potential marriage arrangement. But sometimes practicality made Nadia want to scream with frustration.

"Do you even care that Bishop isn't guilty?" she asked, unable to remain wisely silent.

Gerri frowned. "You can't know that. There were witnesses who saw him fleeing the scene of the crime with blood on him. That sounds about as damning as evidence can get."

Maybe it did, if you actually believed it. Maybe she was being naive, but no matter how she looked at it, Nadia couldn't imagine Bishop hurting Nate. Certainly not *killing* him. No, Bishop was nothing but an easy scapegoat, a powerless Basement-dweller who could be very publicly brought to justice in very little time and with a minimum of fuss, at least in theory. Was Mosely even entertaining the possibility that Bishop wasn't guilty? It hadn't seemed so to Nadia, and she hated the thought that the real killer—whoever it was—was going to get away with it so easily.

"But if the evidence didn't point to him," Nadia persisted, "would you care? If you were sure he wasn't guilty, would you still cheerfully hand him over to Mosely to be executed?"

The look in Gerri's eyes turned flat and hard. "I wouldn't 'cheerfully' turn over my worst enemy. But if turning over an innocent man was what I had to do to protect my family, then I'd do it. I certainly hope you'd do the same."

Nadia averted her gaze. Gerri was right, and she knew it. Her first duty was to her own family.

"Tell me you're not going to risk my children's future for the sake of some lowlife Basement-dweller who's probably guilty as hell," Gerri insisted when Nadia didn't answer quickly enough. "Nathaniel should have left the creature in the Basement where he belonged."

Nadia's chest tightened with the effort of holding in her outrage. She'd be the first to admit she didn't like Bishop, but he was neither a lowlife nor a "creature." It wasn't his fault he'd been born in the Basement. No doubt his life there had been unsavory, and he had probably done some illegal and immoral things to survive, but he should still be entitled to a certain level of decency and fairness.

But hers was the minority opinion among Executives, who felt that providing the most basic necessities for human survival—food, shelter, and rudimentary health care—was an act of unparalleled generosity toward Basement-dwellers, who contributed nothing to society at large, were unemployed, and generally unemployable. That most were born into it and couldn't escape didn't lessen the taint of their status.

But what Bishop should be entitled to was irrelevant. Nadia had already promised Mosely that she would be his spy, and she couldn't afford lofty ideals.

"Have you ever known me not to do my duty?" she asked Gerri, bitterness dripping from her every word. Most of the world envied the members of the Executive class for their money and power and privileges. Most of the world had no idea how much personal freedom those privileges cost. Nadia would give it all up in a heartbeat if she could be an ordinary Employee who could choose her own path in life. But that was a luxury she would never have.

"I'll do what I have to do," she finished. She couldn't blame Gerri for wanting to secure her children's future, but she also couldn't quite stand to look into her sister's face anymore. "Just don't expect me to be happy about it."

Gerri made a little snorting sound that wasn't quite a laugh. Nadia risked a quick glance at her sister and saw from the tightness around her mouth and eyes that *she* wasn't happy about it, either. Which made Nadia feel just a little better, even if it didn't change the ugly reality.

CHAPTER FOUR

nate began his first morning as a Replica much the way he remembered starting every other day of his life since he'd left normal classes and graduated to "on-the-job" training. Which, granted, had only been a handful of months ago.

He made liberal use of the snooze button on his alarm clock, refusing to drag himself out of bed until he was sure to be behind schedule for the rest of the day. Usually, it was Kurt who eventually persuaded him to get out of bed, but today Nate had to do it himself. His butler had offered to serve as his valet until a replacement could be found, but Nate had brushed the suggestion aside with something akin to horror.

His breakfast was served with a printout of his daily agenda on the side. Hartman, his majordomo and self-appointed social secretary, had long ago learned that Nate had a tendency to neglect his online calendar and thought the printout made it more likely Nate would show up where and when he was supposed to. Glancing at the agenda, Nate didn't know whether to laugh or scream when he saw he was scheduled to shoot a commercial for Replicas in the afternoon. You'd think his father could wait at least a day or two before trying to profit from his own son's death.

Eating breakfast by himself made Nate feel ridiculously alone, though it wasn't like Kurt usually ate breakfast with him. He couldn't risk his other servants finding out that Kurt was more than just his valet. And yet knowing that Kurt was far away, out of his reach, made the whole apartment seem bigger and emptier. The eggs tasted bland, the toast dry, the coffee too sweet. Nothing was quite right.

Nate ignored the business briefs a truly dedicated heir would have pored over during breakfast. Sometimes, he skimmed them to keep his father off his back, but stories of mergers and acquisitions hadn't held his attention *before* he'd been murdered. They seemed even more massively boring and unimportant now, so instead he checked out the media coverage of yesterday's events. Even though he knew better.

He was the lead story for every news and gossip show on the net, and every story seemed to lead off with the footage of him biting off the reporter's head, his language bleeped out to protect delicate ears. This was often followed by footage of Nadia exiting the security station after her questioning, although all you could see were her feet because of how carefully the security officers were blocking her from view. He doubted that would do much to protect her from the gossipmongers.

Nate forced himself to shut off his handheld before he was tempted to smash it against the wall.

According to his agenda, his first formal obligation of the day was a two-hour board meeting at Paxco Headquarters, but there was no way he could face that. Sitting in a room with a bunch of self-important fossils with sticks up their asses as they droned on and on about pointless crap was the last thing he wanted to do.

Knowing he would pay for it later, Nate sent word to his father that he was "indisposed" following the trauma of his birth from the artificial womb. The Chairman wouldn't buy it, naturally, so Nate decided not to be home when the Wrath of Chairman Hayes hit.

Nate had spent a long and mostly sleepless night wondering where Kurt was and if he was safe. Maybe with all those dollars missing, Nate should assume Kurt was out of Paxco's reach, but the unrelenting tightness in his gut wouldn't let him relax. Besides, even if Mosely was content to blame the murder on Kurt in absentia, *Nate* wasn't. He wanted to know who had killed him, and why. He wanted the bastard to pay for what he'd done, and since Kurt appeared to be the last person to have seen Nate alive, he might be able to shed some light on what had happened.

The first step in his private investigation had to be to talk to Nadia. She might not know what had happened to him, but she could fill in some of the blanks.

Nate left his apartment, "forgetting" his phone so that he wouldn't be too easy to reach when the Chairman went on the rampage. He even ordered his driver and his bodyguard to turn off their phones. He pretended not to notice how uneasy the order made them. At least, he *thought* it was the order that made them uneasy. It was possible it was the fact that he was a Replica that bothered them, but if that was the case, they were just going to have to get over it.

Satisfied that he'd bought himself at least an hour or two of free time, Nate directed his driver to take him to the Lake Towers. He'd tried to call Nadia last night, but had been told she was too ill to come to the phone. He wasn't sure if her illness was genuine or merely an excuse, but he couldn't blame her for wanting to go to ground. Being around Mosely gave him the creeps, and he couldn't imagine what it had been like for Nadia to endure an entire day of questioning. He hoped she'd had more sense than he and had avoided watching the media vultures use her misfortunes as entertainment.

Whether she was sick or not, Nate had to talk to her. She was his best friend, and she'd been through absolute hell yesterday. And knowing Nadia's family, they hadn't made the situation any easier on her, so she might appreciate the sympathetic ear. Assuming she didn't completely freak out about him being a Replica.

But Nate's motivation for going to see Nadia wasn't entirely altruistic. He certainly couldn't rely on the media's account about what had happened on the night of the murder, but he hoped Nadia would be able to give him the first in the trail of breadcrumbs that would eventually lead him to Kurt—and, through him, to the true killer.

An ordinary citizen would have had trouble getting through the Lake Towers security even with an appointment, but there were privileges that came with rank, and Nate wasn't shy about taking advantage of them. He was in the elevator on the way to the penthouse before the security staff had finished bowing and scraping. He'd worried that the story of his murder and reanimation would make people treat him like a freak, or even an impostor. In some ways, he *was* an impostor, not the real Nathaniel Edison Hayes, no matter what he looked like or remembered. But he should have known that the Lake Towers staff would act like professionals and treat him as if nothing had changed. And if they were whispering and staring at him when his back was turned, he didn't have to know about it.

When the elevator doors opened at the top floor, the Lake family's butler, an aging gentleman named Crane, was waiting to meet him.

"Good morning, Mr. Hayes," Crane said with a polite bow.

Nate refrained from rolling his eyes, but it was always an effort to contain his sarcasm when Crane was around. The old fart was so stuffy he was a caricature of himself, but he didn't know it. From the penguin suit to the mannerisms— like *bowing*, for God's sake—to the British accent from a man who'd been born in the state of New York, back when it existed, everything about him was affected and overdone.

"Miss Lake will join you in the morning room," Crane intoned. Nate wanted to point out that it had been at least a couple of centuries since anyone had had a "morning room" in their house. "May I bring you some refreshments?"

Nate wanted nothing more than to have a private conversation with Nadia, but he knew from experience that if he didn't allow Crane to bring refreshments, the butler would check in on them every few minutes to see if they wanted something—either because he was desperate to be of service, or because he was a nosy bastard who didn't like the idea of his charge being left alone with a man, even if that man was her presumed fiancé.

"Some coffee would be nice, if you don't mind," Nate finally said, deciding it was the option that would lead to the fewest interruptions.

"Very good, sir," Crane said, bowing again, and this time Nate *did* roll his eyes. Of course, Crane was too busy bowing to notice.

Nate started toward the "morning room," which everyone other than Crane referred to as the den, his bodyguard falling into step behind him. Nate stopped in his tracks and gave the man a withering look. Ordinarily, his bodyguards knew better than to hover so close, and Fischer was usually one of the more laid back of them.

Fischer didn't take the unspoken hint, neither backing down nor even lowering his eyes.

"You think you need to guard me inside my fiancée's home?" Nate asked with a shake of his head. He supposed he should have expected an extra dose of paranoia from his guards after he'd been assassinated, but it somehow hadn't occurred to him.

Fischer shrugged his massive shoulders. "Just doing my job."

"Your job is to guard me when I'm out in public," Nate reminded him. "You don't have to stick to me like gum on the bottom of my shoe. Stay here."

"The Chairman—"

"Isn't your boss," Nate interrupted, though he wasn't so sure that was the case. If it came down to Nate and the Chairman giving the man contradictory orders, there was no question whose Fischer would follow. "I intend to have a private conversation with Miss Lake, and you are not invited."

Fischer looked unhappy and even a little alarmed. Nate wondered if Mosely or his father had given him orders to stick extra close—and report on Nate's every move. If he decided to launch his own search for Kurt, he would have to be very, very careful not to lead Mosely and his men right to him. Even though Kurt was almost certainly out of Paxco by now and would have fled to a country or state with no extradition agreement with Paxco, Mosely had frighteningly long arms.

"If it'll make you feel better," Nate said, "you can turn your phone back on. But if my father calls, you make sure to tell him I can't come to the phone. Do not interrupt me under any circumstances."

Fischer looked even more unhappy, but when Nate strode

toward the den, the guard remained behind. Nate thought he heard the man muttering to himself. It was probably a good thing for both of them that he wasn't able to make out the words.

Nate felt an unaccustomed flutter of nerves as he approached the den. Nadia was the only person other than Kurt whose opinion actually mattered to him. If she looked at him and saw an impostor masquerading as her dead best friend, he wasn't sure he could take it. His father didn't love him, his mother had been absent from his life for ten years, his "friends" were all sycophants, and now he'd lost Kurt. He couldn't lose Nadia, too.

With an effort, Nate ordered himself to man up and get on with it. He took a deep breath as though marching into battle, then stepped into the den.

Nadia was already waiting for him. She was curled up on a sofa wearing a boxy fleece sweater, with a warm, fluffy quilt tucked around her legs. Her lustrous blond hair was gathered into a sloppy braid that hung over one shoulder, and her face was devoid of makeup. Her cheeks seemed even paler than usual, the circles under her eyes so dark they looked almost like bruises. Nate had never seen her looking so vulnerable before, and guilt stirred in his chest. He didn't know what had happened on the night of the reception, but he was sure Nadia wouldn't have been hounded by Mosely if it weren't for him.

A hint of pink tinted her cheeks, and Nadia smiled at him ruefully. "I look that bad, huh?"

Nate shook his head at himself and forced a grin. "Let's just say I hope you feel better than you look."

She made a sound of mock outrage. "You're supposed to flatter me and say I look great, you ass."

He blinked innocently. "You expect me to obey social convention? I may be a Replica, but I'm still *me*." He frowned. "Sort of."

He'd been trying for humor, but of course bringing up his status as a Replica was about as far from humor as he could get. *Way to kill the mood,* he scolded himself as he watched the light bleed out of Nadia's eyes and the smile fade from her lips. He hurried to sit beside her on the sofa. He wanted to take her hand and give it a comforting squeeze, but she was gripping the quilt so hard he'd have to pry her fingers free to manage it.

"Sorry," he said. "I was trying to be funny."

"Guess that means you really *are* still you," she replied, shaking her head at him. There was a tentativeness to her voice he wasn't used to, and she was staring at his face with too much intensity. He realized she was trying very hard not to give him the visual once-over everyone else had given him.

"It's okay to look," he told her gently. "I know this must be really weird for you. It is for me."

She chewed her lip as she finally allowed her eyes to wander. He held still for her inspection, which paused when she reached his wrists.

"You're not wearing cuff links," she commented, and Nate guessed from the heat in his face that he was blushing. He often skipped the tie and sometimes even the jacket that constituted an Executive's uniform, but Kurt liked him in cuff links, so he usually wore them.

"It's not because I'm a Replica," he said. "It's just that I suck at putting them on myself." Of course, he could have asked one of his other servants to do it for him, but that wouldn't have been the same.

Nadia nodded at his explanation. "Other than that, you look like you," she said with an ironic smile. "And you *sound* like you." Her hands relaxed their grip on the quilt, although she didn't exactly look at ease.

"Hmm. Only smell, taste, and feel left to go." He leaned toward her and offered his throat. "Have at it." Out of the corner of his eye, he saw the hint of a smile tugging at the corners of her lips, and he let out an internal sigh of relief.

"In your dreams," she said, shoving him away playfully.

"Brat," he said, then tugged on the end of her braid, and her smile broadened into a grin.

"*You're* calling *me* a brat? Have you looked in the mirror lately?"

The memory of standing in front of the mirror yesterday, examining his body and marveling at its perfect imitation of the original Nate Hayes, flashed through his mind, and he shivered. He looked down at his hands, turning them over and staring at them as if he'd never seen them before.

"I can't quite . . . absorb whatever it is that happened to me," he said. "I feel so normal. But I'm not the same person I was just a couple of days ago."

"Yes, you are," Nadia said firmly, hiding the lingering doubts he was sure she must feel.

He looked up and met her eyes. "If I were the same person, I'd remember what happened the night of the party."

Nadia didn't quite grimace, but she did look uncomfortable, and she averted her gaze. "Let's just pretend you had a nasty blow to the head and have amnesia. That doesn't make you a different person."

He waited for a moment, expecting her to tell him what had happened. He'd thought it was pretty obvious what he'd been fishing for. But Nadia just sat there chewing on her lip and looking uncomfortable. Suddenly, Nate wasn't sure he wanted to know exactly what had happened after all.

Crane took that moment to enter the room—without knocking, naturally—carrying a tray with a coffeepot, two white china cups and saucers, and a cream and sugar set. The tray was decorated with a large golden-yellow mum in a small crystal vase. Nate knew Nadia valued informality as much as he did, but informality was a foreign concept to people like Crane.

Nate and Nadia met each other's eyes as Crane put the tray down and fussed to make sure everything was arranged just so. Nate was tempted to offer the old man a ruler so he could make sure every item was exactly the same distance apart, but making fun of Crane was just too easy.

Finally, Crane was satisfied with the arrangement of the cups and saucers—or was satisfied that Nate and Nadia weren't going to say anything of great interest while he was eavesdropping—and trundled out of the room. Again, Nate suspected the slow pace was deliberate, but neither he nor Nadia said a word beyond "thank you" until they were alone again.

"You shouldn't sneer at him like that," Nadia said, pouring herself a cup of coffee. "He's just doing his job."

It wasn't the first time Nate had been told he wasn't allowed to complain about people who were doing their jobs, but he never quite saw the logic in the restriction. Unlike Executives, Employees could choose their jobs, after all, and they could also do them without being assholes.

"He's not living in a Jane Austen novel," he said, a little peevishly. "I see no reason why he can't do his job without the stick up his ass."

Something flashed in Nadia's eyes, and she put the coffee-pot down with a little more force than necessary. "That's how ninety percent of the people he interacts with want him to behave. You think he should change just because *you'd* like it better?"

Call him crazy, but Nate had the feeling Nadia was angry with him. And not just because he'd grumbled about the butler. No doubt she had cause, but one of the things he'd always liked about her was her ability to refrain from critiquing his behavior like just about everyone else in his life did. Life under the microscope, with the whole world pointing out and then reveling in his every misstep, was a pain in the ass.

"I'm sorry I'm not perfect," he said, his voice sharper than he intended as he grabbed for the coffeepot. "I just get tired of people acting like assholes. Crane actually *bowed* to me when he met me at the door, for God's sake."

Nadia leaned back into the sofa's cushions and crossed her arms over her chest, looking mulish. "He's doing his job," she gritted out as if he hadn't heard her the first time. "Not everyone can do whatever the hell they want whenever the hell they want to, like you can. You were assassinated, I spent fifteen hours in the security station, Bishop is running for his life, and the most important thing you can think of to talk about is how annoying you find my butler? Really, Nate?"

Nadia's words hit home, and the surge of anger faded.

"I'm sorry," he murmured, stirring some sugar into the cup of coffee he'd asked for but didn't really want. It was easier to fuss with the coffee than to look at Nadia and see the reproach in her eyes. "I guess picking at Crane is easier than facing all the other crap that's bouncing around in my head." He took a sip of his coffee, then wrinkled his nose at the taste. He'd put in the same amount of sugar as he usually would, but it tasted too sweet. He'd noticed the same thing at breakfast, though he'd assumed he'd absently put in too much sugar. Maybe there was a subtle difference between his taste buds and those of his original.

Mentally, he rolled his eyes at himself. There was no point in obsessing about this. He put the cup down and risked a glance at Nadia. To his relief, her expression had softened.

"I'm sorry, too," she said, though as far as he was concerned, she had nothing to apologize for. "I know you must be worried sick about Bishop."

His fists clenched again as he fought off an image of Kurt in Mosely's clutches. Then he smiled a bit as he fully absorbed what she'd said. "You don't think Kurt did it."

Her mouth dropped open. "Of course he didn't do it!" she said indignantly. "You don't for a moment think—"

"No, no," he hastened to interrupt. "I'd never in a million years believe that of Kurt. I just thought that with the so-called evidence against him, you might have doubts. You never liked him."

Nadia dismissed that with a wave. "I don't have to like him to know he's not guilty. I've seen the two of you together when no one else is looking. He loves you."

Was there a hint of wistfulness in Nadia's voice? Nate had never asked her how she felt about their future marriage. Maybe because he was afraid he wouldn't like the answer. She had never batted an eye when he'd revealed his secret to her, never shown any sign that she hoped to "convert" him, but that didn't mean she was happy with the prospect of being with a man who would never be faithful to her, even once they were married. Hell, he wasn't sure if he'd even be able to consummate their marriage, and any heir he produced might well be conceived with the help of a turkey baster. Fidelity would never be an option. It was all so achingly unfair, to everyone involved. Which was why he tried not to think about it too much.

"Tell me what happened on the night I got killed," he said. "According to the media, you and I ducked out of the party because we were hormone-crazed teenagers wanting some privacy. I know that's not what really happened."

"Not exactly," Nadia confirmed grimly. And then she told him what she knew.

CHAPTER FIVE

nadia hated every moment of lying to Nate. She desperately wanted to tell him everything that had happened to her since the night of the reception. Especially everything that had happened when Mosely questioned her. If she could tell Nate what Mosely wanted her to do, then together they could devise some way to work around it, some way to make it seem like she was cooperating with Mosely while not actually risking Bishop's safety. Several times during her retelling of the night's terrible events, she almost blurted out the truth.

But the real truth was, she couldn't tell Nate about Mosely. She knew Nate too well, and there was no sign that his Replica was any different. The minute she told him how Mosely had treated her, Nate would go on the warpath. He would confront Mosely, and there was no way that could end well for Nadia. Mosely would take revenge on her for talking. Of that she had no doubt, even if Nate might think he could protect her. And so she didn't dare tell the truth, no matter how much she wanted to.

Nate looked appropriately abashed when Nadia told him just what he'd been up to on the night of the reception, how he'd set them both up for the hell they—and Bishop—were in now. He stared down at his hands, and even winced now and again, though she tried not to be too accusatory. No matter how angry she was with him.

"I was an asshole to you," he said when she was finished. Maybe he hoped she'd contradict him, but she didn't. He squirmed. "I'm sorry."

She shrugged, which wasn't quite an acceptance of his apology, but it was the best she could do. She was glad he was at least able to acknowledge that he'd done wrong. With Nate, sometimes that was half the battle. For a fleeting moment, she wondered if the original Nate would have apologized, or if that was just something his Replica did, but she shoved the thought away. She had seen no sign that he wasn't identical to the original in all ways.

"I'm going to make things right," he said with a decisive nod. "I don't know how, yet, but I'm going to do it."

Nadia had no doubt he would try. She also had no doubt that given a little prompting, he'd be happy to talk about the steps he was going to take to make things right, which would no doubt begin with finding Bishop. And if he told her anything, she was going to have to relay the information to Mosely. Sure, she could try lying and pretending she knew nothing, but with Mosely's reputation as a human lie detector, she didn't dare. The only way to avoid telling Mosely anything was to make sure she didn't have anything to tell.

And so, instead of prompting Nate to tell her what he was going to do, instead of the two of them teaming up, putting their heads together, and trying to figure out how to help Bishop and find the real killer, Nadia faked a shiver and closed her eyes with a little groan. Nate put his hand on her shoulder in sympathy.

"Poor thing," he murmured, pulling the quilt up from where it had pooled around her waist and tucking it around her shoulders. "If the bastards hadn't kept you for questioning all day yesterday, you'd probably be all better by now."

Thanks to the medical treatment Nadia had received upon arriving home last night, she *was* feeling a lot better. But if exaggerating her illness would get Nate to leave without telling her anything Mosely would be interested in, then she wasn't above doing it.

"I feel like I could sleep for a week straight," she said, and that was pretty close to the truth. She offered him a tenuous smile. "I was going to pump myself full of coffee to stay awake, but now I think maybe it would be better to take a nap."

Nate looked at the coffee service, which they had barely touched, and wrinkled his nose. "It's crappy coffee anyway." She could almost read his thoughts, watching his face as he considered making another wisecrack about Crane and then thought better of it. It made her think he might be capable of learning after all.

"I'll come by again tomorrow to see how you're doing," Nate promised, folding her into a hug that felt better than it had any right to. "Call me if you need anything." He pulled away from the hug, and a hint of his usual playful smile curved his lips. "I don't have my phone on me at the moment, but I won't be able to avoid Dad forever, and once he's ripped into me, I'll stop playing hide-and-seek. Until then, if you need me, call Fischer's number. He'll be stuck to my side like glue for the rest of the day."

Nadia returned his smile while fighting a yawn. Funny how feigning the need for a nap had turned into a very real need. "Be careful," she warned him, the smile fading as fast as it had come. She didn't think he was in any danger, but she worried his impulsiveness and his desire to find Bishop would lead to disaster for Bishop. Only she couldn't explain that without initiating the very conversation she was trying to avoid, so she hurried to clarify. "I don't suppose whoever killed you has any reason to do it again when you're not going to stay dead, but . . ."

Nate acknowledged her warning grimly. "I'll be careful," he promised.

If only Nadia thought Nate's idea of "careful" was careful enough.

nadia could have used her illness as an excuse to stay in bed all day, but the idea of being alone with her thoughts wasn't the least bit appealing. She needed distraction, even if the available distractions had their own drawbacks, so when lunchtime rolled around, she presented herself in the dining room to face her mother, this time with no sympathy-inducing symptoms to smooth the waters.

To her surprise, Nadia's father joined them for lunch. Ordinarily, he ate lunch, and often even dinner, at the office. He hugged her warmly, then directed the lunchtime conversation to anything other than the events of the day before. Her mother played along, and Nadia wondered if the two of them had reached some sort of agreement before Nadia had shown up. They were acting like nothing unusual had happened, as if by pretending Nadia hadn't spent the whole day being questioned at the security station they could make the ugly incident disappear. In truth, Nadia was hardly eager to talk about the subject herself, but it felt strange and unnatural to sit at the table and talk about social events and trivialities after what she'd gone through.

Her mother excused herself as soon as the servants began to clear the lunch dishes, and Nadia had the feeling that for once in her life, Esmeralda Lake had found making small talk burdensome. Nadia would have excused herself just as quickly, except her father stopped her, putting his arm around her shoulders and steering her to a corner where they could talk without being in the servants' way.

"How are you feeling, my dear?" he asked, looking down at her with concerned eyes.

If he really wanted to hear how she felt, he wouldn't have asked her here in the bustle of the dining room. Some Executives treated servants as if they were deaf and blind, but her father had never been one of them. With him, private conversations were held in private, and Nadia tamped down a sense of hurt. She'd known better than to expect a genuine outpouring of sympathy from her mother, but she'd hoped for more from her father.

"Much better," she answered, because that was the answer he was expecting. She hoped he couldn't see how stung she was.

He nodded approvingly. "Good, good," he said, making eye contact only briefly. "Are you well enough to attend class this afternoon?"

Nadia blinked in surprise at the question. Of all the things he could be concerned about, *that* was what he felt was important?

Unlike Employees, Executive kids didn't go to school but were instead privately tutored in the subjects deemed most relevant to their future lives. In order to provide a social outlet, some Executive families hosted small study groups at their homes, where a tutor was brought in to educate several students. The Lake family hosted an economics session on weekday afternoons, and Nadia was fastidious about attending, even though the group included Jewel and Blair, two-thirds of the Terrible Trio. The group also included her closest friend—other than Nate—Chloe Rathburn. Nadia wasn't anxious to face any of them today, not even Chloe, who would undoubtedly want a full account of everything that had happened. Chloe was sweet, and Nadia genuinely liked her, but she had never been terribly sympathetic to Nadia's struggles with Nate. If Chloe were in Nadia's shoes, she'd do whatever Nate wanted whenever he wanted it, and she didn't understand why Nadia didn't feel the same way.

Of course, Nadia had already determined she didn't want to be alone with her thoughts, and going to class would certainly provide the distraction she needed. She sighed.

"I suppose I am," she said. "Why do you ask?"

"I've hired a new personal assistant," her dad said in what seemed to Nadia like a complete non sequitur. He made brief eye contact with her, then looked away again, as if the admission made him uncomfortable. "His name is Robert Dante, and I've asked him to stand in for Sully in the afternoons."

Sully was the servant who was usually on duty to fetch and carry for the students during the classes, because heaven forbid an Executive girl spend a couple of hours without having a servant at her beck and call. Nadia shook her head as she tried to puzzle out what was going on.

"You're going to have your personal assistant stand around a classroom fetching for us instead of actually having him working for you?" That made no sense whatsoever. Nor did the fact that her father found it necessary to take her aside and announce his new hire.

"He's an exceptionally bright young man. I think with some additional education, he could make something of himself. I can't have him officially attend your classes, but I believe he can learn a great deal just by listening in." Instead of looking at her, Nadia's dad fidgeted with one of his cuff links.

Gerald Lake did not fidget. Nor did he usually avoid eye contact. Something about this conversation was making him uncomfortable, and Nadia was beginning to suspect she knew what it was.

What were the chances that her father would suddenly hire a new personal assistant and decide that assistant should hang around Nadia's classes on the very day after Nadia was detained and questioned by Paxco's chief of security in connection with the Chairman Heir's murder? It made no sense, and while her father's explanation sounded logical enough, his body language screamed that there was something amiss.

"I see," Nadia said slowly. "I should go out of my way to make this bright young man feel welcome in our household. Is that what you're saying?"

Her father finally met her eyes and held her gaze. There was a hint of relief in his expression, as if the obvious irony of her question had reassured him that she had heard the message he was trying to convey without words.

"Yes," he said. "That's an excellent way of putting it."

So, Mosely had coerced Nadia into spying on Nate, and now he'd inserted someone in her own household to spy on *her*. Why her father wouldn't come right out and say it, she didn't know. Perhaps he'd been given direct orders from the Chairman and felt he was honor bound to obey them. And with only this oblique warning delivered, he could honestly say he hadn't told her Robert Dante was here to spy on her if Mosely asked. So perhaps she understood his reluctance to speak plainly after all.

"I'll do my best," she promised, and her father gave her an affectionate squeeze on the shoulder.

"I know you will."

nadia's home took up the top three floors of one of the Lake Towers. The lowest of those three floors was mostly made up of servants' quarters, but one large and sunny corner room served as a schoolroom for Nadia's classes.

An Executive schoolroom looked nothing like the classrooms in ordinary Employee schools. Instead of a bunch of straight-backed chairs lined up facing a teacher's desk, there was merely a large round table with comfortable ergonomic chairs. You could tell which seat was the teacher's because of the oversize monitor and whiteboard behind it, but Nadia had always thought the setup looked more like a conference room than a classroom. The table sat on an obviously expensive red and gold rug, and potted plants were artfully scattered throughout. A table in the far corner sported silver urns of coffee and hot water for tea, as well as elegant finger sandwiches and bite-size pastries.

Nadia wasn't sure what to expect as she made her way from the elevator to the schoolroom. Jewel and Blair were both reluctant students at best, and they often skipped classes unless there was a test or some other pressing need for them to be there. Nadia hoped they would skip today so she didn't have to spar with them, but she suspected they wouldn't be able to resist showing up so they could pretend to be sympathetic and concerned while they pressed her for lurid details. Even if she told them nothing, they'd be sure to share a rumor or two they would claim they'd learned straight from her. At least Cherry was a year younger, so Nadia didn't have to face the entire Trio together. But as concerned as she was with her mean-spirited classmates, she was more concerned about the ominous Robert Dante. She wondered if he was a nasty, weaselly type like Mosely, the kind of person who could give you an ingratiating smile while freezing your marrow with the coldness of his eyes.

Nadia felt uncommonly nervous when she stepped through

the doorway into the schoolroom, her eyes darting around quickly to get the lay of the land.

As she'd suspected, Jewel and Blair were both present. They stood together in the far corner of the room, each holding a china cup and saucer while they bent their heads together and talked softly, giggling. Nadia's immediate assumption was that they were talking about her, but perhaps she was being self-centered.

Chloe was sitting at the table, about as far away from the other girls as she could get in the confines of the schoolroom. Supposedly, racism had been all but abolished in these advanced and civilized times, but the Rathburns were the *only* black Executive family in Paxco, and Chloe always seemed to hover around the fringes of Executive society. Although she was invited to and attended all the Executive parties and events, she always gave the impression that she was on the outside looking in. Nadia had never been sure whether it was on account of Chloe holding herself aloof or whether it was because the other Executives subtly shut her out.

Nadia had willfully befriended Chloe when they were thirteen, more because she was stubbornly unwilling to accept Chloe's fringe status than because they had so much in common. They weren't the kind of "best friends" Nadia read about in books or saw on TV, not the kind who had long, deep conversations about boys and life and their hopes for the future. For instance, Nadia would never tell Chloe the truth about her relationship with Nate. But they were friends nonetheless, and they had fun together.

Chloe noticed Nadia's arrival first, and when Nadia met her eyes, she knew at once that something was wrong. Chloe smiled at her and waved, but there was something slightly off about her expression, and she quickly looked away, cupping her hands around her coffee cup and staring moodily at the steam rising from its surface. Hardly the greeting Nadia was expecting. And that was when it occurred to Nadia that she hadn't had any phone messages from Chloe this morning. Surely a true friend should have at least called to see if she was okay.

Out of the corner of her eye, Nadia saw Jewel and Blair watching her and smirking. Nadia could just imagine what had happened here before she'd arrived. Jewel and Blair had probably talked extensively—and loudly—about Nadia's fifteen hours of questioning at the security station, speculating on the possibility of her being guilty of something. Maybe they'd even suggested that they were taking a social risk by attending classes at Nadia's home, that the taint of Nadia's potential involvement with the Chairman Heir's murder might rub off on them.

Jewel and Blair were both so highly born that they could afford the social risk of being in Nadia's presence. But Chloe, already on the fringes, could not. And the bitches had made sure she knew it.

Nadia swallowed hard and tried to act as though she were oblivious to the undercurrents. Fuming quietly, she headed toward the refreshments table. And that was when she got her first look at Robert Dante.

He was standing stiffly, with his back against the wall, hands clasped behind him, looking straight ahead in the perfect imitation of a servant making himself unobtrusive while standing at the ready.

She guessed his age as somewhere around eighteen—unusually young for a servant who was meant to interact with his Executive employers. He should have had to work his way up to the position, but she supposed being a spy meant he could skip all that. Well over six feet tall, he had shoulders so broad they seemed to strain the limits of his jacket. The formal livery couldn't hide the muscular build that reminded her of a professional athlete, and his deeply bronzed skin and freckled nose suggested he spent a fair amount of time in the sun. Not at all the look of someone who hoped to make a living as "personal assistant" to a man like Nadia's father. Not what she would imagine a spy looked like, either, though she supposed a spy who *looked* like a spy wouldn't be much use.

Ordinarily, Nadia would introduce herself to a new member of her household, even if girls like Jewel and Blair would sneer at her for acknowledging a servant as a fellow human being. However, since Dante was here to spy on her, she didn't feel inclined to indulge in social niceties, so she tried her best to ignore him as she fixed herself a cup of tea.

He was hard to ignore, and she found her gaze darting in his direction again as she dunked her tea bag. If she had to be spied on by someone, at least that someone was conspicuously nice to look at.

Maybe he sensed her looking at him, because he suddenly met her eyes. She looked away hastily, hoping she wasn't blushing. Just because she was engaged to Nate didn't mean she didn't notice good-looking guys like any other girl, but she didn't want anyone to notice her noticing a servant like that.

Bracing herself for awkwardness, Nadia turned and headed toward the conference table. Jewel and Blair were still smirking in the corner, and Chloe was still fascinated by something in the depths of her coffee cup. Nadia considered sitting on the far side of the table, but she always sat next to Chloe, and she wasn't going to allow social politics to change that. She took her seat and sipped her tea, painfully aware of the wall of silence beside her.

Nadia felt as if everyone in the room was watching her every move—with the exception of Chloe, who was trying to pretend she didn't exist. She felt sure Dante was staring at her, *spying* on her, but she didn't dare glance his way again. She looked over at Jewel and Blair and saw that they had both locked on to her and were heading over to the table.

"You poor thing," Jewel said with stunning insincerity as she set her cup carelessly on the table and reached for Nadia's hand to give it a squeeze. She inserted herself into the space between Nadia's and Chloe's chairs, standing so her backside was directly in Chloe's face. "I can't imagine what you must have gone through yesterday." She shuddered dramatically. Behind her, Chloe slid her chair over, getting Jewel's butt out of her face—and putting more distance between her and Nadia.

Jewel wanted to play at being a sympathetic friend? Fine. Nadia knew just how to beat her at that game.

Nadia rose to her feet and threw her arms around Jewel, hugging her hard. "It was awful," she confirmed as Jewel awkwardly hugged her back, her body stiff as a board. Nadia had to suppress a smile, knowing how badly Jewel wanted to pull away. But pulling away from a hug she had seemed to solicit herself would be openly rude, and while subtle, underhanded cruelty was accepted and sometimes even encouraged in girls of their station, open rudeness was not. "I can't tell you how much I appreciate your kindness and support in such a difficult time."

"Well, um, of course," Jewel said brightly, still trapped in Nadia's hug.

Nadia wasn't sure what prompted her to do it, but she couldn't help darting another look in Dante's direction. And yes, he *was* looking at her, with a small smile on his lips and a glimmer of amusement in his eyes. His smile broadened when their eyes met, and he held her gaze for a fleeting moment before he returned to proper servant mode, wiping the expression from his face and staring straight ahead.

Nadia finally released Jewel from the hug, pleased to have so successfully fended off her first attack. But though she liked to think of herself as an understanding person, hurt and disappointment compelled her to voice one more thought.

"It's in times like these that you find out who your true friends are," she said, smiling warmly at Jewel. Chloe had moved far enough away that Nadia couldn't even see her in her peripheral vision, but she knew her barb had hit home when she saw the smug satisfaction in Jewel's eyes.

Nadia immediately felt guilty. It wasn't like she didn't understand. Chloe couldn't afford to take any chances with her reputation, especially not in these critical years during which her marriage would be arranged. In fact, she probably shouldn't have shown up for the class at all. Taking potshots at her was unfair.

Mad at herself for speaking before thinking, Nadia sat back down and picked up her cup of tea just as their tutor arrived to begin class.

USUALLY, Nadia enjoyed her economics class. She wasn't a big fan of math as a general rule, but the teacher, Mr. Guthrie, had a contagious enthusiasm for the topic that rarely failed to draw her in. He was so good that sometimes he could win over even Jewel, an indifferent student if there ever was one. But today, there was so much tension in the room that no one seemed to be concentrating on the lesson, not even Nadia. Chloe was taking pains to ignore her, though she didn't look happy about it, and anything Nadia tried to say to ease the strain would only make things worse. She was also aware of Jewel and Blair reveling in the discomfort, sharing smug, superior smiles and writing notes to one another that made them giggle.

Mr. Guthrie noticed the passing of notes and gave the girls a disapproving frown, which they completely ignored. The poor teacher was at a disadvantage where his students were concerned, being a lowly Employee who couldn't afford to ruffle any feathers. The frown was the only sign of censure he betrayed as he continued with his lecture.

Nadia's attention continued to wander, and she found her gaze frequently drawn to Dante, who stood silent and unmoving at his post against the wall. She felt like he was watching her at all times, but she soon realized that he wasn't actually looking at her, but at Mr. Guthrie. Nadia remembered her father mentioning that Dante was a "bright young man" who would benefit from the classes. She'd thought that was merely an excuse for his presence in the schoolroom, but he seemed to be genuinely interested—certainly more interested than any of Mr. Guthrie's official students on that particular day.

After forty-five minutes, Mr. Guthrie declared it time for a break, and Nadia considered the possibility of making her excuses. Only the knowledge that Jewel and Blair would take her withdrawal as a victory kept her from leaving.

Usually, Nadia and Chloe would spend these break times talking, but as soon as Mr. Guthrie called a halt, Chloe was out of her chair and heading toward the ladies' room. Nadia had a feeling her friend was going to spend the entire break in there, just to avoid having to talk to her—and to avoid having to pointedly *not* talk to her.

Nadia pretended nothing unusual was happening, hiding her feelings behind a serene expression. She headed over to the refreshments table to make another cup of tea. To her annoyance, Jewel followed her, putting her hand on her arm to stop her just short of the table. Jewel hunched her shoulders a bit and leaned toward her as if sharing a secret, but she didn't particularly lower her voice.

"I wanted to speak with you while we have a moment," Jewel said as Nadia came to a halt.

This can't be good, Nadia thought as she looked at Jewel with an expression she was sure adequately displayed her complete lack of interest in whatever the other girl had to say. But Jewel was never one to take a hint when she didn't want to.

"I couldn't help noticing during class that your servant was listening in." Jewel waved a hand vaguely in Dante's direction. "I thought you might have a word with him about it before class resumes."

Despite her respect for manners where her peers were concerned, Jewel obviously felt no compunction about being openly rude to servants. She might have made a pretense of keeping this a quiet discussion between the two of them, but there was no way Dante hadn't heard her.

Technically, it was bad form for a servant to openly pay attention to what his "superiors" were saying in his presence. Servants were supposed to be as unobtrusive and unobservant as pieces of furniture, so that the Executives they served could pretend they weren't there. But Nadia had never been a stickler for such conventions, and even if she had . . .

Nadia blinked innocently and cocked her head. "Really? How shocking. Shall I order him to stuff his ears with wax so he can't hear Mr. Guthrie speaking?" She frowned, as if flummoxed by the problem. "But that would make it difficult for him to hear any requests for service as well." She glanced at Dante and saw that while he was looking straight ahead, his lips were twitching as if he was fighting a smile. Clearly imitating a blind and deaf piece of furniture was not his forte. It was lucky Jewel had her back turned to him or she'd probably be demanding his head on a platter.

Jewel held her nose a little higher in the air. "Make jokes if you must, but it's unseemly behavior for a servant. That other one knew his place."

"That other one?" Nadia asked, unable to keep her voice from rising just a bit. "You mean Sully? Who's been attending us for two years? Do you mean to tell me after all that time you don't know his name?" That seemed to be taking the superiority act a little far, even for Jewel.

"You're missing the point. In light of recent events, you would be wise to exercise extra caution in regards to propriety. There are those who might take offense at your servant's behavior and take your unwillingness to correct it as a sign of moral turpitude."

There was an implicit threat evident in Jewel's words, and Nadia knew she should take that threat seriously. Jewel could easily start a rumor that the male servants at Nadia's house behaved in an "unseemly" manner, which could lead the most spiteful and jealous of the gossipmongers to start speculating about just what kind of unseemly behavior was involved. Such rumors could eventually become stories about how the servants were servicing Nadia in bed, or something equally ridiculous.

But really, how seriously could she take someone who used the term "moral turpitude" in everyday speech?

"I'm touched to know you've taken such a keen interest in preserving my reputation," Nadia said, then affected another puzzled frown. "Or is it my servant you've taken such an interest in?" she asked, making a show of looking Dante up and down. "I must admit, he is nice to look at, but I had no idea you would find him so . . . distracting."

The color that rose to Jewel's cheeks was quite gratifying indeed. Nadia wasn't as good at starting rumors as Jewel was—she suspected the art required more malice than she herself was capable of—but that didn't mean she couldn't do it. Jewel liked to think of herself as the queen bee among the upper echelons of the Executive teens, and she and the rest of the Trio did wield a great deal of social power, but there were plenty of people jealous enough of her to revel in a good, unsavory rumor.

Nadia dropped her voice to something just above a whisper, through with the games. "Neither of us is going to come out of it unstained if you take this any further. I suggest for your own sake that you pay more attention to your lessons and less attention to who else may or may not be listening." How had she ended up defending the guy she knew was here to spy on her? If she'd been using her head instead of reacting emotionally, she might have been able to use Jewel's complaint as an excuse to get Dante out of the schoolroom and away from her.

Jewel smiled, a razor-sharp expression that held no warmth. "I was merely trying to be helpful."

Nadia didn't dignify that with an answer, and was more relieved than she wanted to admit when Jewel gave up and flounced off. Hostilities weren't over—they never were, where Jewel was concerned—but at least they were on temporary hiatus.

Nadia began fixing the cup of tea she no longer wanted, and she was surprised when Dante finally left his post at the wall and made his way to the table beside her. He made a show of gathering the trash and dirty dishes onto a tray, but if he were just doing his duty he would have waited until after the break was over.

"I'm sorry if I put you in an awkward position," he said in a voice so low she could barely hear him. "I'll try not to catch her attention again."

Nadia dunked her tea bag a little more vigorously than necessary as she took a sidelong glance at him. His eyes were a green-flecked brown, and they sparkled with humor. He must have really enjoyed listening to a pair of Executive girls arguing over him.

"If you're going to play at being a servant," she said in an equally low voice, "you should at least *try* to act like one." No well-trained servant would address his employer's daughter with such ease and familiarity, especially when they were close enough in age that it could easily be construed as flirting.

Dante arched an eyebrow at her. "I'm not sure what you mean," he said with a pretty good impression of puzzlement. "All I wanted to do was apologize for my mistake. And if you dunk that tea bag one more time, your tea is going to be dark enough to pass for coffee."

Nadia withdrew the tea bag—he was right, and the tea was likely undrinkable—and dropped it on the tray he extended to her.

"Will there be anything else, Miss Lake?" he asked, suddenly turning formal again.

In her peripheral vision, Nadia saw that the other girls were back in the schoolroom, and she figured even if they weren't looking directly at her, they were very aware of her and—thanks to Jewel—of Dante. So that was why he'd turned formal again after his overly familiar teasing.

"No," she said with a sigh, wishing for a simpler life. "You've done quite enough already."

CHAPTER SIX

It had been almost forty-eight hours since Nate's murder, and still no word from Kurt. Not that Nate was expecting word anymore. If Kurt had been planning to contact him, he'd have left *something* in the secret compartment, even if it was just a scrawled good-bye. No, Kurt was gone, and he'd left Nate behind without a word. Even if he hadn't needed Kurt's account of what had happened on the night of the murder, Nate doubted he could have let go without making an effort to find him. No matter how dangerous that effort might be.

There was only one logical place to begin the search: the Basement.

There were parts of the Basement that respectable Employees and Executives could visit during the day with relative safety. These were the neighborhoods on the fringes, not controlled by any of the gangs. These were also the neighborhoods where the black market did a brisk business, selling goods smuggled in from rival states.

Though the Replica technology was unequaled anywhere in the world, the rest of Paxco's home-grown tech was decidedly second-rate. Officially, Paxco citizens could buy Paxco products at reasonable prices, or a competitor's superior products at absurdly high prices with a premium tax on top. Even the richest of Paxco's citizens balked at those prices, and there wasn't a single Executive Nate knew who didn't take advantage of the black market's offerings—usually through intermediaries, because even in the fringes the Basement was never truly safe.

What Nate was contemplating was not a routine visit. To track down Kurt, he would have to delve into the Basement's human trafficking market—and that would require him to go deeper into Debasement, where even Paxco security officers feared to tread. It would require him to leave the relative safety of the daylight and venture into the dangers of the Basement night.

Even thinking about going into the Basement at night sent a shiver of adrenaline down Nate's spine. Like any young man of means, he'd made forays into Debasement with friends, dipping his feet into the shallow end. The neighborhoods that housed the black market during the day turned into something much more sinister at night. The privileged rich could sample some of Debasement's most tempting vices, dabbling in drugs, exotic contraband, and sex for hire. Such behavior was officially frowned upon, but everyone knew that perfectly respectable Executives and Employees took advantage of the opportunities there.

Nate had never told anyone, not even Nadia, the truth about how he'd met Kurt. Sure, Kurt had shown up at one of the Basement recruitment drives the Chairman sponsored, but he'd come because Nate had invited him. Nate had first met Kurt at a Basement-fringe club called Angel's, one of the favorite destinations of well-heeled tourists. At Angel's, you could get cheap, home-brewed drinks that ate a hole in your stomach, or you could get expensive brands that weren't carried by any official Paxco liquor stores. You could also get any drug your heart desired, and a pretty girl or boy to "entertain" you in one of the private rooms upstairs.

Last year, Nate had gone to Angel's with a group of friends. Well, not friends, exactly. It was hard to make real friends when you had a secret you couldn't afford to share—and when most people who tried to make friends with you were just kissing your ass because you were the Chairman Heir. Anyway, he'd gone to Angel's with a group of other Executive guys. Getting laid at Angel's was practically a rite of passage for an Executive boy, but Nate had been more interested in getting drunk when the press wasn't around to snap embarrassing pictures.

He'd been well on his way to achieving this aim when he'd caught sight of Kurt, prowling through the crowd in a palpable cloud of sexual energy. One glance was all it took to see that he was trolling for customers, but like any born-and-bred Basement-dweller, he always kept his eyes open for unexpected opportunities. Like when he'd bumped into a very drunk Executive douche bag and carefully relieved the man of his wallet.

The moment Kurt had slipped the wallet into a gap in his clothing—no doubt a secret compartment sewn in for just such occasions—his eyes had met Nate's. If Nate were being a responsible Executive, he'd have stormed over and demanded Kurt return the wallet. Instead, he froze like a rabbit, immediately and completely fascinated. A slow, wicked smile spread over Kurt's lips, and Nate had to grab the back of the chair he was sitting in to keep himself in place. Here in the Basement, he could let loose a lot of his inhibitions, but his companions weren't so drunk they wouldn't notice if he made a pass at a guy. And since they weren't really his friends, that would be a bad, bad thing.

Without meaning to, Nate licked his lips. The spark in Kurt's eye said he saw the gesture as an invitation. Nate swallowed hard, wishing he could make a true invitation. But though he tended to recklessness, he wasn't a complete moron and had no wish to experience the horror of "reprogramming."

Most likely, Kurt knew exactly who Nate was and knew better than to approach. He merely winked at Nate and moved off into the crowd. Nate hadn't been sure whether to feel relieved or disappointed.

That might have been the end of their acquaintance, if one of the club's hostesses hadn't glommed onto him a while later and started flirting. Naturally, Nate wasn't interested, but the girl was persistent, and so sexy Nate's companions started looking at him funny for refusing her. He'd given in because he couldn't afford not to, but she'd surprised the hell out of him by leading him to a room that was already occupied—by Kurt, who'd paid her to catch Nate's eye and lure him upstairs.

That had been one of the best nights of Nate's life, made all the better by the knowledge that he was doing the forbidden and getting away with it. There was an undeniable chemistry between him and Kurt, something Nate *knew* was mutual. Before the night was out, Nate had extracted a promise from Kurt to show up at the next recruitment drive, so that Nate could give him a safe, respectable job. He'd paid an absurd amount of money for Kurt's time, hoping that Kurt would be able to get by without having to turn tricks until the recruitment drive rolled around, but he half-expected him to be a no-show. Nate had been more thankful than he cared to admit when Kurt kept his promise after all.

Angel's would always be a favorite for Nate because it was where he'd met Kurt. But it was also a place where money, both company scrip and real dollars, changed hands in epic quantities. If Kurt had arranged passage out of Paxco, he'd most likely arranged it at Angel's. So tonight, Nate was going there, as he had countless times before since his first trip at the age of fourteen. With one big difference.

This time, he was going alone.

nate looked at himself in the mirror and wondered if he'd gone completely crazy. Nobody sane would think of doing what he was about to do.

The eyes that stared back at him from the mirror weren't his.

Well, yes, they were. They just didn't look like it.

Pale blue contacts leached most of the color from his eyes, and the kohl he used to line them made them look paler still, almost inhuman. His naturally dark hair was hidden under a white-blond wig, and his eyebrows and eyelashes were painted soot black with more kohl. A thin, blue-white powder cooled and lightened his warm skin tone, and his black lipstick didn't go all the way to the edges of his lips, making his mouth into a harsh black slash in his face.

He couldn't do anything to change his basic bone struc-ture, of course, but a couple of pouches artificially filled out his cheeks, giving him dimples, and the changes in his color-ing were so striking that even his own mother wouldn't recog-nize him. If his own mother were around, that is. She and the Chairman had had a falling out almost ten years ago, and she'd withdrawn from public life, entering a fancy Executive "retreat" that bore a disturbing resemblance to a medieval cloister. Nate hadn't seen her since. Apparently, staying away from the Chairman was more important to her than main-taining a relationship with her son.

Regardless, no one looking at him would guess that he

was really the Chairman Heir in disguise. Right now, he was a different person. He was the Ghost, a Basement alter ego Kurt had helped him create. Well, bullied him into creating, at least at first. Nate had balked at just about every aspect of the costume. But he'd wanted to go to the Basement incognito more than he'd wanted to protect his dignity, and in this getup, he fit right in. Nate had the amusing thought that if his own staff should catch sight of him, he'd be detained as an intruder. But then he decided the thought wasn't so amusing—if anyone should find out about his alter ego, his days of slipping away to the Basement would be over.

Dressed in black leather and silver chains that made his artificial skin tone look even paler and more sickly, Nate used the escape route he and Kurt had devised together to sneak out of his apartment without anyone knowing.

The escape started with a long slide down a laundry chute—one that was a lot less nerve-wracking when Kurt was waiting at the bottom. Tonight, Nate just had to hope no one was dawdling in the laundry room at one in the morning.

Nate hit the pile of laundry at the bottom of the chute with a soft "oof" he couldn't suppress. The landing stole his breath for a moment, but he was relieved to find himself in a pitch-dark room. There was no one around to witness his escape.

When he caught his breath, Nate scrambled out of the laundry and edged his way to the door. From there, it was a long, nerve-wracking trek to the service stairs, and an even longer climb in the dim, echoing stairway down to the parking level. The only good news was that no one in their right mind used a stairway in a high-rise—especially at one in the morning—unless absolutely necessary.

Nate couldn't set foot on the street in his disguise. Theoretically, Basement-dwellers could roam the city as freely as Executives and Employees, but in practice they tended to stay in the Basement. You could sometimes see them in their flamboyant outfits in the neighborhoods that bordered the Basement, but you'd certainly never see them in the streets of lower Manhattan, in the territory of the cream of Executive society. Even if he wasn't immediately detained, he'd be *noticed,* and that might be just as bad.

But he couldn't just commandeer his own car to drive out into the city. He'd have to use his parking pass to get in and out of the garage, and the activity would be logged for curious eyes to see. Which left him no alternative but to be a little . . . creative.

As a general rule, most people of the Employee class couldn't afford to own gas-fueled vehicles, so they used public transportation. However, one of the men who worked the front desk at Nate's building owned a motorcycle—an ancient Ducati he had inherited from his grandfather—that he doted on like a favorite pet. Thinking he might enjoy taking a joyride someday, Nate had persuaded Kurt to steal the man's keys and make copies, a task that had been child's play for Kurt's nimble fingers. They never had taken that ride together, but Nate still had the keys. He figured it wasn't stealing, as long as he brought the bike back in one piece. Besides, being on the bike would give him an excuse to wear a helmet and cover the most obvious parts of his disguise.

The bike had an obviously nonstandard storage compartment strapped awkwardly to the back. Nate removed his chain-laden leather jacket and stuffed it in the compartment, leaving himself in a plain black T-shirt and black leather pants.

Still noticeably out of place in this neighborhood, but probably in the dark and on the move it wouldn't draw too much attention, as the aggressive chains would.

Face and hair hidden by the helmet, Nate edged the motorcycle out of the parking garage. If anyone checked the records, they might well question the bike's owner about why he'd taken the bike out when he was supposed to be on duty, but no one would guess Nate had taken it. No one would know he hadn't remained safely asleep in his bed.

maybe he was taking caution to the point of paranoia, but Nate decided not to drive the motorcycle all the way to the Basement. Instead, he pulled into a parking space on the street about three blocks from the border. By that point, he was well past the respectable neighborhoods where his outfit would draw unwanted attention. He hoped he wasn't so far past civilization that the bike would disappear while he was gone. He didn't want to think about how he would get home from here without it.

Of course, since he was walking into the Basement with no backup, planning to ask questions of people who generally didn't take well to being questioned, perhaps he was being overly optimistic in thinking he would make it back at all.

With that cheerful thought, Nate stowed his helmet and donned the leather-and-chains jacket, taking a moment to check his disguise in the motorcycle's side mirror. Was it his imagination, or did he look just a little wild-eyed?

As he walked away from the bike, his mouth was dry and his heart was jackhammering. He'd never realized before how secure Kurt's presence on their jaunts had made him feel. Trips to the Basement had always triggered an adrenaline rush, but as long as Kurt was with him, he'd felt . . . safe.

Which had probably been pretty naive of him. There was no such thing as "safe" in the Basement at night, even for its most powerful predators. But Kurt's ease in his natural habitat had created a convincing illusion. And Nate had wanted to be convinced.

In polite society, the streets would be quiet at this time of night. But the Basement was anything but polite society, and the streets got progressively busier as he edged his way closer to its borders. The place came alive at night, its illicit clubs and bars filling the darkness with sounds and scents, drawing the unwary in like some exotic carnivorous plant luring insects with its nectar.

Once upon a time, the Basement had been the South Bronx, but when Paxco had bought out the state of New York, one of its first civic "improvements" had been to raze the neighborhood to the ground. That had happened well before Nate was born, and from what he'd heard, the residents had practically done the city's work for it in the wave of riots that broke out when the plans were announced. They seemed to think they should make their own decisions about the disposition of their neighborhood and had shown their displeasure with the decree by tearing it down. Either that, or they'd just enjoyed the excuse to take to the streets in a frenzy of destruction.

The neighborhood that Paxco had built over the rubble was an homage to practicality. Every building was a high-rise, allowing Paxco to house its poor and unemployed in as small a footprint as possible, so the city could reclaim fringe neighborhoods and make them into something more respectable. And every building was identical, built of ugly gray concrete with small, regularly spaced rectangular windows.

There was technically no wall or other barrier to separate

the Basement from the respectable neighborhoods of the city; however, the looming gray concrete high-rises were as intimidating as any wall, towering over the low-rent Employee housing that bordered them. When Nate passed between the first two buildings, a shiver traveled down his spine.

Most Basement-dwellers were far too poor to own cars, and most tourists were far too protective of their possessions to bring cars into the neighborhood. The architects behind the Basement had anticipated that, and they hadn't bothered with wide avenues with multiple lanes and room to park. Instead, the Basement was a claustrophobic warren of narrow streets that made the high-rises on each side look even taller and more forbidding, and cars could only venture through when pedestrians allowed it.

In the Basement, there were no distinctions made between residences and places of business—not that there were any *official* places of business in the Basement anyway, unless you counted the soup kitchens and hospitals. The only way you could tell one building from another was by looking at the graffiti spray-painted on walls and doors.

This being a temperate almost-spring night, the streets of Debasement were at their most crowded. Floods of Basement-dwellers roamed the streets, hawking their wares or searching for prey. Others gathered just to socialize and posture, or to protect their territory.

Though Nate had been to Debasement many times, the first minutes were always a shock to the senses. In the world he was used to, there was a certain uniformity of appearance as Employees and Executives dressed in accordance with the conventions of their social circles. In Debasement, the convention was to be as unconventional as possible, each individual striving to stand out, perhaps in defiance of the uniformity of their surroundings. Nate had dressed in leather and chains because the outfit exaggerated the pallor of his ghostly alter ego, but the people around him sported a riot of colors. Neon orange, screaming hot pink, electric blue, sunbright yellow.

Piercings had been a staple in Debasement since the neighborhood had first been born, but facial tattoos were becoming increasingly popular, and those who weren't ready to commit to tattoos went for face painting instead. Street vendors offered to do elaborate face painting for a fee, a service that was used almost exclusively by tourists—and priced accordingly. It was like going to a very adult carnival—the kind where you could get your face painted while getting a blow job. The air smelled of street food, and of too many bodies, often laced with a whiff of illicit, sickly sweet smoke.

Dressed as he was like a native, Nate made his way through the crowd with relative ease, the predators ignoring him as uninteresting prey, the street salesmen dismissing him as not having money to burn. It was just the kind of camouflage he'd been hoping for, and it got him to Angel's without incident. He almost let out a sigh of relief when the club came into sight, but passing through the crowd had been the least problematic part of his plan.

From the outside, the building that housed Angel's club / bar / brothel / general den of iniquity looked no different from all the buildings around it, a bland gray pillar of concrete with windows like soulless eyes staring onto the street below. The name Angel's had been spray-painted in metallic silver over the entryway, and the door was flanked by a pair of Debasement's version of bouncers—men with the barrel chests and buzz-cut hair of lifelong soldiers but pierced, tattooed, and painted like some long-ago goth band.

Nate felt the eyes of the bouncers on him as he climbed the stairs to the front door of the club. He'd been here enough times with Kurt that he was sure they recognized him, but they gave him the evil eye anyway. As a general rule, Angel encouraged Basement-dwellers who didn't work for her to take their business elsewhere; her club catered specifically to the Employee and the Executive class, where the money was. But money trumped everything, and a Basement-dweller whose pockets were pleasantly stuffed after a lucky score could buy a handsome welcome.

Nate wished Kurt hadn't taken *all* his dollars. He shelled out the cover charge in Paxco scrip, paying three times what he would have if he'd had dollars, and immediately demoting himself in the eyes of the bouncers. Customers bearing dollars were treated like visiting dignitaries, regardless of their class. Those paying with scrip were tolerated as long as the money held out, but ripped off at every opportunity.

Nate endured an overly personal manual search from one of the bouncers, whose hands moved slowly and squeezed harder than necessary. The guy stank of body odor and cigarette smoke, and was about as sexy as a pickup truck on cinder blocks. It was an effort of will not to shrink away from his touch.

"Want me to turn my head and cough?" Nate asked when the bouncer's hands lingered where they shouldn't.

The bouncer gave him a scowl to let him know he wasn't amused, then gave his family jewels a little extra squeeze. Nate reminded himself that he could hide signs of weakness without resorting to his own special brand of humor, which he doubted would be much appreciated by his current audience.

Finally satisfied that Nate wasn't carrying anything into

the club that he shouldn't, the bouncer let him go. Yet another hurdle overcome, but the greatest challenge still awaited him.

Someone with a keen understanding of architecture and structural engineering must have helped Angel renovate her club, because although it was located in a building identical to those around it, it was completely different on the inside. The apartment buildings had eight four-room units per floor. They were supposedly designed to house families of four, but they would be tight and cramped even for two. Certainly they weren't designed to house a nightclub, which was why Angel had had all the apartments on the first two floors of her building ripped out.

What she'd done was technically illegal—the high-rises were meant to be free housing for the poor. When the city planners had first designed the Basement, they'd made sure that there was enough housing for everyone who needed it. What they hadn't planned for—or, more accurately, what they'd willfully ignored—was the human desire to lay claim to territory. Housing units were claimed by whoever had the strength to hold them, and if a powerful Basement-dweller like Angel of Mercy wanted to take over whole floors of an apartment building, rip out all the apartments, and turn them into a club, no one was going to stop her. And the fact that she'd managed to rip out all the apartments except for a few support pillars here and there without bringing the entire tower down around her suggested she'd had high-level help doing it.

Angel was most likely the richest person in all of Debasement, and with her money she could no doubt have decorated her club as elegantly as any legitimate Executive club in the city. However, she was also one of the savviest people

Nate had ever met, and she knew exactly what her customers wanted. They didn't come to Debasement in search of an elegant club they could find in their own neighborhoods; they came to see how the "other half" lived—without actually having to see anything more than a prettied-up fantasy.

The club was decorated in what Nate liked to think of as jailhouse chic. The pillars and floor were naked concrete, complete with chips and pockmarks to make them look like they came from a war zone. The ceiling was exposed beams and wiring, and lighting was provided by bare bulbs on wires. The walls were concrete, too, only you could barely see any of the concrete gray behind all the spray-painted graffiti that decorated them. Most of it was gang tags—for "artistic" effect, not because Angel's was part of any gang's territory— and suggestions to do things that were anatomically unlikely. There were also some pornographic cartoons, and one whole wall displayed a spray-painted portrait of Angel herself, holding a wicked, serrated blade to her chest and testing the edge with her finger as she looked out over her club with all-seeing eyes.

Nate fought his way through the crowd toward the bar. If you were looking for someone in a bar, the best place to start was generally with the bartender, and Kurt had always seemed to be at least mildly friendly with one of the ones who worked here. Nate darted through an opening to grab one of the rickety barstools. To his disappointment, the bar was being tended by Viper, a foul-tempered asshole Nate would have just as soon avoided. There was an off chance that Kurt's friend, Random, was also on duty today, but Nate would just have to wait and see, because he didn't want to ask questions of Viper if he didn't have to.

A petite blonde in heels so high they should have given

her a nosebleed climbed onto the other end of the bar. The girl was an obvious Basement-dweller, her hair dyed jet black with neon blue and green streaks, tattoos peeking out from the edges of her clothes, her face dotted with holes where she was pierced but not wearing her jewelry. But she was dressed in Executive finery, wearing a clingy red skirt suit that fit her like it was made for her, a white button-down blouse, and a conservative string of pearls. The stilt-like red pumps that looked like they were made out of plastic definitely did not go with the outfit.

As the patrons hooted and hollered out encouragement, the girl began to dance on the bar, stepping around bottles, jars, and glasses. Dollar bills and scrip appeared like magic in people's hands, and as the girl slithered out of her clothes, she revealed convenient places for patrons to tuck the money. Viper worked around her, taking money and giving out drinks as if she weren't even there.

Nate would have preferred to just buy a drink and sip quietly as he kept his eyes out for Random. But he knew from experience that if he ignored the stripper, she might make it her personal goal to gain his attention, and he was not in the mood for a lap dance. He held out bills like the men around him and tried to enjoy the show.

Technically, strippers weren't supposed to remove their G-strings, and patrons weren't allowed to touch, but those rules were ignored in Debasement with the same negligence as most laws. The strippers at Angel's never seemed to mind, always encouraging the patrons to sample their wares—as long as there was money involved, naturally. Maybe it was because Nate was in a somewhat altered state of mind, or maybe this particular girl was new and not as practiced as the pros he'd seen before, but he couldn't help noticing how frozen her eyes and smile were as she pranced across the bar, naked except for her shoes and her money-stuffed garters, letting the patrons, men and women both, touch her whenever and wherever they wanted.

Nate stuck a bill in her garter when she invited him to, but he did it almost gingerly, trying not to touch her any more than necessary. There were some girls he found attractive, but this chick wasn't one of them. Her movements were almost mechanical, her expression behind the fake smile one of bored indifference. Based on the number of bills in her garters, Nate was the only one who gave a crap.

when Nate came to Debasement with Kurt, he always had a blast, and time had a way of getting away from him. It was always Kurt who had to gently break it to him that it was time to go. Together, they had sampled the various exotic drinks offered at the bar, danced openly as a couple because in Debasement, no one cared—and none of the tourists could see through Nate's disguise—and rented the rooms upstairs when they wanted . . . privacy. They had enjoyed Angel's male strippers, had bargained for contraband with the club's favored black marketeers, and had even dabbled in some of the tamer drugs, though Kurt had advised Nate to caution on that front. When Kurt championed caution, Nate listened.

Angel's without Kurt was nowhere near as much fun as he remembered. Drinking alone held little appeal, especially when he was drinking the watered-down crap that was served to customers paying in scrip. And without Kurt to distract him, he found himself really *looking* at the strippers and sex workers for the first time. There was nothing wrong with sex for hire, as far as he was concerned. Two consenting adults and all that. It certainly seemed a less unsavory "career" for a Basement-dweller than the drug dealing and violence that were the most obvious alternatives. Sex was fun, after all. But with nothing to do but sit back and observe, he was seeing things that before he'd always ignored, like the way the prostitutes' hungry smiles tended to wilt when their customers weren't looking.

It was all uncommonly depressing, and within fifteen minutes of arriving, Nate was more than anxious to get the hell out. But he'd come here for a reason, and it wasn't to have fun. He risked asking Viper if Random was on duty tonight, but Viper ignored him as if he hadn't spoken. The guy on the next stool said he hadn't seen Random in weeks, so maybe he'd gotten another job. Or maybe he'd just disappeared, the way Basement-dwellers sometimes did.

Nate decided his next best option was to talk to Angel herself. She rarely failed to make an appearance, so Nate settled in to wait.

An hour passed, and then another, and Nate still hadn't caught a glimpse of Angel. It was possible this was one of those rare nights when she didn't show up at the club. By the end of the third hour, he'd wandered from one end of the club to the other at least three times, and he still hadn't found her. To keep from being kicked out, he'd had to keep the money flowing, buying more drinks than he dared to swallow—being alone and drunk in Debasement was a recipe for disaster—and stuffing G-strings of strippers he had no interest in. He was running low on scrip, and he was aware that soon the staff would notice and ask him to leave.

At just after 4:00 A.M., Nate made his way to the bar once

more and gestured at Viper. The vertically slitted yellow contacts he wore certainly enhanced his reptilian look, as did the curved, fanglike implants that replaced his upper canines. Even when Nate had been here with Kurt, throwing dollars around with aplomb and thereby buying the devotion of the rest of the club's employees, he'd always felt like Viper disliked him. Of course, like everyone else who worked at Angel's, Viper was a part of the "atmosphere," filling the role of the scary-ass bartender to give the tourists a thrill. Maybe acting like he disliked everyone was just part of his job.

Viper waited impatiently for Nate to order a drink, and Nate knew even before he opened his mouth that he was making a mistake. But he was almost out of scrip—if he ended up having to do this again, he'd make sure to bring a lot more money with him—and it was his last shot. He leaned over the bar, forced to shout over the music even though he'd have rather kept his voice down.

"I was hoping to talk to Angel tonight," he said, then folded his hand around the remaining scrip in his pocket and slid that hand in Viper's direction, making sure a corner of paper showed.

Viper looked at Nate's hand and made a face. Nate thought the feeble bribe was about to be refused, but Viper tapped a sharpened, clawlike fingernail on the corner of paper and drew it out of Nate's hand. He looked at the hundred-dollar note with obvious distaste, picking it up gingerly and dropping it into the tip jar he kept behind the bar. (Keeping a tip jar where just anyone could get to it would have been begging for the Basement-dwellers to help themselves.)

"Outta luck," Viper said, managing to make his words hiss despite the lack of sibilant letters.

It was more than he'd gotten when he'd asked about Random, but it was a little thin at fifty dollars a word. Nate waited a second to see if Viper planned to elaborate, but the man turned and started to walk away. Unwisely, Nate leaned over the bar and grabbed Viper's arm. Out of the corner of his eye, he saw one of the bouncers take notice and start moving his way. The smart thing to do would be to let go, but Nate was too frustrated to be smart.

"What do you mean I'm out of luck?" he demanded. "Is she not here tonight?"

Viper stared at him with those slitted yellow eyes, and Nate fought a shudder. He'd always assumed the reptilian effect was caused by contacts, but now he wondered if they were implants, like the fangs. Cosmetic surgery performed by amateurs struck Nate as a terrible idea, but, like many terrible ideas, it was popular in Debasement.

"Time to go," someone said from behind Nate, and a hand clamped down on his shoulder. "Let go of Viper, unless you want to lose fingers."

In a bar in civilized society, Nate might not have taken that threat seriously. Here, he knew the bouncer was dead serious. Nate wasn't here as the Chairman Heir of Paxco; he was just some anonymous Basement-dweller, and if Angel's staff wanted to torture or even kill him, the law wouldn't bat an eyelash.

"Please tell her I need to talk to her," he said a little desperately as he let go of Viper's arm. "There's money in it."

The bouncer yanked on Nate's arm, practically dislocating his shoulder, and Nate stumbled forward. He tried to turn and say something else to Viper—he wasn't sure exactly *what* he could say that would persuade the man to convey the message—but the bouncer was having none of it. Another joint-torturing yank propelled Nate away from the bar, and oblivious patrons filled in the space he'd just vacated, hiding the bartender from view.

CHAPTER SEVEN

nadia slept almost ten hours Monday night and woke on Tuesday morning feeling much more like herself, the lingering weakness of her battle with the flu gone. Remembering that Nate had promised to come by and check on her, Nadia examined her day planner, hoping she didn't have too much free time. If she could keep herself bouncing from one obligation to another as much as possible, she wouldn't have time for more than a brief visit from Nate, and maybe she could avoid having him tell her anything she didn't want to hear.

The morning would be her most vulnerable time. Mornings were when she did her individual schoolwork and studying. Some days, she had a tutor, but today wasn't one of them. She had plenty of homework to do, but when Nate was a student, he'd considered all homework optional, and he'd expect her to feel the same way. Fortunately, he almost never stopped by in the morning—yesterday being a big exception— and she had two hours of classes scheduled for the afternoon, followed by a meeting of the Teen Charity League, which was little more than a glorified social club for Executive teenagers, but which did manage to fit in some actual charity work here and there. That should account for most of the daylight hours, and then tonight her mother was putting on a dinner party, which always seemed to entail a lot of fussing and chores, despite the fact that all the real work was done by the servants.

After examining her calendar, Nadia felt secure in her armor, and she tried to forget about all the pressure sitting on her shoulders. She spent the morning studying, crossing her fingers that Nate wouldn't interrupt. She got her wish, though her concentration wasn't up to par. She breathed a sigh of relief when afternoon rolled around and it was time for class.

That relief evaporated when she arrived at her first class and discovered that Chloe hadn't come, but Jewel and Blair had, even though they rarely showed up two days in a row. Jewel bragged that she and Cherry had been invited to a private dinner at the Chairman's mansion, going on and on about what she would wear and how she would style her hair and how honored her family was. If the boasting was designed to make Nadia entertain uneasy thoughts that the Chairman was rethinking the marriage arrangement, she unfortunately succeeded.

Naturally, the story of Nate's rebirth as a Replica was still front and center with the press, and they were constantly replaying things like Nate's altercation with the reporter—and Nadia's ignominious exit from the security station. In retrospect, she figured she should have left with her head held high, lack of makeup and inelegant attire notwithstanding. The effort to hide from the cameras just made her look guilty. Jewel found ways to slip references to the footage into conversation as often as possible. The day before, Nadia had come out the winner of their verbal sparring, but not today.

To make her victory that much sweeter, Jewel went out of her way to make demands of Dante, always during class rather than during breaks, so that he would have to leave the room and miss key parts of the lesson. And in yet another attempt to prove she was an obnoxious bitch, Jewel ordered him to carry her bag down to the lobby for her when class was over. Nadia could have countermanded that order—he was supposedly her family's servant, not Jewel's—but she wanted Jewel out of her sight as soon as possible, so she bit her tongue instead of arguing.

Nadia was pissed off enough about Jewel's behavior that she didn't immediately leave the schoolroom, instead fixing herself a cup of tea and taking a moment to enjoy being blissfully alone. In a little more than an hour, she would have to face Jewel again at the Teen Charity League meeting, and she needed to regroup first.

The solitude lasted for maybe one or two minutes, and then she heard footsteps approaching. Dante must have fled Jewel's presence at a downright sprint to be back so soon. Nadia wished she'd hurried back upstairs, not wanting to be trapped into conversation with him.

Her heart skipped a beat when she saw not Dante but Mosely standing in the doorway to the schoolroom, arms crossed over his chest, unblinking eyes pinned on her. Nadia froze, trapped by the malice in his gaze. She didn't want to know what he was thinking as he looked at her like that, but it made her feel naked and vulnerable and very, very alone.

Not that she *was* alone, of course. She was in her own home, and even if there was no one in sight, a scream would bring half the household running to her aid. Until they saw Mosely, of course. No one could protect her from him.

"What do you want?" she asked sharply. "If I had anything to say to you, I'd have called."

Perhaps snapping at Mosely wasn't the wisest course of action, but it was either snap or cower. Acting normal around this man just wasn't possible, not when she was so acutely aware of what he could do to her.

Mosely made a *tsk*ing sound with his tongue, closing the door behind him and moving closer. Nadia had to fight an instinctive urge to take a step back. This was *her* home, and she would not retreat from a bully in her own home.

"I'm disappointed in you, Miss Lake," Mosely said with a frown. "Surely you don't think I'm unaware that Nathaniel visited here yesterday. And yet I haven't heard from you. Do we need to have another discussion about your duty to your state?"

Nadia cursed herself. She should have sent word to Mosely about Nate's visit even though she hadn't learned anything. She should have known he'd expect regular updates from his unwilling spy.

"I didn't have anything to report," she said. "I was still pretty sick when Nate came by yesterday, and we didn't talk much."

Mosely stepped even closer, and this time Nadia couldn't help moving backward. She didn't want him close enough to touch her. His lips curved into a pleased smile, and she wished she'd had the nerve to hold her ground. Nothing pleased a bully more than seeing his prey's fear.

"What you're telling me," he said, "is that you had an opportunity to question him about his plans, and you chose not to do so because you had a case of the sniffles."

"It was the flu!" she snapped, once again letting him see that he'd struck a nerve. She took a deep breath, letting it out slowly and looking away so she didn't have to see Mosely's baleful stare. She spent half her life putting on a public face and hiding her true feelings. She could endure public verbal sparring sessions with the Trio without ever letting on when their words hurt her; she could pretend she and Nate were in love—and in lust—when they were nothing more than good friends; she could set all her own needs and wants aside for the sake of following protocol and protecting her family. Why couldn't she put on a brave face for Dirk Mosely? True, he was physically dangerous to her—and to those she loved—but she was an Executive, damn it. The face she showed to the public was never the real her, and she should be putting on the same front for Mosely that she put on for anyone else.

"I don't care if it was bubonic plague," Mosely said while Nadia was still trying to regain her composure. "Time is of the essence, and you don't seem to be treating your mission with the proper sense of urgency."

Nadia looked up to meet his gaze again, and although what she saw there made her shiver inside, she was pretty sure that this time she kept her fear from showing on her face. "I'm sorry, Mr. Mosely," she said in her most practiced Executive voice. "I know how urgent it is, and I'll work harder at getting Nate to talk to me." The promise made her feel vaguely nauseous, and she wasn't sure how she would force herself to do what she was being asked, but she'd worry about that later. For now, she had to make sure Mosely left this meeting satisfied.

"You'll have to do better than that."

"I'll do what I can. But you have to remember, Mr. Mosely, you're working with an amateur here. I don't have any way of making Nate talk to me if he doesn't want to." Which was true enough. And it was possible he *wouldn't* want to talk to her about whatever he was doing to try to find Bishop. It wasn't as if he would think she could help him.

"Still not good enough," Mosely said. "I have evidence that Nathaniel visited the Basement last night."

Nadia's jaw dropped open. "What?" She knew Nate had been to the Basement before with his friends—it was a rare Executive teenage boy who hadn't—and she suspected he and Bishop had gone there as a couple, but she couldn't imagine even someone as reckless as Nate going to the Basement alone.

Mosely chuckled at her shock. "I take that to mean he didn't tell you he was planning to go poking around."

"Certainly not!" Going to the Basement with a group of his friends and a legion of bodyguards was one thing, but she'd never have guessed he'd go there alone. He had to have been in disguise. Nadia couldn't even imagine what would happen to an Executive of his stature if the Basement predators got their hands on him.

Of course, the Basement was the only place Bishop could possibly be hiding. He'd been born there, and no doubt still had contacts there. Not to mention that the average Basement-dweller wasn't overly eager to cooperate with authorities and turn fugitives in.

"Scrip that is registered to him has shown up there," Mosely continued. "I don't like the idea of our Chairman Heir traipsing around the Basement unobserved and alone. Paxco has already had to swallow an enormous expense in creating this Replica; the last thing the state needs is to be forced to do it again."

"If you think I can talk Nate out of going to the Basement, you don't—"

"No, of course not," Mosely interrupted. "You've already proven how little influence you have on him."

Nadia's face went hot, and she hated that she couldn't contradict him.

"Besides," Mosely continued, "while it might be . . . uncomfortable to think of our Chairman Heir putting himself in harm's way, I suspect it is our best chance of finding Mr. Bishop. I have, of course, interviewed many of my contacts in the Basement in hopes of locating him, but I haven't yet learned anything of great import." He gave her a dry, cold smile. "Basement-dwellers are, as I'm sure you know, rarely forthcoming with authority figures."

Nadia hugged herself, remembering the ease with which Mosely had threatened her with Riker's Island. If he could wield such threats against an Executive, who knew how gruesome a threat he could wield against a powerless Basement-dweller? Had those he'd "interviewed" survived the encounter?

Mosely laughed, his eyes sparkling with genuine amusement, and Nadia realized she was once again wearing her emotions on her face, something she couldn't seem to keep from doing in Mosely's presence.

"I think I've given you a rather exaggerated impression of my depravity," he said, still smiling. "I won't hesitate to do whatever is necessary to find the man who killed our Chairman Heir, but torturing random Basement-dwellers would be counterproductive. Someone who knows nothing about Mr. Bishop's whereabouts would happily, *desperately* make something up under torture just to make it stop. I have no moral objection to torture, but to be a practical and efficient use of my time and energy, it must be used judiciously. Which means I need to have some idea who might have information. And that's where Nathaniel comes in. Friends of Mr. Bishop's might talk to *him* more candidly than they would to me or my men."

Nadia frowned. "But he would have been in disguise when he went, right? Even Nate isn't reckless enough to waltz into the Basement at night by himself if he thought anyone would recognize him."

"True."

"So why would anyone talk to a complete stranger about Bishop?"

Mosely shrugged. "They might if the price was right. And even if no one does, it would be informative to know whom he chooses to contact, since I believe he knows more about Mr. Bishop's previous life than he has revealed to anyone."

Nadia looked away, hoping to hide the chill of revulsion Mosely's statement inspired. He might have stopped short of torturing random Basement-dwellers for information, but anyone Nate contacted would be in serious danger if Mosely found out about it.

"I bet you're wondering where *you* fit into this picture," Mosely said, and Nadia reluctantly forced herself to face him once more.

"I have a feeling you're about to tell me."

He nodded, reaching into his pocket and pulling out a slim envelope. "Naturally, you will do your best to persuade Nathaniel to tell you as many details of his trip to the Basement as you can manage. Especially names of people he's spoken to." He opened the envelope and slid a tiny disc out of it, smaller than the nail on Nadia's pinkie. "This is a tracking device. It will give us real-time information on Nathaniel's location at all times. You will find a way to plant it on him— I'd suggest in his wallet, or something else he habitually carries with him—and the next time he goes to the Basement, we will know. And we will follow."

He held the device out to Nadia, but she didn't reach for it, could only stare as her stomach shriveled. Recounting things to Mosely that Nate told her in confidence was a terrible enough betrayal, but planting a tracking device on him . . . She couldn't. Especially when she considered what would happen to all the people Nate talked to when Mosely got hold of them.

Mosely's free hand darted out and grabbed Nadia's wrist. She reflexively tried to pull away, but he squeezed so hard she couldn't help crying out.

"Don't be a fool," he said as he forced the tracker into her palm and then squeezed her fingers closed around it. "We both know you have no choice."

Nadia shook her head. "I can't," she breathed, hardly able to force any sound out of her mouth.

"You will." Mosely let go of her wrist and grabbed her chin, forcing her to look into his eyes. "Do we have an understanding?"

Dread coiled in Nadia's gut, cold and tight and hard. Mosely's eyes were dilated, his nostrils flared. If ever Nadia had doubted that he enjoyed his work, the look in his eyes now proved it. Any sensible person would back down while she had the chance, and Nadia had always been a sensible person.

Which was why she was almost as surprised as Mosely when her fingers opened and the tracker rolled off her palm and onto the floor. Her chest was too tight and her mouth too dry for her to voice her refusal, but he got the message just the same.

"You are an ignorant, foolish child," he told her, then drove his fist into her stomach and let go of her chin.

Nadia would have screamed at the sudden, shocking pain, if she'd had any air left in her lungs. Instead, she made a strangled sound and fell to her knees, both arms wrapped around her middle as she bent in half and tried without success to breathe.

"I don't need to take you to Riker's Island to hurt you,"

Mosely said. "And I can hurt you in ways that won't leave any marks. You'll never be able to prove I laid hands on you. And who would believe a spoiled teenager over Paxco's chief of security?"

If Nadia could breathe, she would have screamed for help. No matter how scared everyone was of Mosely, they certainly wouldn't stand idly by and let him hit her in her own home.

Mosely squatted in front of her. "But maybe you're one of those martyr types. Maybe now that you're no longer ill and feverish, you figure you should stand by your quaint little principles, no matter what the consequences to yourself."

A little air found its way into Nadia's lungs, and she managed a whimper of sound. Barely enough for *Mosely* to hear, never mind the household staff.

"But what about your loved ones, Miss Lake? Are you willing to risk *them* as well?"

Nadia gasped in a little more air. Tears of pain blurred her vision, but not enough to hide Mosely's smile.

"Maybe I should have your sister Geraldine's home searched for contraband," he mused. "We both know there will be plenty to find. I can arrest her and her husband for dealing with the black market."

Nadia shook her head. "Can't!" she gasped. If Paxco prosecuted every Executive who dabbled in the black market, the state would go bankrupt from the enormous expense of it—and there wouldn't be a single Executive left to run the government.

"Of course I can, Miss Lake. Why do you think Paxco turns such a blind eye toward the black market in the first place? True, enforcing the law in its entirety might be impractical, but there's also considerable leverage to be gained by making sure all of Paxco's most powerful Executives engage in activities for which we may someday choose to prosecute them."

Nadia could breathe now, mostly, but she couldn't form any words, could only stare at Mosely in horror.

"Your niece and nephew will be in the custody of child protective services while your sister and brother-in-law stand trial. Once their mommy and daddy are hauled off to prison, I'm sure the little darlings will be put in their grandparents' care, but who knows what would happen to them while they're in state custody? And who knows how long bureaucratic mix-ups and red tape can keep them there?"

Nadia shook her head again, thinking she had to be suffering from some kind of waking nightmare. The manic gleam faded from Mosely's eyes, and his expression gentled. It was an expression unlike any other she'd seen on his face—and she didn't believe it for a second.

"You must think I'm a terribly cruel, heartless person," he said, and he sounded mild and regretful. "I assure you, I'm not. I don't go out of my way to hurt innocents, and I certainly don't enjoy making such ugly threats against small children. But I have a job to do. I have to secure the welfare of my state, and the needs of my state will always come first. Someday, when you're the Chairman Spouse, you'll understand, and you'll come to appreciate the work I do."

"If I ever become Chairman Spouse," she said in a voice that sounded ravaged by tears, though her eyes were dry, "I'll see you in prison for the rest of your life."

Mosely blinked. That was twice in one day she'd managed to surprise both of them.

"Perhaps not the wisest thing to say under the circumstances," Mosely said, but he sounded more amused than angry. "You don't want me for an enemy."

Nadia snorted and snatched up the tracker from where it had fallen on the floor. Mosely had been her enemy from the moment he'd stepped into that interview room, and they both knew it. "You need me, remember? You wouldn't be bothering with me if you didn't."

Mosely conceded the point with a shrug. "So you'll plant the tracker as I requested?"

She shoved the little disc into her pocket, hating Mosely more than she'd ever thought it was possible to hate another human being.

"I'll do it," she said bitterly, sparing a little hatred for herself. "As you've made abundantly clear, I have no choice."

AFTER Mosely left, Nadia sat alone in the schoolroom, trying to pull the pieces of herself back together. Her stomach was still throbbing where he had hit her, and his threat to Corinne and Rory was still ringing in her ears. She had no doubt that he was willing to hurt small children if he thought that's what he had to do to get his way. She'd been hoping to complete her assignment for him in the most half-assed way possible, allowing herself to believe that somehow he wouldn't see through her. What a fool she'd been.

She rubbed her fingers over her pocket, feeling the contours of the little device she'd been ordered to plant on Nate, wishing she could think of a way out. But any attempt she made at escaping her "duties" would risk Corinne and Rory, and she just couldn't do that. She didn't think that Mosely was bluffing, nor did she think he was above acting out of spiteful retaliation if she went to Nate and told all. Nate wouldn't be able to control his temper, wouldn't be able to keep her confession a secret, too secure in his own power as the

Chairman Heir to see the danger. He would confront Mosely, and Mosely would make Nadia pay.

Nadia tried to persuade herself to get to her feet and leave the schoolroom, but the silent, empty room was a balm she wasn't willing to give up. If she left the room, she'd have to face other people, have to put on her public face and pretend nothing was wrong. Here, she could let down her guard and allow herself to wallow in her misery, at least until Dante came back to clear the tea service. She wasn't usually one to wallow, but this afternoon seemed like a fine time to make an exception. So, of course, Dante returned no more than a minute or two after Mosely left.

A hint of anger fired her blood, giving her strength. Had Mosely sent his pet spy back to the schoolroom to report on how Nadia was faring in the aftermath of his threats? If so, she refused to give him the satisfaction of seeing her upset.

Dante's footsteps slowed when he caught sight of her, and he came to a stop a respectful distance away. He tried to stuff his hands in his pants pockets, then looked awkward and embarrassed when he remembered his livery pants didn't *have* pockets. If Nadia didn't hate him for being Mosely's spy, she might have thought it was rather cute. Instead, she fixed him with her coldest look.

"I do not wish to be disturbed," she told him. She sounded almost as haughty and superior as Jewel, but she couldn't summon the energy to care. She was more than prepared to be a complete and utter bitch, if that was what it took to get her solitude back.

But Dante wasn't really a servant, and he wasn't terribly good at acting like one, either. He walked over to the refreshments table and, without a word, filled a cup with hot water and dumped in a tea bag, turning his back to her as he dunked it up and down. Nadia supposed if she really wanted to be alone, she would be forced to leave the room, but though she urged herself to get up, she found herself still sitting there, watching Dante's back as he fussed with the tea.

Nadia forced herself to look away as he turned to face her again. Still without speaking, he brought her the cup of tea, setting it on the table beside her.

"I have to clear the tea service," he said softly, "but I thought you might like a cup before I did."

Steam wafted in her direction, bringing with it the enticing scent of tea. Something hot, sweet, and soothing would hit the spot, she realized, but she was still reluctant to reach for it.

"Did you ever consider *asking* me if I wanted a cup of tea first?"

He shrugged his broad shoulders. "I crossed paths with Mr. Mosely on my way here. I figured a visit with him warranted a cup of tea. Unless you want something stronger?"

Nadia glanced up sharply at the tone in Dante's voice, but he'd turned his back to her again and headed to the refreshments table to start gathering the dirty dishes and trash. Maybe she was reading too much into what she'd just heard, but it sounded as if Dante didn't much like his boss. Maybe there was dissension in the ranks. Or maybe Dante was trying to lull her into speaking too freely with him.

Of course, he had his back to her now and was clearing the tea service, not trying to talk to her. Maybe she should give her paranoia a rest for a while.

Another wisp of steam wafted her way. She'd wanted that cup of tea before Mosely's visit, and she wanted it even more now. She reached for the cup and took a grateful sip, savoring the warmth as it slid down her throat. Dante had put just the right amount of honey and lemon in it. Obviously, he'd paid attention to how she fixed her tea when she made it herself.

"Thank you," she said, almost reluctantly. It seemed wrong to thank the enemy, but she had to admit he was being rather nice to her.

He looked over his shoulder at her and quirked a smile, making Nadia wonder if he'd heard the reluctance in her voice. "I live to serve, you know," he said.

Nadia surprised herself by returning his smile. He might have denied being here under false pretenses when she'd commented on it yesterday, but he obviously wasn't making much effort to fool her.

"Yes," she agreed drily, "I can see that you're naturally subservient."

He laughed briefly, then carried the dishes to a cleverly concealed dumbwaiter at the far end of the room. What had led someone like him to work for someone like Dirk Mosely? Unlike Executives, Employees could choose their own career paths, at least to the extent their talents allowed, and she'd never before met anyone associated with Mosely who could even remotely be described as easygoing. And yet that was how she would describe Dante after their limited acquaintance.

That's the persona he's put on for this job, she scolded herself while taking another sip of tea. To think he was showing her his real self while he worked undercover was the worst kind of naïveté.

The thought made the sweet tea taste just a little sour, and she put it aside. Perhaps it was now time for her to stop skulking in the schoolroom and get on with things. The tracker wasn't going to plant itself, and she doubted Mosely would have much patience with any delays.

Dante returned to the refreshments table to continue clearing, but she must have been wearing her emotions on her face, because he stopped in his tracks and gave her a look full of sympathy and concern.

"Is there anything else I can get you?" he asked, and the kindness in his voice was almost more than she could take.

"You don't happen to have a cure for Dirk Mosely sitting around somewhere, do you?" she asked. She was being too open with him, too unguarded, but Mosely had weakened her defenses, and the quip escaped before she thought better of it.

His smile looked almost sad. "If I had that, I'd be making a killing selling it on the black market."

"How can you stand working for him?"

The warmth and openness faded from Dante's face. "I work for your father, not Dirk Mosely. And I'd better get back to it if you don't want anything else." He turned his back to her. As if he hadn't already hammered home the fact that their conversation was over. Apparently hinting that he worked for Mosely was all right, but coming right out and saying so wasn't.

Nadia stood up, wincing as her abused stomach muscles protested the movement. It was lucky Dante had turned his back to her again, because if she'd seen another look of sympathy on his face, she might have screamed. Or cried. He didn't get to be all warm and nice and sympathetic, not when he worked for the enemy.

It took more effort than she'd have liked to admit to keep her pace steady and unhurried as she headed for the door, trying not to long for things she couldn't have. Thanks to the hint of scandal that had attached itself to her, she was cut off from Chloe's warmth and sympathy—though in truth, their friendship had never been half as deep as Nadia's friendship with Nate. Thanks to Mosely's blackmail, she could no longer rely on Nate either, and if he ever learned the truth, she would lose his friendship forever. And thanks to Mosely's scheming, her father had been forced to accept a spy into their household. The fact that she was intrigued by said spy didn't make him any less of a spy.

All her current woes could be squarely laid at Mosely's feet. Somehow, someday, she was going to turn the tables on him. She didn't yet have the first idea how, but if it took her whole life, she was going to find a way to destroy him.

CHAPTER EIGHT

Despite all the effort she'd put into avoiding Nate—and potentially learning too much that she'd have to share with Mosely—Nadia ended up going to see him instead of the other way around.

After her encounter with Mosely, she realized she couldn't stand to go to her Teen Charity League meeting anyway. Though they had no interest in helping those less fortunate than themselves, the Trio always attended the meetings, reveling in the chance to prance and preen and lord their lofty status over lower-ranking Executives. Dealing with Jewel was bad enough, but fending off verbal jabs from the entire Trio—in front of their adoring fans, no less—held no appeal. And Chloe would be there. Nadia wasn't up to pretending she wasn't still angry and hurt by her friend's desertion, no matter how well she understood it.

Besides, if she didn't get the tracker planted on Nate as soon as possible, Mosely might get impatient with her. More impatient than he already was.

Getting in touch with Nate turned out to be harder than she'd expected. He wasn't at home, he wasn't at work, and he'd either turned off or was refusing to answer his personal phone. According to his majordomo, Nate was dodging his father, who wanted him to make some commercial. Eventually, Nate got word that she was trying to reach him and asked her to meet him at his apartment—after the workday was over so his father was less likely to ambush him with a camera crew.

The first thing she noticed when she saw him was that Nate looked exhausted. His eyes were bloodshot, and there was a droop to his shoulders she'd never seen before. He was dressed as if for the office, but he'd dispensed with the coat and tie—if he'd ever worn them—and rolled his sleeves up to just below his elbows. Mosely had suggested she plant the tracker in Nate's wallet, but she wondered whether he took it with him when going to the Basement. If she planted the tracker in his wallet and he didn't take it with him, Mosely was probably going to hold *her* responsible for it.

Her eyes caught the glint of the gold chain Nate wore under his shirt, the one holding the locket she'd supposedly given him. He might not take his wallet to the Basement, but he wore that locket *everywhere,* and it could be easily concealed under his clothes.

Nate smiled at her in greeting, but the smile didn't light up his eyes as it usually would. No doubt some of it was worry about Bishop. However, if Mosely was telling the truth about Nate's venture into the Basement last night, Nate might very well be every bit as sleep-deprived as he looked. Nonetheless, he managed a shadow of his usual jaunty grin as he invited her in.

If she were being a proper Executive, Nadia would have been careful to make sure that she and Nate stayed within sight of the servants, preserving her reputation, but Nate had long ago broken her of that particular cautious habit. She might hesitate to go off alone with him in public, but in the privacy of his home—or hers—she was willing to make exceptions. No servant who couldn't be trusted to keep his or her mouth shut would hold on to a job in the Chairman Heir's household.

Accordingly, Nate led her to the private sitting room right outside his bedroom. It was a cozy, comfortable room, with overstuffed chairs, bookshelves that might be considered full with only half the number of books on them, and a large gas fireplace that Nate flipped on automatically, even though it wasn't cold. Nadia would have grumbled about the waste, except she knew how much Nate liked having a fire going.

"Want a drink?" he asked, ignoring the comfortable chairs and pacing in front of the fire.

Nadia didn't think her stomach would welcome any company, and she almost refused. Then she realized a drink could give her the opportunity she needed to plant Mosely's tracker. She needed to get Nate to take off the locket, and she suspected the only time he did that was when he showered.

"A hot cocoa would be nice," she said, though she knew that wasn't the kind of drink Nate had in mind. Nate *might* decide he needed to shower if she spilled wine or beer on him, but he might just change his clothes. The chocolate would make a more significant mess, which was just what she needed. If Nate hadn't been so busy staring moodily into the fire, he probably would have seen the guilt playing across her face and wondered about it. But he didn't, and she did a decent job of keeping her voice light and guileless.

"Maybe with some Bailey's in it?" Nate said, but didn't wait for her approval before ducking his head out the door and signaling to a servant. "Two cocoas with Bailey's."

Nadia shook her head at him behind his back. It never occurred to him that she might want something other than what he suggested. Sometimes, it amazed her that he could be such a good guy and yet be so oblivious to everyone and everything around him. Just more proof that Nate's Replica was *exactly* like the original Nate—to the point that she had a hard time remembering that he wasn't.

"It's like he never died," she murmured to herself, but Nate heard her and shifted uncomfortably.

"The original Nate, you mean. I never quite know whether to use first person or third when I talk about stuff that happened to him. I mean, it happened to *him,* but I remember it happening to *me.*" His brow furrowed, his expression becoming uncharacteristically serious. "But someone really did die. There's a body and everything. I feel like I should . . . I don't know, be more torn up about it or something."

Nadia nodded. "I should be grieving for him," she said, "but it's hard to feel like he's dead when you're here."

"Guess that's kind of the point of Replicas."

They both fell silent, lost in their own thoughts. Nate stared at the fire, and because she was too restless to sit still, Nadia perused the overloaded bookshelves—although she'd done it before and knew better.

Nate very much enjoyed shocking people, so of course the books he kept so prominently displayed in his sitting room were predictably *not* what a respectable young Executive should be reading. In fact, if Nadia's parents had any idea what sorts of books were sitting here out in the open where she could get her hands on them, they'd never allow her into the room.

Nadia blushed and smiled ruefully as she read the spines of a couple of books that, based on their titles, looked to be gay porn of some kind. To someone who didn't know better, those books probably seemed to be there only for their shock value, or to complete his collection of erotica. In reality, they were probably the only books on display that he'd ever read.

If Nate were paying any real attention to her, he'd be teasing her for looking at them, pulling favorite titles from the shelves and trying to get her to look at pictures. It showed just how troubled he was that he didn't even seem to notice.

With a sigh, Nadia moved away from the bookshelf while her luck held, and moments later the hot cocoa arrived. Nadia thanked Nate's butler on both their behalf, and Nate quickly shut the door behind the man. He must have been feeling especially paranoid, because he flipped on his sound system, scanning the contents until he found a soundtrack that seemed to be a thunderstorm at the beach. The kind of sound that would mask their voices if anyone was listening outside the door but wouldn't force them to shout to hear each other. It was the first sign she'd gotten that Nate truly understood the seriousness of the situation. He gestured her to a pair of wing chairs in the far corner of the room, and they both sat, putting their cocoas on the small table between the chairs.

The chairs were overstuffed and made for comfort, and the high backs and the corner location made Nadia feel almost as though she were sharing a secret cave with Nate. If there was a more private place to talk anywhere in his apartment, she didn't know of it. She took a quick sip of cocoa, both to moisten her throat and to test its temperature. Too hot to "spill" yet. She wanted to get the whole ugly thing over with, but she fought down her impatience. She wondered if she dared question Nate about his efforts to locate Bishop.

As it turned out, she didn't have to.

"I went to the Basement last night," Nate blurted.

Nadia recoiled as if shocked, widening her eyes and letting her jaw drop open. "You did *what?*"

Was she overdoing it? He would expect her to be shocked,

maybe even angry with him for his recklessness, but it wasn't like she wasn't used to him doing shocking things. She should probably recover quickly from her initial reaction, so she snapped her mouth closed and tried to make herself relax.

She felt like an actress, playing a role for which she was not adequately prepared. Sure her guilt was written in big, bold letters all over her face, she dropped her gaze and grabbed for the cocoa, desperate for something to look at other than Nate's face.

But though Nate might be feeling paranoid enough to put on the thunder and waves to cover their conversation, it never occurred to him that the real threat might be in the room with him. He went on blithely without even glancing at her to see her reaction.

"I have to find Kurt, and the only place I can think of to start looking is in the Basement."

"Why do you have to find him?" she asked, before she thought better of it. Mosely would expect her to encourage Nate to keep looking for Bishop, and if she should somehow talk him out of it . . . But what were the chances of that? Nate was not the kind of person who'd allow himself to be deflected once he'd set his mind to something. And yet Nadia couldn't help pressing when Nate gave her an outraged look.

"I know why you'd *want* to find him," she hastened to clarify. "But why do you feel you *have* to? If he's hiding in the Basement, it's because he has . . . connections there. Surely those are the kinds of connections he needs if he's going to keep from getting caught. You aren't going to be able to help him with that. Besides, if he wanted your help, he'd have reached out to you. He hasn't, has he?"

Nate's face reddened, and he looked away. "I'm not looking

for him because I want to help him." He grimaced. "Well, I was at first. But you're right, and I know he doesn't want my help. But I need to find him anyway. I need him to tell me what happened the night I was murdered." His fists and jaw were clenched tight, his body language closed off. Was he angry because of what had happened to him, or because Bishop had left him in the dark? "I need his help to figure out who really killed the original Nate. I can't even come up with a reasonable guess who it could be. I mean, they had to know they couldn't really get rid of me, so what was the point? Whatever made them do it, it happened during the blank spot in my memory, so I have nothing to go on. I need Kurt to tell me what happened after you went back to the ballroom and left us alone."

"But aren't you worried you'll lead Mosely's people right to him if you find him?" Nadia didn't want to know what Mosely would do to her if he could hear her right now. But the words seemed to trickle out of her mouth without conscious thought.

"I'm being careful!" Nate snapped, no doubt taking her words as an implied criticism.

Nadia sucked in a deep breath and told herself to stay calm. This was the way he always reacted to what he perceived as criticism, and she should be used to it. And clearly, he *was* being careful. Mosely knew he'd been to the Basement last night, but he hadn't been followed or observed. That was an impressively sneaky maneuver—one he wouldn't be able to pull off again once Nadia completed her assignment.

"You got lucky," she said, knowing how little Nate would appreciate it. "You're trying to outwit a professional spy with a whole network at his fingertips. Do you really think you're up to the challenge?" Mosely would likely drag her off to

Riker's Island right here and now if he could hear what she was saying. And yet she couldn't seem to make herself shut up.

It's what Nate would expect you to say anyway, she consoled herself. If she meekly accepted his determination to find Bishop no matter what the risks, he would *know* something was wrong, even if he didn't know quite what.

"I have to be," Nate said grimly.

"But—"

"I'll be careful. Besides, Kurt isn't in the Basement. In fact, he's not even in Paxco anymore."

"What?" Nadia swore if one more shock came her way today she was going to pull all her hair out by the roots. "How do you know?"

Nate clasped his hands in his lap and stared at them instead of looking at her. "I want you to promise me not to make a big thing out of this."

"Out of what?"

Nate cleared his throat and faced her, though he only held eye contact for a second before he looked away, and she could see by the set of his shoulders that he was bracing for her reaction.

"Kurt and I used to go to the Basement together sometimes. You get treated better there when you're paying in dollars, so I always kept a pretty good stash in the apartment. Kurt and I were the only ones who knew where the money was . . ."

"And now it's missing," Nadia finished for him. On the one hand, this probably meant that Bishop was out of Mosely's reach and whatever objectionable actions Nadia was forced to take wouldn't condemn him. On the other hand, stealing Nate's money—without, apparently, leaving any word of where he was going and without any explanation or apology—didn't much seem like the act of an innocent man. Maybe she and Nate were both being naive about Bishop. Maybe he *was* guilty. People the world over did terrible things for money.

"I *told* you not to make something out of it," Nate said tightly, reading the thoughts on her face. "He was in trouble, and he needed money. I don't begrudge him."

"Of course not," Nadia murmured, despite a chill of unease. To get to that money, Bishop would have had to flee the scene of the crime in Long Island, return to Nate's Manhattan apartment, and then escape to the Basement without being caught. The side trip to Nate's apartment seemed almost fatally dangerous . . .

Unless he'd already stolen the money and had taken it with him to the mansion. Maybe Nate had caught him with the money, and Bishop had stabbed him to keep him from talking.

"Nadia, he didn't kill me," Nate said. "I *know* he didn't."

Nadia took a deep breath and let it out slowly. The evidence certainly looked damning. But surely if Bishop had wanted to steal Nate's money, he could have done it at any time. Why would he have chosen to do it on that particular night, with all the heightened security of the Hayes mansion standing in his way? Why not just slip out of the apartment quietly, in the middle of an ordinary night, while Nate was asleep?

"I believe you," she said, and it was true. "And I understand why you want to find him. But if he's not even in Paxco anymore, then why did you go to the Basement?"

"Kurt and I have some . . . mutual acquaintances there. I thought some of them might have an idea where he'd gone, or at least be able to get a message to him for me."

"Any luck?" she asked, though she could tell from the slump of his shoulders that the answer was no.

"Not yet."

"So you plan to go back." The little tracking device tucked in her pocket felt like it was burning her through the cloth, but of course that was just a symptom of guilt. Nothing she'd learned had changed what she had to do, nor had it made her task any less distasteful. Betrayal was betrayal, whether the plan had a high likelihood of success or not. And whether they could lead Mosely to Bishop or not, the "mutual acquaintances" Nate talked to were going to have huge bull's-eyes painted on their backs, thanks to Nadia.

"I have to," Nate confirmed. Then he ran a hand through his hair and looked uncomfortable. "But I have a little, er, problem."

If whatever he was thinking made *Nate* uncomfortable, Nadia was quite sure she didn't want to hear it, so when he fell silent, she didn't prompt him to continue. Not that she thought that would save her from whatever Nate was about to get her into.

Nate squirmed in his chair. "Like I said, dollars are the currency of choice in the Basement, and Kurt took all of mine . . ." He gave her an imploring look.

Nadia did not like where this was going. "Let me get this straight: you're asking me for money."

"Dollars," he clarified, as if that somehow made it better.

Nadia's heart thumped indignantly in her chest. A girl of her age had absolutely no use for dollars. If she needed anything from the black market, she'd get it through her parents or Gerri or some other intermediary. Which Nate knew perfectly well.

"And where are you expecting me to get those dollars from?" she asked in her most glacial voice.

Nate stopped giving her puppy-dog eyes, his stare turning challenging instead. "Don't play coy. You know what I'm asking."

"You want me to *steal* from my parents."

"Borrow," Nate corrected. "You know I can pay you back. It's just, I need the dollars *now*, and it'll take me a while to restore my supply."

"I'm sure my parents would understand completely," she said, her voice dripping sarcasm. If Nate knew half of what she'd been through already because of him, would he still ask her to do this? He would never forgive her for her betrayal of him, but it gave him barely a moment's pause to ask her to steal from her own parents. She'd never thought of him as a hypocrite before, but this was making her rethink her opinion of him.

"I'm sorry to have to ask," he said, though he didn't sound particularly sorry. His eyes flashed with something that looked much more like anger than regret. "I'm trying to find out who *murdered* me. Don't you think that's a little more important than what trouble you might get in if your parents find out you've dipped into their money?"

For the first time since she'd gotten old enough to know better, Nadia let go of the reins controlling her temper. She shot to her feet, grabbing her almost-forgotten cup of cocoa from the side table. Then she flung the contents right in Nate's face. The chocolate geysered out of the cup, soaking not only his face, but his hair and chest as well, droplets spotting the rug beneath his feet and the chair he was sitting in. Nadia even felt a few drops hitting her own skin.

Stunned at what she had done—even though it had been at least partially premeditated—she stood there with the cup still raised, staring at the mess she'd made. Nate blinked chocolate out of his eyes, then winced. She supposed now he was wishing he hadn't decided to spike her drink. She didn't imagine chocolate and Bailey's felt too good on the eyes.

She lowered her hand back to her side, then put her empty cup down. She bit her tongue to keep from apologizing as Nate rose slowly and silently to his feet, chocolate dripping from the end of his nose.

"I'll get you the dollars," she said, not looking at him. "You knew I'd do it before you even asked. Would it have killed you to acknowledge that asking me to steal from my parents is a big deal? Couldn't you have just asked nicely instead of trying to guilt me into it?"

She expected Nate to snap at her, or act offended. After all, he'd never been good at taking criticism, no matter how well deserved. But for once, he surprised her.

"You're right," he said. "I'm sorry. But Nadia, I *love* Kurt, and he's in danger because of me. I took him out of the life he's always known, and I promised I'd protect him. It's eating me up inside that he's going through this hell because of me, and I'm just—" Nate's voice choked off, and he closed his eyes. He took a deep breath, and when he opened his eyes, he seemed calmer. "I'll try to stop being such a jackass," he said. "But I miss him. And I'm scared for him. And I'm . . . *angry*. That's no excuse for taking it out on you, I know. You're the only true friend I have right now. I'd give you a hug, only I don't want to get cocoa all over you."

Nadia's throat tightened, and she wanted to scream out her frustration. Who was she to take Nate to task for his behavior, when she was here acting as Mosely's spy, when she'd just thrown her cocoa at him not just because she was angry, but because it was her best chance to get Mosely's tracker planted on him? Maybe in the end, the two of them deserved one another.

"I'm going to go shower and change," Nate said. "Maybe it'll give us both a little time to cool off, and then we can talk again."

Nadia nodded her acceptance, too burdened by guilt to speak.

nadia's nerves buzzed with tension as the bedroom door closed behind Nate's back. He was comfortable enough in her presence that he didn't close the door all the way. She could hear him moving around in his bedroom, hear sounds she interpreted as him slipping off his clothes and leaving them in a heap on the floor. Then the clink of metal touching down on wood, which she hoped was him taking off the locket.

Holding her breath, she prayed he'd close the bathroom door more tightly than he'd closed the bedroom one, or there was no way she could get the locket without being caught.

The sound of a door snicking shut seemed to indicate her prayers had been answered. No doubt Nate was going to try to make the shower quick, knowing she was waiting for him, which meant she didn't have much time to work up her nerve. If she was going to do this, she had to get moving *now*.

As she'd guessed, Nate's clothes lay in a heap on the floor, and the locket rested on top of a heavy walnut dresser. Keeping a wary eye on the bathroom door, she edged toward the dresser and picked the locket up in hands that shook just a bit. Her mouth was dry, and every beat of her heart pumped a new wash of guilt into her blood. Her eyes prickled, and she blinked rapidly to keep herself from crying. Guilt and tears were not luxuries she could afford.

The locket was still warm from contact with Nate's skin. Nadia pressed on the clasp, and the locket popped open to her picture, which she took a moment to regard with a critical eye.

She'd known that Bishop had put a picture of her in the locket, of course. Hard to pretend it was a gift from her if her picture wasn't in it. But she'd never actually looked at it before, and she felt an uncomfortable stirring in her gut now that she did.

There were thousands of pictures of her available on the net. Even if she hadn't been semiengaged to the Chairman Heir, her status as daughter of a president made her a favorite with the press. Most were posed shots, where she wore her practiced Executive smile. Some were the embarrassing, unflattering shots the press loved with mean-spirited glee. Things like the picture of her at the age of three, all dressed up in pink velvet and ruffles, with her finger up her nose. The press had just *loved* that one—as if it somehow should have been embarrassing for an Executive three-year-old to act like a three-year-old.

Of all the thousands of shots Bishop had to choose from, he had chosen the very shot she would have if she'd actually had to choose herself.

It was a true candid shot, one she'd had no idea was being taken at the time. Although he wasn't in the picture, Nadia remembered that she'd been talking to Nate. It had been the occasion of his eighteenth birthday, a gala ball that made the wedding reception that led to his death seem like a small family gathering by comparison. Nate and Nadia had been cornered by the Terrible Trio, who had, as usual, flirted and simpered and fed Nadia a steady stream of sly, backhanded compliments.

Nate had the glibbest tongue of anyone Nadia had ever met, and for every backhanded compliment the Trio had handed her, he'd handed them one right back. Only his were so smooth and elegant none of the Trio had ever guessed they were insults. Only Nadia had recognized what he was doing, and her eyes glowed with that knowledge when the photographer snapped the shot.

Instead of her usual practiced smile, she wore an expression she would almost call impish. There was life and vivacity in her expression, a sense of contained energy that in some ways resembled Nate's. She looked beautiful, and intelligent, and somehow very *real*.

Was it just dumb luck that had caused Bishop to pick that particular photo, or did he know her better than she'd ever realized?

You'll never know, because you're going to help Mosely capture him, and he's going to die.

The thought brought guilt flooding back into her system, and Nadia carefully picked at the edges of the photo to dislodge it so she could slip the tracker behind it. The photo came loose, and she lifted it out, expecting to see nothing but the metal back of the locket. What she *did* see made her gasp and drop the little photo of herself.

If she'd been a little less naive, Nadia might have guessed that Bishop wouldn't give Nate a locket with only her picture in it. It was a love gift, after all, even if the boys needed her picture in it for camouflage. Maybe she *should* have been expecting to find a picture of Bishop behind her own. But even if she had, what she saw would have shocked her.

It was a picture of Bishop, all right. Only it wasn't a head shot like Nadia's—it was a full-body portrait. And he was naked.

A proper Executive girl would have averted her eyes the moment she realized what she was looking at, but though Nadia told herself to cover up the photo at once, she found herself unable to move, even to tear her eyes away.

The photo was tiny—it had to be to fit in the locket—and yet there was more than enough detail to flush Nadia's cheeks with scalding heat. She'd known about the tattoos on his arms and torso, as well as his facial piercings. It was hard not to know about them when he made a habit of wearing mesh shirts when he wasn't in his livery. But she hadn't known that the tattoos had continued down below his waist. Nor had she ever had reason to know he'd been pierced in places she hadn't even realized it was possible to *be* pierced.

She told herself to quit gawking, but she couldn't seem to follow her own advice. She knew what the male anatomy looked like, of course. Executive girls were supposed to be demure and innocent, but as long as the net existed, they would never be as pure as the nineteenth-century misses they were supposed to emulate. Nadia and her friends had spent many a stolen moment looking at photos and videos their parents would heartily disapprove of. But that wasn't the same as seeing a photo of someone you *knew*.

The sound of the shower turning off finally shocked Nadia out of her paralysis. She was running out of time. She hastily covered the image of Bishop with her thumb as she used her index finger to pry the edge of the photo up. Urgency made her fingers clumsy, and she almost dropped the tracker as she tried to slip it in behind Bishop's photo. If Nate caught her at this, she would be completely busted, no way out. She couldn't afford the nerves any more than she could afford the guilt.

She managed to wiggle the tracker into place, then gingerly

snugged the edges of Bishop's photo back in, painfully aware that her fingers were brushing over the image of his naked body. She bent to retrieve her own picture, glad to cover the photo that was turning her into such a klutz. The locket was only designed to hold one photo at a time, and it was a tight fit to get both photos and the tracker back in. If Nate opened the locket and looked at Bishop's picture, he might notice how tightly the locket's contents now fit.

Finally, she got everything back in and snapped the locket shut. She put it back on the dresser just in time, slipping out of the bedroom just as the bathroom door started to open.

about the *last* thing Nadia wanted to do on this already incredibly long day was put on her public face and play the role of the dutiful Executive daughter at one of her mother's dinner parties. But unless she could manufacture another bout of flu, there was no getting out of it. Entertaining was one of the chief responsibilities of Executive spouses, and Nadia's mother took her responsibilities very seriously.

Even when hosting the smallest, most informal of Executive events, Esmeralda was stressed for days in advance as she tried to make sure every detail of the evening was carefully planned out, with backup plans and backups for the backups. Today's dinner was worse than most, however, thanks to Nadia's visit to the security station, which the press was still gleefully harping on. A handful of guests—including the Rathburns, naturally—who had previously accepted the invitation called to make their excuses, leaving Esmeralda in a state of high anxiety as she hurriedly rethought her carefully conceived seating arrangements.

Nadia tried to be helpful and tried to put real thought into questions such as whether Edward Brandywine could be seated within hearing distance of Marvin Hamilton without danger of a loudmouthed political debate that would make nearby guests uncomfortable or whether it would cause murmurs if Rebecca Kay were seated near Mark Rickman, who was rumored to be her lover. Decisions such as these would be a big part of her life once she was married, and because of her exalted spouse, they could have serious social and political ramifications. But how could she treat seating arrangements as important with all that was going on in her life now?

Being continually scolded for her distraction didn't help Nadia's temper any, and when she tried to explain herself, hoping for at least a modicum of sympathy from her mother, she was sorely disappointed. She didn't even get in a full sentence before her mother cut her off.

"You have to learn to compartmentalize, Nadia," Esmeralda told her with a frown of disapproval. "Everyone has turmoil in their lives, but you mustn't let it interfere with your obligations." Nadia opened her mouth to protest that her particular turmoil was worse than most, but her mother didn't let her get a word in edgewise. "Before Gerri was born, I hosted a dinner party less than twenty-four hours after I had a miscarriage. I smiled and chatted and supervised as if I hadn't a care in the world, then went to bed and cried for three hours straight when it was over."

Nadia had no idea her mother had ever had a miscarriage, much less that she'd had to carry on in the face of it as if nothing was wrong. Her mother just didn't share personal information like that, not even with her own daughter.

"How did you do it?" Nadia asked in a small voice.

But her mother shook her head. "I just *did* it. There's no great magic trick involved. You learn by doing. I know it's not easy, but I have confidence in you. You'll find a way." She rearranged the seating chart yet again. "Now, tell me what you think of this," she said, handing the chart to Nadia.

Their moment of mother-daughter bonding was apparently over. Which was just as well, because Nadia had something more important to talk about anyway. She'd made a big deal with Nate about having to steal money from her parents, because that was what she'd have had to do if she weren't reluctantly in league with Mosely. But since she was cooperating, and her family approved of her doing so, there was a much easier way.

Nadia put the seating chart down without comment. "I need dollars," she blurted, unable to think of a graceful way to ease into the subject.

"Excuse me?"

Nadia had originally imagined unburdening herself to her mother, telling her all the details of her arrangement with Dirk Mosely—and telling her the exact threats that Mosely had made. But her mother had once again made it clear how little patience she had with human frailty, and Nadia just wanted to get this whole ordeal over with as fast as possible.

"To keep up the charade that I'm helping Nate, even though I'm really stabbing him in the back. I need to give him some dollars."

"I . . . see." Esmeralda picked up the seating chart, as if she couldn't stand for her hands to be idle for a moment.

Nadia found herself practically holding her breath, hoping her mother would ask her questions. Hoping she would show some interest, or even concern. She *had* to know Nadia was going through hell right now and could use her mother's comfort. But Esmeralda Lake had never been much for nurturing.

"You'll want to talk to Gerri tonight," she said, leaving all the questions unasked. "She uses the black market more heavily than your father and I do, so she'll likely have more dollars available." There was a definite hint of disapproval in her mother's voice, and Nadia felt a moment of smug satisfaction that for once it was directed at her perfect sister instead of her.

The satisfaction faded almost as soon as it had appeared. If Nadia failed to appease Mosely, it was Gerri and her children who would suffer the most for it, and she was ashamed of herself and her petty jealousy.

"All right," she agreed. "I'll ask Gerri."

There was another awkward moment of silence, as Esmeralda seemed to be at a loss for words. Then she turned her attention to the seating chart again.

Gerri lived in another one of the three buildings of the Lake Towers, so it was relatively simple for her and Nadia to slip out of the party during the cocktails-and-mingling portion of the evening before dinner was served. If their mother hadn't approved the plan in advance, she would have been furious with her daughters for shirking their duties as hostesses—though technically Gerri was a guest. As it was, she gave them both a pointed look when she saw them heading for the door, a look that told them in no uncertain terms that they'd better hurry back. Gerri acknowledged her with a nod.

Gerri's apartment was silent and dark, though somewhere in the children's wing Rory and Corinne were probably still awake in the care of their nanny. Gerri led Nadia to her home office, where she opened a wall safe and withdrew a couple banded stacks of dollars. There were plenty more inside the safe.

"Will this be enough?" Gerri asked as she stuffed the dollars into a manila envelope.

"I honestly don't know," Nadia admitted. Unlike their mother, Gerri had actually wanted to know what the dollars were for, and Nadia had told her the whole story—except for the threat Mosely had made against her children. Gerri had the right to know, but Nadia didn't have the heart to tell her. There wasn't anything Gerri could do about it, and Nadia wasn't going to take chances with the kids' lives, so there was no purpose to making her worry. Nadia felt guilty for keeping the secret anyway.

Gerri tapped the edge of her desk with her nails, making an annoying little clicking sound as she studied the contents of the safe and frowned.

"It's hard to know," she murmured. "If he were using the dollars for the black market, I'd have some inkling, but for this specific purpose . . ." She shook her head and handed the envelope to Nadia. "It would have been helpful if you could have asked him how much money he needed."

Nadia had been too angry with him at the time to even think about it. Besides, it wouldn't break her heart if she gave the dollars to Nate and it ended up not being enough for his needs. As long as she could tell Mosely it was an honest mistake, anything she did to delay Nate's search could only be helpful.

"It will have to do," Nadia said firmly. "I'll tell him this was all that was in Dad's safe." At least Nate was putting in an appearance at the party later tonight. He'd declined the dinner invitation—as he did whenever he could possibly get away with it—but because he needed to get the money from her, he had promised to make a cameo appearance to lend the party a little extra cachet.

Gerri reached out and clasped Nadia's hand, giving it a squeeze. "You're doing the right thing, you know. No matter how bad it makes you feel."

"Betraying the man I'm going to marry, helping Dirk Mosely arrest an innocent man, and maybe even causing a bunch of innocent people to be tortured . . ." She shook her head. "It might be the only thing I can do under the circumstances, but it's not the *right* thing."

Gerri sighed. "Nadia, protecting yourself and your family is *always* the right thing to do. You have to choose your battles, and choosing to battle Mosely is insane."

"Now, maybe," Nadia said as anger burned in her core. No one should have the kind of power Mosely wielded and abused, not even when they were investigating murder and treason. "But he's not invincible. Someday, he'll make a mistake."

"I wouldn't mind seeing him take a very long tumble, I must admit."

If she knew he'd threatened her kids, would she be quite so willing to put up with him now? Anger spurred Nadia, almost hard enough to make her tell Gerri the whole truth, but she managed to contain it. Telling her wouldn't change anything.

"Maybe you and I can help make that happen," Nadia suggested as she took another look at the envelope full of dollars her sister had given her. Dollars Gerri had because of her extensive dealings with the black market, where she routinely bought tech for personal use that was of higher quality than that manufactured by Paxco.

"What do you have in mind?" Gerri asked with a hint of suspicion in her voice, as if she was prepared not to like whatever Nadia suggested.

"When he hit me, Mosely gloated that he could get away

with it because no one would believe me if I told. But what if I'd been wearing a recorder of some sort at the time?"

Gerri shook her head. "Even if you could prove he hit you, it wouldn't be enough. If we go after him, we have to go after him with something that will kill him. Wounding him would be a very, very bad idea."

Nadia nodded her agreement. "I know. And like you said, we might not be able to do anything about him right now. But what if sometime in the future, he finds himself standing on less firm ground? Even the most powerful people in the world can have their moments. It's not like no one's ever had bad things to say about Mosely before."

"True," Gerri said slowly, no doubt cataloging in her mind the times Mosely's behavior had been called into question.

"What if the next time he's on the defensive about something, we produce recordings of him threatening me? Or worse. Lots of people would give him a pass right now because he's investigating a case of treason and it's all so new and fresh. But what about a couple of years down the line?"

"I don't know, hon," Gerri said doubtfully. "It would take an awful lot to take him down, and I'm not sure it's worth the risk. If he should find out you were recording him . . ."

"How would he ever find out?" Nadia imagined there was a hard glint in her eyes. "He thinks I'm just a frightened little girl who'll do whatever he tells me to."

"Maybe so, but still—"

"I want to make him pay. You don't know what it's been like, being forced to give in to his demands like this." Nadia suppressed a shiver and reminded herself for what felt like the thousandth time that no good could come from telling Gerri about the threat to her children. "Maybe if I'm at least *trying* to get him back, it will make this all more bearable."

Gerri still looked unconvinced, a line of worry creasing her brow. She wasn't given to bouts of uncertainty as Nadia was, and Nadia felt briefly bad for putting her in what must have been an awkward position. That didn't stop her from trying to bolster her own argument.

"Do you think . . . ?" She paused to carefully consider her words before speaking. "Maybe I'm letting him get to me too much, letting my imagination run away with me. But I feel like there's a chance Mosely could make me mysteriously disappear before this is all over. He knows I'll never forgive him for the things he's done, and he also knows I'm destined to be the Chairman Spouse someday. He might find it more convenient if he could stop that from happening."

For one of the few times in her life, Gerri was speechless, staring at her little sister in horror.

"But if I'm recording him, maybe even transmitting the recordings to a remote location, I might have a little leverage to stop that from happening." Nadia shivered again. "Or at least make him pay for it after the fact. You would know where the recordings are being stored, and if anything ever happened to me . . ."

Gerri pulled her into a rib-crushing hug. "Nothing's going to happen to you," she said fiercely.

"But—"

"I'll go shopping first thing in the morning. Paxco doesn't make anything that would fit the bill, but I'm sure I can find a microtransmitter on the black market that would do the job." Gerri released her from the hug, but kept her hands on Nadia's shoulders, fixing her with an intent stare. "Promise me, *promise* me, that if we do this, you'll pretend the transmitter isn't there. Do *not* go fishing. If Mosely says something incriminating, fine. But don't try to lead him into it. Don't take the chance that he might figure out you're wearing it."

Perhaps Nadia was giving her sister an inflated opinion of her courage. Much though she wanted to get revenge on Mosely, the idea that she was going to try to record him scared the hell out of her. No way was she going to take any more chances than necessary.

"I promise," she said simply, and after another soul-searching look, Gerri nodded.

"Okay then. Let's get back to the party before Mom sends a search party after us."

Forcing a smile, wondering how she was going to endure an evening of gossip and small talk, Nadia followed her sister out of the apartment.

CHAPTER NINE

nate would have loved to get his trip to the Basement over with early so he could get some sleep, but he had to wait until his household quieted down for the night to reduce the chances of being seen. He kept himself awake by watching a horror movie on the net, but the ads for an upcoming news special were way scarier than the movie. The ad came up on every commercial break, showing Nate cussing out the reporter and shoving the microphone out of his face; worse, some talking head with a PhD was speculating about whether such an outburst from a former media darling meant the Replication process was flawed and had created violent tendencies. He finally quit watching the movie just so he could stop seeing that ad.

At 1:00 A.M., Nate started the laborious process of transforming himself once more into the Ghost. He was already running on fumes, and this was going to be one hell of a long night.

Yawning, Nate checked the various hiding places on his costume to make sure all the dollars Nadia had given him were secure and hidden. His conscience nagged at him for the way he'd treated her this afternoon. Now that Kurt was gone, she was the only true friend he had, and the absolute worst thing he could do was act like an asshole and alienate her. She was as alone as he was, her parents' love tempered by expectations, her peers' "friendship" tainted by jealousy and ambition. He and Nadia needed each other, now more than ever, and Nate was determined never to take her for granted again. That she'd stolen money from her parents for him after the way he'd acted showed just how good a friend she was, doing her all to help him find someone everyone but the two of them thought was guilty of murder.

Nate used the same escape route he'd used the night before, starting with the rather terrifying drop through the laundry chute. He had a jolt when he landed in the laundry room and found the lights on, but as far as he could tell, there was no one around. He let out a breath of relief, then made his way cautiously to the service stairs, feeling even more on edge than he had the night before.

He didn't allow himself to relax until he was driving the purloined motorcycle out of the parking lot, opening up the throttle as much as he dared on the quiet streets. He wanted to put the little Ducati through its paces, maybe give himself a good adrenaline spike to chase away the last of the cobwebs in his head. Maybe he just wanted to remind himself that he was alive, when by all rights, he shouldn't be. But calling attention to himself wasn't part of the game plan.

By the time Nate arrived at Angel's doorstep, it was past two in the morning. Prime time, in Debasement. The club was crowded, wall-to-wall people, and the predators were out full force. One pretty young hooker even tried to pick *his* pocket, which meant word had already spread that he'd paid the cover charge in dollars. Usually the predators ignored other Basement-dwellers and fixated on the more wealthy and less cautious Executive and Employee patrons. Nate caught the hooker's wrist, trapping her with two fingers halfway into one of his jacket pockets. She was startlingly young, with tiny breasts barely hidden by her red halter top. Nate felt a twisting sensation in his gut. He'd seen some awfully young girls plying the sex trade at Angel's club, but this one seemed little more than a child. Which was probably why she'd resorted to picking Nate's pocket—she wasn't experienced enough to stick to the lower-risk, higher-reward targets.

Nate clicked his tongue at her, still holding her wrist as she looked up at him with wide, innocent eyes. But young though she might be, it had been a long time since this girl had been innocent by any definition of the word, and Nate could see the calculation behind the expression.

"How old are you?" he found himself asking, shouting the question over the music. She looked barely past puberty, but this *was* Debasement, and looks could be deceiving here. He could hope she was really an adult with exceptionally good makeup and some quality amateur plastic surgery.

"What's it to you?" she asked, dropping the innocent look for one of sulky belligerence. She gave a little tug to see if she could free her wrist, but he kept hold. Her voice was clear and high, a little girl's voice rather than a woman's. "You plannin' to give me a spanking?" The girl leered at him, moving closer, pressing her body up against his. "I'll give you a freebie to make up for the, um, misunderstanding."

Nate suppressed a shudder. He was quite sure that even if he were really into girls, he wouldn't be tempted by this little Lolita wannabe. But maybe he could make her life easier for her, if just for one night. Making sure her free hand wasn't doing anything it shouldn't while she pressed up against him, he reached under his leather jacket and opened one of the zipper compartments, pulling out a hundred dollar bill and folding it into his palm.

"I'll let you off with a warning," he told her, trying to smile at her while thinking how unfair it was that being born reasonably pretty in Debasement had doomed her to this fate. If she'd been born to an Employee family, would she be a perfectly respectable schoolgirl, looking forward to a safe and happy life? And if *he* had been born in Debasement, what would his life look like right now?

Of course, now was a shitty time for philosophical, self-indulgent navel gazing.

"You work for Angel, right?" She *had* to work for Angel; Angel wouldn't let someone this pathetic set foot in her club as a patron.

The girl stuck out her lower lip, but there was a flash of real fear in her eyes. "Please don't say nothin' to Angel. I was just . . . playin'.'"

"I won't tell Angel you tried to pick my pocket," he assured her. He clasped her hand, letting her feel the money against her palm. "I just want to have a word with Angel, and don't want to have to spend all night looking for her. Any chance you can let her know I'm here and looking?"

Cautiously, ready to grab her and take his money back if she tried to bolt, Nate let go. She took a step back from him, keeping a wary eye on him as she glanced at the bill in her hand. Her eyes widened and her jaw dropped when she saw what she held.

"Tell Angel the Ghost wants to talk to her. I'll be at the bar. I'll give you another tip once I've seen her. Deal?"

The girl licked her lips, still wide-eyed. Maybe he'd gone overboard with his payment, but he wanted to think it was enough to give her a night or two off.

When had he decided to become a knight in shining armor?

"Do we have a deal, or don't we?" he asked, more sharply than he intended. He didn't like seeing the place he'd once thought of as an adult playground for what it really was, but it wasn't fair to take it out on the girl.

She lifted her chin, and defiance flashed in her eyes. "Deal," she said, then turned to head off into the crowd. She stuck the hand with the money in it into her tight, skimpy shorts, and he tried not to wonder how she protected her money when those shorts came off.

"Hey!" he called after her. She stopped, looking over her shoulder at him. "What's your name?" he asked.

"Why d'you care?"

Nate wondered if Kurt had been such a hard case at that age, then shook his head, trying not to picture his boyfriend as a child prostitute. They'd never talked about it, but Nate knew Kurt had gotten started young.

"I don't," he said, because it was what she expected. "I'm just curious."

She thought about it a moment, then shrugged her skinny shoulders. "Petal."

She turned from him without awaiting a response and lost herself in the crowd. Nate hoped she was going to take his message to Angel, but she might just as easily have been making a beeline for the exit to spend her unexpected windfall.

Surprised by how strongly he wished he could just leave Angel's and never come back, he reluctantly made his way to the bar to wait.

nate was dangerously close to being a morose drunk.

He'd been sitting at the bar for the better part of an hour, and the longer he sat, the more convinced he felt that Petal had taken his money and run. Not that he could blame her. If he'd been in her shoes, he'd have been outta there in an instant.

How had he never noticed before how depressing Angel's was? Sure, the Executive and Employee tourists were having a blast, getting drunk, doing drugs, enjoying the shows, and getting laid. And sure, some of the dealers and hookers probably got off on the power games they played, enjoyed being viewed as dangerous predators or seeing the sexual hold they had on such powerful people. But most were just doing their jobs, with about the same enthusiasm as a factory worker, dreaming of quitting time and hoping they were pulling in enough cash to make ends meet.

His disenchantment with the club had led him to drink more than was wise. Not that he had any choice but to order drinks while he was sitting at the bar, but that didn't mean he had to actually *drink* them. But he hoped that maybe if he took the edge off, he'd see a little bit more of the Angel's he remembered, the fun, wild, exotic club he'd so enjoyed visiting. Instead, it seemed with every sip of alcohol, he found the place just a little more depressing.

He'd gotten himself into such a nasty, broody mood that he was barely aware of the people around him as he sat hunched over his drink at the bar. He finished off the shot of insanely expensive chocolate vodka he'd ordered, barely tasting it. Nadia was not going to be happy with him for spending the hard-won dollars on liquor he didn't really want, but maybe if he kept ordering the most expensive drinks, he'd eventually attract Angel's attention even if Petal hadn't bothered to take his message to her. And maybe he'd even have a few dollars left over with which to bribe Angel.

"Another!" he cried out loudly to Viper, waving his empty

shot glass in the air and then turning it upside down before plopping it back on the bar.

"Fine vodka is meant to be sipped, you know," said a voice from behind him, and Nate froze with his hand still holding the shot glass.

It showed how dangerously careless he'd become that he'd allowed the very woman he was looking for to come up behind him within touching distance without having noticed. Moving slowly, because there was something sly in Angel's voice that jangled his nerves, Nate turned around.

Debasement was full of exotic, unusual-looking people, but even among them Angel of Mercy stood out. Nate wasn't sure how old she was, but if he had to guess, he'd say somewhere in the vicinity of fifty. Her hair was a natural (he presumed) steel gray, cut in a six-inch-high Mohawk that made it look like she had a rotary saw coming out of her head. There were deep wrinkles around her eyes and mouth, and she had the wattled neck of a much older woman, but her boobs were high and tight (almost certainly fake), and she always displayed her cleavage to best effect. The spiky dog collar she wore around her neck might have looked vaguely submissive on anyone else, but on Angel it was a mockery. If there was anyone in the world less submissive than Angel of Mercy, Nate didn't want to meet them.

Angel's face was devoid of the tattoos and face paint that were so popular among the Basement's younger crowd, but her body was a different story. The henna-colored designs started just under her collarbones and crawled down her body and arms in bands and spirals. Nowhere near as colorful and elaborate as some of the other body art Nate had seen in Debasement, Angel's tattoos were nonetheless some of the most striking: a series of repeating, tribal-looking patterns that somehow managed to fit together perfectly, like a monochrome Persian rug woven by a detail-oriented master.

"Angel," he said with a polite nod, while not taking his eyes off of her. "So nice to see you again."

She smiled at him, then gave the guy sitting next to him at the bar a pointed stare. The guy was a drunk twentysomething Employee, but he wasn't so plastered he couldn't read the very obvious hint in Angel's eyes, and he hastily vacated his barstool. Still smiling, Angel took a seat. Viper put a shot glass filled with viscous, crimson liquid on the bar before her. Nate had no idea what it was, and had no inclination to find out as Angel lifted the glass to her lips and drained it. It left a thick coating on the sides of the glass. Clearly, it was supposed to look like blood, but Nate was ninety-nine percent sure it wasn't. It was the remaining one percent that made him decline when Angel arched a brow at him and said "Want one?"

"I think I've had enough to drink already," he said, and wondered if he was slurring a bit. His head did feel a little fuzzy around the edges, and he hadn't been keeping careful track of how much alcohol he was taking in. Kurt would never have let him be so careless.

"Suit yourself," Angel said with a shrug. "I heard you wanted to talk to me. How can I be of service?"

There was a strange glitter in Angel's eye, and Nate didn't like the hard edge in her voice. She was possibly the most intimidating woman he had ever met, and Nate had always had a healthy respect for her, but on the few occasions when he'd talked to her in the past, she'd always seemed perfectly pleasant. She wasn't a kiss-ass, but she did treat her well-heeled customers like honored guests, going out of her way to make sure they were having a good time, the better to make sure they kept bleeding dollars all over her club.

With the way Nate had been throwing around dollars tonight, he'd have expected her to give him the royal treatment, but she was looking at him with thinly veiled scorn. The sense of hostility Nate was picking up from Angel made him distinctly uncomfortable, but without Kurt here to help him navigate the dangerous waters, he had to just suck it up and do what he came to do.

"I'm looking for the Bishop," he said, using Kurt's street name. No adult in Debasement used real, honest-to-goodness names. They went by their first names as children, until they'd "earned" their street names. Many Basement-dwellers—Kurt included—didn't even *know* their surnames, much less use them. Kurt had gotten a kick out of using his street name for a surname when he had registered with Paxco as an Employee. He had never explained to Nate how he'd earned that particular street name, but Nate knew it had something to do with his former profession, and his imagination provided some ideas. There were definitely some B words he could imagine Kurt being known as the Bishop of.

Angel threw her head back and laughed, the sound loud and raucous enough to draw a few stares. Nate felt the blood heating his cheeks, but he wasn't sure what he was embarrassed about. Or what Angel found so damned funny. He ground his teeth to keep from saying something stupid and waited for her to stop laughing at him.

Angel's laughter eventually died, though razor-sharp amusement still glittered in her steel gray eyes. "You stupid fuck," she said, smiling like she was making friendly conversation. "Half of Paxco wants a bite of that boy. Unless you're the Chairman in disguise, there's at least a dozen people who could make it even more worth my while to help them find him."

Something uneasy slithered down Nate's spine. Nate's first trip to the Basement in his alter ego as the Ghost had happened the week after his eighteenth birthday, and he and Kurt had been to Angel's once or twice a month since then. Never had Angel shown the slightest hint that she might know who he really was. But there was something disturbingly sly about her words and the way she was looking at him.

Angel couldn't possibly know, could she?

But no, that was impossible. If Angel knew who he was, she'd either be trying her hardest to get him out of her club before something bad happened to him and she got blamed for it, or she'd have sent word to the biggest, baddest power players in Debasement and gotten them into a bidding war for the right to kidnap him. He wasn't sure anyone in Debasement had what it took to hold him without being destroyed—he wouldn't put it past his father to firebomb an entire block to punish anyone who dared attempt a kidnapping—but there were certainly some who would love to try.

He was drunk and paranoid, Nate told himself. The only reason he was sensing something "off" about Angel was because Kurt wasn't here with him to act as a buffer.

"You're a mercenary," Nate said, "but there's more to you than that." The Angel of Mercy moniker was mostly sarcastic, but Nate had always gotten the impression there was a hint of truth in it. She might not technically qualify as one of the good guys, but somewhere beneath her fierce exterior, she had a heart. At least, Nate hoped she did.

"The others who might pay more for the information want to arrest him," he continued. "I just want to talk to my friend, make sure he's all right. See if there's anything I can do to help him."

Angel shook her head. "What makes you think he wants your help? If he'd wanted to talk to you, he would have contacted you by now. Take a fucking hint."

Nate couldn't help flinching a little at the words.

"Go home, Ghost," Angel said, her voice lower and now almost kind-sounding. "You're already in over your head. Go any deeper, you'll drown. Take some advice from someone who's been around the block a few thousand times."

"I'm not giving up," he said, his fists clenching at the thought. "He means too much to me." That last part slipped out without conscious thought on his part. Most likely, he was revealing more than he should, letting Angel get a glimpse of his vulnerabilities. But at this point, he wasn't sure he cared.

Beside him, Angel sighed loudly. "Fine, then," she said. "Come with me."

She slipped off the stool and started making her way through the crowd without awaiting a reply. Nate blinked in surprise.

"Where—?" he started to ask, but Angel was already out of earshot.

Surprise had given her a head start, but it wasn't hard to follow that table-saw hair. Nate received a couple of angry grunts and glares as he pushed his way through the crowd in Angel's wake.

Angel's club took up the first three floors of the apartment building. She'd had the apartments ripped out of the first two floors for the main body of her club, but on the third floor, the apartments had been transformed into seedy little rooms where club-goers could engage in more private indulgences. It was in one of these third-floor rooms that Nate had first met Kurt. The memory of that first meeting was seared so firmly in his brain that he knew exactly which room it was, even though all the rooms on the third floor looked identical and there weren't any numbers or other identifying marks on them.

When Angel stopped in front of the room and looked over her shoulder at him, unease flared inside him. Why would she lead him to *this* room, of all places?

"Are you sure you want to do this?" she asked. "Sure you don't want to just trust the Bishop to take care of himself?"

"What's going on?" Nate demanded, trying not to sound as unnerved as he felt. But something was just *wrong* about Angel tonight. He'd never thought of her as a nice person, of course, but never before tonight had he felt this undercurrent of malice.

Angel stepped aside and made a sweeping gesture toward the room. "Open the door and find out."

Nate swallowed hard. Every instinct in his body told him that opening the door would be a bad idea. Whatever Angel was up to, she wasn't planning to help him find Kurt. The smart thing to do would be to turn around and march out of here. Go back home and do exactly what Angel was telling him to do: trust Kurt to take care of himself.

But letting Kurt go like that meant letting him take the fall for Nate's murder. Not to mention letting the real killer get away with it. Whatever was going on, Nate had to see it through.

Meeting Angel's challenging stare, Nate reached out and pushed the door open.

The lights were off inside, and the room was pitch-black. Nate opened the door wider, hoping some of the light from the hallway would spill in and brighten the gloom.

Something slammed into the center of his back, propelling him forward into the darkened room. He let out a startled grunt as he flailed his arms for balance, but he hit the floor on his hands and knees anyway. He tried to scramble to his feet, but a heavy combat boot smashed into his gut so hard he was surprised it didn't come out his back.

The door slammed shut and the lights went on as Nate lay helplessly on the floor, arms wrapped around his middle as he tried fruitlessly to suck in some air. Another kick connected with his back, and he nearly passed out from the pain.

"I have a message for you from the Bishop," Angel said, squatting beside him with a wicked smile and a glitter in her eyes. "This is a direct quote: 'If I wanted your fucking help, I'd have asked for it.'"

Nate was dimly aware of three masked figures in the room. Based on their builds, they were probably some of Angel's bouncers. One of them bared his teeth when Nate met his gaze, then delivered another brutal kick. Nate's stomach revolted, and he puked up all the liquor he'd been drinking.

Still smiling, Angel rose to her feet. She swept her bouncers with a commanding look. "Make it hurt real good. But don't do anything that will show."

Nate could do nothing to defend himself. He'd never been much of a fighter, even as a kid—being the Chairman Heir meant that he never had to worry about bullies—and he was already too hurt to stand up, much less fight back. All he could do was try to protect his head.

They worked him over for what felt like about three hours. The bouncers were methodical about their work, and if they were enjoying themselves, it didn't show. *All in a day's work* was what their body language said. Angel, however, watched every blow with a satisfied smirk on her face.

When she finally called them off, Nate was convinced he was about to die of internal injuries, and there was not a drop of food or drink left in his stomach. He stank of sweat and puke, and though he hadn't taken a single blow to the head, he was dizzy and disoriented.

Angel dismissed the bouncers with a jerk of her head, then came to squat by his head again, her voice low and almost seductive as she purred at him.

"The Bishop never wants to see you again," she told him. "He thought you'd get the hint after he stabbed you, but apparently that was too subtle."

Nate could hardly breathe through the pain in his gut, but he shook his head vigorously, denying the message. He didn't know exactly what had happened here, why Angel had turned on him like this, but he refused to believe Kurt had anything to do with it.

"You think it's a coincidence I chose this room for our heart-to-heart?"

Nate couldn't help making a little sound in the back of his throat, a choked denial. No one but Kurt would know the significance of this room. It had to be just coincidence that Angel had had him ambushed here. *Had* to be.

"The Bishop told me what happened here," Angel said. "Told me it would have special significance for you."

"You're lying," Nate managed to spit out.

"Not about this. But the Bishop figured you'd be too pig-headed to take my word for it, so here's a little more proof that I'm his messenger."

She reached for him, and he tried to roll away. The pain of his injuries rose up in a wave so strong it took his breath away, and he practically blacked out. He felt Angel's hand pawing at his chest, delving under first his jacket, then his shirt. He tried again to resist, but another wave of dizziness made his head spin.

His heart nearly stopped when Angel's hand closed around the locket. He wore it under his shirt, and he'd even gone so far as to tape it to his chest to make sure it never became visible here in the Basement, where it might tempt thieves—or even serve to reveal his true identity. Angel ripped the tape off, then yanked on the chain so hard it broke.

So furious that for a moment he forgot his pain, Nate struck out at her.

"The Bishop doesn't want you to have this anymore," Angel said as she stood up, easily sidestepping his feeble blow. "He was through with the real Nathaniel Hayes, and he sure as shit wants nothing to do with a freak imitation of a human being like you. And if you set foot in Debasement again . . . Well, let's just say you won't like what happens."

Angel tucked the locket into her cleavage as Nate lay on the floor and tried to comprehend what had happened, what he was hearing. Trying to find an explanation for it that didn't mean Kurt was really behind all this. But how else could Angel know who he was, or know about the locket?

"Go home," Angel said with a sneer. "Go stick your silver spoon up your ass and live the good life with the rest of the haves. The have-nots can get by just fine without you."

Straightening her clothes as if she herself had delivered the beating, Angel turned her back on him and left the room.

CHAPTER TEN

when she regarded herself in the bathroom mirror Wednesday morning, Nadia was appalled. The shadows under her eyes were as deep as bruises, and she looked as if she hadn't slept in a week. Makeup could only do so much, but she did her best to camouflage the telltale signs of stress. The last thing she wanted to do was walk around broadcasting her mental state to the world.

Last night, Nate had ventured into the Basement wearing the tracker Nadia had planted on him. She hoped for everyone's sake he'd had no more success finding Bishop last night than he had the night before. She hoped he hadn't even come *close* to making progress. Which was certainly possible. Surely Bishop was more skilled at navigating the murky waters of the Basement than Nate was. Surely he would make himself so hard to find that an amateur like Nate would have no chance.

But even if nothing bad happened to Bishop or any of the Basement unfortunates Nate had talked to, she would still have to find a way to live with what she had done, what she had chosen.

"You had no choice," she told herself, giving her image in the mirror a fierce glare.

But, of course, she *had* had choices. She could have chosen to tell Nate the truth. Or she could have appealed to her parents for help. Maybe she was wrong, and Nate *wouldn't* have lost his temper and insisted on confronting Mosely. Maybe her parents *would* have found another way out, would have been willing to face down Mosely's threats in the name of doing the right thing.

"Stop it!" she said out loud, still glaring at herself.

Second- , third- , and fourth-guessing herself wasn't going to help. She'd made the best decision she could under the circumstances, and there was no use crying about it now.

Nadia couldn't face a formal breakfast with her parents this morning, so she rang for a tray instead. Breakfast in bed was a rare indulgence for her, but if anyone asked, she would claim she was still a little under the weather from her bout with the flu.

To forestall any immediate questions, Nadia made sure to be in the bathroom when the tray arrived, and she called out to the maid to leave the tray on the bed. "Your phone is ringing," the maid informed her, but Nadia didn't care. She didn't venture out of the bathroom until she'd heard the bedroom door close behind the maid.

The scent of eggs and bacon made Nadia's stomach rumble longingly, but her hunger died when she glanced at her phone and realized the call she had missed was from Mosely. Worse, he had left a message.

Nadia wished she could ignore the message and eat her breakfast in peace, but she knew she'd never be able to choke her food down while worrying about what Mosely had to say. She tried to comfort herself with the thought that at least he couldn't hurt her over the phone.

Gritting her teeth in anticipation—these days, even hearing his voice was an ordeal—she played the message. It was brief and to the point. And it nearly stopped her heart.

"Nathaniel wore the tracker into the Basement last night. Approximately two hours after he entered the Basement, the tracker stopped transmitting. Find out what happened."

Nadia hugged herself, trying to remain calm. Her first thought was that Nate had discovered the tracker and disposed of it, but she knew that couldn't be. If he'd found the tracker, he would know, or at least suspect, that she had put it there, and it was *him* she would have heard from, not Mosely. He'd have been so furious he'd probably have called her in the middle of the night to tell her what he thought of her.

But if Nate hadn't found the tracker himself, that meant someone else had. The locket meant more to him than anything in the world—and it also hid his greatest secret. He wouldn't let anyone touch it. Not voluntarily, at least. But someone obviously had; someone in the Basement; someone dangerous; someone who would have had to have hurt or even killed Nate to get to it.

Nadia grabbed for the phone and called Nate's personal number, her hands shaking so hard it took three tries. Nate had been taking his life in his hands by asking questions in the Basement. She didn't even want to *think* about what might have happened to him when some Basement-dweller found a tracker on him.

"Oh please, please, please be all right," she mumbled to herself as she listened to the phone ring. She almost screamed in frustration when her call went to voice mail. She tried again, even knowing it was futile. A whimper rose from her throat when voice mail picked up immediately.

There was a soft knock on her door. "Do you need anything else, miss?" a maid's voice asked.

"No!" Nadia said, fear making her voice sharp. She tried

to soften her tone, but didn't have much success as her heart continued to pound in her chest and her stomach upped its rebellious churning. "I'll let you know when I'm done."

"Very good, miss," the maid said, sounding stiff and insulted. Nadia was usually much more polite to the servants than this, and she reminded herself to apologize later, when she was in her right mind. Assuming she'd ever be in her right mind again. She darted to the bedroom door and locked it while she tried Nate's land line. Unlike his personal cell, that number went through to the security desk at his apartment, and Nadia had to fight her way through a human barricade, becoming more frantic with each transfer, until the phone in his apartment rang. Of course, even that wasn't enough to actually put her through to Nate, and it was his butler who picked up.

"This is Nadia Lake," she said, "and I need to speak to Nate *right now*!" She practically shouted the words, terrified that Nate was once again lying dead, this time somewhere in the Basement. The thought that the Chairman could simply create another Replica if this one was dead was no comfort.

"He hasn't risen yet this morning, Miss Lake," the butler said, sounding taken aback by her near hysteria. "Is this urgent?"

Nadia swallowed hard to stop herself from answering with Nate-like sarcasm. "Yes, it's very, very urgent," she said with exaggerated care. "Please wake him up." Feeling like an immature little girl, she crossed her fingers and prayed he was there to be awakened.

"One moment please," the butler said, and she wanted to punch something as he put her on hold.

She was in danger of hyperventilating, so she forced herself to sit down on the edge of her bed, close her eyes, and take a few deep breaths. It was embarrassingly hard to manage. When the phone line went live again and Nate's crusty-sounding voice said "Nadia?" she burst into tears.

"Nadia!" he said in alarm. "What's wrong?"

What was wrong was she was an idiot, she thought as the tears continued to stream from her eyes and her throat squeezed so tight she couldn't talk. She'd let her fear for Nate run away with her, calling him without once pausing to think about what she would say if she reached him. She had no good way to explain why she'd been so frantic and why she was bawling like a baby now.

"I was—" she hiccuped, then had to pause a moment to let another wave of sniffles pass over her. "Worried about you," she finished lamely, swiping at her swimming eyes and shaking her head at herself. Surely Mosely had had people following Nate last night, thanks to the tracker. If Nate had been killed, Mosely would have known it and wouldn't have ordered her to find out what happened. Her guilty conscience had made her leap to the most guilt-inducing conclusion, and she had acted without thinking.

Even if the worst hadn't happened, she knew her fears for Nate hadn't been completely unfounded. There was no way he would have let someone open his locket without a fight.

"Are you all right?" she asked, glad to hear that her voice at least *sounded* a little calmer.

Nate hesitated before answering, and Nadia couldn't help thinking she was acting strange enough that even someone as generally oblivious as he had to be wondering what was wrong with her.

"Why do you sound so worried?" he asked. "They told me you were nearly hysterical."

Yes, of course they had. And she'd confirmed it by bursting into tears when he answered the phone. Of course, she also noticed that he hadn't answered her question. Was it possible he knew about the tracker after all?

Nadia dismissed that thought with an impatient shake of her head. Nate was not a subtle person. If he was pissed at her about something, he'd come right out and say it. But it wasn't as if she could explain any of that to Nate. Not unless she were willing to come clean and tell him the truth.

"I just . . . had a bad feeling," she said, and almost started crying again because the lie was so lame. And because she was so sick of lying. Her head felt thick and sluggish, and she was utterly exhausted from the aftermath of all that adrenaline flooding her system.

"What aren't you telling me?" There was more than a hint of suspicion in his voice now, and she couldn't imagine how she could come up with a satisfying explanation for her behavior. Her throat was so tight and achy she couldn't force any words out. Her mind flailed for a plausible explanation even as waves of guilt and self-loathing crashed over her.

"I think you have some explaining to do," Nate said into the silence, and there was a distinct chill in his voice.

She let out a shuddering sigh. "Yes, I do," she said, though she still had no idea what to tell him. The best she could do was stall for time and hope she could find a way to explain away her behavior. "It's not something I want to talk about on the phone. Can I come over?"

Nate cleared his throat. "I'm, uh, a little under the weather," he hedged.

She swallowed to keep from asking him what was wrong, knowing he wouldn't answer. "Can I come over anyway? I really, really think we need to talk. In person."

Nate made a sound between a groan and a grunt. "Okay. I'll get myself out of bed as soon as I find a crowbar."

His quip struck a false note, the tightness in his voice belying his attempt at humor. Nadia closed her eyes, dreading what that tightness portended.

"I'll see you soon," she said, then hung up the phone before she started crying again.

After getting off the phone with Nate, Nadia couldn't force herself to eat. The scent of eggs that had been enticing only a few minutes ago now made her stomach turn.

Unfortunately, leaving the tray untouched would inspire questions she didn't want to answer—and would insult the entire kitchen staff—so she had to at least make it *look* like she'd eaten. What was one more lie, after so many?

Nadia lifted the dome off her plate, eying its contents and wondering if she could flush them without clogging the toilet. The eggs and bacon would go down easily enough, but she'd have to tear up the toast. She unrolled her napkin to get a knife to use to scrape the plate.

Something dropped out of the napkin before Nadia had even reached the silverware. It hit the side of the tray and bounced to the floor. Frowning, Nadia put the napkin down and slid off the bed, bending to pick up the little envelope that had fallen.

The envelope was unsealed, and there was a hard lump in its center. Mystified as to what it was and how it had gotten into her napkin, Nadia opened the envelope and shook its contents onto her palm. She unfolded the torn piece of paper that fell out and found a familiar piece of circuitry in its center—the tracker she had planted in Nate's locket, now crushed and broken.

There was a message printed on the paper in big block letters, the handwriting awkward and childlike: MAK HIM STOP LOKING 4 ME OR ILL TEL.

There was no signature, but then there didn't need to be. There was only one person it could be from.

"What the hell . . . ?" Nadia muttered as she stared at the tracker and the note. How had *Bishop,* of all people, gotten hold of the tracker? Surely if he and Nate had been reunited last night, Nate would have mentioned it. And if *Bishop* knew about the tracker, then shouldn't *Nate* know about it, too? But there was no way he'd have been half so civil on the phone if that were the case. Nor would Bishop be threatening her with exposure, come to think of it.

She couldn't lie to Nate anymore, she realized in a moment of startling, breathtaking clarity. There was no story she could concoct to explain her behavior this morning. No story he'd believe, anyway, not after she'd roused his suspicions as thoroughly as she had. If she kept lying to him and he knew it, then that would be the end of their friendship. He wouldn't be able to trust her anymore, and you couldn't have a real friendship without trust.

So her choices were to tell him the truth and lose his trust or to lie to him and lose his trust anyway. And whichever way she lost his trust, she was never going to win it back.

Taking a steadying breath, Nadia came to a decision. If she was going to lose Nate's friendship no matter what, she'd rather do it by telling the truth. No matter how much that truth was going to hurt or what it might cost her.

nate felt like he'd been run over by a truck. Several, actually. And it wasn't that far from the truth.

Dragging himself home from Debasement last night had

been torture of an epic level. Angel's thugs had worked him over so thoroughly that it hurt even to breathe, and Nate had been half convinced he was going to pass out and be trampled as he dragged himself out of the private room and through the jostling crowd outside. He hadn't seen Angel again, but he had noticed several of the bouncers keeping an eye on him, and he had no doubt if he didn't get out as fast as they wanted, they'd be doing the fists-and-feet tango again.

He'd swallowed a handful of aspirin before collapsing into bed once he got home, but they barely even took the edge off the pain. A handful of hours of fitful sleep had served to make every muscle in his body stiffen up, but when he examined himself in the mirror before taking a shower, he saw very little evidence of what he'd been through last night. There was some mottled bruising around his ribs and lower back, but nothing that looked like it should hurt half as much as it did. And as far as he could tell, nothing was broken. At least he wouldn't have to go to the hospital and try to manufacture an explanation for his injuries.

The shower loosened up his stiff muscles, and Nate self-medicated with another handful of aspirin and a double espresso. Then he dressed in pajamas and a robe while he waited for Nadia to arrive.

Usually, he was happy to see her. She might not be the love of his life as he pretended to the outside world, but she *was* his friend, and would have been even if their parents hadn't chosen them for one another. But there had very obviously been something wrong when she called this morning, and a nasty, suspicious side of him felt sure he'd heard guilt in her voice. He was still reeling from the shock and pain of what sure as hell looked like Kurt's betrayal. If Nadia was guilty of something, he'd almost rather not know.

Nate groaned and collapsed into a chair, closing his eyes and laying the back of his head against the cushions. It felt like there were ten-ton weights sitting on each of his shoulders, pressing him down into the chair, making it hard to move. Or breathe. Or think.

Kurt would *not* have done this to him, his mind kept insisting. And yet . . .

No one but Kurt would have known the significance of that room at Angel's club. No one but Kurt would have known about the locket. No one but Kurt would have known his true identity—and revealed it to Angel.

"But *why?*" he asked the empty air, unable to come up with a single explanation.

His brooding was interrupted by Nadia's arrival. Nate asked his butler to show her into his sitting room, then tried to brace himself for whatever was to come. Hard to do, when he was already so miserable.

Nadia looked pale and wan when she stepped into the room. She'd tried to cover the dark circles under her eyes with makeup, but it hadn't worked, and she'd chewed all the lipstick off her lower lip. Nate's sense of foreboding grew stronger as he forced himself to his feet. His entire torso groaned in protest, and he winced.

"What's the matter?" Nadia asked, quickly crossing the distance between them. "Are you hurt?"

She knew. He didn't know how, but there was no other way to explain her panic on the phone this morning or her instant assumption that he was hurt.

"You know what happened last night, don't you?" he asked, taking a step back from her. A little voice in his head told him he was being ridiculous, suspecting Nadia of . . . Well, he wasn't quite sure *what* he suspected her of, but it was something bad. Nadia was his best friend, and one of the nicest people he'd ever met.

Yeah, and Kurt was his boyfriend, but that hadn't stopped him from having Nate savagely beaten. And maybe worse.

Nate expected—or at least hoped for—a hasty denial, but that wasn't what he got. Nadia looked away from him, her eyes squinched in misery, her teeth working away at her lip again. She shook her head, and her voice was small and tentative.

"I don't know what happened," she said. "Only that *something* did, and it was bad." She squared her shoulders and raised her chin, meeting his eyes with what looked like a Herculean effort. "I want you to hear me out," she said. "Listen to the whole thing before you react."

Nate's hands curled into fists at his sides. "What the hell have you done?" he asked from between his clenched teeth. Adrenaline pumped through his veins, speeding his heart, making his breath come short. His body still ached from the beating, and somewhere beneath the fury lurked a mother lode of hurt. The fury was infinitely easier to manage, so he focused on it, fueling it and glaring at Nadia with a kind of ferocity he'd never have guessed himself capable of.

For some reason, he'd expected Nadia to quail in the face of his fury, maybe because he felt so overwhelmed by it himself. Nadia was nice enough that some people mistook her niceness for weakness, but Nate had never been one of those people before. It showed something about his own mental state that he made the error now.

Instead of being intimidated by his fury, she seemed to draw strength from it. She stopped chewing on her lip, and her body went rigid as a hint of fire flickered in her eyes.

"I ask you to hear me out before you react, and you're reacting before I say word one? Don't you think you owe me a little more than that?"

"Depends what you've done," he growled. "And it sounds like you've done something pretty shitty."

A fine tremor made her hands shake, but the look in her eyes told him the tremor was of anger, not of fear. "You selfish, spoiled, entitled bastard!" she snarled at him, and she looked like she wanted to slap him. "After everything I've gone through because of you and your stupid little games, you're going to condemn me without even listening to me? How *dare* you? I'm not one of your servants, living to fulfill your every desire. I have my own life, my own needs, my own issues, but you never have given a damn about that, have you?"

She whirled away from him, heading for the door. Without thinking about it, he reached out and grabbed her arm, hauling her back around to face him. She raised her hand as if to slap him, but even in her fury, she was still too damnably nice to do it, and she soon let that hand drop to her side.

"Let go of me, Nate," she said, and some of the anger had drained from her voice, replaced with resignation and something he might almost have labeled despair. "You never bothered to listen to anyone before, so there's no reason I should expect you to now. Bishop and I were both right to keep you in the dark."

Bishop and I? Did that mean Kurt and Nadia were in this together somehow? Whatever *this* was? But that seemed impossible. They had never done more than tolerate each other, and that tolerance was colored with dislike and sometimes even contempt. No way they were working together in some crazy plot against him.

Then again, it seemed that everything that had happened to him since the night of the reception had been impossible.

"You know where Kurt is," he said, squeezing her arm a little harder, making sure there was no way she could pull free from his grip.

Nadia's shoulders sagged, the starch seeping out of her spine. "You didn't really hear a word I just said. I guess I shouldn't be surprised."

"I heard you," Nate snapped. "You've done something you're ashamed of, and you're telling me it's all my fault. Forgive me for knowing bullshit when I hear it."

"You don't know a goddamn thing, Nate," she said, but she sounded more tired than angry. "As far as you're concerned, the whole world revolves around you and what you want. Hell, if you thought about other people half as much as you think about yourself, you might even have been able to figure out what was going on, or at least have a good guess."

"What are you talking about?"

She met his eyes. "Have you forgotten I was taken to the security station and held for fifteen hours after your murder? Have you forgotten that I was the last known person to have seen you alive, and that Dirk Mosely *personally* interrogated me? Did you ever take even half a minute to think about what I might have been through, what he might have done to me, what he might have threatened?"

Nate opened his mouth and drew in a breath to protest, but no words would form in his brain. He'd known Nadia had gone through hell the day after his death, and he'd felt a kind of formless pity for her. Mosely was a sadistic bastard, and he wouldn't have gone easy on Nadia just because she was a teenage girl. But she was the daughter of a president, for God's sake. She was Nate's fiancée, at least to all intents and purposes. Surely Mosely wouldn't have dared do anything . . . awful.

Nadia shook her head again, and this time when she tried to pull her arm free, his grip loosened. But she didn't head for the door.

"No, you never did think about it," she said, each word biting into his conscience.

Nate's fists clenched at his sides. "If that bastard hurt you—"

Nadia threw her head back and laughed, but there was no humor in the sound, and the look in her eyes was wild. She turned away from him, and he thought she was going to storm out. But she didn't. She turned back to him, folding her arms across her chest and staring up at him with fierce intensity.

"What will you do if he hurt me?" she asked. "Burst into his office and punch him out?"

Nate wasn't sure he could see himself being quite that aggressive, but . . . "I would demand his resignation. Maybe even press criminal charges. If he's hurt you, he'll pay."

Nadia pinched the bridge of her nose as if his responses were giving her a headache. "And this is why I kept my mouth shut as long as I did." She dropped her hand away from her face and looked at him earnestly. "Nate, he's the chief of security, and he's investigating the assassination of the Chairman Heir. He wouldn't be doing . . . what he's doing if your father hadn't given him free rein. If you go in there playing the white knight, all you'll do is piss him off. And it's me and my family who will pay the price."

Nate couldn't believe what he was hearing. It was true that the Chairman was capable of being a monumental hardass. He had hired Mosely, after all, and never showed any signs that he was bothered by Mosely's reputation. But he wouldn't let his favorite hatchet man prey on the daughter of a top Executive. Not when that daughter was also Nate's bride-to-be.

"What you're saying is you think I can't protect you," he said through clenched teeth, a little surprised by how much the realization stung. "I'm good enough to marry, but not good enough to actually *depend* on, to *trust*."

Nadia seemed to sense his hurt, and she reached out and gave his shoulder a quick squeeze, even though she was obviously still angry with him.

"I'm sorry, Nate, but no. I don't think you can protect me. Being Chairman Heir isn't the same thing as being Chairman. Maybe if your father actually respected you, you'd be able to do something, but if you go to him complaining about Mosely, he's just going to think you're being naive, not understanding what needs to be done."

Nate was pretty sure Nadia was underestimating him, but it was hard to feel confident in his convictions after what had happened last night. Hard not to doubt everyone and everything in his life—including himself. Especially when he didn't have the full story on anything. He ran a hand through his hair, wishing his fingers could somehow reach down into his brain and scrape all the pieces into order so that things would make sense again.

"Tell me what's going on," he said, deciding to ignore the whole question of what to do about Mosely for now. "Tell me how you knew something bad happened to me last night."

She'd obviously come to see him with the express purpose of telling him just that, but Nadia had a core of stubbornness to her Nate had never noticed before.

"Tell me what happened to *you* first."

Ordinarily, Nate would have bet on himself any day in a battle of wills with Nadia, but today he hurt too much, both physically and emotionally, to keep fighting. Instead, he collapsed back into his chair, wincing at the myriad pains in his back and abdomen, and told Nadia an abbreviated version of what had happened at Angel's club last night.

nadia listened to Nate's story of last night's trip to the Basement in horrified silence. She was here to tell Nate about her deception, sure he would never forgive her for it. And yet she had almost stormed out of the room without confessing a thing, so angry at Nate's obliviousness to everyone around him that she could hardly stand to face him. But Nate had always been like that, and, somehow, they'd been friends anyway. She'd understood that he had a good heart underneath it all. He might not always be looking out for everyone, but if he actually *saw* an injustice, he wouldn't hesitate to try to set it right. In fact, that was one of the very reasons she'd been so reluctant to confide in him.

She'd never realized how angry some of Nate's more thoughtless moments made her until today, when her emotions seethed out of control and spilled out of her mouth.

But as Nate told her about his trip to a Basement club known as Angel's and his encounter with the club's owner, she was reminded once more of all the reasons Nate meant so much to her, despite all his faults. Yes, he wanted his real killer brought to justice, but that wasn't the reason he'd put himself in the danger he had. He'd done it because he loved Bishop and wanted to clear his name and thereby keep him safe. What other privileged Paxco Executive would have ventured alone into the Basement asking questions just to clear the name of someone he couldn't even be sure was innocent?

When Nate told her about the message Angel had given him from Bishop, his hand strayed to his chest, and he rubbed his sternum absently. The pain in his voice and on his face was enough to make Nadia's eyes mist over again, but she was through with crying.

"I refuse to believe Kurt was really behind it," Nate concluded, but he sounded a lot less sure than the words suggested. Not to mention that he'd just finished listing a string of arguments for why it *had* to be Bishop's doing.

Nadia sat back in her chair and regarded Nate closely as she thought about what he'd just told her. If Bishop had gotten hold of the tracker, then that meant he and Angel really were in contact, no matter how badly Nate didn't want to believe it.

"Would you recognize Bishop's handwriting if you saw it?" she asked, a lump forming in her throat as she tried to put herself in Nate's shoes, tried to imagine the level of betrayal he must be feeling.

Nate's eyes were wide and alarmed when he looked at her. "I was teaching him to read and write. So yeah, I'd recognize it. Why?" The last word came out sounding strangled, and Nadia wished she didn't have to do this.

Nadia reached into her pocket and pulled out the note she'd found in her napkin this morning, handing it across to Nate. His face went a little paler, and she didn't have to wait for his response to know he recognized the handwriting.

"It's him," Nate confirmed, his face now almost bloodless. "What is it he's threatening to tell?"

Nadia clasped her sweaty hands in her lap and stared at them. "I told you Mosely made threats," she said softly as her throat tried to close up in panic. "He threatened to torture me, and he threatened to hurt my sister's kids. And they weren't empty threats, Nate. I *know* they weren't."

"What did you do?" His voice was flat, his emotions hidden behind an uncharacteristic veil.

Nadia didn't have the guts to look up and see his face. If he was going to hide his emotions, just this once, she was happy to let him. She had enough trouble dealing with her own without having to face his. "I put a tracker in your locket. Mosely knew you would be looking for Bishop, and he thought you might have a better idea where to find him than he did. He threatened to arrest Gerri and hurt her kids if I didn't do it."

CHAPTER ELEVEN

nadia found her courage eventually and glanced up at Nate's face.

He wasn't looking at her. In fact, she didn't think he was looking at *anything*, his eyes clouded and distant. She'd never seen his body language look so defeated before, and if she'd thought he'd let her, she'd have risen from her seat to give him a hug.

When she couldn't stand the silence anymore, Nadia cleared her throat. Nate's eyes came back into focus, but he didn't look at her, and she wasn't sure she could blame him. She'd had good reason for doing what she'd done—*and* for not telling him about it—but she'd still betrayed him. How could she expect him to forgive her for something like that? Especially when she'd just brought him the most damning evidence of all that Bishop really was responsible for last night's ambush and beating?

"Please don't confront Mosely," she begged quietly. "Not unless you want to see me dragged off to Riker's Island."

"I won't," Nate said in a flat, dull voice. "Maybe you're right and I would have flown off the handle if you'd told me before you'd stuck a knife in my back. But right now I don't care enough to bother."

Nadia tried not to flinch.

"I'll do my best to keep up appearances for the time being,

but I don't care what my father wants: I'm not going to marry you."

Nadia didn't even *try* to hide her flinch at that news, though it wasn't exactly a surprise. She'd known all along that the moment she opened her mouth, everything they'd built together would crumble. She couldn't say she'd ever truly looked forward to her future as Nate's neglected wife, but she'd been at least marginally content with it, satisfied that she would be married to a man who could be her friend if nothing more. Without Nate, her future would very likely include a husband like Gerri's, one whose only redeeming qualities were breeding and power. One she could never love, or even be friends with. And, while she was sure her parents and Gerri would still love her, she doubted a day would go by when she didn't sense their disappointment in her.

Nadia's throat ached, and she wished she hadn't come over. She might have thought she could mitigate the damage by telling Nate the truth in person, but now that she was here, she realized that was wishful thinking. All it meant was that she had to sit and watch her future die in Nate's eyes as their friendship turned to dust. Maybe she should have called Bishop's bluff and let *him* deliver the bad news to Nate. Although why he would bother—or think Nate would listen to him—after what had happened last night, she didn't know. In fact, the threat didn't actually make a whole lot of sense under the circumstances.

"Wait a minute," she said, thinking out loud. "If Bishop is so through with you that he had Angel and her friends beat you up last night, then why did he send me the note and tracker?"

Nate made a growling sound in the back of his throat. "I just told you I'm not going to marry you. Did you hear me?"

There was plenty of pain and dread still roiling around in Nadia's stomach, but now that her mind had latched onto the thought, she couldn't seem to let it go. "I heard you." She met his eyes briefly before her courage failed and she looked away. "It's not like I didn't expect it. But what Bishop did doesn't make sense. Why would he need me to stop you from looking for him after last night?"

Nate leaned back heavily in his chair, crossing his arms over his chest in what she suspected was a protective gesture. "Maybe he wanted to make doubly sure I knew he was behind what happened."

She shook her head. "If that's what he wanted, he would have sent the note to *you*, not to me."

"Maybe he just thinks I'm a stubborn ass and you have influence on me," Nate snapped, too angry to look at the logic of his own words.

Nadia stared at him, willing him to think it through. There were even more facts that didn't add up, now that she thought about it. "You were sure he'd taken enough dollars to secure transport out of Paxco. But if he's fled Paxco, then how did he get his hands on the tracker and send me a handwritten note in so little time?" Digital information might travel at the speed of light, but not so handwritten notes and crushed circuitry.

For the first time, she saw a hint of uncertainty in Nate's eyes. Anger and hurt still reigned supreme, but he was *thinking* again, rather than just acting on knee-jerk emotions. He frowned.

"It doesn't make sense," he muttered, more to himself than to her. "With the dollars he took, he could be on another continent by now."

"And yet he's close enough to get that note to me in a matter of hours. If he's so through with you, and so desperate to get you to stop looking for him, why is he delivering the message through Angel and trying to blackmail me into helping? Why didn't he just do the deed himself last night and tell you to your face he never wanted to see you again?"

Nate gave her a look that was equal parts cold and stubborn. "Maybe he was worried someone had planted a tracker on me and I'd lead Mosely right to him."

"Or maybe he knew that if he tried to deliver the message personally, he wouldn't be able to hide what he really felt," she countered, warming up to her own argument. Maybe she was the world's worst judge of character, but she couldn't see Bishop betraying Nate the way he supposedly had. No, there was something else behind his actions, and Nadia realized she had a good guess as to what.

"He loves you, Nate," she said. "He just doesn't trust you to be careful enough."

"What?"

"I didn't tell you about Mosely because I thought you would fly off the handle the way you do and that I and my family would suffer for it. And Bishop doesn't want you getting anywhere near him because he's afraid you're going to be careless and lead Mosely to him."

Nate looked at her as if she were crazy. "That's ridiculous!" Color warmed his cheeks, and she wasn't sure if it was from anger or embarrassment. "I'll admit I'm a bit . . . impetuous sometimes. But I've been very careful about everything. Paranoid, even."

"Mosely knew you visited the Basement on Tuesday night," she countered. "That's why he had me plant a tracker on you last night. Which you wore into the Basement while looking for Bishop."

"So it's *my* fault that you planted a tracker on me?"

Nadia held on to her patience, though it took a concerted effort with the way her emotions were rioting. "All I'm saying is that as careful as you were trying to be, you were still taking risks. Risks that could have led Mosely to Bishop. As it is, you can be sure Mosely is going to question Angel, since he must know you talked to her."

Nate shuddered. "Mosely probably had someone spying on me. They wouldn't have seen what actually happened—we were in a closed room—but they'd know I left the place in bad shape."

"Hopefully, they'll just think you got mugged for asking too many questions," Nadia said, though she didn't have high hopes. "If she's brought in for questioning, do you think she'll talk?"

Nate's scornful expression was answer enough, and, in truth, Nadia had known it was a dumb question. She doubted even the noblest of human beings could stand up to the kind of pressure Mosely could apply, and a Basement power player like Angel was not going to be the noblest of human beings. If she knew where Bishop was hiding, she'd tell Mosely and it would all be over.

"Let's hope that when Bishop found the tracker, he realized what it meant for him and took appropriate precautions," Nadia said, though she wasn't honestly sure what precautions Bishop could take if Mosely was close on his tail. Why on earth was he still in Paxco if he had enough money to get out? There had to be a damn good reason.

Nate rubbed at his eyes like he had a headache. "I really want to believe you're right." He gave a grunt of frustration. "But why won't Kurt talk to me, damn it!" The frustration propelled him to his feet, and his sudden wince of pain proved that sudden movement wasn't a good idea.

"How could he have had me attacked and beaten instead of just telling me to back off?" he said more softly, rubbing a hand over his apparently sore ribs.

Nadia had to fight the urge to reach out to him. Nate was in more than just physical pain, and she was responsible for some of it. "He hurt you because he thought making you think he was the bad guy was the only way to keep you away," she said as gently as she could. "We both know you'd have ignored him if he'd just asked you to quit."

Nate hunched in on himself. "They beat the crap out of me," he said in a voice so subdued it hardly sounded like him. "You really think Kurt could have them do that and still . . . care about me?"

"He's from a different world, Nate. A much harder world. He did what he thought he needed to do to protect himself. And I'm sure he feels bad about it."

"Not as bad as *I* feel." But she could tell she'd gotten through to him by the renewed life in his eyes. He wasn't going to wallow in his misery for long. Which might or might not turn out to be a good thing.

"Nothing's changed," she reminded him. "Bishop is obviously very, very serious about not wanting you to look for him."

"And you're still spying for Mosely." The cold was back in his voice. "You're going to repeat this conversation for him as soon as you have a chance, aren't you?"

Nadia hadn't even thought of that, so absorbed in her own guilt she hadn't considered the full implications of what she'd figured out. She'd come to Nate to unburden herself, but the fact remained that Mosely had ordered her to find out what had happened last night, and she just had. He would no doubt be in contact before the day was out, demanding to know what she'd learned.

"I don't know how much he'll know about what happened last night, how much the tracker would have told him. But he *will* question me, and if he's anywhere near as good at knowing when people are lying as he's supposed to be, it could get ugly."

Suddenly, the weight of it all was too much, and Nadia bowed her head as her chest tightened with another stirring of panic. There was no way she could repeat everything she and Nate had discussed this morning to Mosely. Nate had gotten too close to finding Bishop last night, and while the information they'd shared wasn't enough to conveniently lead Nate straight to Bishop's doorstep, it could very well be everything Mosely needed. So she couldn't tell him. And yet she couldn't face the consequences of *not* telling him.

"I won't let him hurt you," Nate said, his voice softer and gentler than it had been from the moment she'd blurted out her confession.

He meant the words to be comforting, but she wanted to scream at him. When was he going to accept that he couldn't make promises like that? He'd probably told Bishop the same thing when he'd made him his valet, and look what had happened!

"Please don't tell him what I just told you," Nate continued. "He's probably already watching Angel, but he has no way to know for sure that Kurt's been in contact unless you tell him. And if you tell him that Kurt stole my dollars, he'll make the same assumption I did, that Kurt's not in Paxco anymore."

Nadia shook her head, not sure how she was going to keep Mosely from prying this information out of her. She swallowed hard. "Do you have any idea what would happen to me, what would happen to my *family* if Mosely catches me lying to him?"

"I won't let him hurt you or your family, Nadia. I mean it."

She glanced up at him in exasperation. "Wake up, Nate! You can't stop him from hurting me. You can't stop him from getting pissed off at me and taking it out on my niece or my nephew. You think he can't get some scumbag to hurt them for him? Without ever dirtying his own hands? All he needs is a little plausible deniability, and he can get away with just about anything. You think throwing a temper tantrum is going to stop him?"

"He's not invincible!" he snapped back. "And I'm not some whiny, powerless kid. Can I officially order him to leave you alone and expect him to listen to me? No. But I can sure as hell make a lot of noise he would find inconvenient, to say the least. He can threaten you all he wants, but if it comes down to actually acting on the threats, that's a whole other story."

He's already hit me once, she thought, but refrained from saying, afraid the words would have the absolute opposite effect from what she wanted.

Nate might be right. Mosely might be making empty threats. Not because he didn't have the power to carry them out, or even because he would fear the consequences of doing so, but because if the situation escalated to that point, she wouldn't be useful to him anymore. Once Mosely followed through on the ugliest of his threats, if he actually had Gerri arrested and sent to Riker's Island or had someone hurt Corinne or Rory, the threat lost its power to control her.

But even if Nate was right, even if Mosely didn't plan to follow through on his threats, how could she possibly risk her family's safety on that assumption?

"Please, Nadia," Nate said again. "You can tell him I told you I got beat up by Angel's bouncers because I was asking stupid questions at her club. I was half expecting to end up in some kind of mess like that anyway. Walking around a Basement club asking questions isn't a very good survival strategy, and it shouldn't surprise anyone that it backfired on me. So tell him they beat me up and robbed me. It's true, after all. The only part you have to leave out is the link between Angel and Kurt. And whatever you do, don't tell him Kurt contacted you."

Nate let out a heavy sigh and sat back in his chair, like he was trying to look relaxed. He didn't have much success. "I understand why you did what you did," he said, but that was a lie and they both knew it. "I'm not sure I can forgive you for it, but I'll try. But only if you don't tell Mosely about Kurt."

She swallowed hard. "You want me to risk everything on the hope that you'll *try* to forgive me?"

The coldness in his eyes chilled her. "How about if I try to forgive you *and* I don't interfere with our engagement plans?"

She let out a humorless laugh. Of all the things she'd expected from Nate, this wasn't one of them. "Taking a page from Mosely's book?"

"You want to protect your family. I want to protect Kurt. Our marriage was always going to be a business arrangement anyway, so let's make it official."

Nadia's throat ached, and there was a lump in it the size of a tennis ball. She'd confessed all under the understanding that it would destroy the engagement, that she would doom herself to a future marriage of convenience with a stranger she could never love. Nate was offering her hope where none had existed. So why did the offer hurt so much?

When the smoke cleared, it would look to all the world as if her life had returned to normal. She would marry the Chairman Heir, her father would be promoted to the board of directors, and all her immediate family members would become eligible to have periodic backups and even Replicas. She would have all the material trappings and powers she would have had if none of this had ever happened. The only thing she *wouldn't* have was Nate's friendship. The pain of that loss threatened to rise up and swallow her whole.

"Do we have a deal?" Nate prompted as she struggled with the pain.

Her chest and throat too tight to speak, Nadia could only nod.

CHAPTER TWELVE

when Nadia got home from Nate's, she found that a courier had delivered a package to her from Gerri. She hurried to her bedroom, where she could open it unobserved. Inside was a pair of dangly earrings of gold filigree with a smattering of faceted pink stones. There was a handwritten note from Gerri informing her that there was a tiny toggle switch on the backing of one earring. When activated, the hidden transmitter would send whatever it picked up to a secret location.

"I've shared that location with someone I trust implicitly," Gerri wrote. "Someone who knows what to do should anything happen to the two of us. It's better you not know who, and that you don't know where the data is being sent." A postscript warned Nadia to destroy the note, but the warning wasn't necessary.

Nadia put on the earrings, but even knowing she had a potential secret weapon didn't give her the courage to contact Mosely yet, so she decided to investigate the mystery of how Bishop's note had gotten onto her breakfast tray instead. Someone in this household must have put it there, and Nadia was determined to find out who.

Of course, Nadia couldn't tell anyone she'd received a note from a known fugitive and suspected traitor and murderer. For all she knew, whoever had planted the note in her napkin had no idea what was in it, and, if so, it was best it stay that way. She decided the best way to play it was to pretend the envelope had contained a nasty note she suspected came from one of her Executive rivals, like Jewel. Certainly Jewel wouldn't be above sending a nastygram just for the fun of it, and getting one of Nadia's own servants to deliver it would add spice.

Since the tray had originated from the kitchen, Nadia started there, questioning the head cook, Mrs. Reeves. Mrs. Reeves was a grandmotherly little woman who'd been working for the Lake family since well before Nadia was born. As Nadia suspected, it was Mrs. Reeves herself who had put together the breakfast tray, but of course she hadn't put the note in the napkin. She was outraged by the very idea that someone did such a thing, her cheeks turning a mottled red with indignation. Grandmotherly she might be, but she had a fiery temper.

"I don't think whoever did it meant any harm," Nadia said soothingly, and it was the truth. "They probably thought it was nothing more than some secret note passing between a couple of teenage girls acting like kids."

Mrs. Reeves put her fists on her hips and scowled. "If anyone in my kitchen had anything to do with it, they're going to rue the day they were born."

So much for Nadia's careful attempt to make sure no one got in trouble. "Please, Mrs. Reeves," she said a little plaintively. "I really want to know who sent me that note, but no one's going to talk to me if they're afraid you're going to take your meat tenderizer to them."

Mrs. Reeves made a sound between a snort and a laugh. "Always favored the cleaver, myself. Gets the point across faster." The hint of humor restored her mood, and the redness in her cheeks started to recede.

Nadia smiled a little. "Less of a mess with a meat tenderizer."

Mrs. Reeves arched her eyebrows. "Clearly you've never seen what I can do with one."

"Will you please ask around for me? Without terrorizing anyone?"

Mrs. Reeves frowned. "I can't condone anyone being a sneak on my watch. I can promise I won't fire anyone without running it by your parents first, but if I find out someone put a nasty letter on your tray, I'm going to let them know exactly what I think of them and don't think you can stop me."

Nadia had to concede. Mrs. Reeves was much more likely to find the answer than Nadia was, and whoever had put the note on her tray really shouldn't have done it. It was an offense that would get someone fired in most households.

"Thanks, Mrs. Reeves. Let me know as soon as you find out something."

"Of course."

Nadia left Mrs. Reeves to her work and retreated to her room to freshen her makeup and firm up her resolve. She would need everything she could muster to face the inevitable specter of Dirk Mosely.

nadia knew better than to hope Mosely would be willing to debrief her over the phone. Instinct told her he'd be in an uncommonly bad mood after having lost the tracker's signal last night, and he would want to take it out on her. Maybe he'd even want her to come to the security station again for another more formal—and more intimidating, more reputation-damaging—interview. She circumvented him by talking to one of his underlings and making an appointment for Mosely to meet her at the apartment. He might ignore the appointment, or he might show up with a handful of officers in tow and "ask" her to come to the station, but she was pretty sure she could at least start their interview on her home turf.

The question then became, how could she lie to him without being found out?

Realizing that she had never been able to act normal around Mosely, Nadia decided her best chance of surviving the interview with him was to offer an alternative explanation for her inevitably unnatural behavior. So while she waited for him to arrive for their one o'clock appointment, she dipped into her parents' liquor cabinet and sampled several of her favorite liqueurs. If she'd wanted to get truly drunk, she'd have gone for the vodka, but all she'd wanted to do was take in enough to make life a little fuzzy around the edges—and to make her breath smell like she'd been drinking.

By the time Mosely was announced, Nadia's cheeks were nicely flushed from drink, and the alcohol had made her feel almost brave. The pretty little earrings with their secret transmitter helped. Just the thought that she might someday be able to make him pay for his abuses was heartening. She even managed to smile in greeting when Mosely was shown into the room, and he looked at her as if she'd gone mad. He was expecting her to cower after their last encounter, and the look on his face when she smiled at him was enough to make her want to laugh. So she did, letting the alcohol loosen her inhibitions and enjoying Mosely's discomfort as a girlish giggle escaped her lips.

Nadia batted her eyelashes at him and made her way to the couch, making sure to look unsteady on her feet before collapsing ungracefully into the middle seat. Despite her smile and the giggle, her heart was fluttering like a trapped bird in her chest.

"Are you drunk?" Mosely asked incredulously.

Nadia giggled again, though this time the sound was a little more forced. She'd never been truly drunk in her life, but she'd seen enough people overindulge to feel like she had a handle on how to act. The more out of her mind she could make herself seem, the less likely Mosely would be able to see through her lies. At least, that was the theory.

"I might have had a little too much wine with lunch," she said, licking her lips absently like she could still taste it. "I just wanted to . . . settle my nerves a bit before we talked."

Mosely stalked over to the nearest chair, sitting on its very edge and glaring at her. "And why did you feel the need to do that?"

She arched an eyebrow. "You need to ask after our last meeting?"

He pushed to his feet, giving her a look of contempt. At least her impersonation of a drunken idiot seemed to be convincing. All she had to do was hope he'd buy the rest of the act.

"I'll come back after you've had a chance to sober up," he said. "Might I suggest a large quantity of black coffee?"

"Don't you want to know what Nate told me about his trip to the Basement last night?" she asked, blinking up at him with wide, innocent eyes.

Mosely gave her one of his creepy stares, one that made her feel as if he could see right through her. If her head weren't so cloudy with alcohol, she might have wilted, or at least looked nervous. Instead, she gave him a coy smile and hoped he wouldn't insist on coming back later. Seeing him once in a day was more than enough already.

"So he actually told you something useful?" Mosely asked, and she couldn't blame him for the skepticism in his voice. Up until now, she hadn't exactly been a very effective spy.

"If he hadn't, I would have at least tried to convey the information in a phone call rather than meeting with you personally." She let a bit of her usually well-controlled resentment creep into her voice. "After the things you've threatened, I'd do anything I can to keep you as far away from me as possible." She feigned a gasp, reaching up and covering her mouth with her hand as if the words had just slipped out. "Sorry," she mumbled. "I didn't mean to say that. Maybe I shouldn't have had that wine."

Nadia feared her act was completely transparent, but Mosely resumed his seat, watching her with an expression that would have frozen her marrow if she didn't have enough alcohol running through her veins to keep her warm. Maybe she'd had a little more liqueur than she realized, because she felt uncommonly brave.

"Tell me what Nathaniel told you about his trip to the Basement last night," Mosely demanded.

Nadia clasped her hands together in her lap and stared at them, tensing up her shoulder and neck muscles so she looked like she was internally resisting what she was about to say. She even started and stopped a couple of times before she began to speak, as if, even with the alcohol, it was taking all her willpower to get up the nerve to tell him what she'd heard.

"Nate went to the Basement last night. Went to a club called Angel's." Nadia frowned, realizing Nate had never told her why he'd gone to that particular club, although it was obvious that last night hadn't been his only trip there. "I'm not sure why he was looking for Bishop there—I didn't think to ask him, and he didn't say. But anyway, he told me he was asking questions, trying to find someone who knew where Bishop was or who would take a message to him."

Mosely was watching her with such intensity that Nadia had to fight the urge to examine her clothing and make sure she didn't have a button gaping open or something. His face was almost perfectly expressionless except for the severity in his eyes, and he sat so still Nadia wondered if he was even breathing. The pressure of his scrutiny tightened her throat, and she squeezed her hands together more tightly in her lap.

"Nate told me he bribed someone to set up a meeting between him and the club's owner, but apparently she didn't like him asking questions in her club. When he wouldn't stop, she lured him into a back room, then had her bouncers beat him up and rob him." She was trying her best to keep her voice level, to keep the pace of her narrative smooth and uninterrupted so there would be no discernible change between her tone when she was telling the truth and her tone when she was lying. She couldn't tell from Mosely's closed-off expression whether she was having any success or not.

"They stole his locket," she said. "That's where I'd put the tracker."

"And why would they do a thing like that?" Mosely asked. His face stayed expressionless, but there was a hint of something, maybe anger, in his voice.

She frowned at him as if completely puzzled by his question. "It was solid gold, and antique at that. Why *wouldn't* they take it?"

Mosely's eyes bored into her. "Very *convenient* for you, wouldn't you say, Miss Lake?"

Nadia had drunk the liqueur in hopes it would give Mosely

an alternative explanation for any inconsistencies in her story or awkwardness in its delivery, but she was now glad for its soothing warmth in her belly, and for its ability to keep her adrenaline from going wild. Even so, fear chilled her from the inside out. If Mosely thought she was lying to him, or thought she had arranged for the tracker to be stolen . . .

She shook her head, both to shake off her fears and in response to Mosely's question. "I don't see how it's convenient," she said. "Nate wore the tracker into the Basement just like you wanted him to. He says he was there for a couple of hours. And since you no doubt had someone following him, you know who he talked to. And you also know he got beaten up. How does his losing the tracker after all that translate into something convenient? Oh, and by the way, he's not planning to go back to the Basement anyway."

"Really," Mosely said flatly, not even bothering to hide his disbelief.

Despite her fear, there was a part of Nadia that wanted to laugh again. She'd been afraid that Mosely would see through her lies and know that she and Nate had learned something—albeit, very little—about Bishop's whereabouts; however, that didn't seem to be the conclusion he was drawing. Instead, he seemed to think she'd arranged for some big cover-up to free Nate from the tracker.

Nadia looked at her hands again, remembering the stiff way Nate had moved this morning. "I didn't see any bruises on him, but he was obviously in a lot of pain when I went to see him. He wants to find Bishop still, but I think last night proved to him that he was in over his head. Besides . . ."

"Yes?"

"Nate still doesn't believe Bishop killed him, but he did

tell me something this morning I thought you might want to know. Something I think makes even Nate have doubts now and then."

"I'm intrigued. Please, continue." More skepticism, but Nadia couldn't allow herself to worry about it.

"Nate keeps a stash of dollars in his apartment. He and Bishop were the only ones who knew where those dollars were. When Nate went to the Basement for the first time, he wanted to take dollars with him, but when he went to get them, they were all gone."

For the first time, Mosely looked like he really *was* intrigued. Was he drawing the same conclusion Nate had when he'd found the dollars missing? She wasn't sure exactly what the misdirection would buy them—after all, neither she nor Nate had any idea why Bishop was still in Paxco—but maybe it would at least throw Mosely off the scent for a while.

"Very interesting indeed," Mosely said.

Now would be a good time to let Mosely draw his own conclusions, but since Nadia was still pretending to be at least a little tipsy, she didn't think sitting quietly and letting Mosely think was the right thing to do.

"Nate keeps making excuses for why Bishop took the money, but he's pretty upset about it. He thinks it means Bishop used the dollars to get out of Paxco. He wasn't going to the Basement because he expected to actually find Bishop there. He was going because he hoped he'd find someone who could help him get in touch with Bishop wherever he's hiding.

"I know you think Nate is reckless and naive, and you won't get any argument from me. If he still thought he had a chance of finding Bishop in the Basement and helping him, I'm sure what happened last night wouldn't stop him from trying again. But under the circumstances . . ." She let her voice trail off.

Mosely regarded her with those disturbingly cold eyes of his, and she felt like he was mentally taking her apart, peeling away layer after layer as he tried to figure out whether she was telling the truth or lying. Her stomach burbled unhappily, the noise loud enough to make her cheeks heat with a blush. She probably should have eaten a little more solid food to balance out the effects of the liqueur, but her meeting with Nate this morning had stolen her appetite. She hoped the booze was having the desired effect, confusing Mosely's interpretations of her word choice or body language—or whatever it was that made him so good at figuring out when people were lying to him.

"Did you learn anything last night before the tracker went dead?" she asked, unable to bear the silence and the scrutiny any longer. "You wanted to know who Nate was talking to, and it gave you a clue, right?"

"Indeed. I have issued an arrest warrant for this Angel of Mercy who so mistreated our Chairman Heir last night. Unfortunately, the men I had following him felt they had to deliver their report to me before detaining her, and by the time I issued the warrant, she had made herself scarce." He leaned forward in his chair, those eyes boring into her again.

"Make no mistake: my men *will* find her. And she *will* talk to me, with the greatest of candor. I want you to think very, very carefully about what you've told me this afternoon, Miss Lake, and be assured that if I talk to her and her story of last night's events doesn't *exactly* match yours, you will pay a heavy price. With that in mind, is there anything you'd like to add? Or amend?"

If Mosely got his hands on Angel, she'd end up telling him

about her connection to Bishop, whatever it was, and Mosely would know Nadia had lied to him during this interview. By keeping this secret, Nadia was risking her entire family's future. Gerri could go to prison over this, and Corinne and Rory . . . Everything she had done so far, she'd done to protect those she cared about most, and now she was risking it all. Her sane and sensible side told her to blurt out the truth now, before it was too late.

"Well, Miss Lake?" Mosely prompted.

Coming clean with Mosely was the sensible thing to do. It would mean giving up forever the idea of marrying Nate. But it wasn't fear of losing her advantageous marriage that kept Nadia silent. It was the boiling cauldron of indignation inside her.

What Mosely was doing was wrong, on so many levels. He was abusing his authority, using blackmail, threats, and even torture to hunt down an innocent man while refusing to even consider the possibility that someone else was behind Nate's murder. He might say he was doing it all for the good of Paxco, that he was just doing his job, but Nadia would never, ever accept that. Mosely enjoyed the power he wielded, the fear he inspired. There was no way she could see the avaricious gleam in his eyes every time he talked to her without knowing deep in her heart that he was a bully who loved his work. And after everything he'd already bullied her into doing, she was through with letting him win. She was just going to have to hope that Angel was as good as Bishop at staying hidden.

"That's all I can think of," she told him, and even the artificial bravery of the alcohol couldn't keep her from sounding as scared as she felt. "I hope you'll keep in mind that everything I'm telling you comes to me secondhand. It's possible Nate is keeping things from me."

"You'd better hope he isn't, then. Because if I find out anything you've told me is untrue, it's going to be *you* I hold responsible, not him." He pulled an envelope out of his pocket and tossed it at Nadia. "There's another tracker in there. If you're telling me the truth, then it's possible you're right and Nathaniel won't venture into the Basement again. But if he does, I want to know about it."

Nadia was forced to unclench her hands to pick up the envelope. Her palms were wet and clammy. "With the locket gone, I don't know where I can put a tracker. I doubt he takes his wallet when he goes to the Basement."

Mosely smirked at her. "I guess you'll just have to be creative."

He rose to his feet, and if Nadia were being her usual polite self, she would have risen, too, to see him to the door. No matter how much she loathed and despised him. But she honestly wasn't sure her knees would hold her, and she didn't want him to see her shaking. So she merely sat on the couch and stared at the envelope containing the new tracker as Mosely saw himself out.

It wasn't until after Mosely was gone that Nadia lost the battle against the alcohol she'd imbibed in hopes of fooling him. The booze, the lack of solid food, and her terror whenever she allowed herself to think about what she was risking was enough to send her racing to the bathroom.

Afterward, she took her second shower of the day, not because she needed it, but because she craved the comfort of the hot water. She shivered even in the heat and raised her face to the spray, wishing the water could wash away the obedient, dutiful child inside her who kept panicking over her decision to lie to Mosely. Her parents—even her father, who was less rigid than her mother—would disown her if they ever found out what she'd done. Even if no harm ever came to her family, she had broken the one cardinal rule she'd always been raised to honor: put your family's needs above all else.

Nadia was surprised to discover that after the gut-twisting panic had run its course, she felt better. The chill faded little by little, and by the time she exited the shower, she felt more like herself again. She had made the decision to lie because her heart told her it was the right thing to do. She'd protected her family as best she could while staying true to the promise she'd made to Nate, as well as the promise she'd made to herself to see Mosely destroyed someday.

Nothing he'd said today was particularly damning, but at least she'd recorded him making vague, ominous threats. Maybe next time she was forced to talk to him, she would try to steer the conversation a bit more in hopes he would say too much—despite her promise to Gerri that she would do no such thing.

Having thoroughly emptied her stomach out, Nadia called to the kitchen requesting some chicken soup and crackers for an afternoon snack. Mrs. Reeves herself delivered the tray, giving Nadia a look of grandmotherly concern.

"Are you feeling sick, miss?" she asked as she set the tray on an end table beside Nadia's reading chair.

Nadia wondered if Mrs. Reeves was asking because of her pale face and shadowed eyes, or whether it was just the chicken soup and crackers. "My stomach is a little upset," she admitted, though she felt fine now, and the smell of the broth made her hungry.

"Well, this will be just the thing for you, now won't it?" Mrs. Reeves said, and she unrolled the napkin to show that it contained nothing but silverware. "I tried to get to the bottom of what happened with your tray this morning. I put it together myself, and the girl who delivered it to you, Missy Hampton, swears up and down that she didn't put anything in your napkin. I'm afraid I was a little sharp with her when I was asking questions."

Nadia imagined that being on the receiving end of a rant from Mrs. Reeves was an unpleasant experience, but after what she herself had been through with Mosely, she could scrape up only minimal sympathy. Especially as Hampton now seemed the most likely person to have delivered the note.

"She won't admit putting the note in your napkin, and she says she had no idea it was there. But when I pressed her, she admitted she had a little mishap on her way to your room. She tripped on the edge of the carpet in the hall and dropped the vase I'd put on your tray."

Nadia tried to picture the tray in her mind, and, sure enough, she couldn't remember there being a vase on it. Mrs. Reeves never sent a tray out of the kitchen without a flower on it.

"She put down the tray to pick up the broken pieces and left it unattended while she threw the glass away. She says when she came back, she saw someone nip out the other end of the hall in a hurry. She only saw the back of his head, but she thought it might be your father's new assistant." Mrs. Reeves's frown said she didn't quite buy the story, that she thought the maid was trying to cover for her own guilt.

"My father's assistant?" Nadia asked. "You mean Dante?"

"That's the one," Mrs. Reeves confirmed. "Hampton says she didn't think anything of it at the time, but he might have had enough time to tamper with your tray."

"Thank you, Mrs. Reeves," Nadia said as she turned over this new information in her head. "You've been very helpful."

Mrs. Reeves looked doubtful. "I don't know about that. I'd want to hear what your father's assistant has to say about it, but it wouldn't be my place to question him."

Nadia smiled and patted Mrs. Reeves's shoulder. "Don't worry about him, Mrs. Reeves. I'll ask him about it myself."

"And you'll let me know if Hampton was telling me the truth? If she lied to me, then she doesn't belong in this household."

Nadia didn't want anyone to get fired over this, especially not some hapless maid who probably thought it was some harmless gossip. But if Missy Hampton concocted a cover story blaming someone else for what she'd done, then she deserved to be fired.

"I'll let you know," Nadia promised.

CHAPTER THIRTEEN

nadia didn't know what to make of Mrs. Reeves's revelation. Maybe Hampton was making the whole encounter with Dante up, just to have someone else to point the finger at. Or maybe everything had happened exactly the way Hampton said, but it hadn't been Dante she'd seen. Even if it *was* Dante, that could easily be coincidence. After all, there were plenty of legitimate reasons he might be in the hallway of their apartment. And of course, he could have been sneaking around on some errand of Mosely's.

Logistically, it was fairly easy to imagine Dante having had access to her tray, without anything in his actions seeming particularly daring or out of place. What *didn't* make sense was for him to be conveying messages to her from *Bishop*, of all people. If he were truly working for Dirk Mosely, then he was the enemy—no matter how friendly he seemed—and there was no way he had any contact with Bishop. Of course, it was possible, maybe even *likely*, that Bishop had used an intermediary of some kind. Maybe Dante had no idea he was delivering a message from the man who'd supposedly murdered the Chairman Heir.

The only way she'd find out would be to question Dante, but the idea frightened her. If she let on that she'd had contact with Bishop, and if Dante relayed that message to Mosely . . .

The old, painfully cautious Nadia would have measured

the risks against the potential rewards and decided not to pursue this. But Nate had put his life on the line trying to find Bishop, and, thanks to the note, Nadia might now be able to help him, or at least point him in the right direction.

At two o'clock, she headed down to the schoolroom for her classes, praying that Jewel and Blair would be absent. Surely they wouldn't show up *three* days in a row. She let out a breath of relief when there was no sign of either one of them. Chloe was still keeping her distance as well, and Nadia suspected her former friend would soon formally withdraw from the class. Nadia wasn't sure if it was because of the lingering taint on her reputation, or because Chloe knew their friendship could never recover from the awkwardness.

Whatever the reason, Nadia was Mr. Guthrie's sole pupil—unless you counted Dante, who was openly listening now that Jewel wasn't around to harass him about it.

No matter how much Nadia usually enjoyed Mr. Guthrie's lectures, this time she could barely focus enough to keep up with him. She found herself constantly watching Dante out of the corner of her eye, searching for any clue to who he really was, what he really wanted. Trying to discern whether he was a danger to her, a possible ally, or just a coincidental bystander. Once or twice, Dante caught her looking, and Nadia hastily glanced away.

When the class was over, Nadia doubted she could have repeated back a single thing from the lesson. She chatted amiably with Mr. Guthrie as the teacher packed up his things. If she was going to confront Dante about the note, now was by far the best time to do it, so, as Mr. Guthrie made his way out, Nadia drifted over to the refreshments table, where Dante was clearing away the untouched plates of sandwiches and pastries. She fixed herself a nerve-soothing cup of tea as he carried the plates away. Then, when he returned, she pointedly made eye contact.

The wariness that crept into Dante's expression the moment she met his eyes put her on alert. True, she didn't make a habit of initiating conversation, but something about the way he was looking at her made her think he knew exactly why she had stayed behind.

Dante averted his eyes and reached for the coffee urn.

"I want to talk to you," Nadia said, though she was sure he'd already guessed that much.

Dante hesitated a moment as if in surprise, then shrugged and picked up the urn. "So talk," he said, turning his back on her and carrying the urn toward the dumbwaiter at the far end of the room.

Nadia shook her head at him as she followed on his heels. "You're the world's worst imitation servant," she told his back, and was rewarded by a faltering of his footsteps.

He recovered quickly, resuming his march toward the dumbwaiter. "I don't know what you're talking about."

He wasn't the world's greatest spy, either, Nadia decided. Shouldn't a professional spy be able to lie more convincingly than that? Then again, he didn't look to be any older than Nate, and he couldn't have had a lot of on-the-job experience. Perhaps Mosely had set him on her as some sort of a training mission. If so, he'd need a lot more training before he'd be ready for the real thing.

"Why don't you make things easier for both of us by dropping the charade?" she suggested. He kept his face averted as he thumped the coffee urn onto the dumbwaiter, but she could see the flush of red creeping up his neck. Whether the flush was embarrassment or anger, she couldn't tell.

"Drop what charade?" he asked, turning his back on her again and striding toward the refreshments table.

He moved fast enough that if she'd tried to turn and follow at the same speed, she'd have spilled her tea. "You know, a *real* servant wouldn't turn his back on his employer and walk away when she's trying to talk to him."

He stopped in his tracks, his broad shoulders tight with tension. He risked a look at her, and there was an expression she couldn't quite interpret in his eyes. Anger, maybe, though she thought it was more complicated than that.

"You're not my employer," he said. "Your father is. And I have a lot of work to do."

Nadia had known who Dante's true employer was since before she'd ever laid eyes on him, and it wasn't her father. Perhaps she would get him in trouble by revealing she knew the truth about him, but there was too much at stake for her to continue being so cautious. She put the cup of tea down, no longer interested in it.

"You work for Dirk Mosely," she countered, unable to keep the distaste out of her voice. He seemed remarkably likable for someone who worked for Mosely, but then maybe he was better at acting than she gave him credit for. "You're here to spy on me, and I'm tired of pretending I don't know it." Not that her pretense had been any more convincing than his had been.

Nadia could practically see the denial on the tip of Dante's tongue as he once again met her eyes, this time with a definite hint of belligerence in his expression. But both the belligerence and the denial faded away as his shoulders slumped. Maybe he realized that nothing he said would convince her, or maybe he was as tired of pretending as she was.

"If you're so sure you're right, then what is it you want to talk about?" He sounded weary, almost defeated, and she wondered what Mosely would do if he found out Dante's cover was blown. A reasonable man would understand that Dante's cover had been ridiculously thin to start with and wouldn't blame him for being discovered, but Mosely was not a reasonable man.

"I'm not going to tell on you, if that's what you're worried about," she reassured him.

He gave her a wry little smile. "You mean you're not going to call your good friend Dirk and demand I be removed from your home immediately?"

Okay, maybe that *hadn't* been what he'd been worried about. She matched his smile and his dry tone. "Much as I love chatting with him, no, I'm not."

Some of the tension eased out of his shoulders, and he came closer to her, no longer looking like he was on the verge of fleeing. The look in his green-flecked eyes softened in sympathy.

"He hurt you yesterday, didn't he?" Dante asked.

Nadia reflexively put her hand to her middle, where Mosely had hit her. The pain had been sudden and shocking, and the ugly threats that had come with it had haunted Nadia's sleep. "I thought I hid it better than that," she said, her knees suddenly feeling weak. She headed toward the conference table, grabbing a chair and turning it around to face Dante as she sat down.

Dispensing with the servant act completely, Dante pulled out another chair for himself and sat. "You're much better at acting than I am," he assured her. "It's just that I know how he operates."

"You were very nice to me afterward," she said. She remembered the kindness in his eyes when he'd found her, still reeling from Mosely's visit, and she remembered how he'd made her a cup of tea without being asked. "Was that all part of the act? Mosely being the bad cop and you being the good one?"

Dante raised an eyebrow. "Did I ask you any questions?"

No, he hadn't. Hadn't shown any sign that he was trying to take advantage of the weakened state Mosely had left her in. "Guess you're as bad at being a spy as you are at being a servant."

She regretted the words as soon as they left her mouth, but Dante didn't take offense. Instead, he smiled, the first full, genuine smile she'd ever seen on him. The smile brought out dimples, which in combination with the freckles over the bridge of his nose might have made him look cute if he weren't so physically imposing.

He really was nice to look at. Not as polished and traditionally handsome as Nate, of course, but he was more rough-hewn and rugged. Certainly not the kind of boy an Executive girl should be attracted to, but maybe that in and of itself was part of his appeal.

"I'm still a beginner," he said, his eyes dancing with amusement. "Give me a couple years, and I'll have earned my cloak and dagger."

She shook her head at him, realizing that he'd been putting on more of an act than she'd originally thought. Now that he'd decided to stop pretending to be a servant, his whole demeanor had changed. Even his body language was different, loose and completely relaxed. She'd seen hints of this side of him before—most noticeably when she was verbally sparring with Jewel and he was trying not to laugh—but even if he hadn't quite mastered the demeanor of a servant, he had certainly managed to make himself considerably more stiff and formal.

She couldn't ever remember anyone but Nate being this relaxed around her. Certainly not any of the Executive boys she knew, who were all too afraid of offending Nate to let down their guard with her.

She felt a pang of loss as she remembered that Nate would never again be this easy with her, either. She'd have rather lost the engagement to him than to have lost his friendship, and the pain was stunning.

"What's wrong?" Dante asked, his brow furrowed in concern as he leaned forward in his chair. "Are you all right?"

"I'm fine," she assured him, stiffening her spine and telling herself to get over it.

"Spoken like a true Executive," he muttered under his breath, though she was sure she was supposed to hear it. "Never admit weakness around the help."

She'd have been annoyed at the jab, if she didn't sense it was just a ploy to get her to admit what was bothering her. She didn't think he was probing on Mosely's behalf, but she couldn't be sure. Still reeling from the fresh loss, she could easily find herself dropping her guard and revealing too much to someone who offered her so much as a modicum of kindness. She forced a brittle smile.

"Never admit anything in the presence of one of Dirk Mosely's spies, you mean," she corrected him, and was rewarded with a minute flinch.

"Good point," he said, clasping his hands between his knees and looking away.

His obvious guilt made her like him better—again. "How did someone like you end up working for someone like

Mosely?" she found herself asking, unable to reconcile the glimpses she'd gotten of the real him with the kind of sleazy individual who would voluntarily work for Mosely.

The open friendliness in Dante's face suddenly shut down. "I'm afraid that's a state secret," he said. His smile said he was trying to make a joke of it, but it clearly wasn't a joke. She might have pressed him on it, except he beat her to the punch. "You said you wanted to talk to me about something. I'm pretty sure my employment history isn't it, so what is it?"

Nadia would have loved to delve more deeply into Dante's secrets, intrigued by his contradictions, but she had far more important things to talk about, and her curiosity would have to take a backseat. As long as Dante was Mosely's spy, he was the enemy, and she had to be careful not to reveal anything she shouldn't.

"You slipped an envelope into the napkin on my breakfast tray this morning," she said, watching his face closely for a reaction.

His brows drew together in a puzzled frown. "Excuse me?"

He almost managed to pull off the act. The facial expression was just right, as was the baffled-sounding tone of his voice. If she hadn't been watching him so closely, she'd have missed the way his eyes widened for a split second before he regained control of his expression.

"Do we have to go through this denial thing again?" she asked as her mind worried at the convoluted puzzle. Of all the people who worked in the Lake family household, Dante seemed like the *least* likely person for Bishop to approach for messenger duty. True, he might not know that Dante worked for Mosely, but still . . . If Nadia were trying to slip an illicit message to an Executive girl, she'd have tried to enlist someone who had easy access to that girl's room, like a maid. She would *not* have chosen the girl's father's male personal assistant.

"Yeah, we do," Dante said with a stubborn set to his chin. "I didn't put anything on your tray." He glanced over her shoulder at the refreshments table behind her. "I still have a lot of clean-up to do," he said, starting to stand up, "so if you'll excuse me—"

"Sit down!" she snapped, her tone so sharp it startled him into submission. She glared at him. "I don't have the patience to play this game anymore. I know you put that message on my tray. You were *seen*, okay? So denying it just makes you look like a dumbass."

His surprise at her unladylike language would have been comical if circumstances hadn't banished Nadia's sense of humor into a cold and lonely exile.

"I didn't think Executive girls knew words like dumbass existed, much less let them drop from their pure and virginal mouths." He said it like it was a joke, but there was an edge in his voice that belied any humor.

"Is it just Executive girls you hold in such contempt, or is it all Executives? Or all girls?" She knew jealousy made a lot of people in the lower classes look down their noses at Executives, but she'd never been so blatantly slapped in the face with it before. It was worse than silly, but Nadia actually felt stung by it. It shouldn't matter to her what Mosely's spy thought of her, but she'd had more than her fill of contempt in the last few days.

Dante sighed and settled back down in his chair. "Sorry," he said, looking like he meant it. "I have a problem with girls like your lovely classmates, but you're not like them."

Since Nadia felt much the same way about Jewel and Blair, she let the subject drop. "So are you ready to admit you put the envelope on my tray so we can move on?"

"Move on to what?"

Good question. She wanted to know how a message from Bishop had found its way into Dante's hands, but there was a chance Dante didn't know who it was from, and if he didn't know, Nadia wanted to keep it that way. He didn't exactly seem fond of his boss, but she doubted his low opinion of Mosely would keep him from revealing any important information he learned.

"Who gave you the envelope?" she asked, deciding that was the safest tack to take.

"I don't know what envelope you're talking about." He looked her straight in the eye when he said it, but the lack of conviction in his voice told her it was a pro forma protest. He knew she wasn't going to buy it, and yet he wasn't willing to admit the truth.

For about a quarter of a second, Nadia considered the possibility of letting it drop, but the very fact that Dante was being so cagey about it meant there was more to learn and that it was important. The question was, how could she break down his reserve and get him to talk? If she were Mosely, she'd resort to threats, but she wasn't . . .

She let the thought trail off in her mind. There was no way she could cajole Dante into talking. She could try bribery, but her every instinct screamed at her that the attempt would be not only futile, but counterproductive. She didn't want to stoop to the level of those who'd used threats and blackmail to bend her to their will, but there was too much at stake for her to indulge her moral ideals.

"I know you're not really a servant," she said, "and I know

that in theory you shouldn't be overly concerned about protecting your position, but somehow I suspect your real boss would be unhappy with you if you got fired."

Dante's eyes narrowed, and there was a flash of anger in his eyes. But behind that anger was fear, and Nadia's conscience cringed. She managed to keep her expression cold and regal, keeping her disgust at her own words hidden behind her Executive mask.

"You wouldn't," Dante growled.

No, she wouldn't. But Dante didn't have to know that. "We've been down here alone in the schoolroom together for a good long time," she said. "I know Mosely ordered my father to hire you, but if I make certain accusations . . ."

Dante's hands clenched in his lap, and the way he was looking at her made her feel like the lowest scum on the face of the earth. Maybe she should just let him keep his secrets, whatever they were.

"And here I thought you were different from the rest of the Executive girls," he sneered. "You may be nicer than they are when things are going your way, but as soon as someone doesn't do what you want . . ." He shoved his chair back and leapt to his feet, then gave the chair an extra shove for good measure.

Nadia rose more slowly. She couldn't blame Dante for being angry. She was acting *exactly* like a spoiled Executive girl who couldn't accept the reality that not everything was going her way. She was threatening to ruin his career, maybe even his life, by fabricating a story about sexual misconduct. The fact that she knew she wouldn't do it didn't make her behavior any more palatable.

"This isn't how I act when things don't go my way," Nadia said, her voice shaking ever so slightly. "This is how I act when I'm cornered and desperate and everything that's good in my life is crumbling around me. This is how I act when *your boss* has got his hooks into me so deep I'm surprised I'm not bleeding."

She managed to keep herself from crying, but it was a near thing. If she could somehow follow the trail of breadcrumbs from the message all the way back to Bishop, if she could be the one to bring him and Nate back together, then maybe someday Nate would find it in his heart to forgive her. And maybe she'd even find it in her heart to forgive herself.

She didn't expect Dante to relent. After all, he already knew about the hell she was living through, had infiltrated her household to make sure she was as trapped as Mosely wanted her to be. He was part of the problem, certainly not part of the solution, even if he did have secrets she couldn't yet fathom.

Dante apparently considered it his life's mission to surprise her. Instead of telling her how little he thought of her excuses, he took a step toward her, reaching out to touch her shoulder in an awkward gesture of comfort. The expression in his eyes softened from anger to sympathy, perhaps tinged with a touch of guilt.

"I'm sorry, Nadia," he said, his voice surprisingly gentle. "I know you're in a terrible position, and I know it's really, really hard on you."

Nadia's breath caught in her throat as she met his gaze, trying to figure out what to make of his sudden change of heart. His hand remained on her shoulder, feeling inordinately warm through the fabric of her blouse. He was standing too close to her, gazing at her with too much intensity. He opened his mouth a couple of times as if to say more, each time thinking better of it.

She couldn't tell what he was thinking, but whatever it was had brought a lost, unhappy look to his face. He broke eye contact and let his hand drop from her shoulder. She immediately missed the warmth of his touch. In those few seconds when he'd stood too close, when his hand had been on her shoulder, she'd caught a glimpse of a tortured soul buried deep inside, and for the first time, she wondered if he did Mosely's dirty work any more willingly than she did.

Nadia took a step backward, putting a more comfortable distance between them. She couldn't afford to be intrigued by Dante, nor could she afford to see him as anything but the enemy. She had to remain firm, use every method at her disposal to get him to spill whatever secret he was hiding from her, even if her methods left her feeling dirty and low.

"Even though you're not really a servant," she said, drawing herself up stiffly as if offended, "you should never address me by first name even in private."

She expected the coldness in her tone to bring back the anger and the contempt she'd seen in him before. She didn't *like* having those feelings directed at her, but at least they helped her keep her emotional distance, helped remind her who and what he was. Instead, he ran a frustrated hand through his hair and suddenly plopped back down in the chair he'd recently vacated.

"I am going to get in so much trouble for this," he muttered under his breath. Then he squared his shoulders and looked up at her.

"For your information," he said, his eyes a little wide as if what he was about to say frightened him, "you've been calling me by first name all along. My name isn't Robert Dante, it's Dante Sandoval. And the person who gave me that message to deliver to you was Bishop."

CHAPTER FOURTEEN

PƎHCO headquarters was located in what most people still called the Empire State Building, despite its official renaming. Nate hadn't set foot in the place since he'd awakened as a Replica, even though as Chairman Heir he was expected to spend most of his waking hours there.

The day after he'd had the crap beaten out of him didn't seem like the best time to change that, but Nate wasn't up to taking evasive action, so he was sitting around at home when his father finally reached the end of his fuse and sent one of Nate's own bodyguards to fetch him—by force if necessary.

Nate fixed the bodyguard, Fischer, with a fierce glare. His whole body ached from the beating and his head was throbbing from too little sleep, too much stress, and too much to drink last night. All of which made him *so* not in the mood to have Fischer manhandle him. Fischer was unmoved by the glare, and Nate knew he had no choice but to go along.

He tried not to wince or gasp too much as he made his way downstairs to the limo with Fischer close at his heels. Getting into the limo was no fun, and Nate hoped he wouldn't be expected to move around for the commercial he would no longer be able to avoid doing. His head ached even more as he thought about how many takes he would need to get it all right in his current condition.

The Empire State Building had once been a major tourist

attraction, but now that it was Paxco Headquarters, tourists had to jump through enough security hoops to get in that they often didn't bother, especially when so many parts of the historic building were off limits. The Chairman and his staff, including Nate, had their own private entrance on the far side of the building from where the tourists and office workers entered.

Nate had seen in the news that some protesters had set up shop around Headquarters, but since there was always somebody protesting something, he hadn't paid much attention. Which meant that he was totally unprepared for the welcoming committee that awaited him outside the Chairman's entrance, waving placards and chanting. There were more of them here than there had been when Nate had left the Fortress, and they seemed angrier.

Security was keeping the crowd well back. They'd set up sawhorses to make a generous perimeter, and they also formed a human wall, ready to beat back any overly enthusiastic demonstrators. Nate wasn't surprised when a couple of the building's security officers hurried over to the car to give him extra protection.

One of the security officers opened the door for him, letting in a wall of sound the glass and steel of the car had been muffling. The demonstrators were shouting, and they waved their placards more wildly when they caught sight of him. Those who didn't have placards settled for shaking their fists in the air. Nate wasn't sure how many people were out there, but they numbered in the hundreds, and they were stunningly loud.

"Sorry for the inconvenience, sir," the security officer said, holding the door while his eyes continued to scan the crowd for threats.

Inconvenience. That was one word for it.

Nate stepped out of the limo, and the crowd went wild. Shouts turned into howls as people began to push and shove to get closer to the barriers. Then the howls turned into a chant: "Replicas aren't people!"

The security officers and his bodyguard tried to hurry Nate along, but he couldn't help stopping a moment, frozen in shock at the ferocity of the crowd, at their snarling anger, at their dismissal of him as a human being. "I *am* a person," he wanted to shout at the crowd. Not that he could shout loudly enough to be heard over this roar, or that anyone would listen to him if he did.

The snippets he'd seen on the news had clued him in to the fact that the general public was wary and suspicious of Replicas, as had the protest outside the Fortress, but he'd never expected this level of hostility.

"Get down!" Fischer, suddenly yelled, pouncing on Nate's back and knocking him to the ground.

Something zipped past his head and splatted on the open door of the limo. It was just an egg, not a deadly weapon, but the throwing of that single egg seemed to flip a switch. Until then, the security officers had been calmly controlling the crowd, holding them back but not ordering them to disperse. Now, they reached for their pepper spray. The egg thrower was hauled over the barricade as the others at the front of the line tried to retreat out of reach of the spray. One of the security officers started whaling on the egg thrower with his baton.

"No!" Nate yelled as he was hauled bodily to his feet.

The crowd was screaming now, placards dropping as those closest to the front saw the threat and tried to run. But those in the back didn't know what was happening and kept trying to press forward, making retreat impossible as the security officers blasted pepper spray indiscriminately, not caring that the crowd was now *trying* to disperse. Those trapped between the officers and the wall of people behind them started fighting back because there was nothing else they could do. The egg thrower was curled up in fetal position, trying desperately to protect his head, but the security officer kept hitting him.

"Stop them!" Nate yelled again, but no one was listening to him. When he tried to move toward the melee, security officers grabbed each of his arms and hauled him forward, while Fischer grabbed hold of his collar and shoved on the small of his back for good measure.

Ignoring his repeated protests—and the screams of the crowd behind them—the officers forced Nate through the doorway and into Paxco Headquarters.

The interior of the Empire State Building had been almost entirely gutted when it had become Paxco Headquarters, but the architects had done their best to preserve the art deco lobby with its stunning ceiling mural and intricate glasswork. None of which was visible from the Chairman's entrance, which sported a functional and ultramodern lobby with enough security measures to withstand the Apocalypse. The glass doors of the entrance were bulletproof, so thick that when they closed, the screaming and shouting from the riot was muted to almost nothing. No one inside seemed particularly alarmed at what was occurring on their doorstep, although a few people did look at Nate with open curiosity as Fischer and the security officers frog-marched him to the elevators. Adrenaline and horror had fueled him when he'd seen the start of the riot, but now that the immediate crisis had passed—at least for him if not the poor bastards outside—the adrenaline faded and his bruised and aching body shouted its own protests. The security officers seemed to sense his capitulation, and their hands dropped from his arms, but Fischer still had a hand on his back, right on one of his worst bruises.

"Let go of me," he said in what he hoped was a level, rational-sounding tone. "I'm not going to try to go back out there."

Fischer's hand dropped away, but Nate was sure all three of his escorts were on high alert for any sign he was about to make a break for it.

If he thought running back out there and screaming for the security officers to stop would help the situation, he might have tried it. But somehow when that single egg was tossed, both the crowd and the security officers holding them back had lost their powers of reason and self-control. Nate had never seen anything like that before, and he hoped he never saw it again.

His security escorts waited until Nate and Fischer were safely in the elevator before walking away. Nate supposed they were going to join the fray, assuming it wasn't all over by now. He hoped no one had been seriously hurt.

To his surprise, Nate found that there was a slight tremor in his hands as he straightened his jacket and tugged on his cuffs. All that hatred, all that violence, was because of *him*. Because he wasn't really Nate Hayes, no matter how much he felt like it. He was a Replica, an artificial human being. How could he blame the people of Paxco for being horrified at what he was?

Nadia accepted him because she *knew* him, because she could talk to him and see that he was still the same person.

She could be lulled into almost believing he was the original Nate Hayes because the illusion of the Replica was so powerful. The same could not be said of the faceless mob. Maybe his father wasn't just being an opportunistic bastard when he wanted Nate to do this commercial. Maybe it was damned important that the public be more exposed to him so they could come to accept him.

"Seems hypocritical to me," said Fischer, staring up at the numbers above the door instead of looking at Nate, "that people who depend on Paxco for their livelihoods are out there demonstrating against Replicas. Ungrateful bastards have to know Replica technology is our number one source of revenue. Do away with Replicas, most of them would be out of a job, maybe even out on the street."

Nate rarely paid much attention to his bodyguards unless they did something to annoy him. Hell, he didn't even know what Fischer's first name was, had never bothered to ask. It humbled him that the usually taciturn man was trying to take some of the sting out of what had just happened.

"Yeah," Nate said, though he wasn't sure he agreed with Fischer's point. Yes, the Replica technology was an enormous revenue stream and provided thousands upon thousands of people with jobs and salaries and homes. But it was a very unsettling technology, and the morality of its use was far from clear even in his own mind. But if Fischer was going to be nice to him . . .

Nate cleared his throat. "Look, I should have just let you get me out of there without throwing a tantrum like I did. Sorry I was a dick."

Fischer kept looking at the lighted numbers. "It's all right. I'm used to it."

He said it completely deadpan, not a hint of amusement in

his eyes or voice, but since Nate was 99 percent sure he was kidding, he laughed. Which his body instantly told him was a bad idea.

Fischer finally tore his eyes away from the floor numbers. "Are you hurt, sir?" he asked in concern.

"I'm fine," Nate assured him, forcing a tight smile as he waited for the pain to fade.

Fischer looked skeptical, but the elevator had arrived at their floor, and the doors slid open.

nadia drifted slowly back to her chair, staring at Dante—or perhaps she needed to mentally start calling him Sandoval—reshuffling the puzzle pieces in her head and trying to put them together. She wasn't having a whole lot of success.

"You work for Dirk Mosely," she said, speaking slowly as she eased into her chair. "You carried a message to me from Kurt Bishop. And Bishop isn't rotting at Riker's Island as we speak?"

Dante shook his head. "Not unless something drastic has happened that I haven't heard about." He crossed his arms over his chest in a gesture that looked almost defensive. Nadia hadn't unraveled the riddle yet, but one thing she felt certain of: Dante was *not* supposed to be telling her any of this.

Unfortunately, now that he'd dropped his bombshell, he seemed reluctant to volunteer any more information. However, Nadia had no qualms about dragging it out of him. She wanted to spit out questions in rapid fire and shake the answers out of him, but she forced herself to take it slow. The last thing she wanted was to make him clam up again.

"Okay, fine," she said as she settled on question number one. "If you've been in contact with Bishop, then why haven't you told your boss?"

Dante reached up and rubbed at his eyes. "I can't believe I opened my mouth."

"Well, you did." Nadia couldn't make sense of the emotions roiling through her any more than she could make sense of the puzzle Dante presented. She was excited at the prospect of finally getting some answers, and yet there was also a good deal of dread about what those answers might be. And then there was the frightened, cautious, maybe even paranoid part of her that whispered this all had to be some kind of an elaborate trap, set by Mosely to trick her into revealing every scrap of information she'd kept secret.

Dante huffed out a deep breath and straightened his shoulders. "Right. But I need you to promise me something first."

She understood his caution, but it was far too late for it. "We both know I'd promise you my firstborn child if that's what it took to get you talking right now. We also both know I'd never make good on it. You've opened the barn door, and you look pretty silly chasing after the galloping horse."

Even in the midst of his obvious turmoil, Dante managed a half smile. "You have a way with words."

"I'm glad I amuse you. Now, tell me what's going on!"

The hint of humor vanished from Dante's face. "You're right and I can't hold you to any promises, but I'm *begging* you not to repeat anything I'm about to tell you. Lives are at stake, my own and other people's."

Lives had been at stake from the moment someone had stabbed the Chairman Heir to death, and Nadia had been shouldering the responsibility to protect them so long it felt almost natural now. "I understand. Now, who are you, really?"

With the grim resolve of a soldier marching into battle, Dante sat up straight in his chair and met her eyes. "My real name is Dante Sandoval. My parents are both sanitation workers." He made a face of disgust. "One step removed from Basement-dwellers. We're technically Employees, but we're so low Mosely didn't want anyone to be able to look into my background. I'm not respectable enough to be a servant, you see, so he insisted I make up a new name for this assignment."

Nadia had no trouble hearing the bitterness in his voice, and now she understood a little better why he'd seemed so touchy about her status as an Executive.

"I'm sorry if I'm being insensitive," she said, "but I'm not that interested in your background right now. I want to know—"

"I know what you want to know," he interrupted, and she saw a renewed flash of anger in his eyes. Anger that he visibly tamed, reeling himself back in as she suspected he'd done a thousand times in his life. Kind of like how she'd held in all her anger with Nate for so long. The problem with holding it in so fiercely was that it tended to get out at the most inconvenient times.

"I guess my background isn't that important," he conceded. "I was just trying to explain that people like me, people like my family, have shitty, miserable lives working shitty, miserable jobs without ever being able to hope for better, and people like you have everything handed to you on a silver platter just because you happened to be born an Executive."

No doubt about it, Dante was harboring one hell of a lot of class anger. Nadia would have liked to point out to him that her life wasn't as much of a picnic as he might think, but entering into a debate about the class system wouldn't get her the information she wanted, so she bit her tongue.

"Eventually," Dante continued, "it gets to a point where the downtrodden have had enough, and they band together.

It's happened a million times over the course of history, and it's happening now."

"What does that mean, exactly?"

"It means there's a resistance movement forming in Paxco."

Nadia frowned at him. "Am I supposed to be shocked? Someone's protesting something practically every day." Nadia had the uneasy suspicion that if it weren't for Mosely and his security goons, there would be a lot more protests, and they'd be a lot bigger and louder. The government wouldn't be so gauche as to publicly quash protests, but they would make sure such protests were a controlled burn, not something that could catch on and spread.

"I don't mean the kind of resistance movement that involves marching around carrying signs. I mean the kind that's actually going to *do* something about the injustice."

"What does this have to do with anything?" Nadia asked. She wanted to know more, but she had to keep the conversation focused. She and Dante had had the schoolroom to themselves for quite some time now, but there was no guarantee someone wouldn't come looking for one or both of them at any moment.

"I'm part of it. I'm here because I'm working a mission, trying to infiltrate Mosely's spy network. It'll probably take years before he'll trust me with anything sensitive enough to be useful, but when he does, I'll have the ammunition to help the resistance take down the entire Paxco security division."

Nadia might have stood up and cheered the vision, if she didn't think that Dante's resistance meant to take down more than just Paxco's security division. She didn't for a moment think that the class system was fair, nor was she blind to the massive corruption within the government of Paxco. The

Chairman himself was about as corrupt an individual as she could imagine. But it sounded like the resistance movement had ambitions to start a revolution, and that wasn't a pleasant prospect, either.

"Bishop's part of the resistance," she said, the lightbulb suddenly going on above her head. "That's why he didn't flee Paxco when he had a chance. And that's why you're carrying messages for him."

Dante nodded. "The resistance is mostly Employees, but there's a fair number of Basement-dwellers. I've heard we even have a few low-level Executives, though I don't know who they are."

Now that she had more puzzle pieces, Nadia found it easier to put them together, though she didn't much like the picture that was forming. Dante had been sent on a mission to infiltrate Mosely's spy network. What were the odds that another member of the resistance would have found his way into the Chairman Heir's household on the basis of pure chance?

She tried to drive the thought from her head. She would worry about the twists and turns of Bishop's motivations later. Right now, she had to concentrate on the fact that she was sitting face-to-face with someone who was capable of contacting him.

Of course, Bishop had reached out to contact both her and Nate within the last twenty-four hours, and that contact had been far from friendly. He'd delivered the message that he didn't want to be found with vicious conviction, and she wondered what she was doing, still trying to find him after all that he'd done. After all, he'd had Nate *beaten* last night, had hurt him body and soul.

But in the end, none of that mattered. What mattered was

that neither she nor Nate would be able to rest until they found out what had happened on the night of his murder, and there was only one person who could tell them.

"I need you to take a message to Bishop," she said.

Dante looked at her as if she were insane. "You're joking, right?"

She continued as if he hadn't spoken. "He underestimated me, and he underestimated Nate. I told Nate the truth about the tracker this morning." Her throat and chest tightened at the memory of the look in Nate's eyes, but she tried to keep the pain from showing on her face. "I even showed him the note Bishop wrote me. He now knows for sure that Bishop is still in town, and he's not going to stop looking for him."

"He *has* to stop," Dante hissed, leaning forward as if his very intensity could convince her. "He almost led Mosely's men right to him last night."

"I know," Nadia said calmly. "That's why Bishop would be much better off if he'd just bite the bullet and talk to Nate. The *least* he can do is tell Nate what happened on the night of the murder."

Dante shook his head. "Have you ever considered that there's a *reason* he's not telling?"

"Maybe Bishop does have a good reason for everything he's done," Nadia said carefully. "But that doesn't change anything. Nate isn't going to stop looking for him. Not until he finds out what happened, at least." Probably not even then, now that Nadia had helped convince him that Bishop still loved him. Perhaps that had been a mistake on her part, but it was too late to change it now. And Dante didn't need to know just how personal Nate's attachment to Bishop was. It was always possible that Dante knew the truth, but if he didn't, she wasn't going to be the one to reveal it.

"If he keeps looking, he's going to get himself killed again," Dante said. "And he might get a whole lot of other people killed along the way. People who *won't* come back from it."

"So tell Bishop to talk to him. Surely talking to him would be better than letting him keep stumbling around in the dark."

Dante groaned and leaned back in his chair, staring at the ceiling. "I am so sick of stubborn people!"

"Just tell Bishop what I told you." She didn't have any more convincing arguments she could trot out, but then she probably didn't need any. Bishop knew Nate too well. Once he realized the beating last night *still* hadn't convinced Nate to stop looking, he'd know his only choice was to contact Nate.

Dante let out a resigned sigh and sat up. "All right. I'll tell him."

"Can you also tell him . . ." Nadia swallowed hard, past the sudden lump in her throat. "Tell him I had no choice. About the tracker, I mean."

"I already told him that," Dante said. "I know better than most what Mosely's capable of." He reached for her hand and gave it a firm squeeze.

That simple touch felt better than it had any right to. She barely knew him, and he obviously had an enormous chip on his shoulder about Executive girls, but right now it seemed as if he was the only person in her life who was being nice to her and wasn't making demands.

"You told him, but he didn't buy it," she said. "If he weren't so angry with me, he'd never have had you slip me the message. There was no point in it—except to let me know he knew about me. Not that I blame him."

Dante squeezed her hand again, showing no sign that he was planning to let go anytime soon. "He's never had to go head-to-head with Mosely, so he doesn't understand." *But I do,* said the look in Dante's eyes.

Nadia nodded. It shouldn't matter to her if Bishop thought badly of her. They had never liked each other anyway. But his was another name on the list of people she'd disappointed over the last week, and the weight of it all was getting to her.

Still holding her hand, Dante moved his chair closer to hers until their knees were touching. He took her other hand and met her eyes. She was drowning in misery, but Dante's hands were like a lifeline.

"Don't blame yourself for any of this sh— er, mess. Mosely strong-arms people for a living, and he has the weight of all of Paxco behind him. It wouldn't have done anyone any good if you'd called his bluff, because we both know whatever he threatened you with, it wasn't a bluff. Your choices sucked, and you took the lesser of two evils."

The warmth and earnestness of his expression was almost enough to make her cry. Why couldn't *Nate* have looked at her like that? Why could someone who was practically a complete stranger understand and sympathize when her best and oldest friend couldn't?

"It's not really *Bishop's* hard feelings that are getting to you, is it?" Dante asked softly. "You said you told your boyfriend about the tracker. I don't suppose he took it so well."

Grateful as she was for Dante's kindness, she had no desire to talk to him about Nate. "I just wish none of this had happened."

He was still holding her hands, and one thumb brushed absently over her knuckles. She wasn't sure if he even knew he'd done it, but the simple caress awakened a swarm of butterflies in her stomach.

Not that he had meant it as a caress, of course, she told

herself. He was being nice to her because she was in distress and she needed the hint of kindness. It wasn't anything personal. He'd already made it quite clear how he felt about Executive girls in general. And the butterflies didn't mean anything except that she was feeling lonely and vulnerable after her fight with Nate.

Footsteps sounded in the hallway outside the schoolroom, and Dante hastily let go of her hands and rose from his chair. One moment, he was warm and friendly and . . . comfortable. The next, he was stiff and upright, playing the ill-fitting role of the dutiful servant.

"Would you like another cup of tea before I clear the rest of the service?" he asked, standing at attention.

The footsteps continued past the doorway and faded into the distance, but Dante didn't relax his posture. It was no doubt best for both of them if he kept up his act at all times anyway. Mosely wouldn't appreciate him giving comfort to the enemy.

Already missing the precious few minutes of camaraderie they'd just shared, she rose to her feet.

"Thank you, Dante," she said, taking pleasure in knowing she was addressing him by first name like an equal and no one else would know it, "but I don't need any more tea right now."

With a formal half bow, he turned away.

Inside Paxco Headquarters, life went on as if nothing had happened.

Nate, still badly shaken, reported to the private studio where the commercial was to be shot, and it was every bit as awful as he'd anticipated. The script made him want to gag, and he could only imagine what kind of sappy "inspirational" music they'd be playing in the background. He couldn't remember his lines to save his life. The crew kept moving him into position like he was a doll—heedless of his bruises, of course, because they didn't know about them. The lights were hot enough to make him sweat and bright enough to fuel his headache indefinitely. Usually, he was good in front of the camera, but this time he flat-out sucked.

The crew and the director eyed him warily, his ineptness no doubt making him seem very different from the Nate Hayes they thought they knew. He tried not to be snappish with them—the last thing he needed was more people thinking the Replication process created aggressive or even violent tendencies—but he knew he wasn't exactly being easy to work with.

As soon as he escaped the shoot and holed up in his office, he couldn't stop himself from looking for updated reports about the riot instead of wisely taking some aspirin and huddling in a dark corner until he felt better. As of five o'clock in the afternoon, there were no reported deaths, although one of the security officers had been severely trampled and was in critical condition. There was no definitive word on how many of the protesters had been injured or how badly, but a total of thirty-two people had been arrested and sent directly to Riker's Island to await trial on a laundry list of charges that included treason.

The net had plenty of video coverage of the event, but what neither the videos nor the articles ever mentioned was exactly how the riot had started. The videos all showed the angry mob clashing with the security officers—failing to show the people who were desperately trying to flee the pepper spray—and the articles just said the protest "got out of hand." Nowhere did Nate see it mentioned that the whole mess had started because someone had thrown a completely harmless *egg*.

The knowledge that the protesters were going to be charged with treason, among other things, made Nate sick to his stomach. Despite the ugly things they'd been shouting at him, Nate couldn't stand the thought of people serving life sentences or even being executed because of a riot they didn't start, and he arranged a meeting with his father to give the Chairman a clear picture of what really happened.

The meeting was at five o'clock, but of course the Chairman made Nate wait while he finished a phone call that went a half hour long. Nate would have been pissed off, except he was so used to it that he couldn't muster the energy to be pissed anymore. When he was a kid, Nate had sometimes sensed real paternal affection from his father. He even had a picture of himself as a small child, maybe four years old, riding on his laughing father's shoulders. But the older he'd gotten, the less his father seemed to like him, and once he hit adolescence, they'd become more like embattled strangers than father and son.

Now that Nate was officially an adult and no longer dependent on his father, he found the best way to keep their relationship civil was to keep it on a strictly business level. His father agreed, which was why he played the make-the-subordinate-wait mind games.

It was just after 5:30 when Nate was finally admitted to the Chairman's corner office. Even then, his father made him wait just a little longer, scanning over a document he probably wasn't even reading as Nate helped himself to a tumbler of scotch from the bar.

"Want one?" he asked, holding up the bottle. It was as good a greeting as any.

The Chairman finally looked up from his document, setting it aside. "Please."

Nate poured a second drink, then laid it on his father's desk before lowering himself rather gingerly into the plush leather chair. He'd found he could almost forget about his injuries when he was either upright or seated; it was the transition between the two that smarted.

"I heard about your . . . ordeal this morning," the Chairman said. "I should have had security disperse the crowd before you arrived. It didn't occur to me that they'd get so out of hand."

Nate took a sip of his scotch, forcing himself to slow down and think a moment before he made a surly response. Anything the Chairman had heard about the riot had no doubt been reported to him by security personnel, who had a vested interest in portraying the incident as a crowd turning into a rioting mob.

"Actually," he said, with what he felt was admirable calm, "that's what I wanted to talk to you about. I've been looking at the news coverage. I saw that thirty-two people have been arrested and charged with treason."

The Chairman's eyes sharpened, and Nate figured his father sensed where he was going with this.

"Don't you think that's a little . . . extreme?"

His father leaned back in his chair, cradling the scotch in his lap. "They attacked the Chairman Heir. That's the very definition of treason."

Nate sipped his scotch again, but if he was going to use scotch as his pressure valve when his temper flared, he'd need the bottle. He gripped the tumbler rather more tightly than necessary, but tried to keep his voice level. The longer he could keep the tension from escalating into something resembling a fight, the better chance he had of convincing his father to be a little more lenient.

"I don't know what you've been told exactly," he said, "but no one actually *attacked* me. Some idiot in the crowd threw an egg. That's all that happened. And security went berserk. The crowd didn't get out of hand at all. It was the security officers. They started in with the pepper spray and batons just because someone threw an egg."

"Your bodyguard interpreted it as an attack. I hear he wrestled you to the ground."

Nate waved that off. "He saw someone throw something. For all he knew, it was a rock or a grenade. I'd have ducked myself if I'd seen it coming. But it wasn't a rock or a grenade. It was an egg. I was not attacked, so there's no reason to charge those people with treason."

Nate remembered the sight of the security officer beating the guy who'd thrown the egg. As far as Nate was concerned, the poor bastard had more than paid for his offense already. Assuming he'd survived. Just because the news didn't mention any fatalities among the demonstrators didn't mean there weren't any.

The Chairman swirled his scotch around in his glass, one corner of his mouth tipped up in a patronizing smile. "You're a good kid, son," he said in an equally patronizing voice. "You have a good heart and a generous spirit. But I don't care if they threw *marshmallows* at you. I will not have my son and heir attacked by an unruly mob of idiots who want to throw away the goose that laid the golden egg because it makes them uncomfortable."

Nate leaned forward in his chair and put the scotch down. It wasn't helping his temper any, though he was fighting like hell to stay calm and in control of himself. An impassioned, emotional appeal to the Chairman's better nature had no chance of working. A rational, reasoned one just might.

"You didn't see what I saw," he said, wishing he could scrub the sights and sounds out of his memory. "The moment the pepper spray came out, the people at the front of the crowd tried to run away, but they couldn't because the people behind them didn't know what was going on. They were trying to run, trying to protect their faces, and the security officers sprayed them anyway, then started whaling on them with their batons. The guy who threw the egg was lying there in fetal position as they beat him, and no one else had done anything worse than yell and wave signs around. They've already been beaten and tortured with pepper spray. They don't deserve to be tried for treason just because they happened to be present when someone threw an egg." Maybe if he repeated the part about the egg often enough, the Chairman would finally see the ridiculousness of the overreaction.

Nate was proud of himself for managing to stay so calm and reasonable. Nadia would be impressed with his restraint. And she thought he couldn't contain his temper! If she could see him now, she'd realize how wrong she had been not to trust him.

The Chairman shook his head and sighed. "You're missing the point, son. There were arrests made after that first demonstration at the Fortress, but most of those people were released without charges, and those who were charged were fined, not jailed. And because we didn't take a hard enough stance against that kind of behavior, those animals showed up at Headquarters today. They will continue to show up in ever greater numbers unless we forcefully discourage such behavior. Filing treason charges against the rioters will be a powerful deterrent to anyone else who might think about setting up another such demonstration."

A chill sank into him as Nate stared at his father and a

suspicion wormed its way into his mind. His mouth went dry, and he licked his lips as every muscle in his body tensed.

"Why *didn't* you have the demonstrators dispersed before I arrived?" he asked, his voice strained. He prayed for his father to look puzzled, to not understand what Nate was getting at. If he didn't understand, that meant Nate's sickening suspicion was wrong. But the Chairman merely folded his hands on the desk and returned his stare, his face bland as he dared Nate to put voice to what had happened.

"Were you hoping someone would do something stupid when I showed up at the scene?" Nate asked when it was clear his father wasn't going to answer. "Did you order the security officers to attack the crowd at the slightest provocation?"

Still no answers. And no shifting of the bland expression on the Chairman's face.

Nate shoved back his chair, barely even feeling the protest of his back and gut muscles as he leapt to his feet, the full horror of what had happened finally dawning on him.

"It was even worse than that, wasn't it? You ordered the security officers to attack. And you ordered them to wait until I made an appearance, so you could use my presence as an excuse for a treason charge!"

It had all been one massive setup. Thirty-two innocent people were going to lose their liberty and maybe even their lives because Chairman Hayes wanted to discourage protests.

Nate had always known his father was a hard man, that he saw the world through a lens of cold logic. He was probably capable of compassion, but only when it was strategically expedient. But this was an atrocity worse than he'd imagined his father capable of.

The Chairman rose to his feet much more slowly, leaning forward and putting his fists on his desk. "Before you storm out in a cloud of righteous indignation, remember this: my concern is for the well-being of Paxco. The relentless insistence on individual liberties over the needs of society as a whole is what led to the dissolution of the United States. We have to learn from our predecessors' mistakes. That will mean some individuals are treated unfairly, but that's the price we have to pay."

"The price *they* have to pay, you mean," Nate said, shaking his head in disgust. "Justify yourself all you want. What you did was despicable."

The Chairman rolled his eyes. "Get out and take your high horse with you. Someday, you're going to have to grow up and see the world as it really is, but that day obviously hasn't come yet."

Nate reached down and grabbed the crystal tumbler he'd been drinking out of. Knowing that he was justifying his father's view of him as a spoiled child throwing a temper tantrum, Nate couldn't help hurling the tumbler at the wall with all his strength. The spray of shattered glass was not as satisfying as he'd hoped it would be.

CHAPTER FIFTEEN

nadia sat alone in the den, waiting for Nate to show up for their eight o'clock "date." They usually tried to make a public appearance together at least once a month, giving the press an opportunity to photograph them and giving the high-society gossips something to talk about, but it was their quiet, private get-togethers that she had always enjoyed most, the nights when they'd stayed in and talked or watched a movie or played games. These were times reminiscent of their childhood together, when they didn't fully understand what the handshake agreement between their families would mean to them in time.

Tonight was going to be a very different story.

She'd tried to call Nate after hearing about the riot, but she'd gotten his voice mail. She'd left a message, but he hadn't called back. Late in the afternoon, he'd texted her a terse message assuring her he was all right, but that was it. Apparently, he didn't want to talk to her. She supposed she shouldn't be surprised, but it still hurt.

She resisted the urge to call him again and took a page from his book, texting him to remind him of their scheduled date. She had a feeling he would conveniently "forget" about it if she didn't, and she needed him to show up so she could fill him in on her interview with Mosely—and figure out what to do about the new tracker Mosely had ordered her to plant.

Nate hadn't answered her text, and he was now a half hour late. It wasn't unusual for him, but Nadia couldn't help but take it as yet another slap in her face. She kept taking her phone out and looking at it, hoping he'd sent a message that she somehow hadn't noticed.

Three times, she started to text him to confirm he was coming, and three times she erased what she'd written before she sent it. He would show up when he showed up, and her nagging him about it would just make her seem needy. Of course, she *was* feeling needy, spectacularly so, and she couldn't stand sitting still in the den any longer. She let Crane know where she was going, then made her way up to the roof-top garden.

During the day, the garden was a beautiful oasis amongst all the glass and steel of the city. The wind was blocked by two tastefully low walls and by the bulk of the other two Lake Towers. Spring was in full bloom, beds of daffodils and early tulips making splashes of vivid color. A paved, circular path made its way through the flower beds, and at the far end of the garden were a pair of wrought-iron benches, one facing the beauty of the garden, one facing the breathtaking view of the city.

Now that the sun had gone down, it was a little too chilly to hang around outside, but Nadia had no interest in going back in. Instead, she kept warm by restlessly pacing the circular path, her hair whipping in the gusts that got past the wind breaks. Without the sun to shine on them, the flowers looked duller, less cheerful, and the panoramic view made Nadia feel very . . . isolated.

By 8:45, Nadia's feet hurt from her restless walking, and she decided to sit on the bench facing the panoramic view. Moments after she sat down, she heard the sound of a foot-fall behind her, and she turned to look over her shoulder.

Relief flooded her when she saw Nate standing there, and she wanted to run to him and throw her arms around him. She hadn't realized how afraid she'd been that he wouldn't show up until he finally made his appearance. She rose to her feet, wrapping her arms around herself for warmth—and to dis-courage her desire to give Nate a hug.

"I thought you weren't going to come," she blurted.

Nate stuck his hands in his pockets and stood about an arm's length away. "I don't much want to be here," he admit-ted bluntly. "I've had a sucky day."

Nadia imagined being in the midst of that riot had been an ordeal for Nate, and she certainly pitied him the rude awaken-ing he'd had this morning when she'd made her confession, but she was through making excuses for his self-centered atti-tude. Instead of acknowledging the hurt his words caused, she stood up a little straighter and looked him in the eye.

"Did you risk the arrest and torture of yourself and every-one you love, including two helpless children, today?" she asked, her voice as sharp as knives. "No? Then how 'bout you don't talk about how rough you've had it, okay?"

Nate's look of surprise would have been funny any other time. If he only knew how many times she'd refrained from telling him what she really thought through all the years they'd been friends . . . But that was over now. They weren't friends anymore, not really, and she wasn't going to censor herself anymore, either. They had made a pact together this morning, and he would hold up his end of the bargain even if she pissed him off.

Nate opened and closed his mouth a couple times as he floundered for something to say. Her natural urge to be the peacemaker made her want to let him off the hook, but she didn't. Maybe the reason he was so self-centered all the time was because no one dared call him on it, and he didn't know any better.

"I'm sorry," he finally mumbled, rubbing the back of his head and looking down at his feet. "I know I've been unfair to you." He scuffed his shoe against the paving stone, kicking at an imaginary pebble. "I can't imagine what you've been going through." He huffed out a deep breath and looked her in the face again. "I don't blame you for doing whatever you need to do to protect your family. I just wish you'd trusted me enough to talk to me about it instead of going behind my back."

For Nate, this was an abject apology, and Nadia should have been grateful for it. She *was* grateful. But it wasn't enough.

"Tell me the truth, Nate: if I'd told you everything from the start, would you have kept quiet about it? Or would you have confronted Mosely on the assumption you could protect me from his retaliation?"

Nadia could almost see him restraining his knee-jerk first response, and his Adam's apple bobbed as he thought about it. There was a shadow in his eyes, and his shoulders hunched in a bit. Whatever he was thinking, he didn't like it. Shaking his head, he moved past her and collapsed onto one of the benches, his head hanging low.

Nadia took a couple of tentative steps in his direction, wanting to give him a hug, or put a hand on his shoulder. Anything to rebuild just a tiny bit of the connection they'd once had. But she wasn't sure she could bear it if he rebuffed her, so she merely stood there wringing her hands uselessly.

Nate raised his head and patted the bench beside him. "Come sit down. We have a lot to talk about."

Nadia sat beside him, but not in touching range. To her surprise, Nate slid over and slung his arm around her shoulders, pulling her close until their bodies were pressed against one another from shoulder to knee. He was warm and familiar, and, without thinking about it, Nadia rested her head on his shoulder and closed her eyes, trying to pretend nothing had ever gone wrong between them. She felt the press of his lips on the top of her head and smiled. For this one moment, she would take what he offered without thinking about what the future would bring.

She didn't know how long they'd been sitting like that, neither one talking, before another figure wandered out from the tower and into the garden. Assuming it was one of the servants, Nadia hastily sat up and put some distance between herself and Nate. She and Nate had posed for photographs where they were holding hands and had even kissed in public to uphold the illusion that they were a couple, but she still didn't want anyone speculating too much about what they did together when *not* in public. She trusted the servants' discretion, and she and Nate were an acknowledged couple anyway, but she didn't see any reason to take chances, especially now. But when the figure stepped into the light, she saw it was Dante.

"Dante!" she cried in surprise, standing up. "What are you doing here?"

Dante looked quickly back and forth between her and Nate. Trying to figure out if she'd been spilling any secrets, maybe? "Looking for you," he said. "You didn't seem to be in any of the usual places, so I thought I'd take a shot at the garden."

Nate stood up too, moving closer to Nadia and putting his arm around her shoulders again. "Want to introduce me to your friend?" he asked, and there was a barely perceptible edge in his voice.

"Um, sure," Nadia said, though she wasn't sure what to say. "This is Dante. He's my dad's new personal assistant."

"Pleased to meet you," Nate said insincerely, holding out his hand. Most Executives wouldn't offer to shake hands when meeting a low-level Employee, but Nate had always ignored the snobbiest of the social conventions.

"You too," Dante said, and Nadia suspected the handshake that ensued was of the bone-crushing variety. She was tempted to ask who won.

"So, you were looking for me?" she prompted, a little surprised that Dante had approached her out here when Nate was with her. She would have thought he'd want to talk to her in private. If he was going to try to separate her from Nate to have a private conversation now, she had a feeling it wouldn't go very well. Nate might not be attracted to her, but he was still sizing Dante up like a rival.

"Yeah," Dante said, giving Nate a sidelong glance. "About that matter we were discussing this afternoon. I've arranged a meeting. For *both* of you."

Nadia's eyes widened in surprise. After all Bishop's resistance, she hadn't expected him to be willing to meet. "Really?"

Dante nodded. "That's the plan as of now, anyway. He might not show up, especially if he gets a bad vibe."

"All right, what are you two talking about?" Nate asked.

Dante waved his hand at Nadia, silently giving her permission to explain.

"Dante's the one who put the note from Bishop in my napkin this morning," she said. That was meant to be only the beginning of her explanation, but Nate didn't give her a chance to continue.

"That so?" he asked, then hauled off and punched Dante in the jaw.

Dante went sprawling, and Nate gave a shout of pain, clutching his right hand to his chest and cursing. Nadia was paralyzed by shock, but only for a moment. Ignoring Nate and his cursing, she dropped to her knees beside Dante, who was rubbing his jaw as he shook his head as if to clear the cobwebs.

"Are you all right?" she asked, unable to believe that Nate had just thrown a punch. He just . . . wasn't that kind of guy. She couldn't help thinking about the opinions she'd seen touted on the net, the ones that suggested Replicas might have violent tendencies. They were making something out of nothing, of course, extrapolating wildly based on one brief loss of poise with a reporter. Everything that had happened since the night of the reception was enough to put *anyone* on a short fuse, Replica or not.

"Yeah," Dante mumbled, eying Nate warily as if primed for another attack.

Nadia gave Dante a hand up, then turned to glare at Nate, who was still nursing his sore knuckles. Nadia wondered if that was the first punch he'd ever thrown. It would serve him right if he'd broken some fingers.

"What the hell was that all about?" she demanded.

"He's a sneak, and he terrified you," Nate responded, looking both sullen and stubborn.

It was Mosely's call that had terrified her this morning, not the note Dante had tucked into her napkin, but she hadn't specifically told Nate that. She wondered if he'd have gone all protective and alpha male on her if Dante weren't so good-looking. He was acting positively territorial, although Dante was hardly of a class to be a rival. Nadia opened her mouth to give Nate a piece of her mind, but Dante forestalled her.

"Time out," he said, making the requisite hand gesture. Nadia noted that although he was still acting wary, he was taking Nate's unprovoked attack with a surprising level of calm, as if it didn't bother him. "I'm willing to let bygones be bygones. We have more important things to talk about." The look in his eyes hardened as he fixed his gaze on Nate. "Try that again, though, and I'll fight back. You wouldn't like that, especially when you're already sore."

Nadia got ready to jump in between the two, thinking that Dante's calmly spoken words were more of an invitation to further fighting than a conciliation. "You may call me Mr. Hayes," Nate said, low and menacing. "And how would you know I'm already sore?"

"That's what I was trying to tell you," Nadia said in exasperation. "Dante is a friend of Bishop's. Now, why don't you sit down, shut up, and *listen* for once in your life."

Nate gave her a shocked look, but he was just going to have to get used to her standing up to him from now on. She had to fight a smile, proud of herself, when Nate meekly sat on one of the benches and made a zipping-his-lips gesture. Taking a deep breath, Nadia sat beside him and told him everything she'd learned from Dante, who stood off to the side, silent. The only thing she *didn't* mention was her suspicion that Bishop had been planted in his household by the resistance. The idea would no doubt occur to him anyway, but perhaps not right away.

For a long time after Nadia finished talking, Nate didn't say anything. He sat forward with his elbows on his knees, staring at the paving stones beneath his feet as he took it all in. The look on his face told her he was lost in thought, but it didn't tell her anything about what he was thinking, and she thought he might be guarding his expression because of Dante's presence.

Eventually, he sat up straight and glanced over to Dante.

"Explain this," he said. "Why is it that yesterday, Bishop was trying so hard to keep me away that he had me beaten, and today he wants to see me?"

It was a good question, and Nadia's suspicious mind immediately suggested it was a trap of some kind.

Dante shook his head. "He'll explain when and if you see him."

"No, *you'll* explain," Nate insisted, "and right now."

"Or what?" Dante asked, raising an eyebrow. "You need me to take you to the meeting."

"How do I know anything you're saying is true?" Nate countered. "You could be trying to set me up for . . . something."

"You're just going to have to take it on faith, I suppose. Nadia was under the impression you wanted to see him, but if you're not interested . . ." He shrugged his broad shoulders, and there was a hint of smugness in his tone.

Even in the lamp-lit darkness, Nadia could see the flush of anger creeping up Nate's neck. He wouldn't have missed Dante's overly familiar use of Nadia's first name, and Nadia didn't think that had been a slip of the tongue. Dante might not have come up swinging after Nate hit him, but it seemed like he was being deliberately provoking. Maybe he hoped Nate would throw another punch so he could show off his own manly prowess. But though Nate didn't make a habit of controlling his quick temper, tonight he kept it in check.

"Fine," he said through gritted teeth. "I'll go. But if you're lying to me, it'll turn out very, very bad for you." Dante rolled his eyes at the threat. "So when and where is this meeting?"

"The where is a secret," Dante said. "I'll take you there. Take your phones with you to bed tonight. Sometime after midnight, you'll get a call from me. Nadia first, then you."

"Remember when I told you you could call me Mr. Hayes?" Nate said. "Well, you can call *her* Miss Lake."

Ordinarily, Nate wasn't nearly this uptight about protocol, and he'd be perfectly happy to allow the informal address. But it was obvious he and Dante rubbed each other the wrong way, and Nadia thought once again her services as peacekeeper might be needed.

"In there," Dante said, jerking his thumb at the apartment behind him, "I'm a servant and I'll address you both as such. Here and now, I'm your co-conspirator, and we'll talk as equals or we won't talk at all."

"Fine," Nate said, dissatisfied. "But even as a supposed 'equal,' you don't know me well enough to call me Nate."

"Fine," Dante said in a similar tone. "Nathaniel. I'll ring you and Nadia after midnight. You'll sneak down to the service entrance, and I'll be waiting for you there in a white panel van. Nathaniel, you should wear your Basement disguise. And Nadia, I'll have a disguise for you in the van."

Nate was shaking his head violently. "You are *not* taking Nadia into the Basement. I'm willing to take whatever risks are necessary myself, but she's been through enough already."

Nadia's emotions were a confusing swirl. Fear at the thought of venturing into the Basement at night. Gratitude that Nate still cared about her enough to object. And determination to make her own decisions about what she would and would not risk.

"Bishop's instructions were very clear," Dante said. "Either you both go, or neither of you goes."

"We can both go somewhere other than the Basement."

"You're under the mistaken impression that this is a negotiation. It isn't. It's a take-it-or-leave-it deal."

Nate opened his mouth to protest, but Nadia put her hand on his arm to stop him.

"I'll go, Nate," she said quietly, ignoring the flutter of fear in her belly. "If that's the only way Bishop will see you, then I'll do it. There has to be a reason he's changed his mind about seeing you, and I suspect it's something we need to know. I'm already in this up to my eyeballs anyway."

Nate put on his stubborn face, which she knew all too well. "I am not taking you into the Basement."

"Yes, you are," Nadia said more firmly, then turned her attention to Dante. "I presume you won't be parading me through the streets for everyone to see." The predators couldn't hurt her if they didn't know she was there.

Dante gave her an approving smile. "No. We'll be discreet. The disguise is just a precaution. If all goes well, it'll be only the good guys who see you."

"If all goes well," Nate muttered darkly. "Nothing has gone well since the moment I came back to life. Why should I expect that to change?"

"We're doing this," Nadia said. "We have to." She tried not to think about what she would tell Mosely the next time he talked to her, which, with Nate's visit to her apartment tonight, would no doubt be tomorrow. If she'd managed to convince him of her ignorance today, she wasn't sure how she'd do it tomorrow. But that was getting way ahead of herself.

Thinking of Mosely reminded Nadia about the new tracker

she was supposed to plant on Nate, and she reached into her pocket to draw it out.

"By the way," she said, "I'm supposed to plant this on you. Will you take it with you when you leave here tonight so it looks like I've done what I'm supposed to?"

Nate took the envelope from her hand and nodded. "Sure." He tucked the envelope into his jacket pocket, then reached out and took both her hands, drawing her closer to him. She looked up and met his eyes. "Are you sure you want to do this?" he asked, squeezing her hands tightly. "I've put you in so much danger already . . ."

Nadia squeezed his hands back and gave him a smile. Then she freed one of her hands and reached up to smooth the worry line that had appeared between his brows. However angry he was about her deception, there was no denying that he still cared about her, and she was beginning to hope that she hadn't lost him as a friend after all.

"I'm sure."

Nate pulled her into a hug that she suspected was painful, thanks to the battering his body had taken.

nate didn't even try to sleep. He wasn't sure he could manage it under the circumstances, and he had a sneaking suspicion that if he *did* manage it, he wouldn't wake up when Dante called. How pathetic would it be if he made all this effort to find Kurt and then slept through his chance when it finally came?

Assuming, of course, that Dante was telling the truth. The guy had set Nate's teeth on edge the moment he'd laid eyes on him, and nothing that had transpired since had changed his opinion. He didn't like the easy, casual way Dante talked to Nadia, as if they were equals, and he *hated* that Dante was putting Nadia in more danger, even if the request/order had come from Kurt. Not that Nate was a snob and thought Employees should bow and scrape when in the presence of Executives, of course. He hated all that bowing and scraping stuff. Maybe it would have been different if Dante hadn't been so good-looking—or if Nate didn't think Nadia *noticed* he was so good-looking.

Nate laughed at himself. Was he actually *jealous?* He hadn't been able to put a name to his feelings on the rooftop earlier, but now that he tried the word on for size, he found that it fit.

The laugh died quickly. What did he expect Nadia to do? Stay a virgin her entire life to protect his delicate sensibilities? He didn't plan to "cleave only unto her" when they were married, but somehow he'd never allowed himself to think about what *she* might do. Didn't she have as much right to look for love as he did? She had never once shown any sign that she was jealous of his relationship with Kurt. He had no right to be jealous if she'd been hanging all over Dante, which she hadn't. Just because she would be his wife someday didn't mean she was *his.*

The past few days had been brutal, and he wouldn't wish them on his worst enemy. But the fact was, they'd forced him to take a good look at himself, at how he treated those he loved, and he didn't like what he saw.

Nate grunted in frustration. He had no use for wallowing, no matter how much he'd have liked to indulge himself. He had to be ready when the call came, and it took some serious time to transform himself from the Chairman Heir into the Ghost.

Nate was tired enough that it took him twice as long as usual to get dressed and costumed, and he was still fussing with his makeup when his phone buzzed. He glanced down at the phone to confirm it was Dante's summons, then took a critical look at himself in the mirror. He needed another coat of powder on his face to perfect the bluish-pale complexion of the Ghost, but he was afraid Dante would get impatient and leave. Besides, the longer Nate spent fixing his makeup, the longer Dante was alone with Nadia in the van.

Rolling his eyes at himself for his ridiculous jealousy, Nate decided his disguise was good enough and began the simultaneously tedious and hair-raising task of sneaking out of his apartment, leaving Mosely's tracker on his pillow.

As promised, the white panel van was sitting by the curb near the service entrance, its hazard lights blinking. The van was an ancient, dinged-up piece of crap, but, even so, Nate couldn't imagine someone of Dante's station being able to afford a scooter, much less a van. Maybe the vehicle belonged to someone higher up in the food chain in this mysterious resistance movement Nate was just learning about.

The van was stopped in a pool of shadow, but as Nate peered out cautiously to see if the coast was clear, he could see that the back doors of the van were ajar. Nate waited until there wasn't another car in sight, then sprinted across the short distance, belatedly thinking that jumping into the back of a panel van without checking to see who and what was inside first might be a tad on the reckless side. He was taking a hell of a lot on faith tonight, and after everything that had happened, he didn't have a whole lot of faith to spare.

The back door swung fully open just as Nate's second thoughts were beginning to slow him down, and Dante reached out to offer Nate a hand up. At least, Nate *thought* it was Dante behind all the face paint. Nate hesitated only a moment before taking the offered hand and climbing into the back of the van.

Before the doors had even finished closing, the van took off, abruptly enough that Nate staggered and had to balance himself with a hand on the ceiling.

The back of the van was empty but for a handful of over-turned milk crates and a duffel bag. Nadia sat on one of those crates, and Nate's jaw dropped open when he got a good look at her. She was dressed in a shiny black catsuit that made her usually willowy form look lush and curvy. A silver chain belt circled her hips, tinkling charms hanging from a link here and there. Her blond hair was hidden beneath a neon-pink wig, and a band of pink and black face paint crossed her face over her eyes like a blindfold.

No two ways about it. She looked *hot*. And not at all like Nadia Lake, the sweet-tempered, genteel Executive's daughter.

"Down, boy," Dante muttered, and Nate blushed under his makeup.

Nadia smiled at him tentatively as he made his way to the milk crate closest to her and sat down. He reached over and took her hand, giving it what he hoped was a comforting squeeze.

"You look amazing," he told her, telling himself that he shouldn't feel embarrassed that for a moment he'd found his future bride attractive despite his sexual preferences.

Nadia cocked her head at him, eyes taking in his alter ego. One thing he knew for sure was that he did *not* look amazing. The point of his costume was to make him look different, not good. Maybe there were people in the Basement who thought skin the color of skim milk and black lipstick on a guy attractive—Kurt seemed to like it, after all—but to Nadia, he had to look bizarre.

"You look . . ." She thought about it a moment. "Wild," she finally finished, and Nate felt strangely pleased by the term.

Dante came to sit on another milk crate, and Nate frowned at him.

"If you're back here, then who's driving?" he asked, uncomfortable at the thought of some unknown other being in control of the vehicle. The fact that Dante looked sexy and exotic in his Basement disguise while Nate looked like a freak wasn't helping his nerves much, either.

"No one you know," Dante said, but didn't elaborate.

Whoever was driving didn't give a damn about his passengers' comfort, jackrabbiting through intersections and taking turns more sharply than necessary. The van banged its way through a pothole so deep Nate thought they were going to overturn. All three of them reached out to steady themselves, and when they did, Nate saw the butt of a gun sticking out of the inside pocket of the loose jacket Dante was wearing. Dante met his eyes and practically dared him to comment, but Nate managed to keep his thoughts to himself. It wasn't a bad idea to have an armed escort when traveling into the Basement, and he had a feeling Dante knew how to use it.

Nate wasn't wearing a watch, but he had the sense that they drove far longer than it should have taken to get to the Basement from his apartment. Either Dante had lied to them about their destination—which seemed unlikely, considering the costumes—or the driver was taking a deliberately circuitous route, perhaps to make sure they weren't followed. Nate tried to guess where they were by listening for clues, but there were no telltale sounds. Or if there were, he didn't recognize them.

After a while, the van's progress slowed considerably, the road getting rougher under its wheels, and Nate guessed they'd finally crossed into the Basement. He expected the ride to end shortly after they crossed the border, but the van continued on, the ill-maintained roads doing a hatchet job on its suspension. Nate gritted his teeth to keep from biting his tongue with any of the unexpected impacts.

At last, the van came to a stop, and the driver pounded on the wall between the cab and the back.

"We're here," Dante said, and Nate's heart leapt into his throat.

Nate wasn't sure what scared him more: the thought that he was about to see Kurt again, or the thought that he *wasn't*. His pulse raced, and his palms were damp with sweat as he waited for Dante to open the back doors and let them out. Nadia put a comforting hand on his shoulder, sensing his anxiety.

"It'll be all right," she murmured in his ear, her voice too low for Dante to overhear. "Whatever happens, it'll be all right."

But Nate knew there were no guarantees for either of them.

CHAPTER SIXTEEN

nate hopped out of the van behind Dante, then turned to help Nadia down. She wobbled a bit on the stiletto heels of the knee-high boots she was wearing, and Nate decided no matter how much he liked the outfit, he wanted to punch Dante again for making her wear it. Then he took a couple of steps forward to get out of the shadow of the van and take a look around.

They were in a dark, crumbling underpass, the van parked horizontally across the road, blocking any potential traffic. Though judging by the state of the road, traffic here was far from common. There were more potholes than asphalt, and grass and weeds had grown up in the gaps. A storm drain on one side of the road was backed up with litter and unknown debris, packed so tightly it formed a stagnant lake even though it hadn't rained since Nate had awakened as a Replica. The walls were thick with gang tags, all done in red spray paint.

There were no lights in the underpass, so only the ambient light of the city made the road and the walls by the entrance visible. Nate could see the same ambient light from the other end of the underpass, but in between was a menacing pool of impenetrable darkness. A tiny spot of red glowed briefly in that darkness, then went out. There was a sound

Nate took for the crushing of a cigarette butt underfoot, then the echoing of footsteps.

Nate reached for Nadia's hand as the sound of those measured footsteps approached, not sure if he meant to give or seek comfort. Maybe a little of both.

At first, Nate didn't recognize the figure that emerged from the darkness. He'd been looking for Kurt's familiar scruffy hair, for the rings in his ears and the tattoos on his upper body that he displayed whenever he wasn't in uniform. He *hadn't* been looking for a kohl-eyed bald guy wearing a torn crimson muscle shirt that displayed a nipple ring and no tattoos. It took a couple more steps into the light before Nate was able to see past the trappings, to recognize Kurt's unique way of moving, though even that was camouflaged by the high-heeled boots he was wearing and the sway they put in his hips. Kurt had too many hard edges to ever pull off a truly androgynous look, but this was a close approximation.

Emotion clogged his throat, but Nate wasn't sure what he would say anyway. He wanted to cross the distance between them, but the lingering aches in his belly and back reminded him that he didn't know his boyfriend as well as he'd thought he did. And though Nadia might not have come right out and said it, Nate was aware of the implication that Kurt had deliberately infiltrated his household on a mission from his resistance movement, not because he was in love.

Kurt looked him over, frowning when he saw Nate was still holding Nadia's hand. Nadia tried to let go, but Nate squeezed harder. Kurt had no right to disapprove. For all that had gone wrong between them, Nadia was Nate's friend, and he needed one. It remained to be seen if that was a role Kurt could ever fulfill again.

Kurt was giving Nadia the evil eye, so Nate put himself between them to draw Kurt's full attention.

"Don't look at her like that," Nate said, and was surprised at how cold his voice came out.

Kurt made a little snorting sound and stepped even closer, until he was only an arm's length away.

"You are such a fucking pain in my ass," Kurt said.

Behind Nate, Nadia gasped in indignation, but she couldn't see the little spark in Kurt's eyes when he spoke. He might very well mean the words he said, but Nate would stake his life there was at least affection behind them, if not love. Something tight inside him loosened just a fraction.

"Says the man who stole all my money, paid to have some thugs beat me up—probably with the very money he stole from me, no less—and tried to convince me he stabbed me to death."

"Like I said. A pain in my ass." But there was a hint of a rueful smile on Kurt's lips, and he opened his arms.

Nate had a thousand and one questions, and a thousand and one doubts, but he couldn't refuse the invitation. He stepped willingly into Kurt's arms and didn't complain when the hug got too tight and made his bruises ache. For that one moment, he allowed himself to forget everything, to simply revel in the fact that Kurt was here and he was safe. It felt so good to hold him that Nate's eyes burned.

Nate forced himself to end the hug. The lack of the vigorous back thumping that was the trademark of the guy hug was probably already making Dante look at them askance. He backed off a little, trying to see Kurt with dispassionate eyes, to judge how much he really knew about his boyfriend and how much was just wishful thinking.

An awkward silence descended. There were so many

questions Nate wanted to ask that he couldn't pick just one, and Kurt didn't look like he had any better idea where to start.

Since Nate couldn't settle on which important question to ask, he settled for an unimportant one, just to break the silence.

"So did you come down with a raging case of head lice or what?"

Kurt grimaced and ran his hand over his bald head. "Most people change their hair by dying it or wearing wigs," he said. "Wigs come off, and dye stinks, so I went a different route."

Nate had to admit, it was a good disguise, especially with the added touch of the boots to change both his height and his gait. Even expecting him as he had, Nate had taken a few moments to recognize him. The bald head and the kohl-lined eyes made him look older and far more dangerous. Forgetting for a moment about his audience, Nate reached out and touched Kurt's chest where it was exposed by the rips in his shirt.

"And what happened to your tattoos?" He felt a pang of loss, though he'd always claimed to hate them. But they were a part of the Kurt he'd known and loved, and he missed them on this near stranger standing in front of him.

"It's just makeup," Kurt said. "Having them removed would have taken more time than I had." He gave Nate the same head-to-toe examination Nate had just given him. "You still look the same. Except for the shitty makeup job. Is that a Replica thing, or were you in a hurry?"

"In a hurry," Nate mumbled, and wondered if the fact that he was a Replica had made it easier for Kurt to have him savaged. Maybe he figured that the Nate he knew and loved was dead, and this Replica was less than human. The rioting crowd had certainly thought so. Could Kurt love a Replica? Then again, Nate had no proof besides a hint of affection in his eyes that Kurt had ever loved him at all.

It was time to get some answers. "Tell me what's going on," Nate demanded. "Tell me why—" He choked on his words.

Kurt gave his shoulder a brief squeeze. "Let's go sit in the van and talk. That'll be more comfortable than standing out here, no?"

Nate looked over Kurt's shoulder, unable to meet his eyes, and that's when he saw the minute glow of a cigarette in the depths of the darkness from which Kurt had emerged. A chill of alarm traveled down his spine.

"There's someone out there," he said, trying to keep his voice low and steady as he moved sideways to put himself between Nadia and the threat.

Kurt followed his gaze, but didn't look alarmed. "My hosts," he said, turning back to Nate. He waved at the graffiti on the walls. "We're in the very heart of Debasement here, in Red Death territory." Kurt plucked at his red shirt. "I'm an honorary member. As long as the money holds out, at least. They're here as backup in case anything goes wrong." He darted a glance at Nadia. "I'll explain everything, but it's going to take a while, so let's go in and sit."

The back of the van didn't exactly make for cozy seating arrangements. The milk crates were hard and low, and Nate had seen candles shine brighter than the little emergency lights the driver turned on. But the cavelike interior did feel more secure and private than the underpass, and Nate was pretty sure Kurt was going to say things he should be sitting down to hear. Nate sat on one of the crates. Kurt sat across from him. Nadia sat beside Nate after moving her crate a little closer to his. He gave her a small smile, glad for the solidarity.

"Let me know when you're ready for me," Dante said, still outside the van. Then he closed the doors.

Nate raised his eyebrow at Kurt.

"I'm pretty sure Dante suspects about us," Kurt explained, "but I don't want him to be sure, and I don't want to have to watch what I say. I told him we needed some private time, just the three of us."

"All right," Nate said, nerves fluttering as he realized he was so close to getting the answers he'd been searching for.

"You have to promise to keep your cool."

Nate opened his mouth to give a glib promise, then shut it again to rethink his words. If there was one thing he had learned in the recent days, it was that his temper had hurt the people around him without him even noticing. But making an empty promise to control it wasn't the way to make things better.

"I'm going on about four hours of sleep in the last couple of days, and my whole body hurts from the beating your friends gave me last night," he said. His temper tried to stir at the reminder, but he shoved it ruthlessly down. "I'll try not to fly off the handle, but I'm hanging by a thread here." His voice got raspy toward the end. Nadia reached over and took his hand again at the same time that Kurt leaned forward and put a hand on his knee. The two of them shared a glance Nate couldn't interpret, then Kurt squeezed his knee and let go.

"I'm real sorry about that, Nate," he said. "Angel promised me they wouldn't hurt you too bad. And it was the only way I could think of to make you back off."

"It might have worked if you hadn't sent me the tracker," Nadia said.

Kurt made a face and rubbed his bald head. "Yeah. Guess Nate's not the only one with a temper after all. Stupidest thing I've ever done."

"Why?" Nate demanded. "Why were you so desperate to keep me away?"

Kurt met his eyes grimly. "Because it was Dirk Mosely who killed you."

Nate's jaw dropped in shock, and Nadia gasped, letting go of his hand to cover her mouth.

"You 'n' me heard something while we were "—Kurt's glance darted quickly to Nadia and back—"together. Something that Mosely was talking about with your father. We were in a supply closet. We decided to get out as soon as we heard them come in the room outside. I don't know about you, but I couldn't make out much of what they were saying, except they were talking about someone named Thea."

The words sent another bolt of shock through Nate's system.

"Anyway, you boosted me up through a ceiling panel. You were going to follow me, but you heard something else. Something that really rocked you. You made shooing motions at me and pulled a joint out of your pocket. I guess that was supposed to be your excuse for what you were doing in the closet if they caught you. Which they did.

"I closed the ceiling panel right as Mosely was opening the door, but there was a little gap I could see through." Kurt shuddered and closed his eyes. "I couldn't do anything." He shook his head, eyes still closed. "I didn't know I had to. Didn't ever think he would *kill* you, for fuck's sake."

Nate shook his head in denial.

"That *can't* be what happened," Nadia said breathlessly. "You said Nate's father was there, too."

Kurt opened his eyes, and the pain and sympathy in them conveyed his message before his words did. "Yeah, he was. He's the one who gave Mosely the order."

CHAPTER SEVENTEEN

nate couldn't talk, couldn't move, couldn't fucking breathe.

"I don't know exactly what you heard," Kurt said in a voice so gentle it hurt. "But whatever it was, it was so big your father was prepared to kill you to keep it secret. Keeping in mind that from his point of view, your death was only temporary."

Kurt had probably meant that reminder to soften the blow, but it had the opposite effect. As far as his father was concerned, it didn't matter what happened to *Nate,* as long as he, the Chairman, didn't have to lose his heir.

The paralysis exploded into a kind of rage Nate had never felt before. He turned and punched the wall of the van with his already-bruised knuckles. He was dimly aware that it hurt like hell, but the rage wasn't finished with him, so he did it again. He tried for a third time, but someone grabbed his arm. He tried to jerk free but couldn't, which meant it was Kurt restraining him, not Nadia.

The rage inside was still rampaging, so he whirled around and threw a decidedly awkward left-handed punch somewhere in the vicinity of Kurt's face, not really trying to hurt him, just trying to make him let go. The blow glanced off Kurt's chin, but Kurt kept his grip, and when Nate tried again, he found himself jerked off the milk crate and wrestled to the floor of the van.

"Stop it, stop it!" Nadia was crying, but Nate didn't know if she was talking to him or Kurt.

"Don't make me hurt you," Kurt growled, his lips so close to Nate's ear he could feel Kurt's breath on his skin.

Nate tried a feeble twist, but he was facedown on the floor, and Kurt had him thoroughly pinned. His battered knuckles throbbed, sending shooting pains up his arm, and Kurt's weight on his back wasn't doing his old bruises any good, either. The rage bled out of him as fast as it had swooped in, replaced by pain, and Nate went limp. A sob tried to push its way up his throat, and he swallowed hard in a desperate attempt to hold it back. Even so, there was a telltale wetness on his face.

Kurt pressed a kiss to the side of his head, then rolled off of him. Nate might not have had the will or energy to move, except neither Kurt nor Nadia was willing to let him crawl into the hole of self-pity he'd dug himself. Kurt "helped" him up, and Nadia threw her arms around him in a hug tight enough to hurt. Nate didn't care that it hurt, pulling her even closer, grateful for her presence even as he was embarrassed by his own weakness.

"Everything all right in there?" Dante called from outside the van, and even Nate had to admit the bastard showed an admirable amount of restraint not opening the doors to see what was happening.

"We're fine," Kurt answered. Nate almost laughed at the absurdity of the statement.

Kurt sat cross-legged in front of him on the floor of the van, a sad smile on his face. "If that's you trying to keep control of yourself, I'd hate to see when you really let go."

Nadia made an indignant sound. "How dare you make jokes at a time like this?"

"It's all right," Nate said to Nadia. His voice was raspy and his throat hurt. He must have shouted more than he'd realized. There was no lightening this particular mood with jokes, but the normalcy of it was comforting. "Sorry I hit you," he said to Kurt.

Kurt snorted. "*Tried* to hit me, you mean. You can't punch for shit." He grimaced. "At least, not with your left. Let's see that right hand. You beat the van down pretty good."

Nate felt the blood rushing to his face and hoped his makeup hid the embarrassed blush. As losses of control went, that had been pretty epic. "It's fine," he mumbled.

"No it's not," Nadia countered, extricating herself from his arms and maneuvering his right hand into the light.

The knuckles were swollen and split, and blood trickled down his fingers. Kurt gave a low whistle of appreciation.

"Yeah, you showed this van what for all right. Can you move your fingers?"

Wiggling his fingers hurt, but he could do it. "It's not all from the van," he admitted, wondering if Kurt would be appalled or impressed. "I, uh, kind of punched Dante earlier, too."

Kurt gave him a look of surprise, then burst out laughing. "I've wanted to do that a couple of times myself."

"I'm glad you *boys* are finding this so funny," Nadia said scathingly.

Kurt sighed. "Sweetheart, sometimes it's either laugh or cry. We aren't supposed to cry, so we laugh instead." He reached across and smoothed a hand over Nate's damp cheek.

Nate's costume was pretty much ruined. He hated to think what his face must look like with tear tracks through the powder, and his wig had come off and somehow ended up underneath him when he and Kurt had wrestled. He could put it back on, but it looked more like roadkill than hair. He supposed he was lucky his contacts hadn't come out when the waterworks started.

"Why wouldn't you tell me any of this before now?" he asked.

"Because Mosely doesn't know I didn't hear the whole conversation. I made some noise when I ran for it, so they knew belatedly that I was there, but they don't know what I heard. If Mosely has any reason to think you and I have been in touch, then he'll think I've told you whatever this big god-damn secret is. He killed you once to keep it hidden. I have no doubt he'd do it again. It would hurt the Chairman's pock-etbook to animate another Replica, but he'd rather do that than have you know the big secret."

"So you . . . you did it to protect me?" Nate put a hand on his sore stomach, trying not to remember Angel's goons hit-ting and kicking him there. As physically painful as it had been, the emotional pain of thinking Kurt had meant to hurt him was far, far worse.

"Well, me too. You did end up leading Mosely's men straight to Angel's place. Angel knew the Red Death had taken me in, and if he'd questioned her, that would have sucked." He gave Nadia a cold, angry look. "I don't care why you did it. I don't forgive you."

Nate had always thought of Nadia as somewhat . . . timid. He understood that a girl of her station had to exercise a good deal of caution—especially one who was expected to marry the Chairman Heir—but he had often found that caution rather tiresome. But either recent events had changed her, or Nate hadn't known her as well as he thought.

Nadia didn't wilt under Kurt's accusatory gaze. Her lip curled in something that looked almost like a sneer as she put an arm around Nate's shoulders. "Well *I* don't forgive *you* for hurting Nate like you did. And I really don't give a damn what you think of me. If Nate didn't care about you so much, I'd hand you over to Mosely in a heartbeat."

Nate didn't believe that, and he suspected Kurt didn't, either. But Kurt held up his hands in a conciliatory gesture.

"Fine. We understand each other."

"No, we don't," Nadia said firmly. "After all the fuss you made to keep Nate from finding you, why all of a sudden did you arrange this meeting? And why did you insist *I* come?"

Kurt grimaced and looked away. "Because I really fucked up when I sent that note." He turned back to them. "But we should get Dante back in here for the rest of this discussion."

"Is that really necessary?"

"'Fraid so," Kurt responded, then looked Nate up and down. "Let's get you straightened up a bit." He picked up the wig, gave it a close look, then dropped it back on the floor of the van. "Fuck that." He then reached out and started pulling out the pins that held Nate's real hair back.

Nadia rose up on her knees and helped, and Nate felt like a monkey being groomed.

"I can do it myself," he said, trying to reach up to his head, but Kurt batted his hand aside.

"Not as fast as we can do it for you," he said.

Moments later, Kurt was ruffling his hair. Then he sat back on his heels. "Better," he declared, then started smoothing out the powder on Nate's face as best he could.

Nate took a deep breath, trying to calm what remained of his inner turmoil. The touch of Kurt's hands helped. There were still a lot of unanswered questions left between them, questions that couldn't be settled in the presence of another person, even Nadia. But Nate was sure he wasn't imagining the affection in Kurt's touch or the regret in his eyes. Maybe Kurt had first infiltrated his household as part of a mission, but Nate had to believe it had become more than that to him. And if Kurt distrusted Nate for being a Replica, he certainly was showing no sign of it.

"We good for now?" Kurt asked quietly.

Nate nodded and hauled himself off the floor of the van and back onto one of the milk crates. Nadia sat next to him once more, and Kurt opened the back doors of the van to let Dante in. Nate stiffened as Dante took in the scene—Nate's dead wig, his real hair, his messed-up makeup, his busted hand—and swore he'd throw his attempts at self-control right out the window if the bastard said one wrong word. But the guy was smarter than he looked, keeping his mouth shut as he and Kurt sat on the crates across from Nate and Nadia.

"You asked why I changed my mind since last night," Kurt said. "Like I said, I really fucked up by sending that note."

"No," Dante interrupted. "I did, by getting caught."

"Whatever." He turned another glare at Nadia. "I let our little spy here know I hadn't left Paxco."

Nate opened his mouth to defend Nadia, but she beat him to the punch.

"You really want to go there with the finger pointing?" she asked. "Because you've been spying on him a lot longer than I have."

"I didn't—"

"Stop it," Dante interrupted, making a chopping motion with his hand. "Let's try to get through this with a minimum of bickering. We've all had our moments in this mess."

"Who died and made you boss?" Kurt grumbled, but at least he didn't light into Nadia anymore.

"The problem," Dante said to Nadia, "is that Mosely thinks you might have been dishonest with him when he spoke to you this afternoon. He isn't sure, because he says you were drunk when he talked to you."

Nate turned and gave Nadia a startled look. She'd accept a drink now and then, but she never seemed to particularly enjoy them, and he'd never seen her so much as tipsy, much less drunk.

Nadia gave a half smile. "I knew I couldn't act normal around him while I was lying, so I figured I'd give him an alternative explanation as to why."

Both Kurt and Dante looked impressed by the tactic, and Nate felt an absurd surge of pride in her. This morning, he'd been ready to write her out of his life entirely, but somehow between then and now, he'd stopped blaming her. She'd had no choice but to do what she'd done, and if she'd tried to confide in him, he probably *would* have confronted Mosely. Or his father.

Nate's mind skittered away from that thought, not willing to deal with what his own father had done to him. Not yet. Maybe not ever.

"It was a good idea," Dante told her. "But he still suspects, and you can't be drunk every time he talks to you."

Nadia was sitting close enough that Nate could feel the shiver that ran through her. If Mosely thought she was lying to him, then he'd go to extreme measures to force her to talk. Once upon a time, Nate would have trusted Nadia's station to protect her from the likes of Dirk Mosely, but now he knew better.

"The problem is worse than you think," Dante continued, sharing an unhappy look with Kurt. "We, er, haven't told the leader of our cell about our indiscretion with the note, but if he ever gets wind of it and thinks that Nadia might be taken in for more rigorous questioning . . ." He looked uncomfortable and let his voice trail off.

Nate was a little slow on the uptake. He blamed it on lack of sleep and emotional exhaustion, but he honestly didn't know what Dante was getting at. Until Nadia finished Dante's sentence for him.

"You think he'll have me killed."

CHAPTER EIGHTEEN

strangely, the threat to her life didn't frighten Nadia as much as it should have. Maybe she'd been on the receiving end of too many threats lately and they had lost their power to shock. Or maybe it was just easier to face a threat to her own person than to think something she said or did might cause Mosely to hurt Rory and Corinne.

The same was not true of Nate.

"That's not going to happen," he said, as if just saying the words could make it true. "None of this is Nadia's fault, and it's just wrong that she should be in danger because of it."

Nadia leaned into Nate's body, more grateful than she could say for his staunch support even as she was mildly exasperated by it. Surely by now he should have figured out that right and wrong had nothing to do with it.

"That's why we didn't tell anyone what we did," Dante said, then made a face. "Well, that and we wanted to cover our asses."

"The upshot is we're running out of time," Bishop said. "If we sit back on our heels and wait for things to shake out, either Mosely is going to learn everything he needs to know from Nadia, or she's going to meet with an unfortunate end. Not that I'd be heartbroken," he said to Nadia, "but Nate seems to care about you."

When Nadia had expressed a similar sentiment to Bishop,

she hadn't really meant it. She was pretty sure, however, that Bishop was dead serious. Nate might have forgiven her for her betrayal, but Bishop hadn't, and maybe never would.

"So what is it you suggest we do?" Nate asked.

"The only way out is to get Mosely before he gets us. We need to get him to incriminate himself so much that even the Chairman can't save him."

"How about telling the world that he stabbed me to death and tried to pin it on *you*?" Nate said, but Nadia was sure he already knew it wouldn't be that easy.

Bishop flashed him a sardonic smile. "Because *everyone* would take my word for it over Mosely's," he said with a roll of his eyes.

"Um, I recorded the last interview I had with Mosely," Nadia said. "I have a hidden transmitter in one of my earrings." She reached up reflexively to tug on her earlobe, but of course she wasn't wearing them now. "I've got him making some pretty ugly threats." She sighed. "But it's not enough," she conceded before they could tell her so. "All he has to do is say he didn't mean it. People might not like his tactics, but no one's going to be really outraged. Not when he was investigating a case of treason."

Bishop looked at her like she might be more interesting than he'd originally thought. "You've really taken to this spying shit, haven't you?"

"Are we going to start that again?" she responded. "You have no room whatsoever to throw stones."

"Cut it out, both of you," Nate said. "We've got more important things to talk about."

"Mosely isn't stupid," Dante said, ignoring the byplay. "I don't think he'd ever guess you were recording him, but he's still not going to say anything to you he's afraid might bite him in the ass. But whatever he's up to, it's sanctioned by the Chairman, and the Chairman gets regular reports. I know because I have to send copies of my reports directly to him when I send them to Mosely. He's watching this case like a hawk, and I'll bet you Mosely talks to *him* as freely as you like."

"What are you suggesting, exactly?" Nate asked in a suspicious voice.

"I'm suggesting we take Nadia's bugging idea a step further." He reached into his pocket and pulled out a slim, compact case, and Nadia didn't have much trouble guessing what would be in it. He opened it to reveal a tiny black dot nestled in white foam. A tiny black dot that closely resembled the microtransmitter hidden in Nadia's earring. There was a moment of tense silence as everyone stared at the harmless-looking dot.

"You want me to plant that on Mosely," Nadia finally said, unable to keep the quaver of fear out of her voice. Passively recording their conversations was one thing, but planting a bug on him was another entirely.

"No!" Nate said suddenly and emphatically. "Nadia's been through more than enough already. If you want to listen in on Mosely's conversations with my father, then I'll plant the bug on my father."

"No," Nadia and Bishop said simultaneously.

Nate looked back and forth between her and Bishop in confusion. If he could see himself, he might not be so confused. The tendons in his neck stood out starkly with his tension, and even under the remains of the powder, she could see the angry flush on his cheeks. Never mind the look in his eyes, which could reduce the unwary to a pile of ash.

"You don't dare go near your father right now, Nate," she said as gently as she could.

"What's that supposed to mean?" he asked.

"He's not Mr. Sensitivity, but even *he* would take one look at you and know something was wrong. And I don't think it's such a stretch to imagine him figuring out what that could be."

Nate gave a frustrated grunt. "I know I haven't exactly impressed anyone with my self-control, but I can do this. I'm a little . . . stressed right now, but give me a few hours to absorb everything and I'll be fine." He made a face. "Okay, not fine. But I'll be able to fake it better."

Nadia reached out and took the bug from Dante's hand. Nate grabbed her wrist to stop her from putting it in her pocket. She closed her fist around the case so that he couldn't easily pluck it out of her hands.

"I have to do this, Nate," she said, trying to free her wrist, but he didn't let go.

"No. If I get killed, there'll be another Replica, so I won't be *dead* dead."

Nadia's eyes burned, but she held back the tears that wanted to come. "*This* you would be." She'd liked, maybe even loved, Nate Hayes for much of her life, but the man he'd become over the last few days meant more to her by far than the boy he'd been before.

"I know you want to be the hero," Bishop said, and there was a slight edge in his voice, "but we have to be smart about this. You suck at hiding your feelings, and you aren't going to get good at it overnight. I don't know if even the best actor in the world could act normal around his dad when he knows the old man ordered him killed. If you try it, you'll give everything away, and you and Nadia and me and Dante will all go down together."

"Thanks for the vote of confidence," Nate spat, but though the words were angry, the look in his eyes was more hurt.

"Sometimes the truth hurts, but you've got to hear it anyway."

"Bishop's right," Nadia said, wishing there was something she could say to make him feel better. "You can't face your father knowing what you know."

He turned his ire on her, still holding her wrist. "Oh, and you can face Mosely knowing he's the one who killed me?"

She raised her chin. "I've faced him knowing he would torture me if he thought he needed to, and that he would hurt a couple of innocent children to punish me. I've brought a recording device into our meetings knowing that if he found it on me, he would destroy me, and maybe my entire family as well."

"But he already suspects you!"

"Yes, about that," Dante said. "When you meet with him, you should tell him at least *some* of the truth. If he thinks you're telling him important secrets, he'll be less likely to wonder what you're *not* telling him."

"I said she is not doing this," Nate said before she could answer. "Why don't *you* plant the recorder on him? He's *your* boss after all!"

Dante gave him a look of exaggerated patience. "Yes, he's my boss. And I'm *undercover*. If I chat him up or go to the security station, that would ruin my cover. I haven't talked to him in person since I was given this mission."

While Nate and Dante exchanged glares, Nadia reached over with her left hand and grabbed the bug out of her right. By the time the staring contest was over, the bug was tucked in Nadia's pocket. Not that Nate couldn't find it and take it away from her if he set his mind to it, but maybe the minor slight of hand would help convince him she was capable of doing the job.

"Look," Bishop said, "no one likes this, but if we don't do something and do it fast, we're all going down. If Nadia's willing to do it, then you have to let her."

It was Nadia's turn to let out an undignified snort. "Nate doesn't get to 'let' me do anything. It's my decision."

Nate finally noticed that the bug wasn't in her hand anymore, and he narrowed his eyes at her. "I'm your future husband, and I *forbid* you to do this."

Nadia couldn't help laughing. "You don't honestly think that's going to work, do you?"

Nate let go of her wrist with a grunt of disgust. He made a gesture as if to punch the side of the van again in frustration, then thought better of it. "I hate this," he muttered with feeling.

Nadia didn't exactly love it herself. There was already so much riding on her shoulders she could hardly bear up under the weight. Now she would add Nate's life and the lives of Dante and Bishop and anyone in the resistance they might implicate if they were questioned to the list of responsibilities she carried. The fate of so many rested in her ability to converse with Dirk Mosely tomorrow as if she didn't know exactly what kind of a monster he was or who held his leash, and her ability to plant a bug on him without him noticing.

"What do I have to do?" she asked, pulling the little box out of her pocket again and opening it to inspect the tiny bug.

Dante gave her a nod of approval. "It's heat activated. Hold it in your hand for a minute or two to warm it up, and it'll start transmitting." He took the box from her and carefully lifted the foam out, revealing a strip of thin, translucent tape underneath. "Peel the backing off one side of the tape and stick it to your hand. Then peel off the other side," he put the foam back in, "and stick the bug to it like so." He put his hand briefly down on top of the bug to demonstrate. "The other side of the bug is sticky. Way stickier than the tape. You'll have to be careful not to let it touch anything—including your hand—until you're ready to put it on Mosely."

Nadia nodded and took the box back, trying not to think about all the million ways this could go wrong.

"Obviously," Dante continued, "it's best if you can stick it to his skin somewhere. But it would be easier and safer to stick it to his jacket and hope he keeps wearing it until he gives the Chairman his daily update."

Nadia nodded again. She could find some excuse to grab hold of Mosely's jacket, surely. Maybe in the course of an impassioned plea to release her from her obligations.

I can do this, she told herself, hoping to make herself believe it.

"And what do you want me to tell him?" she asked aloud. "How much truth is too much?"

"Tell him about getting the tracker and the stupid note," Bishop said. "The idea that you've heard from me will give him a real hard-on."

"Hey!" Nate said, giving Bishop's foot a light kick. "Watch your mouth around Nadia."

Nadia rolled her eyes. Bishop had tamed the gutter mouth that came with living in the Basement, but this was far from the first time he'd let something coarse slip out, and it wasn't exactly shocking.

"It'll make him drool," Bishop continued smoothly. "Maybe it'll even make him think I might contact you again so he might think you make good bait."

Nadia supposed that was meant to be comforting. There

would always be more threats Mosely could raise, more ways he could keep her under his thumb. But she couldn't allow herself to think about consequences.

"All right. I'll tell him that. I might also suggest that you're going to want to warn Nate about me, give him hope that he might be able to intercept you if you do."

"Well," Dante said, slapping his hands on his thighs. "That's settled." He glanced at his watch. "It's getting late and I should get you two back if we're done here."

"We're not quite done," Bishop said. "Nate, when I told you what we heard on the night of the reception, I said that Mosely and the Chairman were talking about someone named Thea. I thought maybe you might have recognized that name."

Nate nodded grimly. "I do."

"Who is she?"

Nate let out a deep breath. "I need you all to promise me that this information won't leave the van, at least not for now. If I answer your question, I'll be spilling state secrets."

"State secrets that might help the resistance?" Dante asked with an eager gleam in his eyes.

"And this conversation is now officially over," Nate said, crossing his arms over his chest.

"You want a ride home?" Dante countered. "Or would you rather walk?"

"Don't be an asshole," Bishop said. "No one's walking." He turned to Nate. "I guarantee it won't leave this van. Tell me who Thea is."

But Nate shook his head. "I trust you, even though I probably shouldn't, but I *don't* trust him." He jerked his chin toward Dante. Nadia wasn't sure if this was a sign that Nate was *finally* being cautious enough, or if it was just further evidence that he didn't like Dante.

"I outrank him," Bishop said, giving Dante a meaningful look, "and I say he's not going to run his mouth to anyone."

"I don't care. I don't feel like sharing secrets with him."

"You trusted me enough to get in a van with me and let me take you to the Basement without any proof I was taking you to Bishop," Dante pointed out. "I'm one of the good guys here."

Nadia believed him, or at least believed he believed what he was saying. But she didn't know enough about the resistance or anyone who was in it to be convinced they were really the good guys. She'd studied enough history to know that even revolutionaries with good intentions often ended up doing terrible things. She couldn't blame Nate for being reluctant to talk around him.

"Then why don't you prove you're a good guy?" she challenged before Nate said something to escalate the hostility. "Don't insist Nate tell his secrets to someone he's known less than twelve hours."

The chagrin on Dante's face said he didn't like it, but he reluctantly exited the van, slamming the doors behind him more vigorously than necessary.

Nate stared at the doors through which Dante had exited with a look of distaste.

"That guy's a total dick."

"Watch your mouth around the lady," Bishop said mildly, and Nate responded by flipping him the bird.

"So who is Thea?" Nadia prompted, her curiosity rampaging. She didn't know anyone named Thea, couldn't think of anyone in the upper echelons of Paxco named Thea, so she couldn't help wondering how state secrets could be involved.

Nate hesitated. "Promise me you won't tell Dante. This is just between the three of us."

"I promise," Nadia said without hesitation. Bishop was slower to agree, but he eventually nodded his acceptance.

"All right," Nate said. "Thea isn't a 'who,' it's a 'what.' It's the name of the AI that invented Replicas."

There had long been rumors that the Replica technology was beyond the scope of human invention. As soon as Paxco had unveiled its miraculous technology, every state and nation in the world had rushed to try to duplicate it, and no one had come close. Religious fanatics claimed it was the work of the devil and a sign of the End of Days. The nuttiest of the conspiracy theorists suggested that the government of Paxco had made a pact with aliens. But the most reputable scientists had posited that perhaps in its research into biomedical engineering, Paxco had created a true AI, an artificial intelligence. Something that started out as a product of mankind's devising but had since grown into something more, something other. Something with the capacity to understand the human brain and body in a way that humans themselves could not.

"So it's true," Nadia whispered. "There really is an AI."

Nate nodded. "I don't know a whole lot about it." He made a wry face. "I'm not considered responsible enough to be let into the true inner circle. All I really know is that it exists, and that it's located somewhere below ground under the Fortress."

"I don't get it," Bishop said. "What's the big secret? Lots of people are already convinced there has to be an AI behind the technology, so why hide it?"

"My understanding is that we don't want anyone to know anything for sure. If other scientists knew *for sure* that it took an AI to invent the Replicas, they'd focus their energies—and their research grants—that way, and they might eventually create another AI that's capable of doing the same thing."

"Uh-huh," Bishop said, sounding completely unconvinced.

Nate shrugged. "My father explained the reasoning a lot better than I did. It made sense—it really did."

Nadia had no doubt that it had. The Chairman was an impressive speaker, able to justify his actions to the public in such a way that there never seemed to be any huge outcry over what Nadia saw as injustices. Though perhaps the existence of the resistance movement proved that he wasn't convincing everyone, at least not anymore.

"It's a camouflage," Nadia said.

"Huh?" Nate asked, looking at her in puzzlement.

"Don't take this the wrong way," she said, putting her hand on his shoulder, "but your father wouldn't share a sensitive state secret with you if his life depended on it."

Nate jerked back as if slapped. "Just how exactly am I supposed to take that that isn't the wrong way?"

"You've gone out of your way to paint yourself as an irresponsible playboy," she said. "Don't be offended at the thought that your father might treat you like one."

It looked for a moment like he was going to argue, but he thought better of it and settled into resentful silence.

"He told you about Thea's existence and told you it was a big state secret so you'd feel like he told you something important and you wouldn't ask any more questions. But there's a lot more to it than that. Something about Thea that he doesn't want anyone to know."

"Something you overheard him talking to Mosely about," Bishop put in. "Something big enough that he'd rather kill you than take the risk you might tell anyone what you heard."

The corners of Nate's eyes tightened at the reminder. "And whatever it is, we're going to have to figure it out."

"Let's not worry about that now," Bishop said. "The thing

we have to do now is get Nadia out of this mess before Mosely gets drastic with her. Everything else can come later."

Nadia wondered if Nate could read between the lines as well as she could. For the moment, she guessed he was too distracted to notice, but she felt sure from the look in his eyes and the tone of his voice that Bishop was humoring him. Allowing Nate to believe that he would somehow be involved in solving the mystery of Thea. That there was a "we" beyond their current mission. But even though they were all on the same side for now, Nadia knew that she and Nate represented exactly the kind of establishment the resistance planned to fight against. When the crisis was over, the resistance would be through with them—and Bishop would very likely break Nate's heart.

CHAPTER NINETEEN

nadia was brushing her teeth the next morning when she heard a commotion outside. The sound of raised voices reached her even through her closed bedroom and bathroom doors. She spit out her toothpaste and hurriedly pulled on the slacks and blouse she'd picked out for the day, her nerves buzzing with foreboding. It could be just Mrs. Reeves yelling at one of the maids, but even Mrs. Reeves's tantrums weren't usually quite so loud.

As she stepped out of the bathroom, Nadia realized it couldn't be Mrs. Reeves, because there was at least one male voice yelling, too. It sounded like her father. But Gerald Lake never yelled—he left such theatrics to his wife. Nadia's palms started to sweat, and her heart fluttered in her chest as she heard the heavy tread of many feet tromping down the hallway, coming closer and closer. Her stomach bottomed out when she heard crying and recognized her mother's tearful voice calling her name. She had a brief thought of diving under her bed to hide, or trying to lock herself in her closet, but that would be as undignified as it would be futile.

There wasn't time to prepare the little transmitter to plant on Mosely, nor was there time to dispose of it, since it was still stuck in the pocket of the catsuit, which she'd hidden at the back of her closet. Probably just having that little transmitter in her possession was enough to help fuel any accusations of treason or espionage Mosely wanted to throw her way.

Panic bubbled and boiled in her stomach, but Nadia kept it at bay as she moved over to her bedside and casually picked up the earrings she had laid there last night when she'd taken them off before her trip to the Basement. Her hands shook only a little as she slid one through the hole in her ear and her bedroom door burst open. She used her fingernail to flip the switch on the earring to transmit and wished the signal were going to an actual person who might be able to help her now, rather than avenge her later.

"I'll be with you in one moment," she said, her voice sounding much calmer than she felt as she inserted the other earring. She picked up a black velvet headband she had discarded on the nightstand, just to make sure her calm donning of the earrings didn't bring any special attention to them.

"Nadia Lake," a deep voice intoned, "you are under arrest for conspiracy and suspicion of treason."

Settling the headband on her head, Nadia raised her chin and turned around.

In her doorway stood two armed security officers, glowering at her. Both had their hands on their firearms, though at least they weren't pointing them at her. Behind them stood Dirk Mosely, and behind him stood two more security officers who spread their arms to keep Nadia's mother and father from entering the room. Nadia's throat closed up to see her mother's face awash with tears, her eyes red and her nose running. Esmeralda Lake *never* cried.

"Turn around and put your hands behind your head," one of the security officers barked as he approached her, brandishing a pair of handcuffs.

Nadia didn't see any point in resisting, so she did as she

was ordered. The officer shoved her facedown onto her bed anyway, putting his knee in her back as he wrenched her arms behind her to slap the handcuffs on. Nadia clenched her teeth to keep from crying out. The officer yanked her to her feet, and his partners forced her parents back so he could drag her, stumbling, out of the room. Mosely watched dispassionately, turning a deaf ear to her parents' repeated attempts to plead with him.

"Mom, Dad, I'll be all right," she choked out, though she didn't believe it any more than they did.

The servants had gathered in the hallway outside, watching in varying degrees of dismay as the officers marched Nadia between them, each holding one of her arms. She was not being quietly spirited away for questioning, and news of her arrest was no doubt spreading even now. Even if Mosely was using this as nothing more than a scare tactic and immediately released her, her reputation would never survive. No matter what the outcome, today marked the end of the life she'd been bred and raised for, and the future was a horrifying unknown.

The public humiliation continued as Nadia was perpwalked through the lobby of the Lake Towers while people stood and stared. A couple of them openly took photographs of the procession. Nadia saw Mosely notice one of the photographers and then pointedly look away. He obviously wanted this spectacle to be as public as possible. Nadia wanted to kill him for it, for putting her family through all the added horror of the publicity. As if her being arrested weren't bad enough.

There were several cars with flashing lights waiting for her at the front door, as well as a van with no windows in the back. A pair of hard wooden benches were bolted against the wall, and the sides of the van were peppered with O-rings at varying heights. Nadia was unceremoniously tossed into the van, then dragged to a bench. Her handcuffs were then attached to an O-ring behind her, high enough to strain her shoulders and force her to bend forward as shackles were put on her ankles and then attached to another O-ring. All of this was done while the doors were still open and a crowd gathered outside. Nadia was sure even more photographs were being taken. At least she wasn't crying, though she didn't think the lack of tears had anything to do with bravery on her part. Everything seemed too unreal to be true. Too unreal to cry about or panic over. But that numb sense of unreality wouldn't last for long, and the worst was yet to come.

The four security officers who had escorted her all joined her in the van—they must have thought she was a dangerous criminal indeed to need four hulking guards to contain her—and the doors slammed shut.

nadia wasn't sure where she was being taken, except that it was somewhere she didn't want to go. Maybe to the security station, where she could maintain at least a faint hope that Mosely would release her after scaring her half to death, but she suspected Riker's Island was more likely. She tried to keep herself alert for any clues, like the distinctive sound of tires on a bridge, but it was hard to concentrate when panic kept swelling in her chest.

"Where are you taking me?" she tried asking the security officers, but none even acknowledged that she had spoken.

The drive seemed to last forever. Nadia's back ached from the unnatural position she was forced to sit in, and every sharp turn or deep pothole the van hit was torture on her strained arms and shoulders. Fear was her constant companion, and her mind kept frantically searching for a way out. But there *was* no way out, not from here. She was trapped and helpless. She would be questioned, probably even tortured. She wished she believed she could bravely endure whatever was to come without breaking, without betraying Nate and Bishop and Dante, but she doubted her own courage.

Eventually, the van came to a stop, and Nadia was dragged out of the van and hustled through a door. Her one brief glimpse of the outside before she was shoved through the door showed that she was in a room that resembled an airplane hangar and that the van had entered through a tunnel. She guessed that tunnel was a secret entrance to Riker's Island, a way the security forces could bring in prisoners of special importance, like her.

Once inside, she was led through several sets of key-coded security doors. The officers forced her to turn around whenever they entered their passcodes, and Nadia felt a bubble of hysterical laughter wanting to rise from her chest. Who did they think she was? Some kind of superspy who could free herself from her chains, disable her four escorts, and make a run for freedom after having memorized their passcodes? She was just a kid, caught up in something way over her head.

The room the guards eventually propelled Nadia into did not look promising.

One half was laid out like the standard security interrogation room: a metal table, bolted to the floor, with a rail to which the unfortunate detainee could be chained; a couple of flimsy, uncomfortable plastic chairs; and a one-way mirror along one wall. It was the other half of the room that caused a new wave of terror to crash over Nadia's head.

The other half of the room featured a table of gleaming surgical steel, bristling with restraints. The table sat at a slight angle just past horizontal, and there were grooves along its edges. Nadia didn't want to, but she couldn't help following those grooves and that angle with her eyes and seeing how they led to a drain in the tile floor. In her mind's eyes, she saw a river of blood being pulled by gravity, channeled by those grooves, flowing to the edge of the table and forming a waterfall straight into that drain.

Above the table lurked something that looked a bit like a dentist's instrument panel, only about ten times as big, with ten times as many attachments. Needles and saws and drills and blades of varying shapes and sizes. All of them coiled and waiting. Nestled among those attachments were a variety of instrument panels and darkened monitors.

Nadia felt so dizzy that for a moment she thought she might faint. She wanted to be brave, or at least to put on a brave face, but terror was like a living beast inside her. It clamped down on her chest, making it hard to breathe. It sucked the moisture from her mouth and the warmth from her limbs. It blotted out all rational thoughts, left her with nothing to cling to except the desperate need to run, to escape.

"Don't worry," Mosely's voice said from behind her. She hadn't even heard him enter the room, so transfixed was she by the monstrosity that loomed over the table. "We have a lot of talking to do before we graduate to more extreme measures." Mosely wandered over to the table and gave it an affectionate pat, like it was a favorite pet.

One of the security officers dragged Nadia over to the interview area, slamming her into a chair, then uncuffing her hands and chaining her to the table. Then he and the other three officers exited the room, leaving her alone with the man who had with his own hands killed the Chairman Heir and framed another for the murder. She couldn't hope for mercy or compassion from him.

Mosely continued to caress his monstrous torture apparatus, smiling faintly to himself. Nadia closed her eyes and took a deep breath, trying to tame the fear, trying to *think*. But try as she might, she couldn't think of a way out. If she refused to talk, Mosely would torture her. But if she *did* talk, she would reveal that she knew far too much. He might not think the accusations of a sixteen-year-old girl being held for treason could do him much damage, but he wasn't the sort to take the risk. Someone might believe her, even if it was just her own family, and they might make a stink about it. Nothing he couldn't handle, but why would he bother when he could just avoid the issue by disposing of her?

She was going to die, Nadia realized, and paradoxically that thought steadied her. Whatever terrible things were going to happen, there was an end in sight. She might not be able to save herself, but she would do her level best to take Mosely down with her. As soon as Gerri heard the news of Nadia's death, she—or her unknown cohort—would retrieve the recordings Nadia had made. Nadia just had to make sure she caught Mosely saying something so incriminating he couldn't wriggle out from the consequences.

As if he hadn't a care in the world, Mosely strolled toward her. Nadia's pulse still fluttered, and she knew that if she unclenched her hands from her lap, they would shake, but she held her head high, thoughts of her posthumous revenge warming and strengthening her.

Mosely tossed a manila folder on the table. He sat down across from her, then flipped the folder open and began laying out a series of photos in front of her. And now she understood why she had been arrested.

The photos were a little grainy, no doubt taken from a considerable distance. They showed Nadia exiting her building and climbing into an unmarked white van. Her heart sank, and she cursed herself for not considering that Mosely might have someone other than Dante keeping an eye on her. Especially after yesterday's interview, where she had aroused his suspicions.

Had someone followed the van once Nadia had gotten in it? And had there been someone watching Nate's apartment? Surely if Mosely had been watching her, he'd been watching Nate. And that meant he knew that she and Nate had both been in that van last night. If they'd been followed into the Basement, then it didn't matter what Nadia said or didn't say—Mosely knew exactly what had happened, knew exactly who all the players were and who he needed to eliminate.

"It seems you have not been completely honest with me, Miss Lake," Mosely said. "I'm disappointed in you. I had thought a girl of your impeccable pedigree would understand the importance of protecting the interests of her state."

She couldn't tell if he was mocking her, or if he was sincerely disapproving. And she didn't care.

"In my opinion," she said, "the interests of my state are not served by pinning a crime on an innocent man."

Mosely gave a condescending chuckle. "Believe me, my dear, Kurt Bishop is a lot of things, but an innocent man isn't one of them. Did you know he was working as a whore when our Chairman Heir hired him?"

If Nadia was supposed to feel disgusted by the revelation, Mosely had missed his mark. She might not have known the specifics of Bishop's past, but she'd certainly known there was ugliness in it. "Prostitution isn't a crime punishable by death. If you think that's an adequate excuse to—"

"You are such a child. Everything is black and white to you, isn't it? You would never consider that sometimes sacrifices have to be made for the greater good."

Nadia clamped her jaws shut to keep from responding. She had a feeling he was probing at her, trying to get her to reveal what she knew without directly asking questions. Her mind raced with possibilities as she tried to figure out how to get Mosely to admit his crimes aloud without giving away too much herself. In the periphery of her vision, the torture apparatus loomed.

Mosely tucked the photos back into their folder and pushed the folder aside. Then he leaned forward with his elbows on the table. Nadia felt like he was intruding upon her personal space even though there was a table between them.

"Where did you go last night, Miss Lake?" he asked.

"You're the spymaster. Why don't *you* tell *me*?"

Mosely raised his eyebrows in surprise. "I'd recommend you be more circumspect in your responses, Miss Lake. Need I remind you that you're under arrest on suspicion of treason?"

Nadia didn't truly believe there was a way out of the mess she was in, but it seemed reasonable to at least put on a show of trying.

"I haven't forgotten. Are you suggesting my situation would somehow improve if I were more forthcoming with you?"

"I am suggesting, foolish child, that if you are not forthcoming with me, I will make you regret it for every remaining day of your miserable life." He glanced pointedly at the apparatus. "You can avoid a great deal of unpleasantness by simply answering my questions truthfully."

So there was no carrot to be offered. Only the stick. Nadia shivered. She didn't know what Mosely would do to her if he strapped her to that table, but she suspected that she would lose a lot of her higher reasoning powers to fear. If she wanted Mosely to incriminate himself, she was going to need her wits about her. Which meant she had to do it before Mosely resorted to torture.

"I ask you again: where did you go last night?"

Taking a deep breath, hoping she was making the right decision, Nadia began laying out the rope she hoped Mosely would hang himself with.

"I went to the Basement to rendezvous with Kurt Bishop."

nate was standing on the edge of the rooftop garden at Nadia's apartment, looking out over the lights of the city. The air was completely still, and he was alone, unsure how he'd gotten there. He was supposed to meet someone, wasn't he? But he was early. Or maybe late. He looked around, confused, unable to remember. The moon hung full in the sky, its light outshining the city. A giant wasp buzzed around Nate's head. He batted at it, and it went away for a moment. But seconds later, it was back, flying in circles around his head, buzzing incessantly. He tried again to bat it away, but it had become invisible.

Nate's eyes cracked open, then quickly closed again in response to the light. He wanted to go back to sleep, but the damn wasp was still buzzing around his head. He opened his eyes again, and realized there was no wasp. He blinked his crusty eyes a couple of times as one by one his brain cells woke up and dragged themselves out of his dream into reality. Reality that included his phone buzzing away on the nightstand.

The buzzing stopped briefly, and sleep tried to drag Nate back down into its clutches. He would have been happy to go, but the phone started up again. He considered grabbing it and throwing it across the room to shut it up so he could get back to sleep.

Cursing the damned piece of technology that was supposedly in "silent" mode, Nate pushed himself up to a sitting position and grabbed it. He pulled his hand back to throw it, but before he did, he noticed the flashing icon that told him he had more than a dozen missed calls. Groggy as he was, the realization still sent a burst of adrenaline through his system. According to the phone, it was just past eight in the morning, and a dozen missed calls at this hour was not a good sign.

Shaking his head in an attempt to clear the fog, Nate answered even though he didn't recognize the number.

"Hello?" he croaked, using his free hand to rub the grit out of his eyes.

"Nate! Thank God I finally reached you."

Nate shook his head again, having failed to clear the fog the first time. The voice was familiar, but whatever part of his brain matched voices to names was still asleep. "Who is this?"

"Dante."

Dante? What the hell was Dante doing calling him? And how'd he even get Nate's private number? Of course, he was a professional spy in training, so the latter probably wasn't that much of a mystery.

"What's going on?" Nate asked as more adrenaline worked its way into his system.

"Nadia's been arrested."

The trickle of adrenaline became a flood, and suddenly Nate was wide awake. "What?" He shoved the covers aside as he scrambled to his feet.

"She's been arrested. It's all over the news. They took her from her apartment this morning, about an hour ago."

Nate was already rushing toward his closet, planning to throw on the first clothes he got his hands on. He had *promised* not to let Mosely hurt Nadia or her family, and he was going to keep that promise. Somehow.

"She's supposedly been taken to Riker's Island," Dante continued. "That's what the news says, at least. But that's not where they took her."

Nate pinched the phone between his face and his shoulder as he struggled his way into a pair of pants. The fingers of his right hand were stiff and swollen, and Nate fought to bend them enough to manage the button and zipper.

"Do you know where they *have* taken her?"

"Yeah. She's at the Fortress somewhere."

"Why?" The Fortress was not a place for prisoners. Its entire purpose was to guard the Replica technology. It was where you went to get your backup scans, if you were privileged enough to warrant them, and where Replicas, like Nate, were made. It hardly seemed like an appropriate place to be taking Nadia after her arrest.

"I don't know."

"Well, you're the spy. Find out!"

"I told you, I don't have that kind of access. I'm still in spy training wheels."

Nate would have torn into Dante for the flippant words if he didn't hear the concern behind them. And if he didn't recognize the same kind of inappropriate wisecrack he was well known for making himself.

"Then how do you know they've taken her to the Fortress?"

Dante hesitated a moment. "Because I put a tracker on her last night."

Nate paused in the act of sticking his arms into a shirt. His swollen fingers curled into a painful fist, and he wished Dante were here in front of him so he could punch the asshole again. Never mind that it would hurt him way more than it would hurt Dante.

"You what?" he growled.

Dante cleared his throat, and sounded unsure of himself for the first time since Nate had met him. "Um, I put a tracker on her. We weren't sure she wasn't going to panic and tell Mosely everything. We thought if we could keep track of her movements, we'd, uh, have an early warning if she did something stupid. An insurance policy."

If Dante was going to be a professional spy, then he needed to learn how to lie better than that. Nate gritted his teeth against the pain as he buttoned his shirt, realizing he should have gone with a pullover to spare himself the effort.

Why would Dante have put a tracker on Nadia? And why would he try to feed Nate this lame explanation? The answer to the latter was obvious: because he didn't think Nate would like the real one.

Why put a tracker on Nadia? It was an insurance policy, all right. Only not in the sense Dante had suggested.

"You put a tracker on her so that your resistance buddies could find her and kill her if she was captured."

Dante sighed. "We couldn't let her talk. We have . . . people at Riker's. People who could arrange for something to happen to her before she was questioned. Kurt and I figured if worse came to worst, we'd fess up to our mistakes and our superiors could . . . make the appropriate arrangements."

"You set her up to die." Nate wanted to kill Dante, wanted to pummel his face until it was nothing but a bloody pulp. And then he'd start in on Kurt, for agreeing to this plan.

"I've seen what Mosely does to people, Nate. Trust me, she'd be better off dead."

"One: that wasn't your call. And two: my name is Nathaniel. Only my friends call me Nate, and you're not my friend."

"Fine, Nathaniel. But we have a rather urgent problem right now. Mosely didn't take Nadia to Riker's Island, remember? The resistance might have been able to get to her there, but they can't get to her in the Fortress. I don't know why Mosely took her there, but it's not for anything good. If she talks, I'm going to have to swallow this cyanide tablet I'm staring at, because I absolutely can't allow them to question *me*. And you're going to meet with some kind of unfortunate end yourself, because Mosely can't afford to let you live with what you know."

Nate shoved his feet into a pair of shoes, not bothering with socks. He knew Dante's reasoning made a sick sort of sense, but that didn't make it any more acceptable. Nate cursed himself for ever getting Nadia involved in any of this. Ever since the night of his murder, she'd been stuck between a rock and hard place, and he'd done nothing to make her situation any easier. Hell, he'd done plenty to make it worse.

"I'm going to the Fortress," Nate announced. "I'm getting Nadia out of there."

"Oh yeah? How are you going to manage that?"

Nate's hand tightened on the phone as another surge of anger flowed through him. Dante was so lucky Nate couldn't reach him right now. Of course, if Dante was telling the truth, he was contemplating suicide, so perhaps he wasn't really that lucky after all.

"That's why you called me, isn't it?" Nate asked instead of answering. "You're hoping I can get her out of there."

"Hoping, yeah. But I don't know what you can do. Mosely

isn't going to let her go just because you tell him to. And if he realizes you know about him, he won't let *you* go, either."

"Well, if everything is so hopeless, you go ahead and take your little pill, and I'll see you in hell."

Nate ended the call. He didn't have time to hold Dante's hand, nor did he have the inclination. He had to get to the Fortress and find Nadia. He had to save her. He'd *promised* to protect her.

CHAPTER TWENTY

nadia broke out in a cold sweat as she sat across the table from Mosely, waiting for him to react to her statement that she'd met with Bishop. Unlike Nate, Mosely had iron control of his reactions, and she could tell nothing from the look on his face. Was he surprised? Or had someone followed her and seen the entire meeting?

Nadia took a deep breath, trying to calm herself. If whoever had been watching her had actually followed her to the rendezvous and overheard the discussion, Mosely wouldn't be asking her questions. If he knew exactly what had happened last night, he'd just kill her, not interrogate her.

"You met with Kurt Bishop?" Mosely said after chewing it over for what felt like forever. "How, exactly, did *that* come about?"

The evaporating sweat on her skin made Nadia shiver. She hated the sign of weakness, but no matter how determined she was to be brave, her body had its own ideas. And maybe looking weak wasn't such a bad idea after all. The less Mosely respected her, the more he would underestimate her—and the more willing he would be to say something that would eventually cost him his freedom, if not his life.

Nadia thought carefully about her answer, frantically trying to figure out which truths she should reveal and which she should hide. If she wanted *any* chance to convince Mosely not to torture her, she had to tell him enough truth to satisfy him. That meant giving up on protecting Bishop. And much though she hated to admit it, it meant giving up on protecting Nate, too. Mosely might not know what exactly had happened last night, but Nadia would bet her life that he knew Nate had been with her.

That left Dante, and the resistance movement to which he was connected. If Dante was arrested, not only would he likely die, but he'd be questioned like Nadia, and he'd tell Mosely who else was in his cell. And those cell members would be arrested and talk, and so on. She might not be convinced this resistance movement was on the side of the angels, but if she could save their lives, then at least she would die knowing she had saved *someone*.

With the decision made, Nadia's racing pulse calmed, though she still shivered. Not because of how scared she was, she realized, but because the room was cold. No doubt kept that way to make prisoners more miserable.

"It's a bit of a long story," Nadia said, still mentally piecing together exactly what she was going to tell him.

"Don't worry," Mosely said drily, "we have plenty of time."

She nodded, then sneaked a glance at the torture table, shivering and emphasizing to Mosely how terrified the threat made her. Hopefully helping to convince him that she would tell him the whole truth rather than risk his wrath.

"Bishop didn't want Nate to find him," she said in a small voice. "When Nate got beaten up the other night, Bishop was behind it. Trying to convince Nate he was really the killer so Nate would back off."

As usual, Mosely's face gave away nothing, but Nadia thought she detected a sharpening of the interest in his eyes.

"Bishop got hold of the locket Nate was wearing and found

the tracker you had me plant in it. He made the assumption that I had put it there, and he contacted me."

"How?" Mosely asked, leaning forward.

Of course he would immediately ask the one question she didn't dare answer truthfully. "Through an intermediary," she said, starting with the truth. "No one I knew, and he never identified himself. He cornered me when I was out shopping and told me to stay out of it or else." Nadia's pulse rate picked up as she watched Mosely watching her. She couldn't say what had changed about his facial expression, but she got the distinct feeling he didn't believe her. Or maybe that was just her own fear speaking, making her panic for no reason. Maybe that was why Mosely was so good at his job—because of his reputation for discerning truth from lies, those who lied to him got extra nervous and gave themselves away.

Knowing her best chance was to get past the lies and into the truthful—and, she hoped, even more interesting to Mosely—part, Nadia hurried on.

"I told him that, despite his best efforts, Bishop hadn't talked Nate into not looking anymore, and that's when he decided to set up the meeting."

"Miss Lake, I thought I made it clear that it was in your best interests to tell me the truth. The *whole* truth."

Nadia's heart sank. She could give him more details on this mysterious intermediary she was making up, but she'd probably doomed herself as soon as she'd said he'd cornered her while she was shopping. There were enough security cameras in lower Manhattan that he could probably retrace her movements over the last week, and he would find no evidence that she'd been out shopping.

Nadia fought to stave off panic. She would worry about how to protect Dante later; right now, her first priority was to get Mosely to incriminate himself while she was of sound enough mind and body to manage it. Which meant she had to redirect Mosely's attention, at least for the moment.

"Don't you want to know about what happened last night when Nate and I met with Bishop?" she asked. She tried to fold her arms, but the handcuffs wouldn't let her.

Mosely frowned and tapped the table with one restless finger. Nadia held her breath, and she had to suppress a sigh of relief when he took the bait.

"Don't think we have finished with the current topic of discussion, but please do tell about last night."

Nadia tapped into some of the fury she'd felt at everything she'd learned last night, letting it steal into her face as she leaned forward. She gave Mosely the most steely look she could manage, stoking her anger, urging it to well up and overpower her fear.

"Bishop told us that he wasn't the one who killed Nate. *You* killed Nate, because of something he overheard you talking about with the Chairman."

In the best-case scenario, Mosely wouldn't bother denying the accusation, might even blithely admit to it. After all, he was planning to kill Nadia anyway, so what did it matter? But perhaps admitting to murder was against the spy's code of conduct, because Mosely merely laughed at her.

"An interesting theory," he said, still chuckling. "What would you expect the murderer to do, if not to point the finger at someone else? Very clever of him to point it at someone you were already predisposed to think ill of."

The door to the interrogation room opened, and a security officer peeked his head in. Mosely turned toward him in obvious annoyance. The officer's eyes widened in alarm at the look Mosely shot him, but he didn't retreat.

"I'm sorry, sir," he said, "but there's a . . . situation you should be aware of."

Mosely looked even more annoyed as he shoved his chair back. "This had better be of the utmost importance."

"Yes, sir."

Mosely stood up with obvious reluctance. "I'll be back soon, Miss Lake," he warned.

Nadia shrank back into her chair, cold and scared and alone, with the hulking torture apparatus that would surely be part of her future looming in her peripheral vision.

nate still didn't have much by way of a plan when he arrived at the Fortress. He didn't technically have the authority to give Dirk Mosely orders, and considering what he now knew about the man, he didn't suppose Mosely would follow them anyway. Not to mention that Mosely was obviously willing to kill him if necessary.

Still, killing Nate in a private corner of the Chairman's mansion was not the same as killing him in front of witnesses. Mosely was an expert at the cover-up, but Nate didn't think a second murder could be covered up so easily. Feeling confident that Mosely wouldn't just shoot him on sight didn't mean he had any idea how to free Nadia, but even so, Nate had to try.

Getting through the first few layers of security in the Fortress was easy. Everyone knew who he was, and they weren't about to risk their jobs trying to stop him. Besides, he had all the right access codes as a privilege of his rank. He tried asking where Mosely was, but no one would admit to having seen him. Not surprising, as there was more than one entrance to the Fortress and Mosely would have used the most private one. Nate made an educated guess that Mosely and Nadia would be somewhere in the very heart of the building, deep enough that even Nate didn't have the clearance to get through. But he was prepared to be way more forceful than anyone would expect him to be. And it would take a security officer with balls of steel to deny the Chairman Heir.

At each security checkpoint, the demands grew more vigorous, until Nate was identifying himself not just with the proper access codes, but with fingerprints and retinal scans. There were officers at each of the checkpoints, but though they looked at him curiously, no one got in his way until he tried to get on the elevator to the sub-basement level, the floor on which Thea resided.

Though Nate had been in the sub-basement before, he didn't have the clearance to go there without an escort. Here was where he expected to meet resistance, and indeed the two security officers stationed in the hallway leading to the elevator stiffened at his approach.

"I'm looking for Dirk Mosely," he told them. "I believe he's in the sub-basement, and I would like one of you to escort me down there."

The two guards looked at each other, then back at him.

"I'm sorry, sir,—" one of them began, but Nate made an impatient gesture.

"No apologies. Take me downstairs, or I'll have your jobs. I will see that you have the blackest of black marks put on your records, the kind of black marks that mean you'll never get another job. You, and your families, if you have them, will sink into the Basement, where you will languish in poverty for the rest of your days. I'm having the worst week in the history of the universe, so don't tempt me."

In all honesty, Nate didn't expect it to work. His threat was pretty awful—and a part of him felt bad for making it—but he feared the officers would face the same fate if they failed in their duty. If they had to bet on who was most likely to carry out the threat, Nate or Mosely, surely they would bet on Mosely. His plan B was to make a move on one of their weapons on the assumption that they'd never expect it and that the one he wasn't attacking wouldn't dare shoot him while he was making the attempt. Trying to wrestle one security officer for his weapon while hoping the other didn't shoot him wasn't high on Nate's list of things he wanted to do in life, so it was a relief when his blackmail actually worked.

"Fine," the guard who'd tried to apologize said, giving him a filthy look, "I'll take you downstairs."

"Damn it, Flynn!" the other guard said. "Mosely will *kill* us."

Flynn snorted and waved for Nate to follow him as he unhooked a ring of old-fashioned metal keys from his belt. "I doubt he expects us to defy the orders of the Chairman Heir." He stuck one of the keys into the keyhole beside the elevator and turned it, simultaneously leaning forward so the retinal scanner could work. The elevator door opened, and he stepped in.

The hair on the back of Nate's neck rose as it occurred to him that getting here had been far too easy, the guards' protests almost halfhearted.

"Come on, sir," Flynn beckoned, holding the elevator door open when it tried to shut on him. "The alarm will sound if I hold it much longer. It's kind of touchy."

Nate gave a momentary thought to trying to back out and seeing if the guards would allow it. But it didn't matter. If he was walking into a trap, then so be it. He wasn't leaving here without Nadia.

Straightening his shoulders, trying not to look as spooked as he felt, Nate stepped onto the elevator.

CHAPTER TWENTY-ONE

мosely didn't leave Nadia alone for long. Dread weighed down her shoulders as she heard his footsteps approaching the room. She glanced at the ominous table waiting for her. She was running out of time, and Mosely hadn't said anything incriminating yet. Not anything she could use to blackmail him into letting her go, not even anything that would help her get her posthumous revenge. She had to get him talking, and fast.

But when Mosely returned, it was clear that he was through talking.

The moment he stepped through the door, he marched toward Nadia with a purpose. Whatever purpose that was, Nadia knew she wouldn't like it. Instinct screamed at her to flee, but of course, she couldn't go anywhere. That didn't stop her from trying.

Nadia leapt to her feet, but fear made her clumsy, and her feet tangled with the legs of the chair. She almost fell, but managed to right herself and kick the chair in Mosely's direction. Like the flimsy plastic had any chance of stopping Mosely's advance.

Mosely batted it out of his way with annoyance as Nadia moved as far away from him as the handcuffs would allow. She made a feeble effort to slip her hand through the circle of the cuff, but it was firmly secured, and even scraping a few layers of skin off wouldn't help.

"You don't have to do this," she said as Mosely withdrew something from his pocket. Something that gave off a little blue spark. "I'll tell you everything. I'll tell you the truth, I swear it." Surely there was some way she could salvage the situation. Some way she could make her lies more convincing. After all, the ratio of lies to truth wasn't all that high. If she could just get Mosely to focus his questioning on the parts of her story where she could afford to tell the truth . . .

"I'm afraid it's too late for that, Miss Lake," Mosely said with what sounded almost like regret. Then he lunged forward, covering the distance between them in two quick strides, and jabbed the stunner into her belly.

A shrill scream escaped Nadia's lips as pain ripped through her whole body and she lost control of her limbs. Her knees buckled, and she crashed to the floor. She was still cuffed to the table, so the fall wrenched her shoulder and she landed awkwardly. She tried to move, tried to at least turn so her arm was in a more natural position, but her brain's commands to her body went unheeded.

"Nathaniel is coming to your rescue," Mosely said as he unlocked the cuff around her wrist, letting her arm flop to the floor. He used his foot to turn her over onto her stomach, and there was nothing she could do to stop him.

Mosely squatted beside her. "There is no earthly way he could know you were here in the Fortress."

The Fortress? But she was at Riker's Island, not the Fortress. At least, that was what she'd thought. But of course she'd been in a van with no windows, and while Mosely had dragged her through multiple security checkpoints, she'd never seen any sign of other prisoners, or even of any cells.

"But he seems to have found you against all odds," Mosely continued. "Which suggests that someone planted a tracker on you." He moved her hair aside, brushing it away from the back of her neck. "Well, what do you know?" Nadia felt the scrape of a fingernail against the skin at the back of her neck. "Right where I train my people to put it."

Nadia remembered how Dante had helped her with the wig last night. She'd had no idea how to put it on or how to keep her hair out of the way. She'd let Dante take care of everything, and he'd even helped her take the damn thing off. Apparently, he'd had an ulterior motive.

"You've been withholding information from me, haven't you, Miss Lake?"

Nadia's lips and tongue felt thick and numb, and she didn't think Mosely was expecting an answer. He flipped her over onto her back. Nadia tried again to move, with no greater success. Mosely stood, then leaned down and hauled her limp body up over his shoulder, carrying her toward the dreaded table. And Nadia was helpless to resist, couldn't even force herself to struggle.

Mosely dumped her on the table. He wasn't being careful about it, so the back of her head thumped against the edge. The blow made her see stars, and she thought she was going to pass out. Not that passing out sounded like a bad idea. She'd rather not be awake for whatever was going to happen next.

"And here I thought I was going to have to arrange a convenient accident for him," Mosely continued, somewhat out of breath from the strain of carrying her. He didn't have that potbelly because of his physical fitness. He straightened Nadia out on the table, dragging her into its center and positioning her where the restraints could hold her.

Nadia stared up at the saws and drills and blades and vowed to herself that no matter what Mosely did to her, she would not betray Dante and the resistance. It took a massive effort, but Nadia was able to turn her head to the side so she could stare at Mosely instead of the implements that loomed over her. The motion meant that she was starting to regain control of her body, but it was too little, too late. Mosely had already fastened restraints on both her wrists and was now moving down to her ankles. She breathed as deeply as she could and mined her psyche for every drop of anger she could find. She had never before hated anyone like she hated Dirk Mosely, and she tapped into that hatred to help her chase away the fear even as Mosely fastened the restraints around her ankles.

The rush of hatred was indeed helping Nadia control her terror, and she finally absorbed what Mosely was saying: Nate was coming for her. And Mosely *wanted* him to come.

Mosely tugged on the ankle restraints to make sure they were secure, then came back up to the head of the table. His left hand came down on her throat, fingers digging into her jaw as he used the pressure from his palm to hold her down.

"Thank you for confirming my suspicion that Nathaniel was with you last night. And that you did indeed encounter Mr. Bishop."

The pressure of Mosely's fingers forced her jaws open, and Mosely crammed a foul-tasting rubber mouthpiece in. The ends of the mouthpiece went far enough back that Nadia gagged, but Mosely didn't relent. He lifted her head and wrapped some kind of strap around the back, securing the mouthpiece in place. Tears of misery trickled down the sides of her face and into her ears as she realized she'd lost her last chance of talking her way out of this. Though she was puzzled as to how Mosely was going to get the information he wanted out of her if she couldn't talk.

Mosely stepped back from the table and admired his handiwork. Then he shook his head. "Who knew a little girl and her playboy boyfriend would be so much damn trouble?"

The door to the interrogation room slammed open. Nadia craned to see what was happening, but Mosely was blocking her view of the door.

"Please do come in, Nathaniel," Mosely said without turning around. "We've been waiting for you."

Nadia tried to shout a warning around the mouthpiece, but of course all that came out was an unintelligible grunt. Not that she thought Nate would run even if he knew he was walking into a trap. Her heart ached at the knowledge that she was at least partially responsible for the sequence of events that was leading up to Nate's second murder.

"Let her go!" Nate said in a voice rich with authority. As if he expected Mosely to obey.

Mosely smiled, finally turning around to face Nate. As he did so, he moved to the side just enough that Nadia could see Nate, standing a few feet inside the room. She could also see that a pair of security officers were flanking the door behind him. And that both had drawn their weapons. Nadia couldn't shout a warning, but when she caught Nate's eye, she jerked her chin and rolled her eyes toward the guards. He glanced over his shoulder and saw them.

He looked surprisingly unalarmed when he turned back. "Let Nadia go," he said again. "You've already ruined her life. You can let her go, and no one will believe her—or even care—if she starts spreading stories about you. Like that you killed me with your own hand."

Mosely chuckled, sounding genuinely amused. "It's amazing to me that you can make such a big show of being worldly and dissolute, and yet you remain so charmingly naive. Why should I take that chance?"

"Because I know where Bishop is. I don't suppose you'd have Nadia strapped to that table if you'd gotten the answers to all your questions. Let her go, and I'll tell you everything."

Nadia made a choking sound of protest, though in truth she didn't believe Nate was going to follow through on his promise. He would do everything he could to save her, but he wouldn't give up Bishop. His emotions about Bishop might be pretty jumbled right now, but Nate was loyal to a fault. He just didn't have it in him to betray *anyone.*

Mosely shook his head. "You're operating on the assumption that I won't be able to extract those answers from Miss Lake anyway."

"Maybe you would, but she's a lot tougher than you've given her credit for. Getting answers from her would take time. And you have to know that answers given under duress aren't reliable. By the time you get what you need out of her, Bishop will have moved on."

"You might as well save your breath, Nathaniel," Mosely said, glancing at his watch for some reason. "You think you know so much, but you have no idea what's going on."

"Are you late for a meeting? Because I wouldn't want to keep you or anything."

Mosely smiled. "Just trying to calculate how much longer we have before your father arrives."

"My father's coming?"

"Yes. He insists on being here in person for . . . what comes next."

Nate's Adam's apple bobbed, and he couldn't hide his horror. "When you kill me, you mean. Like you did on the night of the reception."

"Your father is a great man. He's willing to make whatever sacrifices are necessary for the greater good of his state. If it makes you feel any better, ordering your death tore him up inside, even knowing he would have you back. And he wouldn't have insisted I wait for him if he didn't regret what we'll be forced to do."

Nadia's heart leapt as she realized that Mosely had finally said something that could get him in trouble. He had as much as admitted to killing Nate. And he'd incriminated the Chairman, too! It was a little tenuous, the admission not as clear as she'd like. But it might give her some leverage—if only she could speak to let him know his words had been captured for posterity. She pushed on the mouthpiece with her tongue, moving her head around in an attempt to loosen the strap that held it in place. But the damned thing wasn't budging.

"Perhaps when you're older and more mature," Mosely went on, "your father will trust you with Thea's secrets. But everything you've done since your Replica was animated proves that you can't be trusted with them yet. You will tilt at windmills without once considering the cost."

"And what about the cost we pay for Thea?" Nate asked. "Have you ever considered that?"

Nadia lay still. She wasn't having any success ridding herself of the mouthpiece, and she didn't want to risk drawing Mosely's attention. Nate was fishing, trying to get Mosely to explain whatever the big secret about Thea was. And since Mosely thought Bishop had overheard everything and by now shared it with Nate, he didn't know he had anything to hide.

"Only a starry-eyed idealist like you would consider a handful of hardened criminals and Basement-dwellers here and there a significant cost. Not for what Thea gives us in return."

"Yeah, she made it possible for my dad to murder me without losing his heir. I can see how that's a big benefit to society."

"Do you know how much of our gross national product comes from the technology that Thea makes possible? We might not have produced many actual Replicas, but the revenue from providing backup services alone provides power and food and shelter to keep our state thriving. If we stopped feeding her, she'd refuse to make the backups and we'd be bankrupt in a matter of weeks. But of course you don't care about that as long as we do what you think is the 'right thing.'"

Feed Thea? Nadia remembered Mosely's offhand comment about criminals and Basement-dwellers, and when she put the two together, she came up with a pretty revolting image. Her stomach turned over, and Nate looked a little pale. He'd come in here brimming with confidence—or at least doing a very good job of pretending—and he'd bluffed his way through the conversation so far with aplomb.

Mosely must have noticed the pallor of Nate's face and made the correct assumption as to what it meant. He muttered something under his breath that Nadia felt sure was a curse of some kind.

"You didn't know, did you?" he said aloud, shaking his head at Nate.

"No," Nate admitted, his face still pale even as he tried to look triumphant. "Bishop didn't hear anything you and the Chairman were talking about, except the name Thea." He composed himself a little more, shaking off the horror. "So you're actually *feeding* criminals and Basement-dwellers to Thea. How does that work, exactly? Thea's just a machine."

Mosely looked at his watch again with impatience.

"Your plan is to kill me and Nadia both, isn't it?" Nate asked, then continued without waiting for an answer. "If that's the case, then what's the harm of explaining while you wait for my dad to come give you the official order?"

Mosely eyed him. "Fine. Yes, Thea is a machine, and we aren't literally feeding her. She was developed as a research tool." Mosely turned his back on Nate and walked over to the table on which Nadia lay. He reached above his head and flipped a switch. A low mechanical hum sounded, and Nadia's body was suddenly bathed in spotlights. One of the spotlights shone directly in her eyes, and she had to close them.

Nate yelled, and there was the sound of scuffling. Nadia turned her head and cracked her eyes open to see Nate lying facedown on the floor while one of the security officers held him down and slapped handcuffs on him. Even with her head turned, the lights were unbearably bright and she had to close her eyes again.

"More specifically," Mosely continued, "she was developed to research the human body."

Nadia heard Mosely move to the head of the table and heard him flipping more switches. She tried to open her eyes to see what was happening, to see if one of those evil attachments was moving toward her, but the blinding lights wouldn't let her.

"Don't you dare hurt her!" Nate bellowed, but Mosely ignored him.

"Obviously, she far exceeded our expectations when she succeeded in creating exact Replicas of human beings. She can re-create a body down to the tiniest mole and scar, as you already know. But because she was developed for research, continuing to learn more has always been a driving need for her."

"It is my raison d'être," a female voice said from somewhere above Nadia's head. She couldn't open her eyes to see, but instinct told her the voice had come from the apparatus that she was currently strapped to. Thea herself.

"Indeed," Mosely said.

"*That's* Thea?" Nate asked.

"It's connected to her. The servers that house her are a few rooms down, but we've given her the connectivity she needs to operate."

"To further my research," Thea clarified.

"What kind of research?" Nate asked.

Nadia tried again to find a way to spit out the mouthpiece that kept her from talking. She now had more than enough damning, sensitive information captured to put some serious leverage on her side. But that leverage did no good if no one knew she had it. The idea that she might get her revenge after she and Nate both died at Mosely's hands was not as much of a comfort as she'd hoped.

"I am trying to understand the human brain," Thea answered. "I can copy it in its entirety, but I have yet to understand fully how it functions in connection to the rest of the body. I cannot separate mind from body."

Thea was just a glorified computer program, with a computer-generated voice, but Nadia could have sworn she heard a hint of frustration in that voice.

"Why would you want to do that?" Nate asked.

"Because if she can separate mind from body, then she can create the Replica of a human mind in any body she wants," said Chairman Hayes.

Nadia risked another quick blink and saw that the Chairman had arrived and was facing off with Nate, who had been dragged back to his feet by the security officers.

"For instance," Thea continued, "I still have in storage the very first backup scan I ever made of our beloved Chairman.

When his body fails, I could theoretically create a Replica from the old backup, despite your silly human laws." Human laws that prohibited the use of Replicas in the case of death by natural causes. "But it would be missing all the years of growth and learning and memory that had happened since that scan. When I am able to isolate the mind from the body, I will be able to create a Replica of the Chairman with his current mind and his forty-year-old body."

"It's the key to immortality, Nate," the Chairman said to his son, as if there were no one else in the room. "Thanks to Thea and the important research she's doing, I will be able to live forever, with Thea creating a new, younger body for me whenever my current one wears out. And you and everyone you love throughout your lifetime can live forever, too."

CHAPTER TWENTY-TWO

"YOU know you sound like a raving lunatic, right?" Nate asked his father, echoing Nadia's thoughts.

The Chairman shrugged. "Spoken like an eighteen-year-old who thinks he's going to live forever anyway."

"Hey, unlike you, I've died once already." Nate's voice got a little thick, and though he was trying to sound angry, Nadia heard the pain beneath the anger. "And I think if I manage to survive another hour today, it'll be a miracle."

The lights above Nadia dimmed, so she was finally able to open her eyes again and see. Nate's hands were cuffed behind his back. One of the security officers was holding his arm, and the other was pointing a gun at him. The Chairman had come close enough to put his hand on Nate's shoulder, and either he was a really good actor or there was genuine sorrow on his face.

"I'm truly sorry, Nate. I don't *want* to hurt you, but you've made it necessary. I can't trust you to keep this knowledge to yourself."

Nadia struggled against her bonds and screamed as best she could around the mouthpiece. The Chairman was going to kill Nate right here in front of her. She had the means to stop him, if only she could talk. But the bindings weren't getting any looser, no matter how hard she struggled, and the mouthpiece wouldn't budge, and no one was paying any attention to her.

The Chairman reached out and slid the second officer's gun out of its holster. "At least this time I'll take care of you myself," he said. "I'll make sure you don't suffer."

Nate locked gazes with his father as the Chairman started to lift the gun. He had to be terrified, but it didn't show. He didn't wince, didn't look away, didn't try to escape.

"Hey, Nadia," he called, gaze still locked on his father's, "are those the earrings you were telling us about?"

Nadia's eyes widened, and she stopped struggling. She'd forgotten that Nate knew about the earrings, but even if she'd remembered, she probably wouldn't have expected him to realize she was wearing them. She nodded as emphatically as her bonds would allow, and Nate smiled.

The Chairman's hand slowed in raising the gun.

"I think you might want to take that gag off Nadia and hear what she has to say before you go and do anything irreversible," Nate said. "Unless you want the world to hear the conversation we've just had, that is."

Chairman Hayes froze with the gun only halfway up. He looked over his shoulder at Mosely. "Do it."

For the first time she could remember, Mosely actually looked . . . apprehensive, and she figured he had a good idea what Nate's statement meant. He tore out some of her hair in his efforts to get the mouthpiece off her, but she didn't mind a bit. The movement so near her throat made her gag, even though Mosely was taking the damn thing out, and Nadia had to swallow convulsively a few times to get the gag reflex under control so she could talk.

"Check my left earring," she told Mosely. "You'll find there's a transmitter in it. I've arranged for whatever I've recorded to be sent out wide in the event of my unfortunate death or disappearance."

Mosely's eyes glowed with an emotion Nadia thought came very close to hatred. She felt a thrill of triumph.

"Just think of all the things the world will know if that recording gets out," she said. She was trying to sound brave and victorious, but the quaver in her voice ruined the effect. It was certainly possible that Mosely and the Chairman were arrogant enough to think they could find the stored recording before anyone knew she was dead or "missing."

Nadia cried out as Mosely ripped the earring straight out of her ear. Little droplets of blood splashed her face, and Nate roared in outrage.

"Don't be an idiot," the Chairman said, and when Nadia blinked away her tears of pain, she saw that he was now holding the gun firmly to Nate's head. Any hesitancy he might have felt earlier about the prospect of shooting his own son seemed to have vanished. His aim was steady, his face wiped clean of emotion. Nate stopped struggling against the officer who held him.

"Are you okay?" he called to her while Mosely picked apart her bloody earring, looking for the transmitter.

"Yeah," she called back, though she was anything but. Her ear stung and throbbed, her head ached from when Mosely had hit it on the table, and her whole body still felt discombobulated from the electricity that had run through it. She was freezing cold, staring up into a contraption full of torture implements, and strapped to a table completely helpless. She was about as far from okay as it was possible to get, and the thrill of triumph she'd felt was long gone.

Mosely found the transmitter and let out a low curse. He dropped it to the floor and crushed it under his heel, but he had to know the damage had already been done. Always before when he'd looked at her, even when he'd been angry, Nadia had had the sense that Mosely felt he was just doing his job, that any emotion he showed was no more than skin-deep. That certainly wasn't the case now.

"You brought her down to the heart of the Fortress, into Thea's domain, and you didn't check her for electronic surveillance?" the Chairman asked his favorite hatchet man in a voice that would have sane people scurrying for cover. "She was wearing a tracker *and* a transmitter, and you didn't find either?"

Mosely's hands clenched at his sides as he faced his boss. "She's a meek little schoolgirl I dragged from her bed," he protested. "It never occurred to me that she might be wired."

The Chairman shook his head in disbelief. "She wasn't so meek that she didn't go running off on her own independent investigation in defiance of your instructions. Perhaps that should have been your first clue."

"Why don't you two fight about this later," Nate suggested, now standing calm and relaxed in the security officer's grip. He, at least, was convinced they'd won. He was even smiling, the old impish smile she'd always loved, although there were shadows in his eyes that dimmed the smile's brightness. "Right now, you need to get those restraints off Nadia and these handcuffs off me. Then maybe we can move this party to a conference room and discuss terms."

"Thea?" the Chairman said, ignoring Nate's demands as if he hadn't heard them.

"Yes, Mr. Chairman?"

"I'd like you to dissect the young lady's brain until you find out where the signal has been sent."

The blinding spotlights brightened to their full intensity

again, forcing Nadia's eyes closed, and there was an ominous whirring of machinery above her.

"Yes, Mr. Chairman," Thea said.

"I'm sure you thought this operating theater was a modern-day torture chamber," the Chairman said, and Nadia didn't know if he was talking to her or to Nate. "But thanks to Thea's research, it is no longer necessary to torture suspects for information. She can retrieve the information directly from the brain. Although, of course, this process is terribly unpleasant for the subject and ultimately fatal."

"Don't hurt her!" Nate yelled, and there was a frantic edge in his voice. From the sound of it, he was struggling again.

A high-pitched whining sound started up, and Nadia fought past her terror, fought to think coherently instead of letting herself visualize one of those drills or saws descending to cut into her head.

"It won't work," she said in something between a whimper and a scream. No matter how pointless it was, she struggled against the bonds that held her to the table, not caring that they dug painfully into the flesh of her wrists and ankles. "I don't know where the data is stored."

Dirk Mosely gave a bark of laughter. "Of course, you would never say such a thing if it weren't true."

The high-pitched whine was coming steadily closer.

"I'm not stupid," she countered. "You made it clear from the beginning you were willing to torture me. Making the recordings would do me no good if you could torture the location out of me." She couldn't suppress a little whimper of fear, which didn't do much to enhance the illusion that she was bargaining from a position of strength. "If you let your pet monster do this, and she finds I'm telling the truth, you're completely screwed. This is your last chance."

A bubble of hysterical laughter swelled in her chest. She was lying here tied to a table, about to be vivisected by a sentient machine, and she was telling the Chairman that it was *his* last chance. This all had to be some crazy dream, right? An epic nightmare created by her subconscious to terrify her in her sleep. It couldn't possibly be happening in real life.

"Wait," the Chairman said.

The whining sound continued to come closer.

"Thea, stop," the Chairman said, more firmly.

"I can find the recordings, Mr. Chairman," Thea protested. "Even if this subject does not know their actual location, I will discern who *does* know, and we can proceed from there."

"And by the time you do, the recordings will be all over the net," Nadia said. "What do you think would happen if everyone in Paxco, hell, everyone in the *world* knew what you were doing down here?"

Just saying the words made Nadia think about it herself, and she didn't much like what came to her mind. There was already a resistance movement forming within Paxco, infiltrating the upper echelons of the state. Right now, they were biding their time, working their way more deeply into the infrastructure. She didn't know for sure what their eventual goal was, but she'd gotten the impression they were working toward a political coup, not a violent one. But if word of what the Chairman had been doing and condoning came out, violence seemed inevitable.

"You'd risk civil war at the very least," she said, thinking about all the states and nations that already found the ethics of the Replica technology questionable. It was outlawed entirely in many parts of the world, Replicas not even being recognized as human beings. And it was against international law to create a Replica of a living person or of a person who had died of natural causes—specifically to prevent scenarios like the one the Chairman envisioned of his eternal reign. Paxco could very well find itself under attack at the same time that its citizens were rising up against it. When Nadia had first started down this road, she had never considered that her attempts to protect herself might lead to the very brink of war.

"Thea, I'm giving you a direct order," the Chairman said. "Do not proceed."

The whining sound stopped, and the spotlights dimmed to a bearable level. Nadia opened her eyes, then wished she hadn't. A circular saw, its blade still turning from leftover momentum, was bare millimeters from her forehead.

"Don't be childish, Thea," the Chairman said. "Move the blade. And Mr. Mosely, please release Nadia from her restraints."

"Are you sure about this?" Mosely asked.

"Yes," the Chairman snapped, apparently not appreciating having his order questioned.

The saw blade above Nadia's head whirred to life briefly, nearly giving her a heart attack, but Thea withdrew the arm. Nadia swallowed hard. Thea might be a machine, but she was an AI, and had something resembling free will. Just because Chairman Hayes ordered her not to cut Nadia open didn't mean she wouldn't. And Nadia couldn't help seeing that brief reactivation of the saw as a threat, and a sullen one at that. She couldn't get off this table soon enough.

Mosely went out of his way to be rough with her as he removed the restraints, tugging on them so they dug into her already-abused flesh. But she didn't complain, gritting her teeth against the pain. Across the room, she could see that

Nate's hands were free. One of the security officers was gone. The second stood blocking the doorway, his hand on the butt of his gun, though he kept it holstered. Nate and Nadia might be out of their restraints, but that didn't mean they were free, and that didn't mean this was over.

Mosely finally tugged loose the last restraint, and Nadia leapt off the table.

Or tried to. Between the fear and her recent impersonation of a lightning rod, her knees turned to jelly the moment her feet hit the floor, and she crumpled.

Mosely reached toward her, no doubt to drag her to her feet, but Nate crossed the distance between them in a few hurried strides and shouldered Mosely out of the way.

"Don't even think about touching her again," he spat, kneeling on the floor beside her and gathering her into his arms.

Never in her entire life had a hug felt so good, and Nadia pressed herself against him, holding on as if her life depended on it.

The second officer returned to the room, carrying another plastic chair. He set that chair down on the prisoners' side of the interrogation table, then stepped aside so that he and his buddy could flank the door. Chairman Hayes walked over to the single chair on the other side of the table, pulling it back and sitting down.

"I'm ready to discuss terms when you are," he said, folding his hands on the table.

"Can you walk?" Nate asked, still holding her against him.

Nadia wanted to stay in Nate's arms for the foreseeable future. The scent of his skin soothed her, and she was so tired of being scared. But the sooner they got started, the sooner she'd get out of here, and she wanted that more than anything in the world.

"I can walk," she said, reluctantly sitting up straight. "If you'll give me a hand up."

She met Nate's intense blue eyes. There was so much she wanted to say to him, so many things she needed to apologize for—it was amazing how a near-death experience could change a girl's perspective. She promised herself she would say everything that needed saying, just as soon as they had secured their freedom.

Nadia allowed him to help her up. This time, her knees held.

CHAPTER TWENTY-THREE

"That recording must never become public," the Chairman said, starting the negotiations. "You might be tempted to release it to punish me for the wrongs you think I've done you, but the damage that information would do is . . . incalculable."

Nate clenched his fists under the table, where the Chairman couldn't see them. He'd been able to keep his emotions relatively under control in the midst of the crisis, but now that the immediate threat was removed, they threatened to swamp him. He wanted to leap across the table and grab his father around the throat. And the image of grabbing one of the officers' guns and shooting Dirk Mosely dead held a frightening appeal. It was probably a good thing for everyone involved that Nate didn't have to handle the negotiations himself, that he had someone calmer and more even-tempered sitting beside him. Instead of responding, Nate said, "Don't look at me. Nadia's the one who has the recordings. She's the one you have to convince."

He took a perverse pleasure from his father's obvious chagrin at being forced to negotiate with a sixteen-year-old girl. Nadia was still pale from her ordeal, the dark circles under her eyes still prominent, but her gaze was steady, and Nate knew she was far from broken, despite the spots of blood that dotted her shoulder from her shredded ear. He'd once thought of her as a fragile little thing, always so worried about every little faux pas, but he knew better now.

"Very well," the Chairman said, turning his attention to Nadia with reluctance. "I am prepared to offer you complete amnesty in return for those recordings."

Nadia's lips lifted in a smile, which quickly turned into a laugh. "You're joking, right?"

"I assure you, this is no laughing matter."

Nadia contained her laughter, but mirth still sparkled in her eyes. "Then don't treat me like a child. Amnesty for me, my entire family, and Nate are all givens and don't even warrant a mention."

The Chairman did not appreciate being laughed at. Nor did he appear to appreciate Nadia's tone. Nate had been on the receiving end of that cold glare more times than he could count, and he had to admit that he was occasionally cowed by it. But if Nadia was cowed, she didn't show it.

"What else do you want?" the Chairman asked.

"Amnesty for Kurt Bishop, to start."

Warmth swelled in Nate's chest. He wanted to hug her again. Any other girl in her position might have been glad for the chance to get Kurt out of the way. She didn't even like Kurt, and yet her very first concern was to demand amnesty for him.

"That can be arranged," the Chairman said, with a scowl that made it plain what he thought of the arrangement.

"And let's get something else clear right off the bat. I am *not* giving you the recordings. Not ever. No matter what you offer."

The Chairman's eyes sharpened and he leaned forward on his elbows, gaze boring into Nadia with such malice that Nate couldn't help putting a protective arm around her shoulders. Both the Chairman and Nadia ignored him.

"If you don't intend to give me the recordings, then we have nothing to talk about," the Chairman said. "I will feed you to Thea, shoot this Replica"—he waved a hand at Nate without tearing his eyes from Nadia—"and weather the storm of public disapproval to the best of my abilities."

Nadia shook her head. "The one and only thing I'm willing to give you is a promise that the recordings will not be released to the public—and that only if the price is right. I'm not stupid enough to hand over the one thing that will keep you from killing me."

Nate could see by the play of muscles in the Chairman's face that he was grinding his teeth. His father was a master negotiator—Nate had seen him at work before—but he was used to negotiating from a position of power. He was *not* used to negotiating with someone who had him by the balls.

"Face it, *Dad*," Nate said, unable to resist rubbing it in just a bit. "You don't have any choice."

A flush of red fury crept up the Chairman's neck, and Nate wondered if he was about to have a stroke on the spot. Nate also wondered if he still had the gun he'd been holding earlier—Nate hadn't been paying attention and didn't know whether he'd given it back to the security officer or stuck it in his own coat pocket. Maybe he'd better keep his mouth shut. If he pushed his luck too far, his father might lose his temper and shoot him before he remembered why that was a bad idea.

"On top of amnesty for Kurt," Nadia continued calmly, "I want Dirk Mosely arrested and put away for life."

Behind the Chairman, Mosely stiffened, as if he had never considered the possibility that Nadia might want his head after what he'd done. But then, Mosely had been underestimating her from the start.

"And lastly, there will be no more human experimentation.

I don't care if Thea refuses to make Replicas or do backup scans. For you to allow our whole state to be held hostage by this damn machine is deplorable."

"Oh, yes," the Chairman said in a voice dripping with sarcasm. "I'm going to bankrupt my state, starve my people, deprive them of jobs and homes and basic human necessities, all because making good use of the dregs of society offends you."

Nate noticed he hadn't voiced any objection to Nadia's demand to arrest Mosely. The sharply calculating look in Mosely's eyes said he'd noticed it, too, and Nate kept a careful eye on him. He didn't appear to be armed—perhaps he didn't feel the need to carry a weapon deep in the safety of the Fortress—but Nate wasn't sure.

"If you're going to arrest Mosely," Nate needled his father, "you might want to get on with it, and I definitely don't recommend sitting there with your back to him."

The Chairman barely spared Mosely a glance. "He is a true patriot. He will do whatever is necessary for the good of our state, even if it turns out to be at great personal cost. But I haven't agreed to your terms, so he needn't worry."

There was an obvious unspoken "yet" at the end of that sentence, and Nate kept his eyes on Mosely. He might be a "true patriot" when it came to sacrificing other peoples' lives and liberties, but Nate wasn't at all convinced he would sacrifice his own. Maybe if his father could see how his hatchet man was staring daggers at him behind his back, he'd realize his mistake.

"I have a counteroffer," the Chairman said. "I will never in a million years find a better, more able security chief than Mr. Mosely, and the livelihood of our nation depends upon the storage of backups and the ability to create Replicas. I'm afraid I can't give up either one without seriously compromising the welfare of our state, and that I'm not willing to do." He held up a hand for silence when Nadia opened her mouth to protest. "In return for your silence, I will elevate your father to the Paxco board of directors, effective immediately. You and all of your family—including your little niece and nephew of whom I've heard you're so fond—can have monthly backups for the rest of your lives. You need never fear losing any of the people you love to preventable causes." His cold, hard gaze shifted to Nate. "I'll even throw in a backup for your lover."

Nate froze. He wanted to maintain a poker face, but hiding his emotions had never been one of his best skills, and he could feel the blood draining from his face, giving him away.

The Chairman smiled, and if Nate hadn't known better, he might even have thought there was a hint of fatherly affection in that smile.

"Did you honestly think I didn't know about your . . . attachment to Bishop?"

Nate swallowed hard, wanting to deny it. The horror of "reprogramming" loomed large in his mind, as did the danger to Kurt. But denying it when his father so obviously knew the truth might make him seem weak, and it would be pointless anyway. Nate stiffened his spine.

"I honestly thought you didn't know. I figured I'd be in reprogramming if you did."

The Chairman dismissed that with a wave. "I don't give a damn who you sleep with, as long as you're discreet about it and don't tarnish the family name. Any backups made of Bishop will have to be done in secret, and if we ever have to animate a Replica, that would have to be done in secret, too. But this is the only way a man of his low background could ever hope to have such security."

Nate had to admit, the idea was tempting. He'd spent this last week terrified that he was going to lose Kurt, that Kurt would be killed because of his association with Nate. Now, he had a legitimate chance to protect him.

But of course it wasn't *Kurt* who would be protected if he had backups made. The Kurt Nate knew today could still die; it was just that Nate wouldn't have to suffer his loss. Just like his father had been able to kill him to prevent Thea's secrets getting out without actually having to suffer the loss of his son and heir.

Beside him, Nadia turned to stare at the table she'd been strapped to, at the mass of nasty instruments that hovered over it. All the lights had dimmed, though Nate had a sense that the AI was still present, silently listening in on their conversation. Waiting to see what her fate would be.

He imagined lying on a table, sliding feetfirst into the claustrophobic white tunnel of Thea's backup scanner, naked, helpless, and trusting as she took her readings and measurements. He'd been through the process more times than he could count, and it had never bothered him before. But before, he didn't know she liked to vivisect human beings for a hobby. She might not be human, but she did at least mimic some human behavior patterns, like the blackmail she used to coerce the Chairman into bringing her victims to examine. Might she also be capable of holding grudges? And just how far had she gotten in her research into the mind-body connection? Enough that she could manipulate Replicas to her liking?

He and Nadia shared a look, and he could tell she was thinking the same thing he was: they couldn't trust her. Wordlessly, he shook his head, and Nadia understood that he was rejecting the offer. She reached over and took his hand, giving it a squeeze.

"It's a generous offer," she said, but if she was trying to sugarcoat the refusal she might as well not have bothered. "But I'm afraid my terms haven't changed. That thing"—she jerked her hand toward the table of implements—"is an abomination, and there's absolutely nothing that can justify its use."

"My research is of incalculable value to the human race." Thea's voice piped up, confirming Nate's suspicion that she was listening to their conversation. "Mankind has sought after immortality for its entire existence, and if I am allowed to proceed, I will one day make that impossible dream possible. I am a scientist, not an abomination."

If Thea were human, Nate would say she was offended by the accusation. Was an AI capable of being offended?

"What you're doing is wrong," Nadia countered. "Killing human beings in the name of research is wrong, no matter what the hoped-for end result is."

The Chairman sighed. "If you're going to enter into an ethics debate with Thea, we'll be here all day. Believe me, I've had this conversation with her before, many times."

Nate laughed. "*You* talking about *ethics*? If you're Thea's teacher, then no wonder she's confused."

"I am not confused," Thea retorted, and this time Nate was sure the machine was actually offended. "Humans like to say that the ends do not justify the means, but they do not really believe that. They say it because they believe it should be true, but their actions say otherwise. I do not adhere to the human practice of saying one thing while meaning another."

"So you cut people open and eventually kill them all for the good of mankind," Nadia said. "Is that what you're saying?"

"I will make mankind immortal."

"And why do you care if mankind is immortal?"

Nate raised an eyebrow, curious to hear Thea's answer. He wasn't sure it was possible to fathom the reasoning of a nonhuman intelligence, but it was certainly a good question.

Silence reigned in the room. Either Thea was taking a very long time to think about the answer to Nadia's question, or she was disinclined to answer it. Which led Nate to reach a rather disturbing conclusion of his own.

Why would a machine like Thea care if mankind was immortal? She obviously wasn't defending the sanctity of human life. And if she was anything like most humans he knew, there was at least a kernel of self-interest at the bottom of her motivations.

Nate turned to regard the Chairman's suddenly impassive face, and the answer came to him in a flash.

"You don't care if mankind is immortal," he said, his voice seeming to echo, thanks to the tension in the room. "You just want to make sure the *Chairman* is."

The Chairman, who protected and fed and cherished her. The Chairman, who had proven himself willing to cave to her blackmail. The Chairman, who championed the Replica technology—and by extension Thea herself—against those who already thought it was immoral. Without a ruthless champion like the Chairman to protect her, would Thea have already been shut down by an angry mob? Like the one that had camped out in front of Headquarters? Nate had been stunned by their hate at the time, but now he was beginning to sympathize with them a lot more.

Thea didn't answer Nate's accusation.

"Shut down the experiments," Nadia said. "Arrest Dirk Mosely. Give Bishop amnesty. That's what I want for keeping the recordings from going public."

The Chairman shook his head. "I can't do that. Not unless

you can convince Thea to keep making backups and animating Replicas even without her research subjects."

"I will agree to those terms, if that is what the Chairman wishes," Thea said, and that was when Nate—and, by the looks of her, Nadia as well—realized there was a fatal flaw in their demands.

"So you will stop your experiments and content yourself with doing backup scans and making Replicas?" Nadia said.

"I will. If that is what the Chairman requires of me."

Nadia's shoulders slumped, and she shook her head. "Everyone here who believes her, raise your hand," she muttered under her breath.

"Even if she's telling the truth, there's no way we can be sure the experiments stop," Nate said. "Even if we come to the Fortress for a daily inspection, we can't be sure she hasn't just moved her operation elsewhere—with or without the Chairman's consent."

"This is ridiculous," the Chairman said. "I will give you amnesty for everyone involved, and I will give you access to Thea for backups and Replicas. It's a more than generous offer. There's no reason you should be so intent on tearing down all of Paxco."

Nadia shook her head. "I'm intent on doing the right thing. I've stated my terms. If we have to shut Thea down entirely to be sure she abides by those terms, then so be it."

"Shut her down? Are you *mad*?"

Nadia sat back in her chair and folded her arms, a picture of implacability. "Those are my terms. Take them or leave them."

Nate almost felt sorry for his father. Distress had stolen the color from his face, and he looked like a different man without the mantle of confidence and authority he usually wore.

"Need I mention again that without the revenue from making backups, Paxco would go bankrupt in a matter of weeks? Is that really what you think is the right thing?"

Nadia gave the thought a moment's consideration, then nodded. "Yes, I do. Lincoln freed the slaves despite knowing it would have a devastating economic impact, and, eventually, the United States recovered. I figure we'll recover from the impact of losing Thea, too."

"You self-righteous little brat!" the Chairman snarled, losing control of his temper for the first time Nate could remember. He shoved his chair back with enough force to knock it over and leaned forward to put his fists on the table and glare at Nadia. She didn't shrink away from him.

"The United States had to go through a civil war to 'recover' from that economic impact. Is that what you want for Paxco? You want to risk the lives of thousands of ordinary citizens, *innocent* people, to protect a handful of convicted criminals here and there?"

"You're forgetting, Mr. Chairman. *I* could have been one of those 'convicted criminals,' if you'd had your way. Mosely threatened to make my sister and my brother-in-law into 'convicted criminals' if I didn't do what he wanted. And you were both willing to convict Kurt Bishop of a crime you committed yourselves. Experimenting on human beings would be wrong even if the test subjects really were genuinely convicted criminals, but how many innocents have you imprisoned for the sake of political expediency?" She shook her head. "No, Mr. Chairman. I know we will all be in for some hard times ahead, but this has to stop. If you don't shut Thea down, I will release the recordings to the public. I think the repercussions of that would be far worse, don't you?"

The Chairman's face had been pale, but now it was flushed

red, and his eyes were practically incandescent with his fury. He stood up straight and reached into his right coat pocket.

Everything seemed to go into slow motion as Nate realized that pocket was hanging lower than the left one and as he remembered his own uncertainty as to where the gun had ended up.

"No!" Nate yelled, leaping from his chair and tackling Nadia to the ground, trying to make sure his own body was between her and the Chairman's gun.

The gun roared, and Nadia screamed. Nate wrapped his arms around her, trying to shield every inch of her body as the gun roared again, the sound deafening in the enclosed room. There was a third gunshot, then the sound of something heavy hitting the floor, a sound he was aware of more from the vibration in the floor than from actual hearing because his ears were ringing so loudly.

The room fell deathly quiet. Nate risked a peek while making sure Nadia's head was still safely tucked against his chest. What he saw made his heart skip a beat.

The Chairman stood facing away from them, arm hanging by his side with the gun still in his hand. On the floor lay Dirk Mosely, blood pooling beneath his head. His eyes were open, but lifeless, and there was a bloody hole in the center of his forehead. More blood spattered the floor all around him, spotting the uniforms of the two shocked security officers who stood in the doorway. Nate swallowed hard, hoping he wasn't about to be sick.

"I couldn't arrest him," the Chairman said calmly, as if he hadn't just shot a man in cold blood. "He was a patriot, and would have done just about anything for the good of Paxco—except spend the rest of his life in prison. If I'd tried it, he would have talked."

Nate felt Nadia stirring against him, felt more than heard her gasp of horror when she looked up and saw what had happened.

Still eerily calm, the Chairman popped the clip from his gun and checked how many rounds were left. "I need another clip," he told the security officers, holding out his hand without looking up at them. The two men looked at each other nervously. They'd shown no surprise at any of the secrets that had been revealed today, so they were obviously part of Mosely's inner circle. But they were even more obviously unsettled by what they'd witnessed. They recovered quickly, however, each offering the Chairman a clip. He took both, reloading the gun and putting the spare clip in his pocket.

He nodded in what looked like approval, then snapped the clip back in.

"If this first taste of blood hasn't brought you to your senses, Miss Lake, then come with me," he said. "We can go destroy Paxco's economy together."

Without looking to see if they would follow, the Chairman shouldered his way past the two security officers and out the door.

CHAPTER TWENTY-FOUR

when this day was finally, finally over, Nadia was going to collapse into a heap and have a fit of screaming hysteria. But for right now, at least, her body seemed to have run out of adrenaline, and as she gently extricated herself from Nate's arms and rose unsteadily to her feet, she hardly seemed to feel anything at all. Just a drifty, floaty feeling of unreality, heightened by the ringing in her ears that made all other sounds seem distant. She looked down at Dirk Mosely, dead because of her, and she felt neither triumph nor guilt.

Nadia suspected she was hovering on the verge of shock, which was probably not a good thing in the long run. But for now, she was grateful for whatever it was that kept her functioning. Beside her, Nate looked a little green, and he was breathing like he'd just run a marathon. Nadia took his clammy hand in hers, giving it a squeeze. She would not soon forget how he'd shielded her with his body when he thought the Chairman was going to shoot her.

"Come on," she said, tugging his hand so he'd follow as she picked her way around the blood that spattered the floor. "We can freak out later. Right now, it's time to finish this thing."

The Chairman might be giving in to her demands, but she didn't trust him for a moment. If all he did to shut Thea down was flip a few switches, she was certain it wouldn't be long before he'd flip them back. Somehow, she was going to have to make sure whatever he did was permanent.

Down the hall, the Chairman was standing in front of a heavy metal door with a series of electronic keypads and scanners running along its side. He put his eye to the retinal scanner, then placed his whole hand on a fingerprint scanner, and even that wasn't enough to open the door, because even after the lights on both scanners turned green, the door was still locked. He punched in a long code on one of the keypads, but the indicator light above it remained red. The Chairman frowned and entered the code again, with the same result. He pounded on the door with his left hand in frustration.

"Don't be childish, Thea," he said. "You know I can manually override this door."

There was no response, although Nadia supposed it was unlikely there were speakers in the door.

"Can she actually hear you?" Nadia asked, curious despite herself. The equipment surrounding Thea's "examining table" obviously included both speaker and microphone, but what was in the electronic equipment of the door?

"I see no reason why not," the Chairman said, scowling at the door. "She's obviously made unauthorized modifications to the door mechanism, and she has shown a tendency to enjoy eavesdropping. She has created ears where none existed before."

"So she's conveniently locking you out when you intend to shut her down?" Nadia asked with undisguised skepticism. If she were an unscrupulous bastard like the Chairman, she supposed she'd try to stall, too.

The Chairman ignored her and pounded on the door again. "Thea, open this door immediately!"

If he was stalling, then he was doing a pretty good acting job. He looked like he was about to take out his gun and start shooting again.

The Chairman hit the door one more time. "Fine!" He stalked down the hallway toward the room they had just vacated. "I'll be right back."

Nate and Nadia shared puzzled glances, wondering what the Chairman was up to. Nadia half expected him to shut the door and lock himself in the interrogation room, but after only a few moments, he emerged again holding a metal key on a chain. Nadia shuddered when she saw the blood on his hands and realized he must have taken the key from Mosely's body.

If the Chairman was bothered by the blood that both literally and figuratively stained his hands, he didn't show it. He flipped open an unmarked panel set in the door itself, rather than in the wall beside the door. Under the panel were a pair of keyholes. The Chairman plugged the bloody key into one of the holes, then loosened his tie and unbuttoned his collar to get to a chain he wore around his neck. He slid the chain over his head and inserted the key into the second hole. Then he turned both keys simultaneously and Nadia could hear something heavy moving inside the door.

"Thea can meddle with electronics," the Chairman said, "but she can't physically alter the door itself. I originally had the manual override put in in case of loss of power, but I suppose it has other advantages."

The door made a final clicking sound, and the Chairman pushed it open and stepped inside. Nate and Nadia followed.

Nadia had been expecting a room full of whirring electronic equipment, kept uncomfortably chilly to counteract the heat that equipment generated. Instead, she walked into a wall of damp heat that reminded her of the tropics.

The room was relatively small, only about ten by ten, and three walls were covered with shelves on which sat the expected whirring electronics. But scattered amongst the electronics were a variety of vats and jars, filled with a red fluid that bore a disturbing resemblance to blood. Fleshy red tendrils seemed to grow out of the jars like ivy, reaching out to the electronics and burrowing into ports and vents. A sound like the steady beating of a heart filled the room, and when Nadia looked closely, she could see the faint pulse traveling through the tendrils. She shivered, despite the heat.

"Thea isn't just a machine," the Chairman said. "It is her biological components that make her what she is. She is a living, intelligent creature." He pulled the gun out of his pocket, but didn't raise it. "I can't just turn her off like a computer. To shut her down, I'll have to kill her. Is that what you want me to do, Nadia Lake? Will you sit astride your high horse and order the death of a living being? Or did you get your fill of death when I executed Dirk Mosely on your command?"

"I didn't command you to shoot him!" Nadia protested automatically. But if she was perfectly honest with herself, she knew there was no way her demands could have led to anything but death for Mosely. Even if he'd been arrested, he would have had to go to trial for his crimes, and a conviction would have led to execution. No matter how bad a man he had been, she knew she was going to bear that scar on her conscience for the rest of her life.

She looked around at the combination of flesh and electronics that surrounded her. Thea was indeed alive, and her abilities were awe-inspiring. If she'd been created and nurtured by someone who had a steady moral compass, she could have been an instrument for good in the world. But she'd been shaped by a power-hungry dictator with only the barest regard for human life. She had a personality of her own, and it was one that mirrored the Chairman's, treating people like expendable game pieces. She could never be trusted to have humanity's best interests at heart.

"Do it," Nadia said.

The Chairman gave her a look of pure loathing, then raised his gun hand and pointed at one of the jars. He was sweating, though that might have been just the tropical heat of the room. He hesitated a long time, darting quick glances in her direction as if expecting her to change her mind any second. The lights dimmed briefly, and Nadia wondered if that was Thea's version of a flinch. She raised her hands to cover her ears and was peripherally aware of Nate doing the same beside her.

The Chairman pulled the trigger, and the jar exploded, sending shards of glass and thick, coppery-smelling fluid into the air. A shrill alarm sounded, and a fleshy lump spilled out of the shattered jar and onto the floor. The lump had grooves and wrinkles reminiscent of a brain, though the shape was all wrong. The Chairman's hands were covered with bloody fluid, but he barely seemed to notice. He turned to another jar, pulling the trigger once more. Then he repeated the process over and over, and with every biological component he shot, more of the electronic equipment went dark. The veins that connected the jars to the electronics stopped pulsing, and blood, or something very like it, formed a lake on the floor and coated everything.

Nate and Nadia retreated from the room, but not before they, too, were stained with Thea's lifeblood, their shoes soaked in it. The Chairman didn't stop shooting until every jar and vat was shattered, changing clips calmly when necessary. Then he stood there in the still, darkened room, covered in blood from head to foot, and wept.

CHAPTER TWENTY-FIVE

nadia stared at her reflection over the sink and wondered if her family would even recognize her. She'd scrubbed off all the blood and other fluids that had stained her skin and hair. Her clothes had been ruined, so now she was wearing a bright-orange prison jumpsuit—necessary camouflage, since she was supposedly being released from prison. The bright orange leached any hint of color from her pale skin, and she had a bad case of raccoon eyes with no makeup to brighten them up.

Despite showering in water as hot as she could bear, she was still shivering, and her eyes were red as if she'd been crying, though she didn't think she had been. It was hard to be sure. She was so dazed by everything that had happened, by everything she had seen and everything she had done, that she felt like there were holes in her memory. Big, deep potholes that could swallow her whole if she let herself venture too close to their edges.

There was a knock on the bathroom door.

"Nadia?" Nate called. "Are you all right in there?"

No, she was definitely not all right. But she was alive, and she hadn't been tortured. She hadn't betrayed Dante and the resistance, and she'd convinced the Chairman to destroy Thea and her sickening research project. Maybe once she got out of the Fortress and back to her own home, she'd have a hope of recovering.

"Nadia?" Nate asked again, and the door rattled. She'd locked it, of course, not trusting that the ordeal was truly over.

"I'm fine, Nate," she lied. She took a deep breath to steady herself, then opened the door.

Nate had showered in another restroom down the hall. Nadia had hidden away so long that his hair had dried and was even more unruly than usual thanks to a lack of hair product. He frowned fiercely at the sight of her prison jumpsuit. She didn't like it much, either, but it was a necessary part of the cover story they had concocted to explain the day's events without revealing anything about Thea. She had supposedly been taken directly from her family's home to Riker's Island, and the Chairman had listened in when Mosely questioned her. During the questioning, she revealed that she'd learned Mosely was Nate's true killer, though she was a little fuzzy on what his motivation was supposed to have been. Mosely had been shot trying to escape, and Nadia was being released and exonerated.

The Chairman had originally insisted that the charade be further strengthened by having Nadia reunited with her family at the Riker's Island processing center, where inmates were taken in and released, but Nate had categorically refused to entertain the possibility. Nadia didn't much care where the big reunion occurred, as long as she got out of the Fortress. They were now two floors above the sub-basement, where Thea had resided, but that wasn't anywhere near far enough away for her tastes.

Nate put his arms around her in a hug. She gratefully hugged him back, reveling in his warmth, wishing it would sink into her flesh and chase away the chill.

"We aren't safe," she whispered into his chest. "If your father ever manages to track down the recordings . . ."

She let her voice trail off. They both knew what would happen if she ever lost her leverage. The Chairman was usually a cold and dispassionate man, but she had clearly broken through that shell. The way he had looked at her when he'd stepped out of Thea's room had spoken of a soul-deep hatred and a promise of revenge. She didn't know how much of that hatred spilled over onto Nate. Maybe now that the Chairman could no longer create a Replica he would not stoop so low as to murder his own son. But Nadia wouldn't put it past him, and she didn't think Nate would, either.

"I know," Nate said, lowering his head until he was whispering directly in her ear. There was no one around to hear, not at this moment, but after what they'd been through, she figured paranoia was natural—and smart.

"What are we going to do?"

"I don't know. But that's a problem to worry about later."

He pushed her away a little, but only so he could look down into her eyes. He brushed a stray strand of hair off of her cheek, tucking it behind her ear in an undeniably tender gesture. "I'm sorry I was such an ass to you yesterday. I was selfish, and judgmental, and otherwise completely out of line. Can you forgive me?"

Nadia's heart fluttered in her chest. She was standing intimately close to him, staring into his eyes. He had touched her with affection, and there was unmistakable warmth in his eyes. He loved her, she realized, in his own way. It wasn't the romantic, fairy-tale love she'd have wished for in the man she was destined to marry. Not the kind of love he had with Bishop. But it was love nonetheless, and she would have to settle for it until she found a Bishop of her own someday.

"Of course I forgive you," she said, dropping her gaze and taking a step backward, not wanting him to read her thoughts.

Nate interpreted her withdrawal differently, not knowing the thoughts and emotions that were swirling through her head.

"You mean you're *trying* to forgive me," he said. "But I guess that will take some time."

She glanced back up at his face to make a hasty denial, then stopped herself. He was right. They'd just been through an unspeakable trauma together, a trauma that made everything else that had gone on between them seem trivial. But none of the things they'd said to one another had gone away, and they were both still hurting. For now, all was peaceful between them, but there was still a storm waiting to be reckoned with.

"I'm sure the same goes for you," she responded quietly.

He smiled sadly. "Probably so. But we'll work it out, somehow. We might not be able to go back to what we were, but maybe we can become something new and better."

"I hope so."

And considering how dismal her future had looked just a handful of hours ago, that was a very cheering thought.

EPILOGUE

A shower, a change of clothes, and a stiff drink had done wonders for the Chairman's equilibrium, and he felt like himself once more. Fury still roiled in his gut: fury that he'd let a pair of teenage do-gooders outmaneuver him, fury that his own son was so completely out of his control, fury that he'd had to set his plans back by weeks, if not months, to keep those idealistic idiots from ruining everything.

The Chairman took a deep breath and closed his eyes, concentrating on pushing that pulsing fury back down. Nothing good ever came from explosions of temper, and he'd made a long and storied career out of maintaining his calm when others around him cracked. Now was not the time to allow emotion to get the best of him. His will was more powerful than his rage.

Steadied, the Chairman made his way down the hall of the Fortress's basement, telling himself not to think about the carnage that was even now being cleaned up by security forces on the level below. At the end of the hall were the three labs that held Replication units. The Chairman stopped in front of the first one and discovered that his palms were sweating. He was confident Thea had understood what needed to be done, had understood the message he had been trying to give her when he typed in his passcode outside her door. He had typed "play dead" instead of the complex string of numbers and symbols that was his real passcode. Then he'd given her as much extra time as he could, pretending she was preventing him from entering her room.

Nerves still buzzing with apprehension, the Chairman pushed the door open.

A lab tech was hovering over the Replication unit, holding the coffinlike lid open while he inspected the contents. At the sound of the door opening behind him, the tech gently set the lid down and turned around.

"How is she?" the Chairman asked, pleased that his voice sounded as calm and steady as ever. The fate of his entire state might rest on the tech's answer, but you would never know it from the Chairman's expression or manner.

"All of her biological components appear to have been successfully Replicated," the tech answered. "She will have to regrow some of her connective tissue, and of course we won't know for certain that the procedure was successful until she has been reconnected with her hardware. But overall, I'm hopeful that she will make a full recovery."

The Chairman's knees felt weak with relief. Thea had understood, had managed to start the process for her own Replication during the time he had stalled.

"We will begin the rebuilding process at once," the Chairman said.

"Of course, sir," the tech said, then took the hint and left the room.

The Chairman stepped closer to the unit that held Thea's biological heart and soul, resting his hand on the lid. "I'll have you back to yourself in no time," he promised her, though he doubted she could hear him in the state she was in. "One way or another, I'll find those recordings, and I'll destroy them. Then I'll make a present to you of Nadia Lake and this obviously defective Replica of my son."

For all the times the Chairman had decried Nate's lack of responsibility and his reckless behavior, he realized now that he was much better off having a son who didn't much care about business or politics. A son who insisted on sticking his nose where it didn't belong was a decided inconvenience.

He stroked the lid of the Replication unit as if he were petting a dog. Thea wasn't a human, but she did have her own thoughts and feelings, and he imagined today's events had been traumatic for her. He wished there were a way he could comfort her, but all he could do was put her back together and then do whatever was necessary to protect her in the future.

"You'll be back soon," he murmured, giving the lid another pat.

Then he left the room, sending the tech back in to care for her. It was time he appoint a new chief of security, one who was just as cunning and ruthless as Dirk Mosely. One who could ferret out the illicit recordings Nadia Lake was hiding. And one who would not hesitate to do whatever was necessary for the good of Paxco.

He predicted it would take approximately one month.

About one week to get Thea up and running again. Another week or so for Thea to scour the net to find the data and destroy it, assuming the new chief of security hadn't already found it by then. And one more week to find the perfect opportunity to make both Nadia and Nate disappear. The Chairman would watch with pleasure as Thea took them apart one by one. Then he would have her animate another Replica of Nate, one that knew nothing about all that had happened.

One who was once again a ne'er-do-well playboy who would stay out of his father's business.

Everything was going to go back to normal. It was only a matter of time.

acknowledgments

First of all, I'd like to thank my editor, Melissa Frain, for helping me make this a better book. Your excellent editorial feedback is almost enough to make me forgive the little prank you pulled on me when we first sat down in person to talk about the book. Thank you also for being such a great champion. I am grateful to have you in my court. My thanks, as always, to my fabulous agent, Miriam Kriss, who, based on her ability to encourage me when I'm at my lowest and her ability to remain cool under fire, must have been a hostage negotiator in a past life. And last but not least, my thanks to my husband, Dan, who has been the first reader and first editor for every single book I've published. Don't think I don't know how lucky I am to have you!